Christobel Kent was born in London and educated at Cambridge. She has lived variously in Essex, London and Italy. Her childhood included several years spent on a Thames sailing barge in Maldon, Essex with her father, stepmother, three siblings and four step-siblings. She now lives in both Cambridge and Florence with her husband and five children.

THE
SUMMER
HOUSE

Christobel Kent

SPHERE

First published by the Penguin Group in 2005
This reissue published by Sphere in 2018

A CIP catalogue record for this book
is available from the British Library.

ISBN 978-0-7515-7117-2

Typeset in Bembo by M Rules
Printed and bound in Great Britain by
Clays Ltd, St Ives plc

Papers used by Sphere are from well-managed forests
and other responsible sources.

Sphere
An imprint of
Little, Brown Book Group
Carmelite House
50 Victoria Embankment
London EC4Y 0DZ

An Hachette UK Company
www.hachette.co.uk

www.littlebrown.co.uk

For my mother

Author's Note

In writing *The Summer House* I have tried to be as faithful as possible to the geography of the town of Levanto and of the lovely, mysterious region of the Cinque Terre on whose edge it stands. There is, however, no village called Grosso in the hills above the town, although there are several villages very much like it, and in Levanto the railway line no longer runs beside the sea, although it once did.

Chapter One

Genova sprawls on the northern Mediterranean between two mountainous spurs that dip into the sea, a snarl of industrial steel, bridges, tunnels and peeling tower-blocks. Between the buildings swoop the motorways, roaring through the centre of the city inches from bathroom windows and washing lines; arterial routes coming from across the top of Italy from Venice and Eastern Europe, down from Turin and the Alps, here to join the coast road to the south or heading west to the glitz and sophistication of the Côte d'Azur. And even where the land flattens and slips into the water, where ships slide in and out, jetties and pontoons and harbour walls creep out from the city like fingers encroaching on the Mediterranean itself.

Above the glittering, roaring city one of Europe's last great forests stretches unhindered and almost impenetrable across the border, through France and all the way to the Camargue. From the funicular that climbs the hills away from the sea the extent of the forest becomes apparent. It lies across the inland hills for as far as the eye can see, its canopy of pine and acacia, rowan and holm oak velvet-black as the light fades on an August evening.

Down by the water, though, in the deeper twilight that lies at the foot of the cliffs, a shabby little train is winding its way out of the city to the east. The noise it makes comes and goes, the irregular rattle of ageing rolling stock, only occasionally audible from up high as the train creeps through the tunnels and over the bridges that lead out from Genova towards the rarefied atmosphere of the Cinque Terre. The train, its dull beige paintwork emblazoned with graffiti that glow luminous in the gathering dusk, seems sometimes to defy gravity, hanging suspended over the sea before disappearing into a dark hillside; impossibly slow. Once, when the geography and poverty of the region didn't allow for the construction of roads, this railway line was the main artery of Liguria; without it many of the villages and fishing ports scattered along the coast would have been accessible only by boat.

Motorways have been built now, in abundance, but the trains still run, and although the occasional shiny Intercity darts like a snake along the coast to Naples, for the most part they shuffle along. The notorious *regionali* and *locali* stop every five or six kilometres along the coast, at every fishing village and seaside town, their paintwork peeling and their upholstery worn thin, carrying another load of bottom-rung travellers: prostitutes, backpackers and itinerant workers, fare-dodgers, illegal immigrants and students.

But this hot evening at least the train is moving, however slowly, and at La Spezia it will turn south to leave the industry and civilization of the north behind. Until that point, that bend where the Italian boot begins to stretch out from mainland

Europe towards Africa, the train will run along the coastline of eastern Liguria, a place of sunshine and holidays, scalloped prettily with little bays and promontories, ornamented with wrought iron and stucco. It is the week of Ferragosto, the public holiday that marks the Assumption of the Virgin and the zenith of the holiday season across Europe.

In her darkened bedroom perched on the hills above the small seaside town of Levanto, Elvira Vitale, the Contessa, comes to. Her head is muzzy from wine and sleeping pills, and as often happens when she wakes she is not absolutely sure where she is, nor even whether it is early morning or late afternoon. Through the door, which is ajar, a thin silvery light is visible that could be dawn or dusk; what gives it away, as Elvira lies and gazes without focusing up at the embroidered canopy of her bed, is the sound of the insects. They are singing in the umbrella pines on the hill behind the house, a shrill high sound they only make once the sun has begun to go down.

Slowly Elvira gets off the bed. There is not a sound in the house; is Jack there? She doesn't know where he is, her handsome husband, but that isn't unusual. He could be drinking cocktails by the sea or asleep in his room; distinctions between night and day don't mean anything much to Jack. He thinks it very middle-aged to keep regular hours. Elvira walks out on to the balcony and looks down.

She is known as the Contessa in the town below, a town which was once no more than a fishing village, because when she bought this house, a million years ago when she was twenty-five, smooth-skinned, full-breasted and flush with success, she was married to a Count. The tide has stuck – something, perhaps, to do with Elvira's natural authority – although they all know the Count is no more, dead of a drug overdose

3

in a London hotel room one long-ago August. Elvira had left him by then, but even now she doesn't like to think of him looking out through dusty hotel windows at some dismal city view, a lightwell or a fire escape, London in August.

Elvira always spends that month here, by the sea, and, increasingly, adds on some of July and September too. They hurtle down through France on the *Autoroute du Sud*, Elvira gazing silently at the blur of scenery, willing them southwards. Elvira's heart always lifts when she sees the glittering sea, and as they wind up around the narrow hairpin bends, leaving the bougainvillea and hibiscus that overhang the high stone walls fluttering behind them; even now she feels the return of the old familiar excitement. The colours of her own country, the flowers all electric blue, magenta and burnt orange, carelessly bestowed by nature in such glowing profusion on this glittering shore. But most of all the knowledge that holiday time is here, that anticipation of a month or more of *benessere*, the glow of the sun on her skin, the sting of salt water; even if they do wrinkle and roughen, Elvira can't resist.

The Contessa has arrived, the residents of Levanto would say, *with her English boy* no doubt muttered under their breath a moment later. It's not just that Jack is young that they don't like; they disapprove of her turning her back on her own countrymen. If only they knew. As they approach the house Elvira likes to eye up each tall iron gate they pass, craning her neck to see whose shutters are still closed, who is in town and who has not yet arrived, whether they have come too early or too late. But each year when it is time to go back to London Elvira spins it out a little longer, tells Jack to go on back without her for a week or two; each year it seems to matter a little less that she should stay on alone, that she should be the last to leave,

4

after Jack, and after all the fashionable summer visitors too. Perhaps because he is English, perhaps because he has never in fact had a proper job, Jack doesn't have quite the same feeling about the holiday season. Life is one long holiday for Jack.

Outside it is almost dark; the Contessa's house, as they know it down below, faces away from the setting sun. The long, green-shuttered windows, the stone terrace running the full width of the first floor, look across a steep canyon and down to a tiny inlet where the dark sapphire-blue water turns to foam against the rocks. The Contessa's view of the sea is oblique, but she prefers it that way; it seems less bare-faced, less vulgar, and it allows her to look inland too, if she wants to. Down the neighbouring hill tumbles the pretty, near-deserted village of Grosso, and across the valley, looking straight out to sea, sit the turreted and balconied summer houses of her rich neighbours. From here Elvira can look at them, but they can't look back.

The terrace of the Contessa's house is of generous proportions, tiled, balustraded and densely fragrant with roses, jasmine and honeysuckle. Elvira takes a deep breath, and feels her head begin to clear at last; she walks to the edge and stands with her hands on the stone. The far-off iron rattle of the coast train coming out of a tunnel echoes around the valley inland.

As she looks Elvira hears a sound behind her, coming around the cliff, feels turbulence in the air. The menacing thump of a helicopter's rotors that grows louder by the second until it is a deafening scream, then the machine and its noise are past her, receding, swooping along the coast and down. Elvira puts a hand to her hair as it is whipped around her head, pulls her gown around her, and watches. A *carabinieri* helicopter, not the coastguard or the police, it dives like a dark blue dragonfly, down behind the far cliff to sea level. Idly Elvira wonders what they are up to now; a drugs bust, perhaps, a car chase, a smash-up on the coast road. I need a drink, Elvira thinks, giving in at last.

It's late now, close on eleven-thirty. Down in Levanto, at the railway station the platforms are silent and almost empty; the fluorescent lighting makes little impression in the velvet darkness that looms overhead. Ania is waiting for the last train to Genova; she isn't usually so late but tonight she felt like pretending she was on holiday here, wandering through the streets among happy, sunburned children, having a swim after dark. She watches a train pull in on the opposite platform. A man stands smoking in the corridor, pale and unshaven; he is leaning against the window on his elbows and looking across the tracks at Ania. She stares straight ahead, but as the train moves off the man turns his head to look back at her.

On the platform the few passengers the train has disgorged are making their way towards the exit. There's an African guy Ania recognizes, wearing a cheap copy of the black and white Juve strip; effortlessly he shoulders a huge black nylon holdall bulging with merchandise. He's back from a day spent hawking sandals and sarongs on a more upmarket beach; Forte dei Marmi, perhaps, where the rich Milanesi go to stake themselves out in rows on their pre-booked places under expensive striped parasols, and he's back for the night. Some of the immigrant workers sleep on the beach; some of them, like Ania, have a corner of some semi-derelict industrial building, a warehouse or a cold store or a stockyard made to look like home with a rug and thin, makeshift curtains, a shanty town or trailer park half-hidden from polite view by bamboo thickets.

Ania watches as a couple of youngish men with baseball caps pulled down over their faces hunch their shoulders and mutter to each other at the exit, making some hasty arrangement. Ania tightens her headscarf and averts her eyes, looking down the track after the receding train, waiting for hers to arrive. She wants to go home, although that's not where her train will take her.

It's after midnight when the train clanks sullenly into Genova, and Ania is so tired she could lie down and sleep right there in the empty carriage but she rouses herself. It is only when she sees an old man on the west-bound platform with his daughter that Ania wants to cry. The girl looks pale and tired and he has his arm around her, protecting her, it seems to Ania, from all the things that she herself has to steel herself against every day; from the dark, from the noises that echo around the cavernous station, from strangers. He is taking her home. Ania, alone on her platform now, turns away.

Chapter Two

It was, of course, too late by the time Rose Fell began to wonder whether she'd done the right thing. The house was sold by then, and the money divided up, the leaving party held, the promises made to call, to visit, to commission a column. They'd all been trying to warn her, it seemed to Rose in retrospect, even at the leaving party; the careful congratulations and worried looks: why had she so easily persuaded herself they were just jealous?

After all, Rose couldn't deny it had been a kind of rebound thing, out of the divorce courts and into exile, a way of putting it all behind her. Running off to a place in the sun, where she had no roots, no contacts, no friends. A mid-life crisis; the features pages and television schedules were full of them after all, disastrous attempts to start a new life abroad, plucky little Brits battling against foreign customs and hostile legislation, doomed to failure and humiliation. At least she could speak the language; surely that was something?

It hadn't taken Rose long, everyone remarked with the definite implication that she had been hasty, to find her house in Italy. And it was true, anyone else she knew who thought about buying somewhere abroad, even a little holiday home, seemed to mull the idea over for a few years until either they found what they proclaimed to be the perfect place or, much more often, the idea was quietly shelved. But Rose had decided on her area (the nearest part of Italy, not far from the sea), had gone to the internet, found a handful of websites that offered pictures and booked herself on a cheap flight to Genova.

She'd looked at a lot of dumps, for the money. She had half the proceeds of the sale of their small terraced house in Lewisham (the only part of London, it seemed, bypassed by the property boom), less solicitor's costs, some money set aside for Jess at university and a modest financial cushion for Rose's first year abroad. Which left enough for two bedrooms, a bit of a view but not of the sea, a patch of garden.

Things, it seemed, happened very differently in Italy. There were no estate agent's details handed out in advance to warn buyers of a flyover past the bedroom window, a view of plastic pipes in a builder's yard or squalid bathrooms, and all the prettily pictured properties Rose had seen on the net had mysteriously disappeared once she arrived, or morphed into something quite different. Windowless flats in modern blocks, old olive presses without benefit of roof, walls or access, and once, a stuffy third-floor apartment without any bathroom at all, inhabited by an extended family of eight whose cooking smells hung heavy in the air and grubby handprints ornamented every wall.

In two days Rose looked at eighteen houses and flats, smiled politely to disguise her dismay until her cheeks ached. It was quite different, she came to understand, to look at a place with the eyes of a tourist, out of here in a day or two and on to pastures new, seeing only the bigger picture, an exquisite skyline, a purple sunset, picturesque decay. When you looked at a place with a view to permanent residence you started seeing the dogshit and the dustbins, smelling the drains. Rose suddenly couldn't help noticing how tired and poor people seemed as she looked around, not the *centro storico* she would have restricted herself to as a tourist but a sun-bleached, dusty suburb or a down-at-heel sidestreet on the edge of an industrial estate. Her heart would sink at the sight of an old woman hobbling painfully up a grimy, pungent stairwell to a flat on the third floor, the acrid stink of cats locked in an apartment all day, a harassed, ill-tempered mother trying to get her children ready for school. Then the agent brought her up here, to Grosso.

A few miles inland and steeply uphill from the buzzing, faintly vulgar seaside town of Levanto, Grosso seemed a quiet place; almost deserted, in fact, despite its picturesque appearance. There was no shop in the village, nor restaurant, although it was said that a private house at the top occasionally offered meals in a rickety sun room overlooking the valley to the few tourists brave enough to make their way inland. There was also, improbably given the series of narrow hairpin bends that made up the route down into the valley, a bus service to Levanto, and in extremis, Rose decided, already persuading herself as she emerged from the house and looked around, the agent by her side, she could walk to the little town in a little under an hour. In time, of course, she might even get a car.

It was the first time she had found herself thinking like this, thinking that it was actually going to happen. She realized that until she saw Grosso she had resigned herself to failure, to an abject return to Lewisham, and her heart leaped at the thought that she might, after all, be able to do it.

There were no roads in the village itself; the road up from Levanto stopped below the church where a handful of rusting vans and mopeds sat beneath faded tarpaulins in the sun. The narrow, claustrophobic paths that wound up between the village houses were patched together, of concrete and cobbles, cracked and mossy, as though the whole place had been put together piecemeal and resisted gravity and disintegration only against the odds. It was afternoon when Rose first saw the place; every shutter was shut and the cats, thin, grey and half-feral, that appeared out of nowhere and wound mewling around her ankles if she so much as paused to catch her breath, were the only visible sign of life.

The house had been empty for some time; the owner, the agent said, had been an elderly widower who had not long outlived his wife, and the children, a son and daughter now in Milan, had not been interested in keeping it for summer holidays. The interior smelled of damp and neglect, and was mildewed and cobwebby, the rafters stained with smoke, the floor dusty with fallen plaster and the dried droppings of nameless animal intruders. It was made of stone, three storeys high with flaking green-painted shutters. But it had a heavy, seamed oak front door, cotto tiles, dark rafters and a *cantina*, albeit pitch-dark and damp, for storing wine in the rocky bowels of the hillside below. Better still, it was, to her surprise, within her price range.

Rose had stood with the agent on the rocky, uneven ground outside the kitchen door and looked across at the view to the west of another stone village tumbling down another hill further inland, with the flaking yellow steeple and little onion

11

dome of a little church just visible. To the north there was a steep, wooded slope, immediately above her was a straggle of village houses and below her some old olive terraces and a tumbledown pigsty belonging to the land – her land, as she was already beginning to think of it – all overgrown with weeds. You could not see the sea, but Rose imagined that she could sense it shifting, huge and restless, just out of sight, could even detect its wild and salty perfume. She knew it was there, that was the main thing, just around a corner, just beyond the palisaded terrace of a beautiful, decaying villa, a villa belonging to an Italian movie star, so the agent said, naming her self-importantly as though Rose should recognize her. Rose had looked across the valley at the trees, almost black in the August sun, and heard the approaching whine of a Vespa climbing the hill, a sound quintessentially Italian. She inhaled the musty scent of some elusive herb from the warm earth sloping down below her and listened to the creaking of crickets in the trees. A lemon tree in a pot, overgrown with weeds, was in flower on the cracked terrace next door and when a breeze from the sea stirred the air a waft of its sweetness drifted across to her.

Rose had thought of Tom, her ex-husband, and his new home in Chiswick with his new wife, and breathed deeply, deliberately. They held hands, he and the new wife, when they went walking together; Rose had encouraged him to go on the walking tours when he got to forty and seemed to feel that something was missing from his life – or perhaps, from their life. She looked around at the absolute foreignness of the scene, a place where she knew no one and no one knew her, and she thought, all right, then. She couldn't go back. 'I'll take it,' Rose had said, startled at the sound of the words coming from her mouth. The agent had only nodded briefly, incuriously, as though none of this was any surprise to him.

It seemed to Rose now that she had spent the seven weeks it had taken to complete the deal holding her breath, lest she change her mind, lest she see sense. She had a brusque meeting with the house's owners, the middle-aged brother and sister, who seemed not on entirely friendly terms with each other but were businesslike (and, Rose intuited, in a hurry to complete where such an unknown quantity as a foreign buyer was involved). The whispered negotiations over price completed, the agent, the notary, the vast tax and removal bills all paid, she had, at first, felt relief, then triumph. It was only now that she was beginning to wonder if she shouldn't have done things more slowly. Thought about the pitfalls; listened to the warning voices, wondered about why the house had stood unsold for so long.

Perhaps, Rose thought as she clicked on the kettle (being careful to check, instinctive by now, that neither the iron nor the washing machine was on concurrently, for fear of blowing a fuse or perhaps the whole fuse-box, this time), she had reached the end of her honeymoon period. She had arrived in Grosso, with the removal van that had failed to climb the hill more than halfway and had disgorged her possessions on a bend, at the tail-end of the previous summer. A year ago, soon. There had been a week of Indian summer, cool mornings and golden days, then in October it had begun to rain, and the rain had gone on for two months, implacable and relentless.

It had been then that Rose had begun to wonder, as the villas were closed up on the hills looking out to sea, the awnings of the empty market-stalls flapped sadly in the autumn rain, and one by one the bars pulled down their shutters and

13

left them down. She'd wondered whether in fact it wasn't only she who had no roots here; perhaps no one did. Perhaps, like the sun-bleached deckchairs on the private beaches, the relationships too, the old people standing and talking in the dusty square outside the church, the games of bowls, the cheery restaurateur and his regulars, perhaps they were all folded up and put away for another year, too. But then Rose had written a piece about it, dashed off a few hundred words about seaside towns out of season and filed it; it had been published with a nice picture and she'd felt better. She was working, at least, and when she looked at the photograph of the sparkling sea that accompanied her piece she felt satisfied. Who, after all, could possibly prefer London, in winter? Or indeed at any other time of year?

Rose held her nerve through the short, dead days of November, when the rain began to ease, and December, when there was a brief flurry of activity on the hillside, nets were spread and the olives harvested. She kept her spirits up even in January, when hailstorms whipped the coast and an icy wind blew in through the rattling window-frames. She still had no central heating, having foolishly put its installation off, thinking, this is the Mediterranean, and the fierce winds off the sea blew the smoke back down the chimney into the little wood-burning stove and her sitting room, dulling the newly whitewashed walls. In February the weather turned, the mornings glittering with frost, the sky an incandescent blue. But there was barely a soul to be seen on the streets even of Levanto, the silence was profound, and Rose found herself working ever harder to fight off a creeping sense of isolation.

She had steeled herself and gone on writing, and things had been published, here and there. In April the wild flowers came, blue chicory, poppies and vetch and plenty more Rose didn't know the names of. She picked them and put them on her wooden table; she wanted to tell someone about them, but there was no one to tell; she wrote to Jess, didn't expect a response and received none. Her acquaintance seemed to dwindle almost to nothing, and she clung to the human contact she had, two words exchanged with near-strangers in the Arcobalena, the only bar to stay open out of season in Levanto, and the woman who ran the minimarket. Emails from home were scrutinized for news, every drop of warmth extracted from a handful of casual sentences, but no one came to visit over the winter, as she had expected. And all together it didn't even add up to the most basic sense of community, not even the knowledge there were doors you could knock on, the prospect of meeting a gang of friends for a drink, stopping in the street to chat.

Then there was Jess. Rose couldn't expect her to phone, no grants these days, couldn't expect her to spend her student loan on international phone calls. And whenever Rose tried to get hold of her, either the phone rang unanswered in the empty hall or she heard a stranger's voice, some incoherent, uncomprehending fellow student who promised to pass on a message but obviously would not be capable of doing any such thing. She'd had a card at Christmas, an ironic, glittery Woolworth's card, cheerful enough. Jess said she'd visit, maybe at Easter.

Easter came and went, and Jess didn't show, but Rose got a card from Spain. At least she's happy, Rose thought, and after all, I chose to come out here, to abandon my daughter. She resisted the temptation to write Jess a long, pleading letter, suggesting a holiday in the summer. In May Rose had taken the train along the coast to Cannes for the film festival, and squeezed a couple of articles out of that. She managed to secure an interview with Giorgio Venturelli, an art-house director from Turin who'd made his name in the seventies, with a film premiering at the festival, a film about bourgeois attitudes in the industrial heartland of northern Italy. She'd watched the film with growing bemusement, a sense that perhaps she had moved to Italy under the influence of a grave misapprehension of the national character. The film seemed to suggest the Italians were a repressed, melancholic lot, and when she interviewed Venturelli she wanted to say, you should try England, you don't know the half of it. But it was unsettling to be reminded of how little she knew about the people among whom she had decided to live. Part of the learning process, she told herself stoutly; getting to know how things really are.

Rose plugged on; she filed a piece about the behaviour of B-movie starlets on the Croisette, something about rural poverty in northern Italy, a cookery feature on focaccia, wrote a couple of hundred words to accompany someone's photographs of Art Deco Italian beach bars. But the serious commissions she'd hoped for hadn't come along, and deep down, she wasn't surprised. That must have been what those guarded expressions at her leaving party meant; it won't be easy, you know. It's a hard slog, freelance. So Rose was branching out.

The little stone pigsty at the foot of her steep, tumbling garden was to be converted, never mind the fact that she hadn't got around to making a quarter of the changes she'd planned for her own house. Rose was going to try her hand at B and B, in season. The fact that she wasn't much of a cook nor a housewife was not, she decided, going to deter her; it was to be an experiment, she told herself firmly. She had just enough money in the bank, the last of her settlement, to cover the builder's estimate for the work; he would come and start, he said, after Ferragosto and the work should be completed before the rain arrived, October or November.

Rose took her mug of tea — it never did taste the same, perhaps it was the rusty mineral-rich water of the hills, or the dusty foreign teabags, filled with a lower grade of floor-sweepings than even English teabags — and walked outside. The sun was up, although Rose's terrace was still in the shade of the steep, uninhabited green hill opposite her house. A haze rose off the road below even this early in the morning, and Rose could feel the sweat forming on her upper lip in the heat; she hadn't been prepared for that, the heat. She still found it unnatural to sleep without the weight of a quilt or a duvet on her; a sheet seemed too insubstantial, but even that was a layer too many on some of these August nights. Rose didn't sleep well, turning in the bed, wishing she'd had the money for air-conditioning, opening the shutters then closing them again when they admitted not a breath of air.

It was very quiet this morning; it always was. The narrow alleys of Grosso were not only closed up and deserted during the siesta hours; most of those shutters, she now knew, never opened at all. But although it was not long after six she could see a tiny, bowed figure toiling far below her among the silvery olives; Gennaro. Rose sat down with her tea steaming between her hands and watched.

Chapter Three

It was close on ten when Elvira wandered out of her room and looked around the door at Jack; the sun that burned its way through the long muslin curtains on the landing hurt her eyes. It was early for her, but she'd been woken before the sun was even up by another helicopter, and hadn't been able to settle.

Sometimes Elvira thought her life was spent watching her husband sleep. Did he do the same for her? He lay face down on the vast bed, his head against the pale pigskin of his headboard. Elvira had had this room redecorated for Jack, as a surprise, leather everywhere and cedar wardrobes from a specialist shop in Jermyn Street, and it was finished just in time for them to return here for the last few days of their month-long spring honeymoon, after Mauritius, New York and Paris. There had been money, then, for that kind of thing; what with one thing and another, the stock market and a crooked broker in Milan and five years of funding Jack's expensive habits, there didn't seem to be so much money now.

Elvira looked down at him, lying there naked in the heat and snoring faintly, the sheet across his lower back. There was not a suspicion of spare flesh on his back, not even a handful or two just above the hips, nor a little thickening of the waist; Jack took care of himself.

Elvira put a hand to her temple, where she could feel the beginning of a headache, then walked slowly over to the leather club chair and plucked off the dark linen trousers left dangling from one of its well-upholstered arms. There were no keys, no change to jingle to the floor and wake Jack as Elvira swiftly left the room with the prize. Like royalty, Jack never carried money with him when he went out, and when he returned, as he had this morning at one or two, he knew the door would be left open for him.

It didn't take Elvira long to go through Jack's pockets; sometimes, in her happier moments, she was able to laugh at herself for it. His platinum credit card, a book of matches, one struck, from the Luna di Miele. Elvira knew the Luna di Miele, a rather fashionable nightclub in Genova, but she had never been there. She didn't like nightclubs much any more, now that they were full of women less than half her age and men she thought she might have met somewhere else, in another lifetime. The lights in the ladies' rooms were invariably unflattering at two in the morning, particularly if you found yourself standing next to a seventeen-year-old in body glitter and chain mail, and the morning after, these days, even the carefully rose-tinted lights in Elvira's own bathroom didn't work their usual magic. A dog-eared train ticket, an old receipt, folded small, and from the bottom of one pocket Elvira's long, manicured fingers emerged dusted and gritty with a fine powder. She looked down, frowning for a moment or two before flicking

19

the trousers back through the open door where they landed more or less where Jack had thrown them the night before. Jack called it paranoia, this anxiety about where he'd been and who with. He put it down to Elvira's drug use, once upon a time. He didn't know she looked through his pockets; she wondered what he'd call it then.

'Darling,' he'd say. 'The statistics aren't good. I mean, I can see why, better than booze for the skin, the waistline, all that. But long-term psychiatric problems, that's what they say. Moderation is the key.'

Jack had to add the last bit, as he wasn't a stranger to cocaine use himself; just occasional, of course, and the difference was, he knew he was in control. Or so he said. Elvira didn't feel quite able to admit to him that her youthful reputation as a hedonist had been largely manufactured by a series of unscrupulous agents. Painkillers, prescription stuff, yes, and she'd had a taste for champagne, that was true. But although she'd smoked the odd joint with blithe equanimity when it was offered it never seemed to do the trick, and she was too shrewd to go in for the heavy stuff, although she wouldn't have told Jack. She had the impression he liked the thought of her as hard-living and debauched.

Elvira was an old-fashioned girl at heart, that was the truth, but that didn't sell movies, not in the seventies. And she hadn't looked old-fashioned, they'd made sure of that. There'd been a couple of staged shots in a New York nightclub, Elvira in draped silk slashed to her belly button with her pupils dilated black and huge, Elvira in a bikini with her eyes half closed and her arm around a panther on a diamond chain, just to fix the image of debauchery in everyone's minds. Jack had even sold one of those vintage paparazzi prints in the gallery, the price bumped up considerably by the appearance of the photograph's subject in person, a living legend. Elvira was a little uncomfortable being a living legend.

Paranoid. Perhaps she was. Perhaps Jack wasn't bored stiff, perhaps he didn't pick up twenty-year-old girls in nightclubs and go back to their apartments. Elvira could see it as clearly as if she was there herself: Jack in a rich girl's apartment, a couple of nineteen-year-olds sharing for the summer, expensive lingerie hanging over the end of the bed. Perhaps Jack didn't sit on their leather sofas and complain that his wife was too old, was losing her marbles, an alcoholic. Perhaps.

Was it to do with age, some menopausal thing? Certainly it seemed to have come over her only in recent years, this inability to keep things in proportion, a kind of fog that had been gradually descending, distorting things. What Elvira liked about getting back to Levanto every summer was that generally the world came back into focus here on home territory. The thought came to her that if that was to go, if even here the ground were beginning to shift beneath her, it might be time to admit that she had a problem. No, she decided, looking out at the sea, breathing deeply.

Ten o'clock, and Ania still hadn't arrived; Elvira wondered idly where she'd got to but somehow this morning it didn't seem important. The sky was clear and luminous, the hillside rich with the scents and colours of her childhood; in the trees she could hear the delirious chorus of birds, and out at sea a little white foam was cresting the waves. Elvira felt her nerves settle, her suspicions recede; she allowed herself to think of her husband with affection. Jack was deeply asleep; he'd got up just after sunset the previous evening, just as Elvira's tension, and her headache, were beginning to dissipate after a glass of champagne on the terrace. Perhaps the timing wasn't accidental; Jack was very good at choosing his moment, when he wanted a favour or knew he was in bad odour, and it didn't take an Einstein to work out that Elvira was usually the kinder for a glass of champagne. He had slipped down to Levanto, true enough, but he hadn't been late back, not for him. One o'clock, perhaps, that was what he had said, and Elvira could persuade herself she had a dim memory of his return, the click of a door as she dozed, a chair pushed back in his dressing room.

From her terrace Elvira could see a village, the straggle of houses that was Grosso, walls of peeling plaster and disintegrating stone tumbling in a sort of random, neglected way down the slope, brightened here and there by fresh rose-pink or lemon-yellow paint.

At the bottom of the village Elvira saw the figure of a woman emerge from her back door and stand, looking across the valley in the sun in an attitude of contented contemplation that marked her out as a foreigner. Elvira leaned forward in her chair for a moment and rested her chin in her hand, looking. She had seen this woman before, a tiny movement in the silent village, like a green curled leaf coming through winter soil, a sign of life. Elvira felt the faintest stirring of interest in the figure, in the woman's pale skin, the set of her shoulders, her gaze across the valley. In the fact that she seemed to be alone; at this she felt a stirring of the oddest and, to Elvira, the most unfamiliar combination of emotions; could it be envy, of a woman living alone in a broken-down house in the middle of nowhere? She wondered what the woman was looking at so intently, what she saw in the dense green forest; and then the distant figure turned, the small oval of her face framed by dark hair looking across at the sea and Elvira for a moment before she disappeared back inside.

As Elvira surveyed her neighbours her gaze came to rest on the prettiest house on the bay, looking down on her from the opposite slope: La Martinière. It was a lovely house, French in style, six sets of long, delicate glazed doors, intricate iron balconies on the upper windows. A gauzy curtain was just visible, fluttering from an open casement window. The house had a baroque formal garden, clipped hedges forming little rooms and alleys that tumbled down the hillside, pale yellow roses foaming around an arbour that overhung the sea.

Elvira studied the bleached façade, so tranquil, so symmetrical, and as she watched a tiny figure, no more than a blur from this distance but male in outline, opened a canvas umbrella and was swallowed up in its shade. Elvira frowned a little as the figure prompted a memory, like a long-forgotten and troubling dream; last year. She turned her face away involuntarily, feeling a flush at her throat as she remembered and an unease that settled in her stomach. She breathed out slowly; it had been nothing but her imagination, in the end, hadn't it? Slowly she opened her eyes again and the hillside appeared before her, warm and fragrant in the sunshine, La Martinière its beautiful ornament, and last year seemed a long time ago.

It had been a bad patch. A temporary blip, a nervous episode that would not be repeated, not if she was careful. The tranquil symmetry of La Martinière gazed back at her like a smile and Elvira screwed up her eyes in an attempt to see what she had seen there – or thought she had seen last year. Someone watching her. The flash of the sun reflected off a lens she had known with inexplicable certainty was trained on her; a car cruising slowly past her house and back again, and she'd called the police, fled back to London when September had hardly begun. How could she have got herself so worked up about it? Elvira sat back in her chair, closed her eyes and pushed the unease away, replacing it with thoughts of order, symmetry and beauty. Bathed in sun, re-creating the image of La Martinière's garden behind closed eyelids, she heard the creak of her own French windows, and the sound of Jack walking softly out on to the terrace. She did not open her eyes.

Ania had been away from home a little more than a year, home being a small Romanian village on the edge of a deep, dark pine wood near the Austrian border. She had left in September, after the harvest, which she had had to stay to help gather in, but was gone before the celebrations that followed.

She had stood on the platform waiting for the train that would take her north, then east, to France, her father standing by her side. She had been wearing the traditional scarf over her thick curly hair, tied tight under her chin, to please her father. She also wore a coat, as she hadn't been able to fit it into her bag with the jars of pickled cabbage and cucumbers and the two long loaves of rye bread, heavy as bricks, her mother had insisted she would need. Ania had stood there quite still, like an animal in the ninety-degree heat, because if she had moved the sweat would have poured from her, and they said nothing, she and her father. Sometimes he looked up the tracks for the train, then down at his feet, turning his tall farmer's hat over in his hands as if trying to frame his thoughts. But he said nothing, although it didn't matter because Ania knew what he was thinking.

And he had been right, of course; none of them were happy, those who left home to look for excitement and money, even

24

if, like Ania, they weren't doing it for a dream of riches but out of desperation. Even if they looked happy when they came back with enough cash to build new houses and buy whole sets of furniture brand-new, matching sofas and armchairs, beds with little ruffles around the bottom. They looked contented then because it was over and they were back home. That was the obvious thing that had never occurred to Ania, not until she came away herself.

She had made her way through Europe without a final destination in mind; first Paris, for ten months, and as her second summer approached, she had been offered a ride south in the sweaty cab of a lorry belonging to a friend of a friend, to the Côte d'Azur where, the word was, life was easier, the hills were full of millionaires, the sun always shone and the sea was blue. Needless to say, it had not worked out quite that way. The only place Ania was offered to live was a spare bunk in a motorhome owned by a Romanian, parked illegally along with a whole shanty town of similar vehicles on the edge of a landfill site.

Ania had found work here and there, cleaning work in the villas that dotted the hills behind Cannes and Grasse, and some them were, in fact, like paradise. The houses were large, crammed with marble and mirrors and ormolu and carved wooden furniture, all of which required a lot of cleaning, but palms grew in their gardens and every morning the grass was wet and the air scented with jasmine and orange blossom. But she was never needed for more than a couple of weeks at a time, hired and fired and passed around between households like an unsightly piece of domestic equipment that everyone found useful but no one wanted hanging around for too long.

By the end of June she made her decision, and one day

before dawn she packed up her few things and left her bunk neat before leaving the caravans behind her. In the grey morning she crossed the border into Italy; perhaps it didn't occur to her that she was gravitating back towards her homeland, away from northern order and back into overheated chaos, but she was. And that was how she had ended up in Genova, sleeping in the curtained-off corner of a cold store she shared with fifteen or so others, not to mention the ubiquitous trailers parked outside, with the sound of trains, Friday night punch-ups, and screaming rows echoing nightly around her. But Ania had had enough of paradise; this was more like home.

This boiling morning the train from Genova along the coast was delayed because of an incident further up the line; that was what Ania, squeezed in between a couple of talkative student travellers, gathered from their conversation with the guard. She wondered about him; it wasn't often you saw a guard on this line, and Ania was glad she had punched her ticket. She thought she'd seen policemen, too, on a couple of the stations they'd passed through, hands resting on their holsters, watching boredly as the train clanked past. Had there been trouble? The trains weren't the safest place, after all, at night particularly. Ania thought about her journey home the previous night, a feeling she'd had getting off the train in Genova, something that had made her wonder if she shouldn't take some more precautions. Rape alarm, something heavy in her bag that might serve as a weapon. You never knew how you'd react, after all, if it happened to you, whether you'd scream, or fight back, or just give in. Another memory stirred, some old news story about a serial killer – a Tunisian? – on the French trains, a year or so back. Ania was glad that it was broad daylight, and the train was full.

26

Uniformed in dark green, although he had removed his jacket in the heat, the guard had an air of great self-importance, and something about the way he portentously imparted information to his audience – an obstruction, waiting for the clearing crew – gave the impression he was in possession of wider and more interesting facts relating to the delay. Again, uneasily, Ania wondered what had really happened.

She looked out of the window, unseeing, and focused on tomorrow: her day off, Ferragosto. She thought she might take the train to one of the nice resorts – Portofino, maybe, or Santa Margherita Ligure – for the holiday, to walk along the front. She didn't want to come all the way to Levanto, and besides, it was her place of work. She wanted to be someone else just for a day, to look at the yachts and the beautiful houses, smell the flowers in the park.

They were half out of a tunnel, and Ania craned her neck to look out of the window. The day was bright and she could feel the heat from the hillside as they sat stationary on the glittering tracks. On the other side the sea was still and tantalizingly blue but inside the train the air was stifling and the passengers were becoming restless. The guard turned and left to walk towards the back of the train, and in his wake people shifted in their seats. Ania turned her cheap watch on her wrist, where the nickel had marked the skin with grey. An hour late, already. She thought of the holiday to come, a day off. Beneath her something changed in the idling hum of the train's engine and with a lurch it began to move.

Chapter Four

The body had been found at dawn. The year-round residents of the seaside villages were used to the sinister flotsam and jetsam that occasionally appeared on the stony beaches; the sea, after all, was a dangerous place. The deckhouse from a fishing boat lost from the radar a month earlier, condoms, syringes, even a yawning refrigerator, once. And that was the least of it.

The closer you got along the coast to Genova, the more sinister were the finds. A ringed hand, puffed and white after long immersion, a sealed steel barrel containing a limbless torso streaked with tar. One sullen grey March day a year or so back fifteen young Tunisians, on their way to what they thought would be a better life, had been washed up. They had appeared on the shingle of a little beach below Portofino, first one, then another, then two at a time, some stripped of clothing by the sea, their dark skin turned grey, on one a faded T-shirt ballooning in the dark waves. Forensic tents had been set up along the beach, where they remained for a whole week while the gruesome finds were processed. Even a child's sandal, ragged and bleached by salt water, could cause nervous old ladies to gasp and cross themselves, for fear of how it might have found its way into the water. But this was different.

Toto entered the office of Commissario Leo Cirri and dropped the folder on his desk, a couple of sheets of thick, pristine buff cardboard. A new file, just opened. Cirri's heart sank. Toto had been busy already.

The room was bright with August sunshine; Cirri had been up since the body was found, and he was feeling like death. He felt like he needed warming through.

'Well?' he said, the folder lying unopened in front of him. 'You've worked fast.'

'Not a prostitute,' said Toto.

Cirri raised his eyebrows. Toto shrugged. 'You're too old,' he said. 'That's how girls dress, these days. Or maybe you're not old enough; if Chiara was thirteen instead of three . . . ' He stopped, and turned to look out of the window.

Cirri frowned at the mention of his daughter's name, and an uneasy feeling stirred in his belly.

'So?' he said unwillingly, not wanting to know the details, nor wanting to think of Chiara either. When he had left the house she had been sitting in a big red plastic car, pushing herself around the garden in the early-morning sun. The file was still closed in front of him.

'A student,' said Toto, turning back to look at him. He loosened his uniform tie in the heat, pulled at his collar to ease it. Toto was a big man, with dark, heavy skin; he sweated easily.

'Anna-Maria Villemartin. Eighteen years old, mother Italian, father French – they're separated. The daughter

29

was living at home with her mother, in the city.' He jerked his head backwards, to the west along the coast where Genova lay.

Cirri put his hands palm down on the folder. 'Have you spoken to the family?'

'The mother,' said Toto. 'Yes; she lives just this side of the city. Haven't traced the father yet, the mother hasn't spoken to him in some time, she says. Five years or so. There's no answer yet from the number she had for him – no machine, no fax, it just rings.'

Cirri nodded, looking down at his hands. 'So. Keep trying it though. The mother might have lost touch.' He paused, looking up. 'But the daughter, you know. She might have stayed in contact, behind the mother's back?'

Slowly Toto nodded. 'So you think – you're not connecting this with – with last year?'

Cirri chewed his lip thoughtfully. 'I don't think the similarities – no, not yet. Of course I'm thinking about it but – better to cover every angle. To begin with. And he has to be told, doesn't he? The father. In the end.'

Toto was looking down at the folder. 'What do you think?' he said, nodding at the desk where it lay.

Cirri sighed. 'Look,' he said, 'okay, they didn't live far from each other, these two girls. If you want to make a connection between them, go ahead. Check a few databases, I suppose it does no harm. But I don't want you to jump to conclusions. Okay?'

Toto nodded thoughtfully, then seemed to collect himself and realize what he was being told. 'Sure,' he said, reanimated. The door banged shut behind him.

For a moment Cirri sat there, unmoving. Slowly he stood

30

up, turned and closed the shutters, one by one, and only then did he return to his desk. He opened the file.

Bodies found on the beach came from the sea, that was how it was supposed to be. The violence, accidental or otherwise, was done to them elsewhere, and the beach was simply where they ended up. Although the discovery of a body always sent a shudder through whichever community had become its final resting place, the crime, or violence, was not local, or at least so they could persuade themselves. The preliminary impressions of the pathologist, though, were that this one, this girl, this Anna-Maria Villemartin, showed no signs of immersion; no water, salt or sweet, was found in her lungs, her tissues had not been softened and bloated by the sea. That was not to say, however, that she was intact. Cirri picked up the blurry digital print on the top of the folder's contents, the image blown up to the size a grandmother might request a framed graduation picture for her mantelpiece, and held it between his hands.

The body was at an angle on the rocks, an arm across her stomach, a black streak of hair across a white cheek. At the time of her death Anna-Maria had been wearing faded, narrow jeans, very low-slung so that her sharp, pale hip-bones were exposed, and a tight, short-sleeved top slashed between her breasts, half-exposing them. Cirri couldn't tell from the picture if this was the style of the T-shirt, or a sign of violence. The fingernails on the hand Cirri could see were ragged, and one was ripped down to the cuticle, leaving the fingertip raw and exposed. Around her neck was a fine, sharp line, hair-thin and livid purple, and although there was not much blood, Anna-Maria's head was so battered it must have been almost unrecognizable, even to her mother.

Cirri wondered how she had been identified. He laid down

31

the photograph and picked up the sheet of paper, a printed form, that lay below it. It listed an identity card among personal items found on the victim, and a photocopy was attached, dog-eared and grubby. He looked at the photograph. You could tell she had French blood, a sallowness about the complexion, a suggestiveness about the mouth, but she had beautiful eyes. Had had. Dark, long-lashed, curving up a little at the corners. With a sigh Cirri laid the folder down and sat there in the gloom for a long time.

Chapter Five

Rose's house had two rooms on each floor. Above the cellar stood the kitchen, and a little living room which contained the wood-burning stove, a braided rug and a sofa; it was cosy in the winter, but a little dark in summer unless the doors were open to the terrace. So Rose had chosen as her work room the second bedroom, whitewashed, raftered, a new wooden bed all made up for Jess, if and when she ever decided to visit, and a table by the window. With the window open Rose could hear the distant restless sound of the sea and, with comforting regularity, the echoing roar of a train.

Rose liked the sound; by some Pavlovian mechanism it stimulated her to work. In Lewisham, in the little house in which she had spent her whole working life since the age of twenty-two, where her marriage to Tom had begun and ended and where, nineteen years before, Jess had been born, there had been a railway literally at the end of the garden.

The railway line closest to the house had been used largely

for freight, and the trains did not run very often. But when they did, clanking through the hawthorn and gooseberry bushes at the end of the garden, they loomed over Rose at work on her verandah; massive, thunderous, anachronistic, a deafening, unignorable reminder of declining industrial power.

Rose had written out her whole life to the accompaniment of that sound, she sometimes thought; she had written about her wedding at Lewisham Registry Office for *Brides* magazine, about her pregnancy – weight gain, libido, breast size – about toddler-taming and choosing schools in deprived, inner-city areas, about the seven-year itch. She had discussed student loans and top-up fees when Jess was taking her A-levels, and then she had found herself talking about empty-nest syndrome, how to manage your husband's mid-life crisis and the need for couples to develop new interests in middle age. She had written a piece about Tom's walking tours in *Good Housekeeping*.

Rose had developed an interest in her garden, in response to her own advice, and while she had stayed in Lewisham, determinedly creating beds of bearded irises, unusual geraniums and musk roses, carmine and magenta and pearly white, planting, digging, replanting, Tom had gone ever further afield. First it was the Dales, then the Peaks, then the Munros. He had gone to the Alps, the Tour de Mont Blanc, the Atlas in Morocco. Rose had produced a piece for a men's magazine about the masculine need for equipment – lightweight rucksacks, harnesses, carabiners – and speculated that perhaps it constituted a substitute for war. One spring Tom had gone to Greece on a trek through the Peloponnese with a group of botanists in search of early wild flowers, and when, on his return, Rose had tried to milk him for information, he had refused to give her any. She should have guessed then, but she hadn't.

It was another month or two before she knew; Rose had been genuinely astonished when at last Tom had blurted it out. That he was leaving her, that he had fallen in love with someone else, and finally, white-lipped with mortification and as close to being savage as she had ever seen her stolid, patient husband, that he'd had enough of his every movement being documented in one women's magazine or another. Of course, he was right, and she had been wrong; with a sickening, heart-stopping lurch she had known it immediately. But it was too late now.

Thinking about Tom, about her own obtuseness, when she had told herself – how had she convinced herself that it didn't matter? Because she wrote about herself, too? – that Tom wouldn't mind his writing about her, that he wouldn't notice – Rose found herself sighing involuntarily. It was an uncomfortable presence in her thoughts, in her conception of herself, the stubborn fact of her wrongness. She was ashamed. Too late.

Rose sighed again, and raised her head from the humming screen of her computer, where she had been struggling to retrieve a piece of the previous day's output, a work in progress about Italian builders that she thought might be a lucrative by-product of the conversion of the pigsty, and she looked out of the window. The peeling green paintwork provided a pleasing frame to the little church inland across the valley, and the shifting colours of the trees; it was a shame, Rose thought, that she sat here in front of such a view and spent most of the time looking at her computer.

In her chair she shrugged off the shirt she had put on over her sundress; even the thin cotton seemed heavy and damp in the late-morning heat. She blew her fringe out of her eyes, cooling the skin of her forehead, trying to focus. She looked back down at her computer, and frowned. A glowing rectangle had appeared on the screen, a warning of corruption. Corrupted files. Under her breath Rose swore, and pushed her chair away from the table in instinctive refusal; she was no good at this. Tom had always sorted out the technical stuff. As Rose glared at her laptop screen in silent frustration, she heard her name called from outside, barely recognizable as her own had she not grown used to hearing it like this, so thick was the accent in which it was pronounced.

'Signora Fell? Signora Rose-e?' Rose stood, pushed the table aside a little and leaned out of the window. A lean, strong figure stood below her, his tanned face stretched in a grimace or a smile and turned up towards the window. It was Gennaro, and from one hand, held up towards Rose, hung a two-foot bloody drop of skinned animal.

Gennaro had first called on Rose about a month after her arrival, perhaps considering that if she was still there by then, halfway through October, she wasn't just visiting. But even before then Rose had seen him around. Although the other inhabitants of the village she encountered sometimes acknowledged her as they hurried home with their shopping or sat impassive on their doorsteps, just as often they didn't, and Gennaro stood out as unfailingly polite and cheerful. On that first visit he had brought her a dish of his own anchovies, salted and dressed with garlic and parsley and thick green oil, and Rose had been touched as well as impressed by his skill. She had decided that Gennaro represented the local inhabitants, extending the hand of friendship and hospitality, even though no others followed suit. She hadn't known then that in

Grosso Gennaro was considered almost as much of an outsider as she was.

Gennaro lived higher up in the village, in a tiny, pristine, yellow-painted balconied house facing towards the sea, whereas Rose's faced inland. He had not, however, been born in Grosso but in another, larger village higher up in the woods inland, and in addition had, he had told Rose with an expansive wave from his balcony that took in all the brilliant blue sea, spent his working life so far as a steward on the liners in and out of Genova. So he had had no part in the working of the land, in village life, until now. Rose laughed at herself; she had imagined Gennaro, when she had seen him among his olives, as a peasant farmer, a *contadino*, or when he brought her his sardines and anchovies, as a fisherman. She realized it was very English of her to make the distinction, but the thought of this wiry, tanned, capable man serving drinks on a gleaming white liner seemed in some small way unsatisfactory; jarring. A diminution. She told herself she was just thinking as a foreigner would think, an Englishwoman, in particular, judging him by unrealistic, sentimental standards.

Rose had sensed quite early on that Gennaro was a lonely man; why else, after all, would he visit her, a mere foreigner, bringing her cans of oil, anchovies, a greasy bottle of his fiery yellow wine? She knew that he had been married, his marriage had produced a daughter he hadn't seen for some time, but he lived alone now; she had not managed to work out whether he was divorced or a widower. What information Rose had Gennaro had communicated to her casually, not as though it might be of any significance to her to know that he was single, and she didn't want to give him the wrong impression by asking for further detail. She came to understand that he felt no affinity with the other villagers, who seemed to consist almost entirely of elderly women, nor they with him.

In mid-June, when the long summer break began, a handful of grandchildren arrived in the village, left for the summer with Nonna while their parents carried on with their work. They looked to Rose like city children, watchful, taciturn little creatures darting through the narrow streets, carrying out ambushes and covert operations; it was strange, she thought, in a country where children were said to be so highly prized, that these ones seemed so suspicious. Sometimes missiles would arrive on Rose's terrace: pellets, rubber bands, a soft football with half the air leaked out of it, and sometimes she would hear their urgent whisperings amongst the tangle of vines and olives below her terrace.

Rose did learn the names of some of the other villagers from Gennaro, information imparted, only when she asked, with a curious kind of veiled indifference. Tiziana lived the closest, a bandy-legged, sharp-tongued woman of close on seventy; hers had been the lemon tree whose scent had seduced Rose on her first visit to Grosso. She had some vines growing on a strip of land alongside Rose's garden, and fat tomatoes, and a grandson called Marco whose name she could be heard calling every evening with fierce exasperation. Rose didn't wonder Marco spent every daylight hour hiding from her in the ruins at the top of the village.

The front door of Tiziana's house opened, as did Rose's, although hers was never used, on to the main thoroughfare of the village, a dark, slippery alley running directly uphill. Her doorstep was kept very clean and it was here that Tiziana and her cronies would sit on summer evenings when thunderstorms threatened and their dark, shuttered kitchens must have been too oppressive. Here they could be heard complaining desultorily about the children, and the weather, although if ever Rose passed they would fall silent. In the mild early hours before dawn Rose sometimes heard them out at the back and if she looked out of her window she might see Tiziana, bowed under the weight of a tank of some chemical or other strapped to her back for spraying against rot or insects, or watering the wilting rows of leaves she managed to coax out of the hard earth. For the most part, though, they preferred to sit taciturn on their cool doorsteps among all the pungent smells of the alley, cat and moss and drains. Perhaps it was not surprising that these old women eyed cheerful Gennaro with suspicion, and the longer Rose stayed the more she could see that he was not like them.

In her kitchen she looked down on the skinned rabbit laid, too long, across her breadboard. She sighed; she had, she hoped, expressed her thanks adequately to Gennaro. Fretting about what might be wrong with her computer, she had not taken up his offer to show her how to stew it to make a sauce for pasta and she was not sure, now, whether this refusal had offended him. More to the point, now that he had gone, she had no idea what to do with the animal. Crudely she hacked it into more manageable pieces and stowed it in her fridge in a plastic bag. It reproached her through the plastic, red-muscled like an anatomical drawing, all sinew and splintered bone; Rose closed the fridge door on it and went upstairs to collect her laptop. She had twenty-five minutes to catch the train to Genova.

As she left the station and walked out into the scalding heat of the *piazza stazione,* Ania, thinking, *I'll just get through today*

39

and I've got a lie-in tomorrow, no matter if they bawl me out for being late, almost brushed Rose's shoulder. Rose was running in the opposite direction to catch the Genova train that stood, hissing impatiently, on platform one, and neither woman really noticed the other, although Ania instinctively shifted to one side as Rose came close, keeping out of the way.

Rose swung on to the train, just in time, and Ania, almost two hours late, turned out of the station's dusty glass doors to walk up the hill to the Contessa's house. She did not see Elvira on her way up because while Ania began the steep climb in the heat, keeping close to the shade of the fragrant, flower-hung walls, her employer was walking in the other direction. Elvira was walking away from Levanto, across the valley on a road that dipped and rose and wound and narrowed gradually until it became a single track high above the sea.

Chapter Six

By late lunchtime the white police tenting and fluorescent tape that had marked the presence of Anna-Maria Villemartin's body on the rocks at the end of the beach had gone, although a police officer was still there. In pale blue shirtsleeves, his peaked cap pushed back on his head, the policeman was clambering slowly from rock to rock within a narrow radius, perhaps three metres, of the body's position. The beach was crowded and the man was not unobserved by the holiday-makers as he moved to and fro, occasionally bending to examine something invisible, some scrap of waste paper or ancient beach towel caught between the stones. If any inquisitive or merely ignorant sunbather approached the area he could be seen sternly warning them off.

The forensic scientist, it was said in the bars along the seafront as their customers were tucking into their plates of *frutti di mare*, had given his preliminary verdict and gone back to Genova. The girl had been already dead when her body was left there, the barman at the Mare Blu announced with confidence and some indignation to an appreciative audience; she had fallen on to the rocks and sustained the injuries to her skull, but she had already been strangled. Fallen, or more likely thrown, on to the rocks from the cliff above, or from a moving train.

The barman's account was reasonably accurate, as it happened, although he wouldn't give his sources; Toto had been into the bar shortly after Cirri had dismissed him from his darkened office, and had felt the need to give vent to his frustration and to express his theories about the girl's death. Like the barman, Toto felt it as a personal affront that Anna-Maria's murderer should have chosen this particular beach, their beach, to dispose of his victim, plus he was offended at his boss's refusal to take his loyal second-in-command immediately into his confidence. So a coffee, then a beer, then a tirade in the bar had been necessary to relieve his feelings. Once, unburdened, Toto had fallen silent a little shamefacedly. He wondered whether to offer his theory that this death, might be connected with another murder, almost exactly a year before, of a young Albanian prostitute garrotted on the evening train from Genova to Florence and thrown carelessly out to lie beside the tracks like a piece of rubbish. Myriam Bosnic.

Toto decided, on balance, that he should not encourage speculation; all the missing-persons cases for years back would arrive on his desk: backpacking foreigners, runaways, depressed housewives. He knew without looking how many disappearances there were on this holiday coast in high season, girls swallowed up by the crowds. The Albanian girl's body had been found the day before Ferragosto in a bamboo thicket beside the track only a couple of miles to the east of Levanto;

out of sight of the town, and involving a prostitute to boot, this murder had made no waves in the Mare Blu.

The body was already gone, though, along with almost all the paraphernalia of police investigation; things were already beginning to return to normal in the town, and despite the barman's commentary the conversation in the Mare Blu was settling back into its usual grooves. The handful of ladies sipping an afternoon Campari from cocktail glasses at the bamboo tables had reverted to talking about the bank holiday – and the undesirables it attracted to their little idyll – about who had been wearing what on the previous evening's *passeggiata*, about the heat and the wind.

They did sometimes talk about Elvira, too, but on this occasion, perhaps because she had not been seen about very much to prompt gossip, they weren't discussing her. Perhaps they might have been if Toto had mentioned her visit to the police station the previous year, convinced that her neighbours were spying on her, imagining stalkers and men with telescopes and God knows what. It had only been Cirri's kindness that had kept the matter out of the public eye. But Toto had an inkling of the volcanic gossip he might set off if he were to drop the Contessa's name into the conversational mix at the Mare Blu, and he didn't want to get into all that.

The Mare Blu was delightful on a day like today; not too much wind, the heat building to scalding point outside in the streets, but over the bamboo tables the air-conditioning was working, the fans were turning lazily and no one moved too much. Everyone was happy, on holiday. Even Elvira, walking away down the coast path with her straw hat in her hand, looked happy.

In Genova, thirty miles to the west, it was a different story.

When Rose arrived at the central station the city seemed close to deserted in the intense heat. More than half the shops were shuttered up for the summer, and her timing left her less than half an hour to spare before the rest closed for lunch. She walked up and down the great arterial boulevards that crossed the city, the pavements blinding white in the sun, and found nothing that resembled a computer workshop, and the nylon briefcase that held her laptop was beginning to feel as though it was full of bricks. It had been a mistake to come; a cock-up. By two o'clock, when the heat in the broad, empty streets was close to unbearable and Rose was sweltering and thirsty and exhausted and ready to head for home, she realized she was lost.

An all-too-familiar sensation of being absolutely isolated in this paradise of a place overcame her and, close to tears, she stopped. She was in a pedestrian street that led uphill between chain stores and fast-food restaurants; there was a deafening metallic rattle as across the street the manageress of a shoe shop pulled down her shutters. Fastening the padlock at pavement level, she looked up curiously at Rose, who was standing there in the middle of the street: hot, indecisive, helpless. Transferring the heavy case to her other hand in an attempt to look purposeful, Rose looked around and saw a narrow sliver of a street leading sharply uphill to her left.

It must, she thought, be Genova's old town, an airless, tumbledown cat's cradle of alleys and tenements where the city had begun, and which, she calculated, stood between her and the station. The alley that led away from her was piled with rubble on a bend higher up and on top of the pile a stray dog, tail between its legs, looked down at her. Taking a deep breath and giving up all hope of finding someone to mend her computer, Rose set off up the steep, uneven slope and left civilization behind.

The dog limped away as Rose began to climb, and in the deep, chill silence she could feel settling around her she could even hear the sound of the animal's unclipped nails on the stone. In sharp contrast to the massive nineteenth-century stucco and stone buildings lining the avenues below, the shiny plastic and bright lights of the chain stores, the buildings here much more closely resembled the decaying streets of Grosso, but were steeped in some kind of more concentrated poverty and squalor. Humble, shabby houses, their plaster crumbling and dirty, jostled against one another; the paint on the front doors was peeling and their wood cracked with age and neglect. There was no sunlight in the street, and it was so narrow Rose could imagine some of these houses remained dark all day. Looking up for a glimpse of sky, she could see that the structures were built into and on top of one another, little precarious jetties supporting illegal extensions and dangerous balconies. She stopped, turned, and looked back.

She had climbed some way and now, far below, Rose could see a tiny glittering strip of the harbour. Somewhere amongst the chaotic jumble of dwellings around her she heard a shout, a surly, threatening sound that went unanswered. She turned to go on walking up, thinking that she could go over the top of the hill on which the old town was built and come back down the other side to civilization, and saw an old man looking down at her from a first-floor window up ahead. Elbows on the sill, in, a dirty white vest that hung loose on his scrawny frame, he was quite motionless, and pale as a ghost. His skin was bloodless, he was white-haired, even his stubble was white; only his eyes, hooded with age, were dark, in dark, deep sockets, and Rose felt them follow her as she walked below him. Although she didn't look up she detected a movement over her head, and walked faster; behind her she heard a rasp and the tiny splat of a gobbet of spittle hitting the ground. She couldn't help herself, turned to look back, and saw that the window was empty; as she watched, a fleshless white arm pulled the shutters to.

It took Rose another ten minutes to reach the top, where the alley disgorged her on to the uneven brick of a small piazza. It contained the blackened facade of a church half-concealed by corrugated iron, and the faded sign of a *mesticheria*, a hardware store long since defunct to judge by the dusty windows and heaped-up junk mail visible inside. A doorway decked with sun-bleached plastic roses stood open beside the shop, behind it steps leading down to a cavernous basement where she could hear music crashing and caught a waft of dope-smell drifting up into the light. Genova nightlife, by day. A few pigeons scratched about on the dusty stones. Rose leaned wearily against a wall, feeling its heat against her back, wiped the sweat from her forehead and wondered what on earth she was doing there.

Chapter Seven

Elvira had come a long way. She had traversed the valley facing out to sea between her house and La Martinière, each on its separate spur of land dipping down to the water, along a narrow path that served as a hiking track. She had, in fact, passed several hikers on the way, walking up from the Cinque Terre towards Levanto, woollen socks, climbing boots, ergonomic rucksacks and bush hats, and to a man – and woman, although it was difficult to tell the difference in those outfits – they had looked at Elvira as though she had arrived from outer space, in her expensive straw hat and dainty sandals.

Elvira paused and looked out to sea. She was on a rocky outcrop, bushy with gorse and juniper that disguised the fact that a few steps away from where she stood was a sheer drop three hundred feet to the tiny inlet below. She took a deep breath and as the clean, hot, aromatic air filled her lungs she felt an access of unreasonable exhilaration. The air glittered with heat around her; the sea was dazzling. Then from the straw bag slung across her shoulder came the bleat of her mobile phone, and the feeling evaporated.

'Darling,' she said slowly, looking at the display. 'Jack.'

She could picture him sitting on the terrace in his clean white linen, waving Ania away to make his coffee; if she turned to look she might even be able to see him from here. But she didn't; she stepped into the shade of an overhanging acacia, and turned to look the other way. On the other end of the line, his voice crackled with bad temper.

'Where are you?'

'I went for a walk, *caro*,' said Elvira. 'You were asleep.' She heard an angry sigh.

'Yes, well,' he said. 'I didn't know. The bloody woman – what's she called? The maid? Woke me up. Bloody woman. And do you know what the time is? She's late.'

'Ania,' said Elvira. 'She's called Ania.'

'Right, yes, Ania.' There was a pause, and Elvira heard a muffled instruction issued with exasperation, probably to Ania.

'Are you at the beach?' Jack's voice was suddenly loud again in Elvira's ear, and she flinched. 'Why didn't you take the car?' His voice was careful, probing.

'I wanted to go for a walk,' she said, reluctant. She heard Jack snort a little with disbelief.

'You hate walking,' he said, coolly amused. 'How are you feeling? Have you taken your pill?'

'Yes, yes,' said Elvira. 'I took it. I'll be back soon, darling, all right? Ania will make you some lunch.' Jack made a sound of grudging assent.

'See you soon, darling,' she said. She held the little silver phone up in front of her and switched it off.

Take your pill. Jack had everything under control. That had been the appeal, to begin with, something cool and unflappable, nothing ever got to Jack. Clinical, almost. She'd had enough of darkness and mess in her life. She'd run into him at the bar of some hideously expensive London nightclub where she'd been drinking champagne out of sheer, terrible boredom after six years living in this flat or the other, one in Switzerland, one in Milan, borrowing a friend's summer house in Sardinia. She'd decided she didn't need a real home, didn't belong anywhere, didn't deserve it. The house by the sea, this house, stayed shuttered up; the truth was, she was scared to death of getting bored if she stayed in any one place too long.

Even in the club's expensive, stifling gloom Jack had seemed to see straight away what she needed. Not passion, not genius, not love. He had a reputation, of course, killer looks, but she wouldn't have wanted anyone dull, would she? And what people didn't see about Jack, what only Elvira saw, was that he was like a doctor himself, in a way, controlled, careful, his hands cool and clean.

'Come along,' he'd said, laughing at the bar. 'Let me take you away from all this.' He'd driven her to the coast, to a hotel in some obscure eastern coast resort where they'd woken to a cold, brilliant winter day and a slate-grey sea. The hotel had been warm and silent, with the hushed, discreet atmosphere and rich, padded luxury only a great deal of money can buy. He had managed to surprise her just enough, and to please her, and Elvira felt herself surrender to the comfort he offered. Champagne, pills, carefully measured out, and life could be pretty civilized after all. *Why not?* she'd thought. *Who needs real life?*

Jack took care of it all now; he'd said she shouldn't be so slapdash about it, after all, medication was a serious matter, she needed a regime. They visited a man in Harley Street, carefully explained Elvira's needs, and it was all sorted. Jack filled the prescriptions for her, set the tablets beside her bed before going out in the evening. It was sweet of him, really. Occasionally, of course, Elvira found herself wondering about Jack's solicitude, but in a detached, dreamy sort of way; she couldn't somehow focus on what he really wanted from her.

She looked up; high on the cliff above her she could see a turret rising out of the trees. La Martinière. She listened for a sign that the house was inhabited, guests chatting around the long blue pool cut into the rock, the chink of glasses, but she could only hear the rasp of the cicadas in the midday heat. Elvira stopped and sat down on a rock in the shade. It was around here somewhere, the path that led up to the house; not much used; she'd been to a party here, long ago when she was young, and modelling. It had been then, walking back down to Levanto from here with her sandals in her hand as the sun came up over the headland, that she'd seen her house for the first time and thought, *that's the one*. Thirty years ago.

Elvira stood up; she could see the path now, the path lined with overgrown box and rosemary that led up to La Martinière; it was marked by an umbrella pine that leaned with the prevailing wind. For a moment she stood motionless, frowning into the distance, then she turned away, picking her way slowly and carefully down the stony path back the way she had come. By the time she got home the afternoon was well advanced, Ania had gone, and so had Jack.

There was chaos in the station; some kind of wildcat strike, and no trains were coming up from the south. Everything was delayed. When, at last, Rose climbed on to a train home it was after four and she was tired and hot; she should have been hungry too but the heat and her sense of failure had robbed her of appetite. The carriage was stifling, and despite the delays it was almost empty. At the far end sat an elderly couple; she in a shiny print dress, clutching an old-fashioned handbag on her knee, he, astonishingly, in a three-piece suit, his shirt buttoned up to the neck. Rose thought about getting old, the blood thinning, becoming impervious to heat and fearful of cold. There was another passenger in the carriage, closer to her, but she couldn't see his face, only a high, broad forehead, thick dark hair springing up from it. She watched as he turned to look out of the window, and reflected in the glass she could see a profile. His eyes were narrowed, as though he was looking along the platform for someone.

The train started off with a jolt and a creak; Rose was still idly examining the man's reflection in the window when he stood and reached up into the luggage rack. He took down a book, an old, battered, cloth-covered hardback, and Rose registered the fact that he was attractive. Something about his profile, his colouring, his broad shoulders, his strong, solid presence; she couldn't have said what. Then he turned and looked at her. Flustered, Rose looked down; for want of some distraction she pulled her laptop on to her lap and unzipped it. Although the man sat down again and was hidden from view, it was as though she could still feel him looking at her. And when she raised her head again, some moments later, it seemed to Rose that he had moved. Whereas before he had been hidden from her, now she could see his down-turned face – the thick arch of his eyebrows; a straight nose – between the head-rests. He might have been looking, might have turned away when she looked back. Rose felt stupid; *he's not interested in you,* she told herself. *You're deluded.*

The train stopped five times between Genova and Levanto and each stop, it seemed to Rose, suddenly in an agony of impatience to be home, seemed more painfully, creakingly slow than the last. But eventually, after a little more than an hour, they ground noisily into the shabby, familiar gloom of Levanto station. Eager to be off, Rose was already at the door. The northbound platform was packed, and she remembered the strike. There were hundreds of them, student travellers sitting disconsolately on their backpacks, old ladies holding their hands across their stomachs and scowling up and down the tracks. Some were striding up and down, arguing angrily, but there were plenty of others sitting patient and quiet, the invisible ones resigned to spend their lives waiting, the immigrant street sellers and cleaners, care workers and home companions. Rose felt a stab of guilty relief that she had made it home herself while these had God knew how long before they could get to their beds.

Impatient to be out of the dusty confinement of the train, through the crowds and on her way, Rose reached for the button that would release her and suddenly there he was, beside her, an old canvas holdall in one hand and his book in the other. She could see the title: *Passaggio a Trieste*. Rose opened her mouth, but she had nothing to say, and she closed it again.

The man smiled a little, and she felt his gaze rest on her, considering her somehow. She looked back, dumb. 'After you,' he said, in perfectly accented English. Rose stepped off the train ahead of him.

Chapter Eight

The day of Ferragosto dawned bright and hot. The climax of the summer season, prepared and longed for since January in the resorts along the Riviera coast. Dreaded by some, particularly those working in infernal restaurant kitchens without air-conditioning in the August heat; all covers booked, the kitchens would sweat and smoke and tempers would fray. Chefs collapsed with heat stroke or threatened their underlings with boning knives. Every campsite and hotel was fully booked, and in the dining rooms, whether they were the dim front parlours of back-street guest houses or the glittering, panoramic, silver-service ballrooms of seafront grand hotels, every table was laid for breakfast on the morning of Ferragosto.

In Levanto, out of the centre things were quiet, the police station was shuttered up, only a desk officer on duty for emergencies. Reports and intelligence gathered on the death of Anna-Maria Villemartin sat orderly on Cirri's desk.

They had found the father, Cirri and Toto, late the previous evening. One Yves Villemartin, a miserable, scrawny drunkard of a man hunched over a glass of Vecchia Romagna in a filthy bar by the border crossing in Ventimiglia. The bartender, a fat man in a dirty vest, had no compunction about pointing him out straight away to the police and then observing their proceedings with undisguised interest as he ineffectually passed a greasy cloth over his bartop. Yves Villemartin was a man with few friends, then, but he did have what seemed to be a cast-iron alibi for the time of his daughter's death. He was of no fixed abode but on the night in question had been on a drip in casualty, waiting for a bed. He had been found on the street in Ventimiglia the morning before his daughter died and had been taken in, unconscious and dehydrated after a three-day bout of alcohol-related vomiting. Anna-Maria had been alive and well and drinking coffee with her college friends in the suburb of the city where she lived with her mother, far away from her father whom she had hardly known at the time of her death, and just as well, in Toto's opinion.

A double shot of the cheap brandy in front of him on the smeared aluminium table, Yves Villemartin had still had a grubby sticking plaster on his forearm where the drip had been inserted. His watery, bloodshot eyes gazed hopelessly from the mugshot on Toto's report on Cirri's desk. A poor excuse for a next of kin, was the consensus at the police station, where clandestine pity was beginning to stir in earnest for the dead girl, but not a murderer.

Elsewhere in Levanto the holiday was in full swing by ten o'clock. Outside the expensive bars, among them the Mare Blu, that lined the street one in from the promenade, every table was occupied for the duration by those who would rather watch than walk through the thronged streets. In the dusty park beneath the promenade a bouncy castle and some decrepit, overpriced carousels had been set up, towers of candyfloss and helium balloons in the shape of Pokemon and circus animals bobbed through the crowds. Below the promenade the beach was already packed, bright with umbrellas and loungers and oiled bodies prone and gleaming in the sun.

This morning had seemed like any other when Rose had woken in the quiet cool of the hills; if anything it was perhaps even more silent than usual. There had been no sign of Gennaro down among his vines, and Rose had spent a desultory half-hour at her desk, tapping on the computer and trying to see what worked and what didn't. At least her email was still functioning, and she had a stack of mail – from England, where obviously no holiday atmosphere prevailed – waiting after her day in Genova. Mostly junk, but one of her regulars, the features editor on a mid-market women's monthly, was asking if she fancied setting up an interview with some faded celebrity – due for a revival, they thought – with a holiday home nearby. No address, no phone, just a number for the woman's agent in Rome, as if that would be any good in August. Rose dialled the number absently, all the same, to hear a sepulchral answering machine announcing the agency's closure until September.

The woman might not even be in town, anyway. All they had was a name. Elvira somebody; Rose wondered if she'd heard that name recently, and thought perhaps she had. *Tomorrow, maybe, I'll ask around*, she decided, pushing the computer away and standing to look out of her window. Just now she thought she might go for a walk; she had things to think about.

Rose could hear the holiday sound as soon as she turned downhill out of Grosso, though she didn't know what it meant, Ferragosto having slipped her mind for the moment. There was a party buzz in the air, a distant brass band, and as she approached Levanto she could see balloons bobbing here and there and the striped awnings of stalls. Bewildered, she wandered into the Arcobalena, only to find it crowded with unfamiliar faces, and she stopped, irresolute, in the doorway.

The Arcobalena was not fashionable and faintly down-at-heel, the decor still the zinc bar, speckled marble floor and elderly cooler cabinet it had had since the seventies. It was unfashionably located, on the edge of the centre, in what might optimistically have been called a garden square, a rectangle of dusty bushes surrounded by stuccoed holiday apartment blocks that had no period charm but were clean and inoffensive. The bar's proprietor, Paolo, was a tall man with a shock of greying curls who wore a leather bracelet and had a ruddy complexion that, to Rose, indicated that he liked a drink. But he was always polite and friendly, in an unfocused sort of way; he didn't overcharge her for sitting down under the grubby umbrellas outside and cautiously Rose began to consider herself a regular.

Occasionally, in expansive mood or on a quiet evening, Paolo would supply her with a free glass of this or that or an extra dish of stale crackers with her *aperitivo*. Today, though, Paolo's colour was heightened, perhaps because of the heat and the extra custom, or perhaps it was down to the glass of brandy on the bar in front of him at ten in the morning, and he didn't seem to notice Rose hovering in the doorway. She turned away, a little downcast, and noticed that someone was standing to leave one of the aluminium tables outside; making up her mind, she darted across and claimed her place on the edge of Paolo's terrace.

Once established, Rose sighed, pushing away the evidence of the previous occupant's breakfast: a cappuccino cup containing a sticky swirl of collapsing foam, a lipstick-stained tissue, a moisture-beaded glass with a cube of ice melting at the bottom. At moments like this – and every day there were several – she was made aware of how tenuous her place here was, how far she still remained from belonging. Today it was not knowing about Ferragosto, and not finding the place she had come to expect at the Arcobalena, but it could be a hundred different things. Forgetting to stamp her train ticket, bringing the wrong combination of documents to the Questura for her *permesso di soggiorno*; asking for a cappuccino instead of a *caffè* after lunch. That quizzical look, the heavy sigh would be the result, reminding her she was a foreigner and always would be.

In Italy, she had come to realize, although the rule of law was barely respected, there were other, invisible rules governing every small detail of daily life that must be rigorously adhered to. Where to go on holiday and when, what to eat and most of all what to wear. Looking down the crowded street that led away from Paolo's towards the centre of town, everyone Rose could see wore the same summer uniform in subtly varying colours. Her own approximation of the same outfit, she could see now, just wouldn't do, but she found it fascinating, all the same, this perfect, happy conformity, no desire to be different. The appeal was obvious, when you came to think of it. She craned her neck looking across the narrow road into the bar, and managed to catch Paolo's eye. He nodded, smiling back mechanically, and at last Rose allowed herself to relax and think. Yesterday.

They had talked, Rose and the stranger on the train, for about as long as it took to walk to the station portico; no more than a hundred yards, a couple of minutes if you walked slowly, and listened. He had a house, he said as he stopped just outside the glass doors and indicated the direction he was taking – not, as it happened, the same direction as Rose's; his house was just a little way out of Levanto, up on the far hill. He gestured towards the sea.

She had no idea how he had known she was English. Her fair skin, her clothes, her lack of make-up? Any one of a hundred giveaway signs, to an Italian, although she still didn't know if that was what he was.

'Have you been at work?' he had asked her first as they stepped down from the train, nodding at the laptop in her arms and with something faintly disbelieving in his tone. And in the scalding heat rising from the pavements it seemed incontrovertibly an odd day to be working, or, for that matter, to be walking the streets of Genova looking for a computer repair shop. He sounded friendly, though. A natural question.

Rose had shrugged, feeling a blush rise from her neck. She tried to smile.

'No,' she said. 'There's something wrong with it. The computer. I was looking for a repair shop.'

He looked sympathetic. 'It's difficult to get anyone to mend anything around here,' he said. 'Particularly in August.' He paused, frowning a little. 'Is it a problem? Are you on holiday?'

Rose straightened. 'No,' she said, and cautiously she felt the thrill of ownership that she had been missing since she moved. 'I live here. I have a house in Grosso. I live on my own.'

Why had she said that? Even remembering, she felt the flush spread across her cheeks again. But he had just nodded, then transferred *Passaggio a Trieste* to beneath his arm, fished in his pocket and handed her a card.

'If I can be of any help,' he said a little formally, looking away over her shoulder as if to save her embarrassment. By then they were standing in the shade of the station's arched doorway; Rose took the card slowly, and held out her hand.

'Rose Fell,' she said. 'Thank you, Mr –' she broke off, and looked down at the card. 'Mr Bourn.' There was the name, and a phone number.

'Richard,' he said gravely. 'Richard's fine.' Then he had turned and set off away from her, walking confident and square-shouldered down towards the avenue of trees that led to the sea.

A harassed waitress Rose hadn't seen before – taken on for the holiday, perhaps – wearing a grubby frilled apron brought her a cappuccino and a glass of water, and absently Rose paid her and sighed again. She felt too old. Too old and tired to be starting all this again, thinking about a man she hardly knew, feeling those prehistoric emotions and insecurities stir again after more than twenty years. Was he interested in her? Her stomach churned. Just being nice? Was he – safe? She had no idea.

I'm only forty-two, Rose told herself robustly, it's not that long ago. But then, she had hated all that courtship thing even when she was eighteen, was so glad to be done with it and settled down with a baby and a house in Lewisham by twenty-three. She realized with a shock that she was not, in fact, too old to start it all again, not even too old to have another baby. The thought was astonishing, and Rose almost laughed. What had brought all this on? A man she met on a train. But perhaps that was what she wanted, what she was waiting for, why she couldn't settle, why she felt lonely. Love. I am lonely sometimes, Rose thought, admitting it.

Furtively she pulled out Richard Bourn's card and looked at it, dog-eared already. Was he English, then? American? His accent hadn't been quite native nor quite foreign. She didn't think she'd call him. No.

In her pocket, Rose's mobile rang.

Chapter Nine

Elvira had woken in Jack's bed. They still made love, at least, she had thought as she lay and looked at the ceiling, never mind that she couldn't remember much about it. Perhaps it didn't happen often these days, but then, that was normal. As if she had any idea what normal was. Did she even know if love came into it, either? Jack seemed barely there, so cool, detached, fingertips resting lightly on the slope of her buttocks, barely touching her and then falling instantly, soundly asleep. Was that love? Was it normal?

Elvira had never been attracted by normal, as so many others had, the girls she'd grown up with on the modelling circuit who'd seemed to have a way of seeking out the reliable, the uxorious, the faithful, love-struck man. The man who'd always worship them, provide for them when – soon enough – they couldn't quite make the grade and were reduced to catalogue work or a gracious retirement, he'd support them, curb their excesses. Who kept track of the bills, paid into a pension scheme and kept the life insurance up to date. Her first husband, the Count, hadn't done any of that; he'd gone through his own money like water and would have got around to Elvira's if she hadn't been careful. Even when she'd been mesmerized by him, by his pedigree, his grand gestures, she had somehow known enough to keep him off the deeds to the house, her prize. So she had some kind of instinct for self-preservation, at least, even if it was buried deep.

Most of the time, though, Elvira wasn't interested in self-preservation, having her excesses curbed; she hadn't wanted happiness, or comfort, or what people called family life, she told herself she wasn't built that way. Didn't need it. So when the Count suggested, out of God knew what capricious, hallucinatory perversity, that they should have a child together, a pretty little green-eyed child, she knew their days were numbered. The girls on Concorde, the drugs, the entourage of freeloaders and the pool parties she could handle, but not this.

Elvira hadn't wanted – had never wanted – a child. Of course Stefano hadn't either, not really, but Elvira wouldn't have even idly wondered about it. When she saw a woman with a baby she felt – angry, somehow, at the suffocating, sacrificial nature of the relationship, and so willingly accepted. Madness. She could not imagine a time when she'd be ready to take it all on, the nurturing, the scolding, the coaxing, the thousands of tiny, infuriating tasks that seemed to accompany child-rearing. The massive, intolerable burden of anxiety. Why did people do it? It seemed an extraordinary sacrifice, and after all, the world was full enough already. Elvira wasn't one to worry about the future, about the world going on without her after her death, empty of all trace that she'd ever been. So what? It was enough that she was here, now.

And all at once she had seen their marriage for what it was; a game, an idiotic game, and she'd thought, *time to get out*. Then she'd auditioned for Marcello Battista, and that had been that. Look where he'd got her. Elvira turned over on her side, her back to Jack, thinking about Marcello. Her stab at love. He'd been in love with her, at least, had fallen for her before she'd even opened her mouth to begin her piece at the audition. Making the film had been like love, all that intensity, all those intimate discussions of her character. It had seemed to Elvira, who after all had still been young, only twenty-five, twenty-six, as though Marcello wanted to know her through and through, and in a kind of dream of love she surrendered herself to him.

For a while she'd allowed herself to think that all his flamboyance and passion, the violent, jealous rages and his need to know all about her meant something. Meant that she'd found a soulmate. But all Marcello had wanted to do, it turned out, was to use her to make that film, to pick away at her life and her past, her flaws and failings and vulnerabilities, and expose them on the screen. Once he'd succeeded and they'd got whatever prize he'd been after, he had to make a different film, and that wasn't so easy. The first time he hit her, she left. Hardly surprising, then, that Jack had seemed the perfect antidote, their life together a matter of pampering each other, making sure that no unpleasantness interfered with their pursuit of pleasure.

The air in Jack's room was heavy with the exhalations of two bodies, and all at once it seemed too small, and stifling, the space made smaller by all that expensive padding, leather and cedar. Elvira got up from the bed in a rush, wanting to be out of the room; she grabbed at something to cover her – a dressing gown over the chair. Was it hers? She frowned at it in the half-light. It was. Strange that she couldn't remember putting it there. She went downstairs.

The drawing room, its shutters closed, was dim and cool; Elvira stopped there for a while, leaning her cheek against the cool marble of the mantelpiece, and listened for the sounds of the day beginning. Ferragosto: you could hear the sound of it drifting up from the town; Elvira thought of summers long gone, fourteen again and walking along the front at Portofixio looking at the yachts. *Perhaps*, she thought, *we could go out together, a nice walk, a little lunch in the Mare Blu.* She felt as though she was floating above her body, looking down on herself standing in the high-ceilinged room among her white sofas, and none of it was real. *How many pills did I take last night?*

Jack appeared in the doorway, a cup of some flowery tea in his hand. Elvira pulled the dressing gown around her and looked at him, perplexed; she hadn't heard him get up. He held the cup out to her.

'What's the time?' she asked.

'Oh,' he said vaguely. 'I don't know. Midday?' He crossed to the long shutters and pushed them open. Light flooded the room, dazzling Elvira; she could feel the heat, too, a sweat beginning to break on her upper lip. She looked around, feeling as though something was missing.

'Ania . . .' she began absently. She wanted to shake things into place in her head, but it felt tender. There was something about the way Jack was looking at her too, quizzical, concerned, that made her feel even more helpless, and obscurely infuriated.

'It's a holiday, remember?' he said. We've got the day to ourselves.' He smiled, handsome and flirtatious in the half-light.

'What's left of it,' Elvira said, hearing the petulance in her voice, uneasy at the thought of all that time slipping through her fingers.

Jack shrugged, still looking down at her indulgently. 'You needed the sleep,' he said. 'Didn't you?'

Elvira looked down into her tea and frowned, wondering why she couldn't bring up the previous evening's events in her mind; her memory seemed like a mad old woman's knitting, loopy and loose, full of holes. 'Perhaps I did,' she said vaguely, giving up the attempt. She turned to him and smiled, making the effort. 'Let's go out, shall we? To the Mare Blu, maybe?'

'Whatever you want,' said Jack, and he leaned across and kissed her, his lips cool and dry on her cheek. 'We've got till the weekend to please ourselves, then Luke and Annabel will be here.'

'What?' said Elvira, aghast. This weekend? That's only two days away. Why didn't you say?'

'Darling,' said Jack, frowning, 'don't be silly. I did say. I've told you twenty times they're coming. For the weekend? Luke's thinking about investing in the gallery.'

Elvira felt nauseated suddenly; the sweet fragrance of the tea was cloying in the dim, shuttered room. 'No,' she said, I'm sure you ...' but suddenly she didn't know, and it made her afraid. She turned her face away and studied her own reflection in the mantelpiece mirror, but she could hardly have said who she was looking at, so little did she recognize herself. Her eyes were too big, too dark, and her face so thin. Elvira looked like her own mother, she realized with a start. She could hear Jack's soft footsteps as he left the room but she didn't turn back to watch him go.

*

There had been some discussion about how best to celebrate the holiday among the inhabitants of the old cold store and of the caravans that stood in the lee of the stained concrete building. A communal meal in the evening had been suggested, as a few of them wouldn't be working: stuffed cabbage, a piece of meat, some demijohns of wine. There was a couple who were friendlier than the rest and more settled – they lived in the biggest caravan, set off for work together at six every morning and cooked for themselves almost every night – and they'd asked Ania if she wanted to come along.

'We can fix up some tables outside,' Marta, the wife, had said, all motherly, trying to be nice. 'Hang up some lights.' The young men would be out among the crowds, selling cigarette lighters or roses in cellophane, no day of rest for them. Ania, who they all thought was too shy to have survived this long, had ducked her head in an ambiguous gesture that could have been agreement or could have been evasion. But when the morning of Ferragosto dawned, light filtering in late to the cool, dark, fetid interior of the cold store, and Marta stuck her head round Ania's curtain, she seemed to have already gone. Her bed was made, her little corner neat, the plaster Madonna and wooden rosary on the box she used for her clothes, all undisturbed as if she hadn't even slept there. No one thought twice; Ania kept herself to herself, after all. They all did, didn't they?

As Rose answered the phone she saw him, in the distance, walking across the top of the road, Richard Bourn, and for a moment she wasn't listening. He was walking slowly, a hand in one pocket, head lowered as though he was thinking. As she looked he disappeared around the corner.

'Sorry?' Rose said into the mouthpiece, frowning at the display. No one ever phoned her on the mobile, far too expensive, and she hardly bothered to take it out with her any more. It must have got left in a pocket; the battery, she could see, was low.

The voice on the other end suddenly became distinct. 'Rose?' It was Cookie Pearson. Rose stood up suddenly at the table and out of the corner of her eye she saw Paolo's head turn inside the bar, tracking her instinctively through his beery bonhomie in case she was a customer trying to leave without settling up. She smiled and nodded, sat down again. Paolo turned away.

Cookie Pearson was a brisk, capable woman imbued with old-fashioned virtues – hard work, common sense – who might a century earlier have filled her childless life with good works and the Women's Institute. She was pushing fifty now but she had good bone structure, was fair, broad-shouldered, with a gap between her front teeth; a strict dressmaker curbed a secret fondness for floaty dresses that did not quite suit Cookie's solidity. Hearing that firm, clear voice always made Rose's heart sink a little: it made her think of beds unmade and floors unwashed, a daughter who had never attained Grade 5 in the violin. No failing could be concealed from Cookie.

Rose tried not to sigh. It was a mystery to her how Cookie had come to edit a magazine targeting (youngish) mothers, commissioning articles bolstering their self-esteem, telling them how to dress to cover the post-childbirth figure, where to find a cranial osteopath for the newborn. A few photographs of the Oscars to provide some escapism among the practical tips, the occasional interview with an abandoned Hollywood wife to show the mothers they were not alone in their insecurity.

In life, Cookie did not treat anyone with such indulgence, but perhaps that was why she was such a successful editor.

'Cookie,' Rose said faintly, sitting back in her chair.

'Did you get my email?' Cookie said. She sounded impatient.

'I got one from you this morning,' said Rose. 'Is that the one? About – um, Elvira Whatsername? It's a holiday here today ...' She trailed off, aware that she was embarking on an excuse already, although in fact Cookie could not have expected to hear from her so soon and, in any case, she never accepted excuses.

'All right, all right,' Cookie said, interrupting her briskly. 'Yes, that's the one. Did I mention she's married to Jack Robbins? He owns that gallery in Mayfair, bit of a ladies' man?'

'Mmm,' said Rose, racking her brains. She could picture him: tall, lean, dark-haired, smooth-skinned. Always in black tie at some launch or other, and not quite trustworthy. 'Yes, I think so,' she said. 'I didn't even know he was married.'

'Yes,' said Cookie, thoughtful for a moment. 'I think he does that deliberately. She's a bit older than him, and seems to be kept out of the picture unless it suits him. Wheeled out for private views, that kind of thing. Reclusive, perhaps?' Cookie sounded hopeful. 'Anyway, Jack Robbins is always good for a whiff of scandal, he's a bit of a rogue, you know. Not very reliable with money, lots of – *socialising*, if you know what I mean. Can get a bit out of hand. I've heard all sorts ...'

Cookie trailed off momentarily, sounding vague, which, knowing Cookie, could only be calculated. Rose wondered what she could be up to. But after no more than three seconds' silent consideration of Jack Robbins' weaknesses Cookie returned to her point. 'So it wouldn't do any harm to line up a nice photo piece of their lovely home on the Riviera, just in case? Focusing on her, of course; I've been looking at some archive pictures of her, and I think she's just the thing, you know, seventies glamour.' She paused, reflecting.

Rose nodded absently; for an old-fashioned girl Cookie was surprisingly sharp at picking up trends. Her heart did sink a little at the thought of setting up such a piece, not to mention writing it, all puff and insinuation. She was trying to work out where she might even begin to track Elvira – what *was* her name, Robbins? – down with her agent on holiday, when Cookie went on again, picking up speed.

'Anyway, she – Vitale – was a model – supermodel, really, one of the first. Call her a trailblazer? In the piece. And she was in a Fellini film once, you know, not a big part, but still. And an art-house movie, some cult thing. There's plenty of pictorial. Just do a bit of homework, see if you can get into the house. If she's really a recluse, might be a bit of a scoop.'

Rose made an effort to sound positive; Cookie didn't approve of pessimism. 'All right, Cookie,' she said, rousing herself. It was all part of the job, after all. 'Sure. I'll get going.' She frowned as the name echoed back at her. *Elvira Vitale*, she thought. *Where did I hear it?*

'Righto,' said Cookie with an air of finality. 'Marvellous.' There was a pause, then, very much as an afterthought: 'And how's it all going? Settling in?' Taking a personal interest was not Cookie's forte.

'Yes, yes, fine,' said Rose, her standard response. 'Lovely. Weather's good.' She knew this was all people wanted to hear. 'The house is working out well, I think.' *Was it?* She thought of the taciturn old ladies, Gennaro appearing uninvited at her back door.

'Right then,' said Cookie, never patient enough to listen for long. 'Let me know how it goes.' And with a loud and definite click, she was gone.

Rose shook her head at the phone, smiling despite herself. It was coming to something if she was missing Cookie. She stood, stretched, and, her confidence returning, waved merrily to Paolo inside the crowded bar before walking off into the crowd.

Chapter Ten

Inland it had grown quite dark but in Levanto crowds were reluctant to see the last of the day's festivities. Beneath the dusty trees in the little park at one end of the town's promenade coloured bulbs were strung between rows of stalls, and business seemed to be brisk. Rose, like the rest of them not quite ready to go home yet, paused in front of a stall run by a smiling African vendor in a long, tie-dyed djellabah. She looked absently at a great heap of leather sandals, green, red and yellow, tasselled and braided, some tarnished silver jewellery in a case, and wondered whether she should get something for Jess.

The traditional parade had passed through the town, a deafening din of drums and trumpets, flag-throwing and flowered floats, the town's young men and women sweating in Renaissance costume, heavy swagged and pearl-encrusted velvet. There had even been a troupe of visiting Morris men. As she turned away now from the sandal stall and walked on towards the sea, Rose could see some of the parade-goers still in costume on a street corner below the promenade. An exquisite young woman, her hair as black and shiny as liquorice in its beaded chignon, stood with her bodice half-unlaced at the back to reveal a smooth curve of olive-skinned back, smoking a cigarette. Rose could not imagine that in the entire British Isles you would be able to muster as many beautiful young people prepared to dress up in historical costume on a hot summer's evening.

The girl was chatting to a handsome boy with shoulder-length hair, his coarse linen chemise untucked from velvet hose, a mobile phone incongruously visible in the shirt's breast pocket. There were five or six of them, unwinding after their passage through the town, and they seemed as fresh and cool as if they had just emerged from the sea. The transplanted Morris men, on the other hand, whom Rose could see leaning in silence against the wall below the promenade, were pale and sweaty, and apparently rather drunk. *Fish out of water*, she thought, *just like me*. And then she spotted Gennaro further along, standing beneath the promenade in the shade in his dust-coloured trousers, leaning against his little van, alone. She realized that she hadn't seen him for more than twenty-four hours and that it felt liberating; his solicitude had been beginning to make her feel guilty. He was looking the other way, and Rose hurried on before he could turn back and see her.

A few yards on Rose could see the neon sign of a bar, a blue wave symbol announcing the Mare Blu over heavy cream canvas umbrellas. She knew the bar; she had passed it almost every day since her arrival, but its exclusivity, its luxury, its exorbitant prices, proclaimed themselves too clearly for Rose ever to have been tempted in. This was the bar to which, that afternoon, Paolo had directed Rose when she had eventually summoned the courage to ask him if he knew anything about a retired film star called Elvira Vitale. Something in the sardonic tilt of Paolo's eyebrows, the sharp look he gave her, had eloquently conveyed the fact that Elvira Vitale was out of his league, and hers.

'She comes for the summer, but she doesn't mix much,' he'd said with a snort. 'You might see her in the Mare Blu, if you're lucky. She's got a place up there,' he said, nodding up at the cliff to the east of the town. 'But she doesn't exactly keep open house. A private person.'

Paolo paused in the act of pulling a *birra alla spina*, and looked down at the pale gold liquid beading the glass, frowning. 'Why d'you want to know?' He looked up at her then, with something like curiosity.

Distractedly Rose shook her head, because just as Paolo had nodded up the cliff she had remembered where she'd heard the name before. The estate agent, pointing at the balustraded villa perched between Rose and the sea, had said it. 'The summer house of Elvira Vitale,' he'd said, proudly, and she hadn't even recognized the name.

'What?' she said to Paolo vaguely. 'Oh, I'd like to talk to her. I've been asked to write about – oh, her house. Her life. I'm a journalist.'

Paolo had looked at her with some scepticism, and just a hint of grudging respect. Rose obviously didn't look like his idea of a journalist, but she felt satisfied to have made some impression, at last, and she had smiled.

Now, though, as Rose stood outside the Mare Blu and hesitated, her brief flush of professional confidence seemed to be evaporating fast. In the bar's glittering interior everyone looked Italian, or very rich, or both, and they had all obviously dressed up for the evening. The terrace was crowded, and there were no free tables; Rose told herself she couldn't afford the prices outside anyway. Carefully she smoothed her hair, straightened her dress and headed inside, edging between the crowded tables from which rose a heady cloud of expensive fragrance, tuberose and ambergris; the smell of money.

Reaching the bar inside, Rose clung to its cool solidity as though it was a life-raft. She asked for a Campari with soda; the first thing that came into her head. The barman seemed friendly enough, in a cool sort of way; he didn't immediately look at her, at any rate, as though she shouldn't be there. Watching him prepare the drink, wipe the bar and polish it off, refill his silver sugar bowl and adjust the bottles in the cooler, Rose straightened up and then, sipping the bitter, aromatic drink, she turned to survey the room.

'I don't see why we couldn't have come down in the car,' Jack was grumbling. 'Christ, anyone'd think you were English, this obsession you've got with walking everywhere suddenly.' He glanced at her, making a slightly ill-tempered attempt at mischief. 'Or German. It'll be hiking boots next. Rucksack. Hairy legs.'

Elvira wasn't really paying attention, but she looked across at him at this, unfocused.

'What?' she said. 'Oh, yes. I'm sorry, darling. Fresh air. I needed some fresh air.'

She looked at Jack a little more closely. He seemed quite bad-tempered this evening, and it occurred to Elvira that every time she was feeling better, clearing her head, it appeared to put him out of sorts. She stretched a hand out to him, wanting him to see that she still needed him.

They were almost down in the town now, just rounding the last bend under a wall loaded with jasmine and heavily fragrant in the warm dusk. Jack looked handsome in the half-light, tanned and saturnine, but he had his hands jammed into his well-cut linen pockets like a recalcitrant schoolboy deprived of his newest toy. Jack liked to roar down into town in the convertible, tossing the keys to a flunkey and walking no more than the three steps it took to get from the pavement inside the Mare Blu.

Still, she thought hazily, it wouldn't do him any harm to walk for once. In the fresh, warm evening she was still trying to work out why there were so many things that seemed to have slipped her mind lately. For one thing, and most urgently requiring her attention, there was the imminent arrival of Luke and Annabel. Her heart sank; she couldn't stand them: she found Luke pompous and cold, and Annabel was a singularly humourless woman, smug at having produced two strapping heirs. As if any fool couldn't have a child. And they didn't seem so attached to their children as to want to bring them on holiday with them, at least Jack had been able to reassure her on that point. Just Luke and Annabel. Unwillingly, she returned to fretting over how she could possibly have forgotten their visit in the first place.

Surely if, as Jack said, he had told her about the coming weekend, she would have begun to make arrangements, for someone to come in and cook, and she would have spoken to Ania about making up the spare suite? *I'll ask Ania*, she thought, surprising herself by thinking of Ania with a kind of gratitude, as an ally. *She'll know.* But then there was the previous evening, which was still, for the most part, little more than a blur. Ania had gone home, hadn't she? She'd gone before Elvira got back from her walk. They'd had a drink or two on the terrace ... had they eaten? Elvira had ended up in Jack's bed, obviously, that was where she'd woken up, but her memory of what happened there remained disconcertingly fragmented. She looked across at Jack, loping ahead of her on the bend, eager to get to the bright lights.

'Darling,' she began, then uncharacteristically she faltered.

He stopped, and turned to look back at her. 'Yes?'

'Do you think I've been – forgetting things? I mean, you said you'd told me ... about Luke and Annabel.'

'No, no,' he said, putting an arm through hers, his old thoughtful self. 'Nothing to worry about, I'm sure. Perhaps we just need to adjust the tablets; or it could be some – hormonal thing? We'll talk to Seymour-Smith when we get back. How about that?'

Somehow this was not quite what Elvira had wanted to hear. Hormones? Did he mean the menopause? And the thought of seeing Seymour-Smith, the cold leather of his Le Corbusier couch, the bland, unctuous, five-hundred-dollar smile broadcast at her across his mahogany desk in Harley Street, was suddenly and profoundly repellent. I'm not sick enough yet, she thought indignantly, to need regular appointments with that man.

'Mmm,' she said vaguely. 'Maybe.' Jack's arm felt heavy against her, the physical contact bringing her out in a sweat, and casually she detached herself. They were almost at the bottom of the hill now, coming into Levanto beside the pretty, green and white striped marble church. Jack was quickening his pace, his shoulders thrown back, at the prospect of company, the well-dressed, sauntering crowd ahead of them. Elvira saw him look across at her quickly, in appraisal, she thought. Was she up to scratch? Would a day come when she wasn't?

They were talking about murder. There were four men, one of whom seemed considerably better informed than the others, a stocky, dark-skinned man who kept plucking at his shirt where the perspiration was holding it close against his skin. The body of a girl had been found on the beach the day before, it seemed; a student. Rose, trying to suppress the dread she felt rising in her at the thought of her own daughter, somewhere in Europe and presumably no less vulnerable, leaned closer.

Listening to the swarthy man responding with weary reluctance to his interrogators, Rose thought he sounded like a policeman; something about his clipped, matter-of-fact delivery. A body had been found in the early hours of the previous day by a couple of foreign girls who had passed a restless night sleeping on the beach, had woken just before dawn and gone for a walk. They'd thought she was asleep, until they saw the head wound, and the blood. Rose could just imagine them, the hysterical screams in the cold blue dawn, the girls running to get away, not feeling so grown up any more about being away from home. She tried not to think of where Jess was just now, on her travels.

Rose knew that pile of rocks, an untidy jumble where the train came out of the tunnel and ran along the beach before turning inland to the station. An uncomfortable place to sleep, she thought, on the rocks, trying not to visualize a dead girl on the edge of that homely, familiar beach scene, children paddling, playing in rock pools. How could they be sure it was murder? It was inconceivable. Couldn't the girl have drunk too much at some beach party, drowned, fallen on the rocks, choked on her own vomit? Was that any more reassuring? Not, perhaps, to Rose as a mother; any of those things could be happening to Jess, too; she'd be just as dead. It seemed, however, that in any case accidental death was not an option, where this girl was concerned. Rose could see that a number of the seated drinkers in the Mare Blu were also listening in, with at least half an ear, alerted perhaps by his air of authority, to the policeman's account. If he was a policeman.

'She was dead already, the forensics guy says.' The stocky man leaned back against the bar, drained his glass of some viscous, dark red liquid and set it down with an air of finality.

Silently the barman removed the empty glass and ran a cloth over the marble where it had left a ring. His face was quite without expression; they might as well have been talking about train times or the weather in front of him. Rose wondered just when the body had been found; perhaps this was old news already. Or perhaps in such elegant surroundings a barman was expected to maintain a pose of absolute discretion; it would be *brutta figura* to display too much interest. This was hardly a backstreet dive. Rose made a mental note to ask Paolo about the body; in his bar, no such discretion would be observed, and from the Mare Blu, Da Paolo's looked a lot like home.

'When she was left there. And she was wearing jeans; no one goes to the beach in jeans, not in August. Not even in the evening.' At this they all fell silent, nodding.

Rose contemplated the man's assertion, and she supposed it was true. The women on the beach wore a kind of uniform; bright, high-cut bikinis, cheap batik sarongs bought from the Moroccan vendors, plastic wedges. Rose thought of a girl in jeans; tough, practical, on her way somewhere; not a holidaymaker. Not teetering along the promenade in micro-shorts and high heels, flesh exposed to the maximum, straps moved every twenty minutes, turned in the sun like a bird on a spit. Not, of course, that that would make them fair game.

'Of course,' he was saying now, meditatively, 'it'll have been a foreigner. That killed her.' They nodded again.

Rose turned away a little uncomfortably, and looked through the door at the street. *A foreigner*, she thought, pondering. There were so many foreigners: tourists; gypsies; Rose herself. Richard Bourn. She looked down at her expensive drink and hauled her thoughts back on track. For a moment, listening to the story of the dead girl, she had forgotten what she was doing here, and when she remembered it seemed foolish that she had thought she might just bump into Elvira Vitale and her husband. *This was a daft idea*, she thought. *I should get home.*

Rose went along the bar to the cashier, paid for her drink. She caught a glimpse of a face in the mirrored cabinet behind the till, through the rows of upturned champagne flutes; at first she didn't recognize herself. Her skin was darker, and had an unfamiliar glow, from the warmth of the evening and the Campari perhaps, and her hair was bright from the sun. Then she became aware of someone behind her in the queue and she scooped up her change and moved aside. As she turned she found herself almost face to face with him, looking a little impatient perhaps at having to queue, or at the fact that there were no tables free and he would have to drink at the bar. Rose knew him at once; Jack Robbins.

'Sorry, darling,' he was saying over his shoulder. 'Something'll come free soon. Or we can go and eat?'

At the bar stood a tall woman, dark-haired, not young,

and looking tired, but there was something about her that prevented Rose from looking away, a beauty branded and indelible in her skin and the combination of her features. Even the way she stood, one elbow on the bar, one delicate brown sandalled foot curled behind the other on the terrazzo floor, was out of the ordinary, from a different world. A movie star. Rose felt herself gawp. Her immediate conscious thought was, *what is she doing with him?* Next to this woman Jack Robbins, with his piercing blue eyes, his sharp cheekbones, shiny black hair, seemed entirely insignificant.

Suddenly Rose was properly interested in doing that interview; she wanted to know – what? What such a marriage could be like? It seemed to her something was going on between these two, something not entirely healthy. And at the same time she knew immediately that she couldn't do it now, couldn't importune them here under the bright lights and the inquisitive eyes of the regulars at the Mare Blu. *But I know where you live*, she thought, and in her mind's eye there appeared the elegant profile of Elvira Vitale's villa on the cliff, shuttered and enigmatic.

She stood looking at the woman at the bar for a second or two, and it seemed to Rose that she saw a flicker of interest in Elvira Vitale's face. Decisively, buoyed up with a sudden euphoric sense of purpose, Rose turned away from the bar: Jack Robbins, moving up to the till, caught her look as she passed and smiled, a flirtatious reflex, a practised, knowing smile that no doubt had opened plenty of doors. But Rose kept moving past him, through the tables and outside into the warm, dark night. Behind her a man came to the door of the Mare Blu and watched her go. The street was brilliantly lit and still thronging with people, and as Rose turned towards the road home she was soon swallowed up in the crowd.

Leaving the town, past the church and into the velvety darkness, Rose walked on unafraid, not thinking of the hill's steep incline, the length of the road ahead, the immense expanse of black that lay inland and surrounded her. There was no moon tonight, but as she walked up through the almond trees towards Grosso, Rose's way was lit by the occasional porch lamp and the fireflies glittering in the warm hedgerows. She walked steadily, and smiled in the dark.

Ania was not, as everyone imagined, out among the market stalls enjoying the holiday; she was a long way from the bright lights of Ferragosto. Where she was hidden it was very dark indeed, a deep, damp, stinking darkness, a dead place. Where Ania lay, curled motionless in the dust, there was not a glimmer of light.

Chapter Eleven

Anna-Maria Villemartin, her mother's only child, lived at home in the holidays. She had been studying economics at the University of Cremona and had obviously been a good student, to judge by the number of photographs, certificates and commendations ranged on the wall of her mother's stuffy *salotto*. They were on the thirteenth floor of a block in a shabby but respectable suburb of Genova, on the way out to the east.

Cirri had arrived early for the appointment Toto had made for him and had stood outside the apartment for some time before he rang the bell. The tiny, dilapidated lift had lurched alarmingly before depositing him in a claustrophobically small lobby between two apartments. As the lift groaned open he saw one of the two doors open a crack, a shape behind it. Stiff grey hair, a wattled chin; an old woman, was his impression, but that might just have been prejudice. But obviously the Villemartins' neighbour – he looked at the brass nameplate and filed the name away, just in case, a policeman's reflex – had seen enough, because no sooner had it opened than it was pulled smartly to again. A dismal, heavy shuffle could be heard retreating behind it. Cirri felt renewed sympathy for Anna-Maria Villemartin's mother, the object of gossip and pity, spied on by the neighbours. With a sigh, he raised a hand to knock at the door.

Cirri's eyes had by now adjusted to the profound gloom in the room, lit only by a low-wattage Tiffany lamp beside the shabby sofa, but he was finding it harder to adjust to the atmosphere of misery, thick and palpable as fog, that combined with the intense muggy heat of the day. Anna-Maria's mother sat opposite Cirri on the sofa; even in her grief she had given him the only good chair, and he felt guilty. She was, he could tell, a decent woman; perhaps, in her youth, she might have resembled her slender, straight-backed, black-haired daughter but now her face was puffed and swollen with crying, her eyes sunken. A bomb site; a disaster area. Her thin, brittle hair was home-dyed red, but growing out at the roots, drawn back loosely from her face in a cheap elastic band, and she pushed back a lank strand with a hopeless gesture.

'So, Signora,' he prompted gently. 'She went out at about six? With her friends?' The woman nodded miserably.

'Silvana Martinelli. They've been friends – oh, since nursery school. Anna didn't want to eat. She eats – she ate like a bird.' At this her voice cracked, but she recovered herself. 'She said she'd pick up something while they were out. We – we'd had words, you see. A disagreement.'

'What about? The argument?' But the woman shook her head.

'I can't – it was, you know, a private thing.' She was

83

becoming agitated. 'A women's matter. I – I don't think she would like me to say.' Her head bowed, he could see her lips pressed tight together and trembling.

Cirri knew he should insist, but the woman's misery prevented him. It was to do with sex, probably. He tried another tack.

'A boyfriend? If there was a boyfriend, you must see, we would need to talk to him?'

Her head jerked up. 'No, no,' she said, anguished. 'Really, nothing to do with anyone else. Just her and me.' He could see she was telling the truth.

'But you expected her home?'

Anna-Maria's mother looked down at her hands abjectly. 'Yes, of course. But perhaps – perhaps I was wrong.' She looked despairing at this thought. Cirri imagined her reliving however that conversation had gone, making it up with her daughter so that she would come home safely. Had Anna-Maria Villemartin gone home with someone she met that night, just to show her mother?

'She wasn't the kind of girl to stay out all night, then?'

'No. No, not here, I mean, in Cremona, she – she leads her own life. But not when she's at home. I didn't wait up for her but in the morning when she wasn't there, I knew there was something wrong. Her room – she hadn't slept in her bed. So I called Silvana.'

The woman stopped, staring bleakly across the room, and Cirri could tell she was contemplating the silence, the emptiness of a future in which her daughter no longer existed. He felt a heaviness in his chest, like a stone, but he laboured on.

'Yes,' he said softly. 'Martinelli. We spoke to her.' The girl had been in shock, incoherent. He waited.

With an effort the woman dragged her gaze back from the framed pictures on the wall, and looked at him hopelessly.

'She said they went to the Greco – a bar, for students, on the front.' Cirri nodded. 'They had a pizza.' She spoke dully. Cirri thought of the analysis of the girl's stomach contents, the pizza still only partially digested at the time of death. 'And then?'

Anna-Maria's mother looked up at him. 'Silvana said they went to a nightclub, down behind the docks.' She seemed distraught, confused. 'I don't know why they like those places; in my day you'd never go there, where the tankers come in. It's not a nice part of town.'

Cirri shrugged slightly, and tried to smile. Genova's docks had changed, he knew that much; artists, foreigners who liked to see the seedy, authentic side of life, they'd popularized the area somewhat. He'd been to have a look, a year or so ago. He didn't like Genova. There was the odd café and nightclub, shiny new tables and chairs laid out incongruously on the cobbles. Once there had been only grimy bars where scabby pigeons scratched and flapped beneath the tables, but to Cirri's mind the changes were largely cosmetic. Underneath it was the same; the streets still stank of fish and urine, and there were still plenty of alleys you wouldn't go down after dark.

'Young people . . . ' he said, uncomfortably. 'They like that kind of thing these days. It's not as bad as it was.' He wanted to save the woman her agonizing, but it couldn't be denied: if the area was safe, why was her daughter dead? Cirri chewed his lip.

'Silvana left before her?' He consulted his notebook. He knew this already from his conversation with the girl but he wanted to know what she'd said to the girl's mother. She nodded. 'Silvana said Anna was having fun. Dancing.'

'But not dancing – with anyone in particular?' He tried to put the question delicately.

'I asked her that too,' said the woman, looking up at him, bleary with exhaustion and the effort of understanding. She looked down again. 'She said not. Not that she could see. But you know what they're like, these places. You can't see a thing, anyway.' Anna-Maria's mother twisted a handkerchief in her lap and brought it up to her eyes, as though trying to blot out the last picture of her daughter, dancing in the dark among faceless, nameless others. People who hadn't cared enough to make sure she got home safely, and perhaps among them someone who wanted to make sure she didn't. Despite himself Cirri sighed.

They didn't talk about how she was planning to get home? How did she usually come home?'

The woman wiped her eyes. 'She always thought the train was safe,' she said. 'She didn't like to take a taxi, because you're on your own, you see? But after midnight, there aren't many trains that stop out here, and she doesn't – didn't – like walking up here in the dark. But she didn't usually – mostly she'd be home early. She was always careful – we're not city people, you see. Not really.' She looked up at him imploringly.

'No?'

'I'm from the country.' She named her *paesino*, a little village north of the city. 'It's my fault for bringing her here. But when Yves left, I had to come here. No work in the country any more.' Her eyes were dull with useless remorse.

Cirri leaned forward earnestly. 'Signora, that's likely to have made her more careful, not less. Really, you mustn't blame yourself.'

It was true, too, he reflected, but if it was him, if his little

Chiara – he stopped that train of thought, patted the woman gingerly on the shoulder.

She looked up at him, desperate. 'It's not such a bad place, that's what I thought. And we're all in the same boat, these days, no one stays where they're born. No one in this building wanted to be here – the old lady next door, she's from somewhere else, the doorman ... We help each other out. Her son, he's a good man, always visiting, like a father to Anna-Maria. He'll be so upset ...' She buried her face in her hands. 'How will I tell people?'

Hopelessly, she wiped her eyes. Cirri knew what she was thinking, that she'd never have a daughter to visit her in her old age, not now. He tried to focus on the girl at the station; had she been persuaded on to the wrong train? To judge by the time of death, it seemed that she couldn't have been on a train that stopped at the nearest station to her home, because the last train that would have stopped in the suburbs would have long gone. She must have been going somewhere else. Would she have done that alone? It seemed more likely to him that she was with someone, that someone persuaded her. So far they'd found no ticket on Anna-Maria's body, and that bothered him.

Almost as though talking to himself he said, 'She wouldn't have travelled without a ticket, would she? I somehow – thought she wouldn't have been that kind of girl. She was the kind of girl who always bought a ticket, stamped it properly?' A stamped ticket would have shown him – what? Timing, for one thing; that was what the stamp was for, after all, to show exactly when you used your ticket. It would tell him for sure what train she was on. But for now, of course, there was no ticket.

Anna-Maria's mother gazed at him 'Yes,' she said. 'How

did you know that? Of course, she would never break the law. Never.' Her voice was almost firm now, but then she seemed to realize that her good girl was gone, and she put her face in her hands, rubbing and rubbing.

Cirri looked down at the woman's bowed head, the pale roots growing out at the hairline, and felt a great weight descend on him. He thought of the girl, afraid of the dark. *She got on that train, though, didn't she?*

He let himself out at the foot of the apartment block, with its depressing hall-smell of polish and minestrone, and stepped into the sunlight with great relief. He took a deep breath, climbed into his unmarked car and headed for the docks.

The nightclub the girls had visited was called the MonteCarla, the letter 't' in its blue-white neon sign twisted oddly into a crucifix, giving the place an immediate air of blasphemy and perversion. The club occupied the basement of a dirty, crumbling baroque building, and the rusting grilles over the windows, strung with plastic roses and fairy lights, looked like the bars of a low-rent dominatrix's dungeon. There was nothing glamorous about the place, nor smart; it didn't even look clean. There was another place, all chrome and glass, a little way up the street, but it was here they'd chosen to come. Cirri couldn't see the appeal, despite what he'd said to Anna-Maria Villemartin's mother, but then what did he know? Perhaps it was a kind of joke. The heavy panelled door had been sprayed patchily with metallic paint; Cirri pressed the bell-push beside it, marked 'Members Only'.

Inside, the MonteCarla was as tacky as it appeared from the street. The floor was sticky and the air smelled of stale beer and full ashtrays and strong disinfectant. The glass behind the barred windows was tinted and a feeble orange light fell through it and down on to the low plastic tables. A dark-skinned man was sweeping the floor – very dark-skinned, with shiny black hair. Indian, perhaps, though Cirri could not be sure; he felt vaguely uncomfortable that he didn't know. The man didn't meet his eye; he just pushed the broom ahead of him, its handle pressing into his stomach. Cirri cleared his throat, and an answering voice came through a door half-open behind the bar.

To his surprise the manager of the MonteCarla, framed by the doorway, looked quite respectable. A shortish man, about thirty perhaps, Cirri thought, in a dark suit of some expensive, lightweight material and an open-necked white shirt. He smiled cheerfully and held out a hand. Cirri shook it cautiously.

'Emilio Scarpuccia?' he asked. 'You own this place?'

Scarpuccia nodded, still holding Cirri's hand. He had a warm, dry grip. 'Among others. Yes.'

'I'm Cirri. From the police in Levanto. They called you from the station?' He extracted his hand.

The manager's face took on a serious expression. 'It's about the girl, then? That's what they said.'

'Yes,' said Cirri. 'She was here last Tuesday, with a girl-friend.' He brought out Villemartin's picture, and a snapshot of her friend. Scarpuccia took them. He shook his head slowly.

'Sorry,' he said. They could have been here, I don't remember them. The place was packed.'

'Do you have a doorman? Bouncer?' Scarpuccia shrugged sleepily, and jerked his head towards the dark-skinned man standing watchfully in a corner, summoning him over.

'George doubles as a bouncer Tuesdays. But he's not paid to remember who leaves when.' He held out the pictures and Cirri watched as the man looked down at them briefly before shaking his head, his black eyes opaque and incurious. Scarpuccia nodded, dismissing him, and turned back to Cirri.

'Are you here every night?' Cirri asked.

The man smiled expansively and spread his hands. 'Well, in and out. You know. I have a number of – business interests.'

Cirri's curiosity sidetracked him. 'Other nightclubs? The same – kind of thing?' He looked around the cavernous room, unable to disguise his distaste for the place. Scarpuccia's smile remained, blandly indulgent.

'Commissario,' he said, with a short laugh. 'You obviously don't go in for nightlife yourself. And why should you, a man of your position? But this is a very popular place. Democratic, if you see what I mean. We get all sorts; old, young. Rich. Not so rich.' He eyed Cirri narrowly.

Cirri nodded slowly. 'Ladies' night, was it? I saw a sign outside. Tuesday night, ladies' night?'

Scarpuccia shrugged. 'A few fairylights and some crates of alcopops go a long way, if there are plenty of pretty girls. That's how the world works. Even in your day.'

Cirri coughed, changed the subject. 'D'you have security cameras?' he asked.

Scarpuccia shook his head. 'Not in my budget,' he said. 'They have to ring for entry, so we're safe enough in here. What happens on the street isn't my concern. What happens when they leave here.'

'No,' said Cirri, feeling unaccountably furious, hogtied by the man's smooth, easy manner. 'I suppose not.' He got the picture, though. Even decent girls, nice, careful, impoverished girls like Anna-Maria Villemartin, might come to a dump like this if entry was free. If you were with a friend you could keep the creeps at bay, and presumably not all the men were creeps. Not at first glance, anyway.

'I might need to come back,' he said.

'Sure,' said Scarpuccia. 'Any time.'

Cirri climbed out into the scalding air of the street, blinking in the light. He looked up and down the narrow pavement. At the flashy club up the road someone was hosing down the pavement and setting out aluminium chairs and tables, but otherwise the street was empty. There were no restaurants, half the buildings were old warehouses, others had their windows boarded up. It wasn't a comfortable residential area; that was the problem with trying to inject life back into these parts of the city, there was no human infrastructure. Once you were out on the street, in the dark, you were on your own.

Cirri sat in his car for some time, letting the air-conditioning run, watching the street. He didn't like the city. City people. They paid no attention to who came and went, not like a little place like Levanto, or a village where everyone knew everyone else's business and people could be trusted. Why would an intelligent girl like Anna-Maria Villemartin, a good country girl, studying for a degree, go off with someone she met in a club? Some flash city wideboy. He leaned his head back, his eyes fixed on some faraway point, and mused.

After a while George, the Indian bouncer, emerged from the MonteCarla, head down, hands in his pockets. He did not, as Cirri expected, walk straight on by; he leaned down and tapped on the window, and the policeman wound it down. The man's skin was very dark, his features fine for a big man.

'She left on her own, that girl,' he said, his Italian foreign and musical. 'But she got to the end of the road okay.' He nodded up the narrow street to where the shiny aluminium tables perched, where the traffic thundered past on the big *viale*. 'You've got to be careful, see. She was only young, I didn't want – anyway. None of my business.' George jerked his head back in the direction of the club. 'He doesn't pay me to watch out for the customers once they're off the premises. Like he said. But I kept an eye on her, and there's lights up there, it's safe enough.' Cirri nodded thoughtfully. 'Thanks,' he said, but the man had already set off again. Cirri watched him for a moment as he walked away towards the sea, then he turned the key in the ignition and drove away.

Rose opened her fridge to get the milk and there it was, a congealed, sticky mass of bleeding muscle, one milky, glazed eye staring back at her through the polythene. Quickly she shut the fridge door again. Bloody thing. Horribly bloody. Rose resolved to do something about Gennaro; her attitude towards his visits was beginning to harden into definite discomfort. But what could she do?

Rose had no intention of cooking the rabbit; the very sight of it inspired a kind of dread. She'd take it down to the dumpsters where the village left its rubbish when she went down to Levanto; in the meantime, she supposed reluctantly, the best place for it was the fridge. It would begin to smell if she left it with the other rubbish in tied plastic by the door. Come to think of it, she didn't know how long it might sit in the dumpster in the scalding heat. The thought turned her stomach. There was no indication of when the rubbish would next be collected from Grosso, what with Ferragosto. At least that was over; Rose had a residual childhood dislike of public holidays of which not even Italian festive spirit had cured her; dead time, life suspended for meaningless ritual, or meaningless at

92

least to her, the Assumption of the Virgin. Hiatus. And besides, now Rose had something she needed to get on with.

Outside the day was hot and hazy; the air was so heavy and humid that it obscured the usually sharp outline of the hill opposite. Overhead the sky glared almost white, and it hurt Rose's eyes as she stepped out on to the warm tiles of her terrace with her coffee. Reluctantly she looked down towards Gennaro's land, knowing he would be there working while it was still cool. She could see the ramshackle hutches where he kept his rabbits, a gas cylinder, a scattering of rubbish, plastic bottles and old planks. She couldn't see Gennaro and with a kind of relief she looked away. Putting a hand up to shield her eyes, she turned in the direction of the sea, and Elvira Vitale's house.

The house, or what Rose could see of it, faced east and was bleached by the morning sun. It was perhaps three or four miles away, but she could see that the shutters, on this side at least, were all closed, the jutting terrace empty. Rose wondered whether she might simply turn up, unannounced; she decided she couldn't. A letter, perhaps? She could write a letter of introduction. But that would be too easy to ignore. She thought for a while, then it came to her, a possibility: Venturelli. The director she had interviewed at Cannes; they'd got on well enough, and he might give her advice, or background on Elvira Vitale at least. She had his number somewhere still, she was sure of it.

Venturelli's voice, when it came on the line, sounded hollow, echoing as though in a vast marble hall. Rose could picture the cavernous gloom of his Turin flat, which sounded cool somehow even in the city, even in the August heat; she'd seen him photographed there for a magazine, sitting among vast pieces of heavy Art Deco furniture. In the film she'd watched at Cannes Venturelli had portrayed Turin as a place of massive, fin-de-siècle apartment blocks, endless stone porticoes, thick walls that kept out the sun. A shuttered, repressive place where the light, and much else, was denied. He barked a laugh when Rose expressed her surprise at finding him at home in the city in high summer.

'You don't know me very well,' he said. 'It's the best place to be, in August, the city.'

Rose thought of the scalding pavements in Genova, the bleached, silent backstreets, shuttered and ominous in the heat. Perhaps Turin was different.

'It must be quieter, anyway,' she said cautiously. 'Levanto is heaving.'

'Ferragosto,' said Venturelli, his voice rich with contempt of everything the holiday represented. They're like sheep, the lot of them, bleating off to the beach the minute August arrives, then bleating back to the city when it ends. You won't catch me at the seaside.'

Rose thought of Venturelli's pale, bespectacled face, his fifty-year-old intellectual's body in swimming trunks, on a lounger beside the girls in their sarongs and foam sandals, and she could see what he meant. It was inconceivable. Anxious not to try his patience, she got to the point.

'Ah,' he said, thoughtfully when Rose mentioned Elvira Vitale's name. 'Yes, she does have a place there, now I come to think of it. Not a sheep, that one, though.'

'No,' said Rose, feeling sure, even from her one glance at the woman standing at the bar of the Mare Blu, that he was right. 'You know her, then?'

Venturelli sighed. 'Not well,' he said, and Rose heard some

regret in his voice. Although I think we – clicked, if that's the right expression. She was a good actress. She hardly did anything, and when she did you couldn't really tell if she was acting or if that was her. That bit-part in a Fellini film, then she was in *Giulia*. Played the lead.' Rose made a mental note to try to get hold of it. 'Very dark, a – minority inter-est film.' The phrase sounded odd, euphemistic, to Rose, and she waited for Venturelli to expand. After a pause he sighed again.

'It was called pornographic, full of fetishism, sadomaso-chism, bound up with the war, the camps. But she was – she made it something else. She played a young Jewish woman who became the mistress of a guard. But then again, it might have been art following life; she married the director, you know, after the film was finished. They tried to keep it quiet but the papers got hold of it straight away, implied she'd been having an affair with him even when she was married to her first husband. Then she just – stopped. Stopped acting.' Venturelli's voice tailed off, as though he was pondering this fact and it perplexed him still. After a moment he spoke again, more matter-of-fact now.

'Well, so, I used to – see her now and again, on the circuit, you know. We used to get together at those terrible parties, oh, twenty years ago, premieres and such. I always had the impression that she was like me, there on sufferance, but she would go. Lately, I think – in the last five years, she hardly goes out. I asked her to be in a film I was trying to get made four, six years ago, and she turned me down flat. She wasn't rude about it, wrote me a letter herself but –' He stopped again. 'She's a closed book, pretty much, now; you'd be lucky to get anything out of her.'

'But,' Rose prompted, 'I could try? It would be interesting to try, by the sound of it?'

Venturelli sighed. 'Well . . . ' he said, reluctant.

'Do you think – is there any chance you could put in a word for me?' Rose held her breath. 'Please?'

'Look,' he said, 'I like you. You're intelligent. You might make it work – I don't think you will, but . . . ' He stopped, then started again. 'Okay. I'll drop her a line. Today, if you like. For all the good it'll do. But I will. But please, for my sake, don't be stupid. Don't ask any stupid questions; she's too good for all that.'

Rose nodded to herself. 'No,' she said. 'Don't worry. I won't ask about her husbands.'

'That would be a waste of time,' Venturelli said. 'They've been – trash, the lot of them. Even the director; never made a good film again. He just fed off her. As for this one – he's the worst, if you ask me.' He didn't elaborate, but there was something like disgust in his voice, and flat incomprehension. Rose wondered for a moment whether it was because Jack Robbins was English that Venturelli particularly disliked him, or for some other reason. She decided not to pursue it.

'Listen,' she said, 'thank you. Really – thank you. I'll do my best to make it worth it.'

'All right, all right,' said Venturelli roughly. 'That's enough. Just give me another good write-up, next time around.'

It was only then that Rose remembered, with a lurch of relief, that she'd been effusive about the film, and about Venturelli, in the piece she'd written in May. The receiver went silent in Rose's hand, and she wondered if Venturelli had already hung up. But then he spoke again. 'I'd be interested to know – how she is. If she lets you through the door, that is.' And then there was a click, and he was gone.

Slowly Rose replaced the receiver and sat back on the sofa, gazing out through the door to the brightness beyond. She felt an access of elation at the thought of approaching Elvira Vitale's front door, even if she was armed with no more than a promise of an introduction from Venturelli. A note would arrive when, tomorrow? That would give her time to do a bit of research; a video of the films Venturelli had mentioned, and some cuttings she should be able to get hold of on the internet, or through Cookie. Monday morning, then.

The room was still cool but the terracotta floor was warm under Rose's bare feet as the rectangle of sun falling through the doorway lengthened. As she sat, contemplating the availability of obscure art-house movies from the seventies on video in Levanto, unwilling to shut the sun out quite yet, she became aware of a subtle alteration in the usual morning sounds outside. As she listened, the nature of the difference began to consolidate; there was the usual early birdsong, women's voices, the two-stroke whine of a *motorino*, but beneath it something deeper. The rumble and thud of a heavy vehicle somewhere below, a clanking, like machinery, and men's voices, growing louder, coming nearer. Out of curiosity Rose went to the front door and opened it on to the cool, narrow alley. Tiziana was on her doorstep two doors up, looking down the street in the direction of the sound; she gave Rose a cursory nod. Then from around the corner lower down, silhouetted by the sun under the overhanging vine, came three men in dusty overalls, hauling a concrete mixer and a pneumatic drill between them. Bringing up the rear was Leonardo Giunti, the builder Rose had last seen in June when he had given her an estimate for the rebuilding of her pigsty. *Of course*, she thought. After Ferragosto, he'd said. And here he was.

Elvira stood in her bathroom and watched as the pills swirled in the lavatory pan and sank, a whole handful of them, brown and white, capsules and tablets. She wondered what she had done; she was beginning to feel jumpy already, after a sleepless night. But for once she had woken in no doubt of where she was, and although the previous evening seemed long and dreary, at least she could remember it in every detail.

They'd stayed at the Mare Blu a while, been found a table, then gone for a meal, nothing special, seafood consumed in near-silence in a comfortable trattoria. She'd been careful what she drank. A glass or two of champagne, no more; she'd caught Jack looking at her in a certain way, puzzled, then a little suspicious, but he'd said nothing. She didn't want a discussion of her drinking habits, not yet, and for some reason she particularly didn't want Jack to know what she was doing; the thought of him discovering her pathetic efforts to take control made her oddly afraid. It was something to do with the conversation she knew they'd have, about taking things slowly, not doing anything drastic, with guests about to arrive, a conversation that would leave her feeling weak and helpless. *I'll do this on my own.* But she had to admit she wasn't feeling good on it. Her mouth was dry, her skin itched and her head ached with what felt like toxicity.

Jack had gone out after she'd gone to bed, she knew that, although she was fairly sure he didn't know she knew. She wondered where he'd been this time; not far, she guessed, as he'd been back before one and was already up. Elvira could hear him downstairs, moving around, and she thought Ania must have arrived, to rouse him so early. Remembering why she needed Ania particularly today Elvira's heart sank. Luke and Annabel.

Jack was on the terrace drinking coffee, his big Olympus on the table in front of him. Automatically Elvira bent to kiss his cheek; it was smooth and scented with cologne and she felt as though all her senses had been heightened this morning, to an almost painful degree. She sank into a canvas deckchair beside him. The sun hurt her eyes and she shifted until the umbrella's shade protected her.

'I thought I'd head off to take some pictures,' he said, gesturing inland in the direction of Grosso. 'Before it gets too hot. And the light's good.' Elvira nodded absently, thinking only that the light seemed terrible to her, flat and glaring. But then she wasn't a photographer.

'Have you spoken to Ania?' she asked. 'About getting things ready for Luke and Annabel? I thought she might cook for us, on Sunday maybe?' She made an effort to make her voice light and steady, as though she was looking forward to the weekend.

Jack frowned. 'Ania?'

'Yes,' said Elvira, not quite suppressing her impatience. 'Remember her? Where is she? In the kitchen?'

For a moment she thought he looked genuinely worried about her. *Am I losing it?* she thought. *What did I say?*

'She's not here yet,' he said, shaking his head. 'Did you think you heard her?' He looked at her with concern.

'No,' said Elvira. 'No. I just assumed – she's usually here by now. Isn't she?'

Jack's face cleared. 'Don't ask me; I'm always asleep when she arrives. She's probably just had a night on the tiles, you know, Ferragosto. Slept in. Anyway, I'll be back before lunch.

We can talk about where we'll eat then, about the weekend. It'll be fun, won't it?' He looked at her.

'Yes,' said Elvira. 'Oh, yes.' She tilted her head a fraction to receive his kiss, no more than brushing her cheek, and heard the almost imperceptible rustle of the voile curtains as they admitted him to the house. A few moments later the front door slammed below and the unnecessary roar of Jack's engine reverberated in the narrow road outside, receding as he descended to the town.

For some reason, as she listened to the sound of Jack's car, Elvira found herself thinking of the foreign woman at the bar, the woman who'd been leaving as they arrived. There'd been something faintly familiar about her, in outline anyway, and when she had looked at Elvira – at them – it had been as though she knew them too. A wondering look, judging them, and Elvira knew what she'd been thinking. *What are you two doing together?* Suddenly Elvira, who had never in her life before accepted the judgement of others, wondered the same thing. It was as though she could see herself from the outside for the first time, the kind of men that she chose. Stefano; Marcello; Jack. *There are things –* Elvira wanted to say in her defence – *things you don't know about. Kinds of attraction you might not understand.* But somehow she was no longer sure. In the pit of her stomach she felt a queasiness stir at the thought that she might have made a mistake with her life. With her whole life. And it might be too late to put it right.

It was very quiet now that Jack was gone; behind Elvira, through the long windows, the dark, cool interior of her house lay silent. She looked out to sea, at the tiny leaning sails far out towards the horizon. She took a sip from Jack's coffee, cooling on the table, but it tasted bitter, and she put it down again. *Ania*, she thought with some impatience. *Where are you?*

100

Chapter Twelve

The hard, cold floor where Ania lay had once been polished but now was thickly overlaid with a patina of mildewed dust and neglect. It was no longer completely dark inside the building, however. There hadn't been electric light here for thirty years and the rotted windows were almost choked with ivy, but through the broken floorboards of the floor above Ania a hazy shaft of greenish light filtered through the gloom.

Some ten years earlier a freak spring downpour had allowed water to collect in one sagging corner of the building's roof and eventually the rotting beams beneath had given way. The light had penetrated first the roof space, then the upper floor of the building, then, when the floorboards had succumbed to wind and weather and marauding children, a shaft or two, on bright days like this one, made their way down here where Ania lay. Originally this space, it seemed, had been two rooms: one large one, with three long windows on one side, and the other narrow, with a small aperture high up on one wall, a row of basins, a sour-smelling soil pipe and the broken porcelain remains of a lavatory pan. At some point, though, the stud wall must have partially collapsed, turning the two rooms into one cavernous, fetid space.

It was not completely silent here, either; there were the insects, of course, the cicadas and grasshoppers as well as other slithering, creeping, clicking things, but there was the noise of a road too, not too far away, although not apparently a busy one. A sharp ear might also have distinguished the sound of chickens scratching and clucking at the boundary of their coop higher up and the occasional, far-off murmured exchange between old women, watering their tomatoes in the morning cool.

Ania didn't move; it wasn't clear whether she would be able to see or hear these things even if her eyes were open, her ear not pressed to the ground. Her face, one cheek resting on the dirty floor, was very pale except where it was smudged with dust, her mouth open a little, and there were bruises at her neck and on her upper arms. Her ankles were bound with a piece of faded blue nylon rope; her wrists too, although they were hidden below her body. Then another, new sound intervened, very slight at first; a light scratching from immediately outside. There was a door at one end of the room where Ania lay and this opened slowly, carefully, scraping across the floor. A man paused at the threshold for a moment, looking at the humped shape on the ground before crossing the room to stand over her. She didn't move even then, didn't flinch from the foot no more than an inch or two from her face.

The man looked down for some moments then slowly knelt, putting two fingers gently to the side of the girl's throat as though feeling for a pulse. After a moment he took his hand away and awkwardly, as though it was not a gesture he was familiar with, stroked her cheek and carefully tucked a strand of hair behind her ear. He straightened her legs a little, took the arm that was twisted across her body and rearranged it as though to disguise the fact that it was bound to the other, as though to make Ania look more natural. Then he walked around her for a while, stopping, head on one side as if to look at the arrangement he had made.

When he had finished, he walked across the room to the door by which he had entered, slipped back through it, and was gone. All that he left were marks on the dusty floor, dragged and swirled here and there, revealing the cracked, greasy tiles beneath.

For a long time the tableau the man had left behind him remained just that, quite still. The sound of his passage back to where he had come from had long since receded, to leave only the insects and the chickens to hold sway over their forlorn, deserted kingdom, when at last, almost imperceptibly, Ania's eyelids trembled, and her eyes flickered open in the gloom.

'Are you sure this is all right?' asked Richard Bourn, looking across the table at Rose as the huge silver platter of seafood – langoustines, squid, marinated anchovies and half a dozen other fish she didn't recognize – was set down between them. The waiter poured the cold wine, bowed slightly, and left.

Rose wasn't quite sure at all. They were sitting in the window seat of one of Levanto's prettiest restaurants, it was beautifully cool and from the interior behind them, hung with old mirrors and set about with exquisitely mismatched antiques, rose the relaxed hum of lunchtime conversation. Rose wasn't at all sure what she was doing here.

There hadn't been much time to prepare for this. It had been close to midday when she had felt that at last, she might be able to leave the builder and his men to it. There were four of them altogether. The builder himself; a bricklayer built like a weightlifter, huge-shouldered and massive-thighed; a red-faced man with a large belly whose expertise seemed to be demolition, and a shy young one, not much more than a boy, who barely spoke and seemed to have the dogsbody role. They seemed eager to get under way and Rose could tell that like all builders, they'd rather she was out of the way too.

At the beginning of the project, in May, there had been a *geometra* – a kind of surveyor or architect, as far as Rose understood, if not a very elevated kind, and it was with him that she had drawn up the plans Giunti now held in his hand. But put on the spot, Rose could hardly remember what they had decided all those months earlier; the *geometra*, being a professional, was away for the entire month of August but Giunti was obviously in need of the work and keen to get started without him. Painstakingly they went over the plans again.

'Okay,' said Rose finally, once they had reached agreement that the builders would begin by levelling some of the land below her house and no actual demolition would begin until the following week. 'Yes; go on.' She could see that she should not hold them up; she supposed they were builders just like in England after all, and she should be grateful that they were there and ready to work.

When she turned to go inside Rose saw that Tiziana was out on her terrace for once, leaning on her cracked concrete balustrade to get a good look at what was going on. Rose smiled at her and was rewarded only by an almost imperceptible nod. You could never tell what Tiziana was thinking; her expression was always the same; squinting suspicion. Further up the village along the hillside Rose could see two, three heads craning out of usually shuttered rear windows, and she nodded as cheerfully as she could manage in their direction. Her building project was obviously attracting attention. She had looked back down the hill towards Gennaro's land, wondering, with some apprehension, what he would think of all this, but there was no sign of him.

Rose had hurried off down through the village, aware of time passing, of her Monday morning deadline. She had no idea whether there was anywhere at all in Levanto that sold videos, let alone one that might stock Elvira Vitale's screen appearances, but she had to try.

The sight of the dumpsters ranged beside the bus stop, though, had brought Rose up short, reminding her as they did of the bagged rabbit in her fridge, not to mention the two carriers full of rubbish decaying at her back door which she had overlooked in the rush to get away. But then she heard her name and turned away. She had seen first an unfamiliar car, not dun-coloured, covered in dust or shrouded by a tarpaulin as all the residents' vehicles were, but cherished, gleaming, an old red sports car. Standing beside it was Richard Bourn.

'I thought you said you lived here,' he had said, smiling tentatively as though not quite sure of his welcome. 'I took a chance. I felt like a drive, anyway.'

Rose had stood there, frowning a little. He looked quite relaxed, standing in his shirtsleeves in the sun beside his beautiful car and looking at her, but she felt flustered, wrong-footed. Pursued. The seductive smell of warm leather and petrol rose from the car and she tried a smile.

'Ah – that's nice of you,' she said. 'Lovely car.'

Richard Bourn stayed where he was, hands in his pockets, and shrugged a little.

'You looked so hot and bothered, getting off the train, with your computer,' he said apologetically. 'I could have been more helpful, couldn't I?'

Rose shook her head in protest. 'No,' she said. 'You were very kind, as far as I remember.'

'Anyway,' said Bourn. 'We should stick together, expats, shouldn't we? If that's what we are. And I've finished work for the day so I wondered – would you like some lunch?'

Rose had opened her mouth, closed it again, looked down at what she was wearing. 'Well ...' she said, thinking of all the things she had to get done. But she could hardly complain of being lonely if she turned down every opportunity for company that came her way. She smiled cautiously. 'That'd be lovely,' she said. 'Do you mind if we stop somewhere on the way? There's something I've got to do first.'

It turned out that there were several video shops in Levanto, including Blockbuster, a big American video rental chain, but although they tracked down the Fellini film in which she had a bit-part, none of them stocked Elvira Vitale's only starring role. Richard Bourn was obviously made curious by Rose's determination, and Rose found herself explaining, a little reluctantly.

'Ah,' he said slowly. 'Yes; I think I've seen that Fellini film, at least. Don't remember her in it. But she's – if she lives up there,' he nodded up the hill, 'then she's my nearest neighbour.' He smiled pleasantly.

Rose looked up at the palisaded villas that clung to the hillside, Elvira Vitale's at the top, its shuttered yellow façade solid and comfortable as it nestled into the rock; beyond it she could see the pale, elegant rectangle of another house, more refined in style. Richard saw her looking.

'That's it,' he said. 'La Martinière.' Rose nodded but said nothing; she didn't want to sound as if she was angling for an invitation. But she went on looking; the house's outline was quite beautiful from here, with its long windows set alone among the trees and overlooking the sea.

They'd found the video, in the end, at the back of an odd little general store on the edge of the old town to which a help-ful assistant at Blockbuster had directed them, its interior a dim jumble of ancient coffee machines and ugly floral dinner services. There on a shelf with cheap dog-eared paperbacks was a row of dusty videos and among them, almost like a miracle, there it was. She was a local girl originally, Elvira Vitale, the shop-owner had explained proudly, wiping the dust from the cassette's spine with a damp cloth. Only then had they gone to eat; Rose had been apologetic about her errand and the fact that it had turned into such a lengthy one, but Richard Bourn betrayed no impatience. The restaurant, he said, wasn't far from the old town, but then in Levanto nothing was very far from anything else.

It was immediately obvious that Bourn's chosen restaurant, behind a loggia overgrown with the deep blue trumpets of tropical convolvulus and next to the striped marble church, wasn't just a humble trattoria, and Rose's immediate reaction had been dismay. But now, the restaurant was so pretty, the food smelled so good that her discomfiture began to subside. Richard certainly seemed entirely at his ease in this environ-ment; it was obvious that the waiters knew him, and Rose wondered if he usually came here alone.

'So what kind of work do you do, then?' she asked. 'To be able to finish at midday?'

Bourn looked at her for a moment as though not quite sure how to answer.

'I don't — well, I don't really have a job, strictly speaking,' he said. 'I started a company in England, oh, fifteen years ago. Developing medical instruments.' He stopped, looking at her, frowning a little. 'Valves, for the administration of drugs. Not exciting. I sold it last year and came out here. I don't really need to work any more, but . . . ' He shrugged self-deprecatingly. 'I do bits and pieces for them. Sort out problems that come up. They kept me on a retainer just in case the company fell apart without me, but it doesn't seem to have.'

Rose nodded, and took a mouthful of her wine. She wondered where Richard Bourn's wife, or partner, was. It did not seem plausible that he was single; she was, of course, but then she was a woman, and not wealthy, whereas he . . . Rose tried to be level-headed, to resist the soporific influence of the warmth, the alcohol and the food. *You're too good to be true. What are you doing out here on your own?* She didn't ask though, only smiled, picking up a langoustine and prising it apart. Richard was looking at her shrewdly, and she wondered if he knew what she was thinking. Perhaps there are plenty of us, she thought, our age, on the shelf, divorced, widowed, split up. Perhaps he'd just rather be alone.

'There's no attractive way to do this, is there?' she said, laughing as the buttery, garlicky juices dripped from her fingers, taking up her napkin.

'I was married,' he said, pushing a fingerbowl across the table to her. 'In case you're wondering. My wife left me, though; she said I worked too hard.' Deftly stripping a razor clam of its meat he laid the long striped shell neatly at the side of his plate, next to an orderly tower of oyster shells. Rose's plate, in contrast, was heaped messily with debris, a half-lemon squeezed of its juice and the transparent, whiskery husks of shrimp and langoustine.

Rose contemplated this evidence of Richard Bourn's orderly habits, and wondered whether it meant anything. 'Is that why you stopped work?' she said. 'Sold your company? Not that it's any of my business, of course.' She smiled at him cheerfully, but he sighed.

'Perhaps,' he said. 'But it was too late by then.' And for a moment or two neither of them spoke. The waiter came back, poured them each another glass and removed the heaped plates. Drinking the wine, looking out at the electric blue flowers, a marble corner of the church and an elderly couple sitting peaceably on a bench in the shaded piazza beyond it, Rose felt a sense of well-being descend on her.

'Do you want coffee here?' said Richard suddenly, pushing his chair back and signalling to a waiter. 'Or would you like to see my house?'

Chapter Thirteen

'For heaven's sake,' said Jack. 'It's not the end of the world, is it, just one day? We'll manage without Ania for a day. She's probably just sleeping it off somewhere.' He paused. 'Do you want me to phone Luke, put them off?'

Elvira knew that her reaction was disproportionate, but her head ached, she couldn't help thinking of the tub of painkillers in the bathroom cupboard, and she needed Ania. It was all getting on top of her, somehow, and there were so many things she needed Ania for suddenly; she wanted to ask her about Luke and Annabel's visit, whether she'd mentioned it, wanted confirmation that she wasn't losing her mind, wanted an ally against Jack. And besides, Ania had never missed a day's work. Even if she hadn't quite obviously needed every penny she could earn, she wasn't the type; she wasn't a risk-taker, she was a grafter. *Perhaps that's my trouble*, Elvira thought with a flash of insight like a break in the cloud; *I should be working. I've got too much time on my hands.*

They were sitting at the kitchen table. Elvira, who never cooked, had come down to the kitchen once it had become clear that she would be facing this weekend without hired help, to see what there was in the way of food for their guests. She had descended the stairs with a feeling of approaching her nemesis, but it was an attractive room, taking up half of the *piano terra*, pleasantly gloomy with cool, rough stone floors and a wall of old, cream-painted shelves. There was a big range and a recessed larder as well as an outsized American fridge, and opposite Elvira two wide-spaced, deep-set windows looked out to sea through the greenery that hung down from the terrace above. Elvira realized that she hardly ever came down here. It put her house in a new perspective, the view from below stairs; she could imagine Ania down here, busy in the cool, while her employer baked on the terrace in the sun, or lay restless in her canopied bed. She found herself wondering what Ania thought of her; not much, perhaps. It was a novel experience for Elvira; she didn't usually care what anyone thought, and here she was, anxious that her cleaner should know that this wasn't really her, this idle, wealthy, pointless middle-aged woman.

Is that me? Frowning at the thought, Elvira looked across the table at Jack. He had come back from his expedition in high spirits, a roll of film ready for developing in his darkroom, to find her pacing the terrace in agitated despair at Ania's lateness. Now he was looking back at her with what seemed to be genuine concern. She smiled at him, only a little shakily.

'You're right,' she said. 'It'll be fine. Don't put them off.'

'Are you sure?' said Jack, looking at her searchingly. 'I'm sure they'd understand.'

Elvira narrowed her eyes at this. *Understand what, exactly?*

She wondered how Jack would phrase it to them. *She's under a lot of pressure. I think she needs help.* She made up her mind.

'Nonsense,' she said coolly. 'It's not as if I've never cooked a meal in my life, is it?'

Jack raised his eyebrows at this, but he patted her shoulder. That's the spirit,' he said.

'Well then,' said Elvira with a confidence she didn't feel. 'I'd better – go down to Levanto. I can order some dishes from the delicatessen. I'm sure you've got things to do in town, haven't you?'

As it turned out, Jack did; he left Elvira in the busy main street in the sun with a wave of his hand. He didn't say where he was going, and Elvira didn't ask; they had arranged to meet back at the Mare Blu for an *aperitivo* an hour later.

The *gastronomia*, Levanto's most celebrated delicatessen, was approaching lunchtime closing when Elvira entered, and it was packed after Ferragosto with locals and tourists, some stocking up for the weekend, some buying for a picnic on the beach or the cliff path. On first entering the shop's dark, crowded interior, Elvira experienced an acute crisis of self-consciousness. She was convinced that the other customers were all looking at her surreptitiously; she thought she detected an exchange of looks between the matrons with their string shopping bags, an alteration in the timbre of the conversation and in their body language expressive of disapproval and judgement. Elvira felt perspiration bloom unexpectedly at her temples and between her shoulderblades.

But there was nothing she could do about it; there was already someone else waiting in the doorway behind her and she could hardly run out. So Elvira stood her ground and the queue was so long, the trade so brisk and noisy, that quite quickly she was able to persuade herself that any heads turned in her direction had turned back again and that indeed it was quite possible that the whole thing had been in her imagination. Perhaps after all she was just another customer. She tried to listen to their conversation, a bit of harmless gossip, that would do it. But the two women at the head of the queue, both grandmothers and Levanto natives by the look of them, were talking in tones of hushed outrage about a murder; a strangled girl. As he wrapped a package of roast ham, sliced as thin as paper, the portly shopkeeper was shaking his head in solemn agreement. 'It's not the kind of thing we're used to,' he said. 'You can bet your life it was a foreigner did it. All these immigrants. Anything else, Signora?' His customer pointed at a fat buffalo mozzarella, and the conversation moved on.

A strangled girl, thought Elvira, as though emerging from a dream and still unsure of reality. Here? His words buzzed in her head; *a foreigner did it*. She stared at the man, but he was calmly taking down a caciocavallo now. Perhaps she had dreamt it; delicately she patted at the perspiration on her forehead with a forearm, looked around so that normality could reassert itself.

She gazed at the pomegranate-red bouffant hair of the woman in front of her in the queue; over her shoulder she could see herself reflected in a mirror behind the counter, her own coiffure sleek and muted and tasteful. London hair. Bond Street hair. She experienced a sudden urge to march into the local salon and ask for a shampoo and set, a nice bright flame colour to cheer herself up, turn herself into a Levanto matron.

The interior of the shop was dim and fragrant with salted and air-dried hams hanging from the ceiling, big salami, fat provolone and gigantic, sausage-shaped cheeses covered in wax and trussed with string. The shelves bent under the weight of bottles of all kinds: oil, wine, grappa and fine vinegars, and the glass cabinet was full of dishes of grilled vegetables, aubergines, peppers, courgettes swimming in oil, tomatoes stuffed with rice. On top of the counter glistening slabs of focaccia studded with artichokes or overlaid with thinly sliced potato and spiked with rosemary were stacked high. As she looked, and began to decide what she should order when her turn came, Elvira felt soothed, found herself in the grip of an unfamiliar sensation. A distant memory of meals past, an elusive, long-forgotten sense of pleasurable anticipation, of flavours and combinations and table settings and good wine: Elvira, after perhaps twenty-five years in which the satisfaction of this particular appetite had been more or less irrelevant, realized that she was feeling hungry.

Cirri watched the Englishman in his monstrous car roar off up the promenade towards the more fashionable end of the beach without more than passing interest, and that more in the car than its driver. He disliked these new cars with a passion; grown unnecessarily, hideously vast, with their cramped, leather-padded interiors, their chrome and bull-bars and fat tyres, they seemed to him to represent everything that was wrong with the modern world. Ugly, wasteful, selfish, domineering, heedless. Cars for men who liked to throw their weight about, for pampered couples for whom one child was too much trouble, for hairdressers and pimps and idiots.

He recognized the driver, though; Elvira Vitale's husband. Her husband was more visible in Levanto than she was, though he didn't have what might be called the common touch; barely spoke Italian according to the barman at the Mare Blu, and that with a strangulated English accent. As for her – Cirri assumed she was a spoilt, rich woman whose judgement had been addled by decades of flattery and high living, but he had to admit that he didn't know whether that was accurate; he had only her husband, and Toto's opinions, to go on. He'd never seen any of her films, never met her, seen her perhaps on a handful of occasions in the town over his ten years at the Levanto station. Beautiful, though, you had to give her that. Even now.

Cirri thought of Anna-Maria Villemartin's mother, and her ravaged face. The girl had been asphyxiated; garrotted, in fact, with some kind of fine, strong wire. Fishing line, or cheese-wire. And that, he knew, could only suggest premeditation. He tried to think of a case in which a garrotte was improvised in a moment of anger, and couldn't, unless it was a trained assassin doing the improvising. Admittedly Cirri's experience of violent killing was small, a gap in his education for which he was grateful, but to him the use of a garrotte rather than one's bare hands or an item of clothing suggested a perpetrator who went out equipped for murder. Equipped to murder either this girl in particular or, and he registered this possibility with a creeping, dreadful sense that it was the more likely, to kill any girl. He thought of Myriam Bosnic, found further up the same railway line a year earlier, and he found himself pleading with a God in whom he did not believe that it should be no more than coincidence. A murderer who came here every summer, for his holidays? Heaven forbid.

In his pocket Cirri's mobile shrilled. It was Toto, in a state of high excitement.

'They found a ticket,' he said, barely able to catch his breath. 'She'd tucked it into a book, that's why we didn't find it before. A ticket to Levanto, stamped twelve twenty-two. She was definitely on that train, and she was going to get off here.' The words came out in a rush.

Cirri nodded, forgetting Toto couldn't see him. The kind of girl to stamp her ticket.

'Boss?'

'Yes ... yes, thanks, Toto,' he said. 'You're right. It means she was coming here.' Cirri felt a terrible despondency as the responsibility for the girl's death settled heavily on his town, his patch, and on his shoulders in particular. It wasn't just by chance, then, that Anna-Maria Villemartin's battered body was found here and not in Monterosso, or Deiva Marina, or Bonassola. She was coming here. Slowly he weighed his mobile in his hand, gazed at the children on the beach.

A small girl in sunhat and sandals was toddling unsteadily on the stones towards the sea, her mother following, bent over and clucking anxiously behind her. On impulse Cirri clicked his mobile open again and dialled home.

'Gloria?' he said, feeling his heart lift as he heard his wife's voice. 'Any chance of some lunch?' He listened patiently as she grilled him and scolded him, why hadn't he told her this morning, was there something wrong?

'No,' he said, smiling at last. 'Nothing wrong. Just wanted to see you, and Chiara, and a man's got to eat. I'll be there in ten minutes.' He snapped the phone shut, and turned for home.

When she entered the Mare Blu with her arms full of the *gastronomia's* brown-paper sacks, loaded with cartons and tubs and flat packages, sliced ham, cheese, quail stuffed with almonds, olives and God knew what else, Elvira was feeling almost triumphant. After the delicatessen, she had bought wine – a particularly nice Barolo – from a *cantina* down a

116

sidestreet and, pausing outside the butcher's, had on impulse bought a big piece of pork, rolled loin well larded with fat. From somewhere long ago she remembered pork stuffed with fennel and coriander and cooked in milk, a dish her mother had reserved for special occasions. Elvira was astonished that the memory existed, intact; she had stopped eating when she was fourteen or so, repelled by the monstrous changes taking over her body, so the image must have pre-dated her adolescence. Thirty-five years ago. Elvira's mother had never been what you might call a role model, either. What had she ever done, after all? That was how Elvira had always seen it, until now, anyway. A packhorse, a dumb creature, she had produced a son and a daughter and brought them up without benefit of a husband, using up her life in dead-end jobs. This had never before seemed much of an achievement to Elvira, rather an act of sentimental irresponsibility. *You'll understand, when you have children of your own*, her mother would say wearily in response to some accusation or row, but Elvira had never made that mistake, had she? Never would, now.

Elvira's mother had worked, of course, because where else would the money have come from? She had had a succession of jobs she fitted around the children's school hours; down at the harbour filleting fish with raw red hands at five every morning, working behind a bar pouring cheap brandy for abusive sailors and surly fishermen, sweeping up in a sweat-shop. On the streets now and again in extremis and before her looks went, although Elvira wasn't supposed to know about that, wouldn't have known if a sweet-faced schoolfriend hadn't informed her that was why Elvira didn't get invited round.

Elvira's brother, Nino, infuriating, golden-skinned and beloved, had started work on the tankers and cargo ships as

117

a third hand at the age of fifteen and by twenty had gained a deep-sea first mate's certificate. At twenty-eight he had gone missing, presumed drowned, along with the rest of the crew, when their ship and its load of truck-tyres en route for South Africa went down in a storm off the Cape of Good Hope. Elvira had been on an assignment in New York when she heard the news; by the time she got home, her mother had been as good as dead too, although in fact it took another two years before the drink carried her off, swollen-faced from alcohol and relentless, unceasing grief. All gone now; did she really belong here any more, without her mother or her brother? The meat weighed heavy now in Elvira's arms; it was beginning to feel like a burden she should not have taken on, and in the doorway of the Mare Blu she straightened her back, resisting the unwanted memories the purchase of food seemed to have brought along with it.

Jack was already there. Not at the bar, but at his favourite table, adjacent to the owner's, his long legs stretched out, a house *aperitivo* and a dish of crisp golden whitebait untouched in front of him. An odd expression passed over his face as he saw her; he looked almost aghast, Elvira thought, although by the time she had crossed the threshold he had toned it down to an expression of amused dismay.

Elvira looked down at herself, puzzled; she was not, she had to admit, looking her best. She could feel her hair sticking to her temples in the heat, and the oil from one of her tubs had leaked out, streaking her sleeve at her elbow. Jack did not leap up to help her with her packages and so she dumped them on the table and sat down, feeling the last of the elation bestowed on her by the success of her shopping mission drain rapidly away as she did so.

'My God,' said Jack. 'What's all that?' He looked almost disgusted at the sight of so much food. 'I didn't mean – darling, you don't have to cater all weekend. We don't want you stuck in the kitchen, it's such a bore, isn't it?'

'Why should I mind?' said Elvira, defiantly. 'It'll be a change. I can cook, you know.' And in fact the thought of spending the weekend in the silent, subterranean kitchen still seemed preferable to spending it with Luke and Annabel. Frowning, she rubbed at her sleeve where the grease had stained it.

'Do you think we should contact the police?' she said. Jack looked startled. 'About Ania,' said Elvira. 'Her – disappearance?'

Jack snorted. 'And say what? Our illegal immigrant cleaning lady didn't turn up for work this morning? They may be an idle bunch but I'm sure even they can think of better things to do than track Ania down the day after Ferragosto.'

'All the same,' said Elvira slowly, thinking of the conversation she'd heard at the deli counter, 'she's never missed a day's work, has she? It's not like her. What if – something's happened to her? I heard – there's been a murder, after all, so they were saying in town.' She uttered the words with a kind of dread, knowing she hadn't dreamt it after all. *It was real, wasn't it? A girl had died.*

Jack responded with indifference. 'So they've got enough on their plate, already, haven't they? The police.'

'So it's true, then?' Elvira looked at Jack, and he shrugged. 'I'd heard something, yes. Chucked off a train. Probably a – you know. A prostitute. Happens all the time, doesn't it?'

'Does it?' Frowning, Elvira bit her lip, and looked down. Perhaps he was right. She would only make an idiot of herself if she went to the police station.

119

Jack seemed to have forgotten the conversation already. 'Now,' he said, smiling, 'do you want a drink?' And without bothering to look round he raised one hand for the waiter, with the other pushing the dish of whitebait away from him slightly. Elvira realized, after her near-epiphanic experience of hunger in the *gastronomia*, that she had never seen Jack take pleasure in eating anything. Suddenly she felt nauseated by the vision of her life, of their life, that this realization conjured up, and very tired. Perhaps there was no way out of this, and no point in trying.

'All right,' she said. 'Champagne.' *What the hell.* She looked up with grim resignation at the waiter approaching their table and fixed a smile. 'Bring us a bottle, will you?'

The light was ebbing again now, the green gloom inside the derelict building was turning grey and the black shadows in the corner of the room had lengthened and merged. Ania was against the wall, frozen, her eyes darting from one corner to another of the long, dark room.

When she had first opened her eyes, Ania had thought she was in the barn at home, asleep with the cattle on the dirt floor in the warm dark. Then she had tried to move, found herself unaccountably unable to free her hands, and had fallen back and struck her cheek. And as she lay there, her hands and feet bound, looking at broken planking over her head, tasting something sour in her mouth and feeling the blood pulse in her temples, all at once the terror had broken over her like a great wave. Frantically she scrabbled and shuffled across the floor towards the wall, humping her back like a caterpillar, painfully slow, her heart pounding with fear and effort until she thought it would burst. And there she had stopped, her back pressed into the damp, powdery plaster, trying to bring her nerves under control. Trying to think.

It was her body getting in the way, shattering any concentration Ania could muster. Her temples throbbed, her chest felt tight and bruised and her wrists and ankles were chafed raw and bleeding from the ropes that bound them. Unwillingly she looked down, and saw an odd pattern of bruising on the inside of her thighs where her skirt had ridden up. She had a sickening feeling that something was not right with her body, that she had been taken apart and jammed roughly back together, her tendons and joints and cartilage all stretched and sore. Her clothes felt sticky and uncomfortable, as though they weren't hers, as though she had not put them on herself.

Where am I? Who did this? Where Ania's memory should be was nothing but a blindingly empty space, like a broken television screen, a jumble of fractured pixels and meaningless luminescence. Her head ached with the effort of trying to bring it back. The station, that was all she could remember, standing beside the track, the sound of the train on the opposite platform. Or was that yesterday? The day before? Ania realized slowly that another thing she didn't know was how much time had passed, how long she had been lying here. Her bladder was tight, her body as stiff as though she had lain here for days. Her stomach felt hollow and empty; she calculated it had been empty for some time, but she was too afraid to feel hunger. She knew that whoever brought her here would come back, and that when he did, when she saw him, he would kill her.

Ania tried to stand, pressing her back against the wall and pushing up, but she was tangled in her own bound arms, and her legs, boneless as rubber, gave way beneath her. She toppled sideways, landing painfully on her elbow, and as she lay there, her eyes filled with tears of self-pity, the accumulation of eighteen months' misery and despair far from home. They burned shamefully on her cheeks. *I'll die, then*, she thought. *Let me die.*

Chapter Fourteen

Rose sat up late watching Elvira Vitale on the small screen. She was a revelation. Even in the bit-part she had been given in the Fellini movie – a girl sitting at a bar, her character barely sketched, asking for a light – she was rivetingly, distractingly watchable, as full of meaning as a girl in a Hopper painting. When she looked up at the camera her dark eyes seemed to speak for her, full of loneliness and longing.

The second film, *Giulia*, in which Vitale played the central role and eponymous heroine, was a different matter. The plot was not original, the film was not well made and the other players were insignificant, but Elvira's performance was extraordinarily convincing; it made Rose lean forward to gaze at the long, luminous face that filled the screen. She'd married the director, Rose remembered, and she wasn't surprised. As Venturelli had suggested, at certain moments she seemed not to be acting at all. Watching her, it seemed extraordinary to Rose that Elvira Vitale had not gone on acting and become a household name, a new Anna Magnani.

The sun had dipped behind the hill as, curled on the sofa, Rose focused on the glowing screen. She had enjoyed television in England; it had, she realized, become her tranquillizer of choice – a soap, a nice detective series, the sober, comforting face of a familiar newsreader – but she didn't often watch it here. The Italian schedules were packed with incomprehensible game shows, the contestants blinking as they were thrust into a brightly lit atmosphere of whipped-up euphoria, and the gaps filled in by ancient, badly dubbed feature films. Italian television was a reminder of the cultural divide that remained between Rose and the local population, of her incomplete integration.

At first, she had to admit, Rose had missed her evening dose of television, but gradually she adjusted; it seemed that the things she couldn't get in Italy, like Marmite, Ribena, a ready meal or a choice of seventeen different breakfast cereals in the supermarket, hadn't really been worth having in the first place. And she had become pleased with the space that opened up in her life in its stead, for sitting on the terrace, wandering in Levanto, looking in the shops that were still open at eight in the evening, mixing with people even if she never spoke to them. She had bought the combined television and video recorder at a discount store thinking she might borrow the occasional film on cassette, but this was the first time she had used it.

Around Rose the room grew dark as she watched the screen, and outside the valleys filled with mist drifting pale among the trees and making the distant lights of other villages twinkle. Towards eleven a warm wind had begun to blow in through the long doors and when around midnight Rose stood up to switch off the television she felt the soft, balmy air on her arms. She stretched luxuriously in the sudden dark, but she wasn't quite ready for bed yet. The twenty-year-old image of Elvira Vitale was imprinted on her mind and waiting to be processed, and besides, too much had happened today. She decided to take the rubbish down to the dumpsters.

The village was dark and silent as Rose set off down the narrow alley. In one hand she held her two supermarket carriers stuffed with compacted rubbish and from the other swung the dismembered rabbit, triple-wrapped in paper and plastic. As with every step the bag bumped against her bare calf, she couldn't help but be reminded of her failure to deal with the rabbit, to turn it into food as any Italian grandmother would have done. At the bottom of the village she took the steps two at a time. A shard of light and a burst of fuzzy applause from some late-night TV show filtered out from behind the closed shutters of one of the houses. Otherwise there was only the rhythmic buzz of the cicadas singing in the olive trees below the village, the sound swelling and ebbing in the darkness.

She had said no, of course, when Richard Bourn had asked her back to his villa for coffee. Not without hesitation; she liked him. She tried to pin it down, the nature of the attraction; he talked easily, intelligently, and listened to her when she talked; he had nice skin, smooth and clean, and strong forearms. And he had asked her to his house, the house on the hill he'd pointed to. La Martinière.

Was that it? She had found herself wondering what it would be like to find herself in closer proximity to him, what his skin would smell like. Were these the responses of a desperate older woman? She wanted to avoid that, at all costs. And besides, it had seemed too ridiculously quick to accept an invitation to his home, alone; this was a first date, after all, and barely a date at that. An impromptu lunch. And there was, too, a stirring of something other than modesty, a reason other than the desire not to seem too eager; a distant echo of her mother's advice to fourteen-year-old Rose not to accept invitations from strangers. But half of her still wished she'd said yes.

'I've got to get back,' she'd said, holding up her cassette, and he hadn't seemed offended. He'd just nodded, lifting his hand for the waiter.

'Another time?' she'd offered. Richard had shrugged, returning her smile although his was more guarded, somehow, and she wondered whether she had offended him after all.

'Sure,' he'd said then, and they'd driven back up in a mutual silence that was not uncomfortable, or at least Rose thought not, and had arrived back at Grosso in mid-afternoon to find it shuttered and empty in the baking heat. He'd kissed her quickly on the cheek and had driven off. Rose had heard the startled blare of a bus horn as it met him on a bend halfway down the hill and her heart had jumped in her chest.

Even now at midnight, in the dark, some of that afternoon heat was still radiating from the stone of the village houses at Rose's back. Reaching the bins, she pressed her foot on the lever that opened their lids and with a sudden, powerful sense of relief swung the bags up and let them fall inside with a hollow clang. When she turned back Gennaro was standing there on the steps in the sodium glare of the single street-light by the bus stop, looking at her and smiling a little. His face was yellow in the artificial light, and hollow-cheeked. Involuntarily Rose gasped a little, a tiny sound, but a perplexed look passed across Gennaro's face.

'*Buona sera,*' he said, holding up his own bag of rubbish to justify his presence. Rose was suddenly convinced that Gennaro knew what she was doing there, that he could see through the layers of paper and polythene and identify his gift to her now lying, rejected, among the chicken bones and old newspapers. She forced herself to smile.

'*Buona sera,*' she said, moving to the side to allow him past. Gennaro didn't move.

'It's a beautiful evening,' he said in Italian a little formally, gesturing around at the soft night. Rose agreed. 'Perhaps –' He hesitated, then began again. 'I will be going out in my boat tomorrow – or today? Perhaps it is already tomorrow?' She smiled a little at him, waiting. 'If I catch some good fish, I wonder perhaps if you will come for dinner tomorrow? I mean, Sunday?' He tailed off again, looked up at the stars as though practising a phrase silently in his head. 'I invite you to eat with me, on Sunday? At about seven o'clock, in my house?'

Dumbly, Rose nodded. How could she say no? The truth was, she couldn't turn him down; at least, unlike Richard Bourn whose invitation she had found considerably more tempting, she had known Gennaro for more than a day. More like a year in fact, and besides, Gennaro's house was in the village, surrounded by gossiping, shutter-twitching old folk, not in the middle of nowhere. Rose wondered where all this caution had suddenly appeared from. Then she remembered the dead girl they'd been talking about in the Mare Blu. She pushed the thought away.

'I would be delighted,' she said, recovering herself, and Gennaro's face split in a smile. He moved aside. 'At seven, then,' he said. 'On Sunday.' And Rose nodded, trying to stop herself bolting past him. Then she took a breath, lifted a hand in greeting and took the steps as quickly as she decently could.

She almost ran back through the village, the air burning her lungs. It was only once she had closed her own door behind her at last, feeling her heart thumping with ridiculous speed in her chest, that she began to wonder. There was something odd about their chance meeting. Could it have really been coincidence that she had arrived at the dumpsters just as Gennaro decided to bring his own rubbish out? At midnight? She thought of Gennaro in his house, imagined him standing behind the shutters in the dark, watching for her, and felt a prickle at the back of her neck.

Rose went outside to her terrace and stood there for some time, listening to her heartbeat slow down as it returned to normal. There was a light on next door outside Tiziana's house that cast a pool of light down on the unkempt paving. It illuminated the old lady's tomato plants, the silvery leaves of the nearest olive trees, the humped shape of the old pigsty and the concrete mixer left by the builders, but below that everything was deep velvety dark. Anything could be out there; it was a thought that occasionally assailed Rose when she was swimming in the sea, that in the cold depths below her there could be anything; slimy, scrabbling sea creatures, decomposing life. She shivered. In the distance the headlights of a slow-moving car followed the winding road around the contours of the hill, heading for the motorway. She stood and listened, but she could hear nothing but the receding car against the background buzz of the night insects. She went inside.

The house felt warm and stuffy now, but nevertheless Rose forced herself to move methodically around it in the dark before she went to bed, shutting the night air out. She locked the doors front and back, closed and shuttered the windows downstairs, and only then, when it was almost two o'clock, did she climb the stairs, slip gratefully between her cool sheets, and sleep.

Chapter Fifteen

Elvira had first met Luke and Annabel at the gallery, of course, something like eight, nine years before, and she had not warmed to them over time; rather the opposite. With a few others they formed the backbone of Jack's gallery rent-a-crowd for private views; an assortment of old schoolfriends, a few rich men and their wives, anxious to seem not only wealthy but cultured, a select group of minor celebrities among whom, Elvira supposed gloomily, she could count herself.

They had been engaged then, Luke and Annabel, no children yet, both working in the City and living in a huge garden flat in a white stucco terrace in Chelsea that was owned by Luke's family. Their future together had been mapped out already, though, Elvira could see that; observing Luke and Annabel had been part of her education in English society or at least that small, privileged but, at least to Elvira, oddly unenviable corner of it occupied by Jack and his friends. They would have children, but not an excessive number, and so it turned out. With typical efficiency Annabel had produced strapping twins nine months to the day after their Mayfair wedding. She had returned to work six weeks later, having provided the requisite minimum of maternal attention and breast milk and employed a maternity nurse and nanny of excellent pedigree and references to take over where she had left off. She had not been obliged, the twins being one of each sex, Hugo and Elizabeth, to produce any more children.

Jack and Elvira saw Luke and Annabel once every two weeks or so, at dinner and cocktail parties, receptions at the gallery, weekends in the country and highly organized picnics. Over the years Elvira had watched, with fascination, as the two small children had been processed by a system the like of which she had never seen. They submitted to a regime of highly qualified care-givers, which gave way to days at uniformed nursery, pre-prep and prep schools selected for them before their conception, their hours filled with dancing and music and riding lessons before they were five. It seemed to Elvira that Luke and Annabel barely saw them, although they were habitually presented to guests, at least before they went away to school, for five minutes before a dinner or cocktail party, scrubbed and clean. She sometimes had the impression, from the look of faint calculation in their pale blue eyes, that Hugo and Elizabeth were not always quite sure which of the assembled company of pink-cheeked, hearty guests bending down to ask whether they'd cleaned their teeth were their parents. The twins unsettled Elvira; it wasn't that they encouraged the slightest pang of maternal feeling, but she did feel sorry for them. Her own childhood, largely carried on without parental presence, had at least had the benefit of a great deal of freedom.

And so, despite their regular and lavish hospitality, Elvira

131

had never grown to like Luke and Annabel, never learned to see what Jack saw in them. He thought they were amusing, well bred, innately discriminating, but the more Elvira saw of them the more she thought them, and many others of Jack's friends, stupid, cold and philistine. She put up with them in London, for Jack's sake; they were rich and well connected, and they brought money and attention to the gallery. But here she felt different; suddenly she didn't see why she should put up with them here, in her own house.

Jack had left Levanto early to meet their guests' plane at Genova airport, in the car. Elvira had suggested that perhaps he might take the train, as Luke and Annabel could drive him back in their hire car, but he had looked at her incredulously and swiped his car keys from the marble-topped hall table in response. Elvira had not been able to get back to sleep once he had gone, before eight; around her the house ticked and sighed, settling back down in Jack's wake, and every creak rattled Elvira and made her head ache. She had a hangover.

She had drunk at least a bottle of champagne in the Mare Blu the previous day. Had they ordered a second bottle? Elvira's temples throbbed with the effort of remembering. Jack had watched, but said nothing, and, she realized now, had barely drunk anything himself. Eventually they had gone to a restaurant for supper, an expensive place up a private road overlooking the sea. Elvira had ordered a salad and eaten none of it, they had bickered a bit over the bags of shopping in the car, over Ania, and had gone home.

At least, thought Elvira, she had taken no pills, although Jack had put them out for her; at least she had the will, born perhaps out of irritation with Jack, to sweep them off the side-table and into the drawer. As a result, she felt, her hangover was a relatively clean affair. If her memory of the previous evening was a little hazy, and left her with a sour feeling in her stomach, she had the feeling it was all there, somewhere, no blank spaces. She also had the feeling, though, that she would need something extra to get her through this weekend.

It was very quiet in the house. Ania had not telephoned, Elvira realized; she sometimes came on Saturday mornings, when asked, and although she had not been asked for this Saturday – *why not, if I knew about Luke and Annabel?* – she might at least have called to explain her absence the previous day. *Where is she?* Decisively Elvira sat up and swung her legs off the storm-tossed bed; suddenly she was aware that she was alone in the house and it seemed like an opportunity, somehow. She walked into her dressing room.

Elvira had a lot of clothes; she had roomfuls in London, too, and winter things vacuum-packed in storage. There were furs and leather coats and boots, crates of vintage clothes, Ossie Clark and Halston and Schiaparelli, things she had modelled in the seventies, boxes of shoes and gloves and scarves and belts. She kept the best stuff here; in this house that was her bolthole, her dressing room constituted an inner sanctum. She didn't come in here and stroke the stuff, bury her face in it, even if sometimes she was tempted to, but it was enough that it was here. Silver shoes she'd danced in at a ball in Venice with Stefano; the dress she'd worn to that party at La Martinière, chiffon and velvet and handmade lace. She could smell it as she came in, the cedar balls to keep away the moths, traces of old perfume, Joy and Fracas. A delicious, heavy, scented nostalgia she couldn't afford to indulge in too often.

Elvira dressed more austerely these days; perhaps it was the English influence, their horror of – what did they call

133

it? – mutton dressed as lamb, their ridicule of the middle-aged Italian matron in her leather skirt and dyed hair, dripping with gold. So Elvira wore charcoal, white, navy, things unadorned and discreet, no gold, no paste. Today more than usual she wanted to refine herself into the background, and she dressed quickly in some dull dark linen thing, narrow trousers and a plain shirt, brushed her hair and carefully closed the heavy door behind her.

The house beckoned, warm and dark below her, and empty. The last hour or so of freedom, she thought, trying not to think of Luke and Annabel bursting through her front door, braying, eyeing her up in that way of theirs. From the landing she could see that Jack's door stood open, and for once it looked tidy in there. Could he have been trying to be helpful, with Ania gone? She was the one who usually picked his things off the floor, laundered them. Elvira stood in the doorway, wondering where his dirty clothes were now, because she certainly hadn't washed them. She felt a spasm of affection for Jack, trying to protect her.

The bed was made, the rug straight, the bedside table empty and polished. On Jack's dressing table, beside two silver-backed brushes and a stud box, sat his camera in its battered leather case, and idly she walked over and picked it up. She wondered what he'd found to photograph yesterday, on his expedition; she had never thought of Jack as a very inspired photographer himself, although he was pretty good at predicting fashions in photography, particularly at the kitsch end of the market. She always thought he dabbled more than anything else, so as not to seem a mere shallow exploiter of others' talents, to give himself a little creative edge. A couple of his pictures were hanging in here; over the dressing table was one of the harbour front at Camogli. Pastel fishermen's houses all of different heights forming a backdrop to the boats, it was pretty but highly conventional; a postcard shot.

Another, hanging over the bed, was more interesting; a shot of a near-derelict building, little more than a mound of ivy and crumbled stone and some shards of roof slate. The composition was good, though: the proportions of light and shade, the intricate variations of green, the faintly sinister humped shape of the ruin made an arresting image. Elvira knew the building; it was the old school on the way up to Grosso, one of Jack's favoured spots. She looked down at the camera in her hands, idly fiddling with its old-fashioned winding mechanism, listening to the heavy click. The camera was empty of film, so Jack must have already taken it out for developing; he had a darkroom here, off the kitchen. He had one in London too; it made a good impression. Jack the craftsman. Elvira sighed. *Perhaps I don't give him credit*, she thought, and put the camera down.

As she walked slowly downstairs, despite a nagging sense of anxiety about Ania's whereabouts Elvira couldn't help but feel pleasure that her house was returned to her, to her alone. After two days without attention a light film of dust, she could see, was already beginning to settle on things, on the polished walnut of the dining table, on the tops of the framed engravings that lined the stairs, on the marble console in the hall. There was a smear on the glass of the front door. But so what? Let Luke and Annabel think what they wanted. On the mat was an envelope, postmarked Turin, addressed to her in a vaguely familiar script. She frowned, put the envelope in her pocket, and continued down through the hall into the kitchen where she paused, indecisive, in the doorway.

The table was bare, the kitchen neat, everything tidied away. Jack must have put the food she'd bought into the fridge: Elvira opened the door and there it all was, two carrier bags jammed in carelessly. The pork was leaking a little blood through its paper and she felt queasy at the sight, but she reached in and pulled it out. The packages thrust in anyhow spoiled a perfectly ordered interior; gleaming shelves, jars clean and wiped, packages of butter and cheese, artichokes in oil, white wine, milk. Evidence of Ania's meticulous, hard-working nature; again her disappearance nagged at Elvira. But Elvira had no number for her, no address, had never needed to contact her because she was always there, without fail. Elvira weighed the clammy parcel in her hand; she dimly remembered Ania promising, at the beginning, to give her a contact number, but it had never materialized. She supposed that wasn't unexpected. She turned to the table.

It took Elvira a surprising time even to assemble the right equipment for the meat's preparation: coriander seeds, garlic, a boning knife, oil, salt, pepper, string to truss the thing together at the end. She had to suppress a childish impatience more than once when her raw material refused to behave as she wanted, when the meat slipped and slid, the papery skin wouldn't come off the garlic, when she couldn't tie the knots as she remembered her mother doing. But when, at last, it was accomplished, a little clumsily but stuffed and rolled and ready for cooking, Elvira was surprised by the satisfaction she felt.

She put the meat into its dish, covered it and put it back into the fridge. Wiping her hands clean at the sink, she saw Ania's headscarf, folded neatly on the side, and almost without thinking she picked it up, held it to her face. It smelled of Ania, faintly musty, spiced, foreign. Elvira hadn't realized she knew what Ania smelt like, until now. She looked out of the window, through the overhanging green of the vine on the terrace, listened to the silence. *I could go now*, she thought. *Down to the police station, tell them she's gone missing . . . To hell with Jack.*

There were plenty of links to Elvira Vitale on the internet, it turned out, not all of them family viewing. She had several unofficial fan clubs, in Holland, Germany, England and America, as well as entries in all sorts of online film directories and nostalgia sites. It was clear that she had a cult following on the strength of her one major film role and a couple of iconic fashion photographs from the seventies. The same shots appeared time and again; one in which she was reclining slit-eyed in satin for an album cover, and the other in which she appeared bound and hooded and naked from the waist down, ostensibly in order to model a pair of perspex platform shoes. Her appeal was not, it seemed, a wholesome one.

From the cutting Rose managed to put together some kind of history for Elvira Vitale. She did not seem to have ever been particularly forthcoming about her family circumstances, and there were no photographs of other members of her family, but it was on record at least that she came from a working-class Genovese background. That much had been divulged by her modelling agency, and the fact that she had been discovered by a talent scout as she got off a train from Genova at Portofino station, at the seaside for a day, at the age of sixteen. It seemed she had ambitions to get out of the great, sprawling, squalid city even then; Rose imagined a girl stepping out of that grubby, nicotine-stained railway compartment, straightening her back, putting on some high heels and trying out a model's walk along the front at Portofino. The stuff of dreams, the big white yachts, the uniformed crew, the glittering restaurants all along the curve of the harbour.

It appeared that Vitale had given up modelling at the age of twenty-two, in 1977, having been offered that cameo role by Fellini. At twenty-three, she married a Count Ribisi, almost twenty years her senior, and bought her villa on the cliff above Levanto; two years later she was asked to play Giulia. Her reviews were sensational, extraordinary, and a rash of profiles followed, puff-pieces, declaring her the greatest Italian actress since Magnani, sign of a renaissance in Italian cinema, suggesting that she had been offered huge sums to move to Los Angeles. A year later she quietly divorced Ribisi; the tabloids assumed as a result of his arrest for possession of cocaine while trying to board a flight to New York in the company of a model even younger than Elvira. But if you looked back through the cuttings the pair had not been seen together for two years or more, since before filming began on *Giulia*.

As soon as the divorce came through Elvira married Marcello Battista, was pictured quarrelling with him publicly at a premiere, photographed leaving their apartment block with a split lip one morning, and within a year they were divorced. Elvira seemed to fall off the radar after that for a while, then, when she reappeared, shown leaving one restaurant or another, it was mostly in the British press, in London and more often than not with Jack Robbins. They married quietly in Chelsea Registry Office, and the publicity picture released showed them standing side by side at the top of some anonymous steps. Elvira stood very straight in a parchment-coloured dress so plain it might have been a hospital gown on a different woman, one without her bone structure and

138

huge, luminous eyes. Beside her Jack Robbins was smiling, expansive in a brilliant white, open-necked shirt, gleaming with good health and grooming.

After that, the coverage dwindled to no more than the occasional paparazzi shot carelessly snatched in the London streets, but Elvira no longer wore red, or high heels, no longer stood her ground and stared the photographers down. She could hardly be seen at all, hidden as she always seemed to be behind dark glasses, a headscarf or her husband's square-shouldered profile; it was as though she had given it all up and was retiring herself before the press had a chance to do it for her. *Former screen goddess.* For almost twenty years, it seemed, Elvira Vitale had been a lady of leisure.

Rose stretched in her chair, leaned forward to look out of the window. It seemed like a waste to her, of all that time. Perhaps after all Elvira was just an actress like any other, shallow, lazy. The day was hot, heavy and grey; a bank of cloud was moving in from the west; out towards the sea the outline of Elvira Vitale's villa was indistinct Rose's head felt fogged, muzzy after a restless night's sleep, and gazing at a computer screen wasn't helping. She'd been making notes by hand, not willing to entrust her thoughts to the computer's failing memory, and she felt tired and cranky. But it wasn't just that; early that morning she had woken with a start, sweating and anxious, under the insidious influence of a bad dream. And it was that awakening, she thought, that had started the day off all wrong. It was Jess; she couldn't get Jess out of her mind.

It had been Jess she'd dreamed of; Jess in one of those shrunken T-shirts and her ridiculously low-slung jeans, getting on a train somewhere in Europe, smiling, fair-skinned, an innocent abroad. A train pulling into a country platform in the middle of a dark pine forest, not an Italian landscape at all but rather somewhere gloomier, more Gothic; it might have been the Black Forest or some Eastern European wilderness of wolves and snow and endless, silent ranked trees. Jess had had a backpack with all her possessions hanging from it, a pan, a scarf and a bedroll. She climbed on to the train, eager and unwary, and suddenly she was surrounded by men. They stood around her in the corridor and jostled her, dark, hollow-cheeked and unshaven, speaking to her in a strange, guttural dialect; they all looked familiar. It had taken Rose some time, on waking, to track down the source of her disquiet, to recall the dream and to realize that all the men had looked like Gennaro.

With an exclamation, part annoyance, part dismay, at the memory, Rose stood up from her computer and walked across the room to the door, then back to the window. Gennaro, she told herself, was a decent man, trying to make her welcome. If he had a romantic interest in her – well, she could put him right, politely; that would be the civilised thing to do. Not to skitter about nervously like a giggling teenager refusing to answer the phone. And as for Jess – about to dismiss her dream as daft, superstition and guilt mixed, Rose realized she missed Jess, needed to know where her daughter was, right now. *Why do I feel guilty?* she thought. *I'm her mother.*

Of course, she wasn't at her student hostel; the girl who answered the phone after fifteen rings or so sounded forlorn when she said there was no one else there. Rose imagined the girl standing in the echoing, institutional green corridor as friendless, bespectacled, only staying on because she had nowhere else to go. Not like Jess, surrounded by friends, the world her oyster. Rose tried Jess's mobile, but only got an anonymous female voice repeating an enigmatic recorded message about the phone user not being available. Please try later. Okay, thought Rose, and taking a deep breath she called Tom.

He sounded impatient.

'Really, Rose,' he said. 'You need to get yourself together. It's all very well heading off to the other side of the world –' Rose tried to protest, her stomach leaden with guilt, that Italy wasn't so far away, but Tom overrode her.

'If you don't want to be worrying about Jess, and I'm sure I don't, you have to make more of an effort. Call her regularly, come back and visit. You have to be firm with her, get her to check in with you, like I do.' Rose's eyes burned, she wanted to make some retort, but she knew he was probably right; it was easier for him, of course, living just around the corner from Jess in London, but Rose had chosen to come here, after all. And he wasn't trying to upset her; despite his obvious exasperation there was a kindly note in Tom's voice. She missed him, she realized. She cleared her throat.

'Yes,' she said. 'You're right.' She paused. 'But you do have an idea where she is?'

Tom sighed. 'She's interrailing,' he said. 'Okay? She's got a month's pass, all of August, and she was in Morocco last I heard. Last week. She's coming back up through Spain, Portugal – that's probably where she is now. She did say she might cut across to the Riviera, and come and see you. Might.'

Rose bit her lip. 'I suppose she'll call?'

'I suppose,' said Tom. 'If I speak to her I'll tell her you'd like to see her, shall I? And you have got her number, haven't you?'

Rose sighed, trying not to voice her indignation. 'Yes,' she said. She sensed that Tom was distracted from her answer; she could hear a voice in the background, a light, cheerful, sing-song voice. Tom's new wife, Jo, was Welsh. She heard Tom answering, his voice muffled by a hand over the receiver; they would be in the kitchen, she thought, they had a glass-roofed kitchen extension, very bright and new and airy. Tom's voice became louder again.

'Jo says she was having trouble getting a signal in Morocco, with the phone, and in Portugal it'll probably be tricky, too. Not much coverage.' Tom's voice was soothing; he was trying to be helpful. They both were.

Rose made a sound of agreement, trying to sound grateful. Thinking of Jo, fresh-faced, practical Jo with no children of her own – yet – getting chatty with Jess, Rose felt herself seething with a toxic combination of guilt, petulance and jealousy and didn't quite trust herself to speak. The worst of it was, she knew she should be thankful someone was keeping tabs on Jess, and it was entirely her own fault if she hadn't managed it herself.

'Okay,' she said. 'Thanks, Tom.' She took a deep breath, then another. 'You and Jo – if you wanted – you could come and visit too, you know. There's some nice walking round here.' She tried to sound genuine.

'Thanks,' said Tom, taken aback, she thought. 'Yes, that'd be lovely. Sometime.' He sounded wary, a little concerned. 'Look, sorry to have to go. Take care of yourself, all right? I'm sure Jess'll call. I'll tell her to call.'

Rose said goodbye and replaced the receiver with deliberate care. Okay, she thought. We'll track her down; it can be done. She went back to the computer.

The screen seemed to have unhung; Rose logged back on and printed out all the stuff she could find on Elvira Vitale, to look at later. She sat in front of the screen for a moment, gazing without focus at the blinking cursor as it waited patiently for her next instruction. Idly she typed in Richard Bourn's name. *Enter.*

The screen filled with references, websites. About a third of them concerned the Richard Bourn she was looking for – it was a common name, after all – and most of those were taken from business magazines or the City pages of newspapers. For the most part they referred to the sale of his company the previous year; some had faintly stuffy-sounding corporate quotes from him stating his enthusiasm for the company's new owners and his confidence in the future for his ex-employees. There were photographs of him in a suit, looking serious and handsome, his hair shorter, but paler than she'd seen him here. She imagined him a workaholic, stuck in a neon-lit open-plan office, and wondered how he was managing without it all, what he was doing with himself. Although the sum Bourn was quoted as having been paid for his company varied a little from one piece to another, it was in the region of twenty-five million pounds.

Rose blinked, taken aback. She knew no one, had never spoken to anyone, worth so much money. She felt a little uncomfortable with the information; was that what she had wanted to know? How much Richard was worth, as though she was some impoverished vicar's daughter out of Jane Austen? She would have said not, before pressing the button, but now – she couldn't deny that it altered the way she saw him.

Rose scrolled down through the references, ready to log off, ashamed of herself. Then, towards the bottom of the page, her eye was caught by a reference to Richard's wife. Ex-wife. She clicked on the reference, waited for the screen to fill with the text of a newspaper article, surmounted by a large photograph.

She was very beautiful, the ex-wife, although not in the way Rose might have imagined, not the expensive, glossy blonde of a rich man's wife but dark-eyed and intense, with something Bohemian about her, not groomed at all. And, according to the article, she was dead.

Chapter Sixteen

Each of the little stations strung along the Ligurian coastal railway possessed its own, quite distinct character, like the ports and fishing villages they served. Levanto was one of the larger and more workmanlike among them, set at some distance from the sea where the town petered out into seedy campsites, car parks and down-at-heel supermarkets. Levanto station was an anonymous grey concourse with plenty of traffic in and out and none of the picturesque, geranium-hung intimacy of the stations attached to the smaller, wealthier towns, Santa Margherita Ligure, say, or Camogli. A cluster of gypsies was generally to be found hanging about outside the main entrance, Romany women with dark, suspicious faces, big printed skirts, trussed babies slung diagonally across their grubby white fronts and their seamy palms held out to passing travellers for charity.

Levanto station, Cirri thought gloomily as he squeezed between the begging hands and a stream of backpackers heading for the sea and the campsites, was not the kind of place where you might find a sharp-eyed, kindly stationmaster with a firm grasp of its daily comings and goings, let alone its nightly traffic. But there was a dingy bar, a newspaper stand, a ticket office, not to mention the assorted panhandlers and touts in search of a tourist to fleece, and the station was unlikely to have been deserted, even at one or two in the morning.

The train whose recently disgorged passengers Cirri had had to fight his way past in the ticket hall was still there when he reached the platform; a *locale* from Genova. Anna-Maria Villemartin might have been bundled out of one of these very carriages. Cirri didn't like to think of it, the girl's dead weight manhandled, hitting the rocks. Bearing in mind the time of death forensics had established to within an hour, it seemed clear that there was only one train she could have taken out of Genova: the 0.32, coming into Levanto at close to one in the morning. They'd asked for footage from security cameras at Genova's main station covering that time, but the technical support people were being slow, and Cirri had a nasty feeling the cameras had contained no cassettes that night. Still, you never knew. Perhaps it was just Ferragosto.

Cirri paused on the platform, looking along at the grimy windows; here and there where they stood open the faces of passengers standing in the corridor were visible resting on elbows to get a breath of air or to say goodbye. The couplings clanked and shifted a little, the faces drew back from the open windows, and with a creak the train set off slowly down the track towards La Spezia and the Tuscan coast. Behind the dirty glass, shuffling along to find a seat or loitering in the corridor, the faces all looked opaque to Cirri now, as though hiding secrets even in the bright afternoon.

Cirri wondered how he'd done it. He could imagine the ill-lit, half-empty late train, the few passengers dozing against their backpacks. There would be the odd homeless person trying to get some sleep, the senile insomniac asking again and again when the train was due to arrive of any fellow traveller unwary enough to open an eye. And then the misfits, the strangers; African traders and Eastern European mafiosi travelling through the night for their own nameless, sinister reasons. Those trains were full of untrustworthy types but somehow Cirri, who had begun to think of Anna-Maria as a thoughtful, sensible girl, didn't believe she'd go anywhere near them.

Had he done it before? Cirri assumed it was a man; it would have needed strength to overpower the girl, to shove her out in the dark and not be dragged after her. He would probably have been aware that some of the doors could be opened when the train was in motion; he would have known he would be able to get rid of her, after. How could he be sure he wouldn't attract attention? In his mind's eye Cirri inhabited that sleazy night train, saw the darkness of the tunnel and then the open sea alongside, the girl's slight body bundled out through the window, and then, almost immediately, the train would have turned inland, slowing as it approached the station.

A thought began to stir, and Cirri waited while it took shape, hardly breathing, not wanting to disturb its unfolding. He went back to the beginning, started again. Anna-Maria had bought a ticket to Levanto. Why was she coming here?

There were two possibilities, it seemed to him. Either she was coming here alone, because she knew someone here, and had been murdered at random en route, or she was coming here with someone who lived in Levanto. Someone she'd met in Genova? Cirri frowned. The mobile phone in her backpack had recorded no calls made that evening, no arrangement to stay over. Had she met someone she knew, between the club and the station? He imagined her arriving at the station, having missed the last train home. He rocked on his heels, thinking. If – and it was, Cirri agreed with himself, not certain but a good chance, a chance worth pursuing – if she was coming here with someone else, someone who killed her, then he got a ticket to Levanto, too. If he lived in Levanto and had invited Anna-Maria back with him, then this is where he would have got off. Killed her, then calmly walked off the train that arrived in Levanto station at one in the morning.

Cirri stood on the platform, deliberately subduing the excitement he felt and letting the possibility settle in his mind. Through narrowed eyes he watched the train's sinuous progress up the track, clanking and sparking across the points, winding away from him and into the tunnel beneath the great cliff that separated Levanto from Monterosso. It was very hot, and the sun glared off the dusty white stone between the tracks in front of him. *Yes*, he thought. *It's possible*. He walked along the platform towards the stationmaster's office.

Cirri drew a blank there – the stationmaster was a jobsworth who went off duty at nine in the evening, and wouldn't have been helpful if he could, puffed up with his uniform and self-importance. The same went for the newsstand, which closed at ten-thirty, and the ticket office; after eleven there was only a machine that issued standard fares.

Discouraged, Cirri turned and went into the station bar. A cavernous, gloomy room that opened directly on to the platforms on one side and the station car park on the other, it was almost empty; lit by a couple of low-watt bulbs in garish red glass pendent lights, one of them fizzing and obviously on the blink. Two foreign girls were sitting in the corner nursing a Coke between them, a half-eaten slice of pizza pushed to one side, and a couple of workmen in dirty vests and reflective tabards were finishing their beers. A hefty middle-aged woman stood behind the tacky fifties wood-veneer counter, listlessly polishing a glass.

Cirri asked for a beer and pointed at one of the curling sandwiches in the glass cabinet; silently the woman gestured towards the cash desk to indicate that, although he was her only customer, she was not prepared to make an exception and serve him before he had paid. With a sigh Cirri turned and went to the cash desk; at least he got a smile from the cashier, a nervous, willing woman who took his money in a great hurry and furnished him with his receipt as though eager not to keep him waiting.

Taking his toasted ham and fontina sandwich, Cirri noted with disgust the sign in the glass cabinet that indicated that some of the products might have been previously frozen. What was the world coming to, he thought, when no one can even be bothered to make up a sandwich fresh any more? And in Liguria, too, where you can find a lovely piece of focaccia dripping with green oil for a couple of pence on any street corner. He masked the taste of the dry, pulpy bread and chemical ham with a slug of cold beer, and eyed the woman behind the bar doubtfully. She didn't look cooperative. Wiping the last crumbs from his mouth with care, he pulled out the photograph of Anna-Maria.

The woman shrugged, apparently indifferent. 'She's Italian?' she asked. 'No, I can't say I recognize her. But then ...' She tailed off, gesturing around at the room as if to say, how can I be expected to notice what my customers look like under these circumstances? As though the bar was packed. She didn't seem inclined to look very hard at the few customers she did have.

'When does the bar close?' Cirri asked. 'At night?'

Again she shrugged. 'Midnight or so,' she said. 'Or one. Depends.'

'Were you working Tuesday night?'

The woman's brow furrowed in an almost comical effort to remember. 'Yes . . . no,' she said. 'I usually work Tuesdays, but my legs were bad.' She looked down at something hidden from Cirri by the shiny wood of the bar. 'Veins,' she said darkly, raising her head with a sharp movement as though to catch Cirri trying to see her legs. *As if*, he thought, quailing.

'So?' he said hastily. 'Who would have been on, that night?'

She nodded across the room towards the cashier. 'Giovanna,' she said. 'You were on, weren't you?' Cirri turned with relief, setting his empty glass down on the bar and as discreetly as he could disposing of the remains of his sandwich in the brass litter bin at his feet. The woman behind her cash desk looked startled, then faintly excited at the prospect of participating in the conversation.

'Er, yes, yes,' said Giovanna, looking around nervously as though a horde of customers might suddenly appear and rob her of this chance to be of use in a police investigation. She wiped her hands on her clean overall and came around from behind her till, craning her neck to see the photograph Cirri held out to her.

'No,' she said, looking crestfallen. 'I don't know who she is. Could be anyone, couldn't she?' Cirri nodded.

'What time did you close up, then?' he asked carefully. 'Tuesday?'

'Now,' she said. 'Tuesday? Yes?' Cirri nodded, curbing

his impatience. 'Because Tuesday my husband, he works late himself, I don't mind when I get back. So, I think, yes, about one-thirty. There was a lot of — you know, the Albanesi, playing cards in that corner, it was hard to get rid of them. Drinking grappa, though I'm sure they had their own bottle under the table, I only served them a couple of drinks. You know how it is.' She looked at him apologetically, and he nodded in an understanding sort of way.

'Anyone else? There's a train gets in around one, isn't there, from Genova? Would be around the time you close up? Did you notice anyone get off?'

Giovanna chewed her lip anxiously, frowning. 'Let me think,' she said nervously, hesitating. 'Well, yes, now you come to mention it, I think I did notice — quite often that train, it stops and no one gets off at all, not at that time of night. Tuesday — I think —' Cirri followed her gaze through the smeared glass on to the platform outside. You could see figures moving along the platform. 'I think so. All men — you don't see women travelling late, only sometimes the foreign girls, but they're daft, aren't they? No sense. So yes, four or five, maybe.' She ran on nervously as if talking to herself, and Cirri wondered if she wasn't a bit soft in the head.

'Were they together? A group?'

More thoughtful now, Giovanna frowned. Slowly she shook her head. I'm almost sure — they weren't; they certainly weren't talking to each other, and I'm pretty sure they all went off in different directions. There were a couple of kids, boys in those baggy shorts they wear, hanging down. An old man, a *contadino*, with a bag full of something, and a smarter type.' She frowned in an effort to remember 'White shirt, maybe even a tie, you know. I'm not sure. Sorry.'

'No,' said Cirri, patting her hand. 'No, that's great. Very useful. You make an excellent witness.' He thought for a moment, looking around the dismal room, imagining the scene, a gang of Albanians playing cards, shouting in their outlandish language, one woman trying to get them to leave. Something occurred to him.

'But you weren't alone, that night? If you were behind the bar, who was working the till?'

'Oh, yes,' said Giovanna, with some hesitation in her voice. 'Actually, it was Alberto Nannini, yes.' From her voice Cirri wondered what there might be between Giovanna and this Nannini. Perhaps her husband didn't like her working with a man, late at night, particularly if he was working nights himself and not there to keep tabs on her. She seemed the twitchy sort, the kind who might be terrorized by a brutal husband.

'And?' he said encouragingly.

'He left before me,' she said, her voice growing firmer. 'Alberto. I locked up. So – so he wouldn't have seen anything. Unless the train was already in –' Cirri recognized the sound of someone improvising, covering up, and kept his face impassive. 'No, he probably didn't see anything.' She was biting her lip.

Cirri nodded. 'All the same . . . Is he around? Now, I mean?'

Giovanna shook her head. 'He worked Ferragosto, got the weekend off instead. I think he's gone away, down south to his parents' place in Campania. Maybe.' Cirri wasn't quite convinced by her casual air.

'And he'll be back in when?' He was encouraging.

Giovanna sounded resigned when she answered. 'He should be in Monday. The early shift – he starts at six-thirty, goes through till midday.'

'Okay,' said Cirri. He could see the stout woman behind the bar eyeballing them while pretending to polish another glass. 'Thank you. You've been very helpful.'

He picked up his cap and turned to leave. Grateful for once for the light and heat that greeted him at the door after the listless gloom of the bar's interior, he stood on the threshold for a moment, soaking it up. He could see across the two sets of tracks to the cracked wall on the other side, and the parched hillside above it. There would be more fire-setting this summer, he realized; such a drought was the perfect cover. He sighed.

Back at the station, Toto was in a state of ill-disguised excitement.

'Well,' he said. 'You'll never guess who's been in to file a missing person's report.' Cirri sighed. 'Go on then,' he said. 'Who?'

Elvira had expected to find Luke and Annabel at the house when she returned from the police station, at close to one o'clock; if the truth be told she had been tempted to stay out longer so as to postpone to the maximum the moment at which she would have to play hostess. But when she got back the place was as she had left it, Jack's car gone, the windows shuttered. She didn't know whether to be relieved or irritated.

It was very hot, perhaps the hottest day of the year so far, Elvira thought. She'd driven down to the police station in the little runaround she kept here, an old Lancia her first husband had given her which spent most of the time gathering dust in the garage. But even without the walk, even motionless in the car, she had felt the heat rising off the cracked leather of the upholstery, and she wondered if it was all down to the weather, if perhaps her body was turning against her at last. Hot flushes, and all that. It was an uncomfortable feeling. She went upstairs to shower and change.

As she climbed the stairs Elvira thought about the thick-set, perspiring policeman she'd spoken to in the messy office, the sceptical look in his eye as she'd taken her statement, his familiarity. She thought she recognized him from somewhere, and realized how little she mixed, in fact, in the town these days. She didn't even know who the policemen were. Was he the one she'd talked to last year? When she had asked whether it was true there'd been a body found, he'd turned more serious. Elvira hadn't got much out of him though. Yes, there had been a body, a young woman beside the train tracks as they emerged from the tunnel at the end of the beach. That much she could have discovered at the Mare Blu. An Italian girl. They were keeping an open mind but yes, the death did appear to be suspicious, but if she didn't mind – he was coolly polite, now – if that was all? He'd keep her informed and if, as he assumed she would, Ania reappeared a little the worse for wear in a day or two, perhaps the Contessa would be so kind as to let them know?

Ania wasn't out on the razzle, though, was she? Elvira knew she wasn't; since her head had begun to clear, since Ania's failure to appear on the day after Ferragosto, the girl's life had for the first time come into focus in Elvira's mind. It was as though it had its own momentum, it reached out to Elvira from her own past. She knew, after all, the limitations of poverty; she had grown up with them. Ania hadn't picked up a man, she hadn't decided on the spur of the moment to take a ferry down to Panarea to mingle with the jetset, she hadn't gone back to Romania without the full amount of money she'd planned on bringing back to her family. She was in it for the duration. Elvira had attempted to explain this to the desk officer at the police station but he had just looked at her, expressionless, and she had lost patience. Perhaps, it occurred to her, he thought she had lost her marbles too.

Peeling off her linen shirt in the bathroom, Elvira felt the crackle of paper in her pocket, and felt around in there, pulling out a crumpled letter. She frowned at it for a moment, then her brow cleared; it was that letter; the one with the Turin postmark. She read it wrapped in her bathrobe, pulling the thin fabric around her reflexively as she stood barefoot in the window overlooking the sea. Well, well, she thought, and despite herself she smiled. Venturelli.

Elvira had barely reached the end of the page when from below she heard the crunch of tyres on gravel. She looked up unwillingly from her letter; she could hear Annabel's voice, high-pitched, querulous, aristocratic, issuing an instruction. They had arrived. She stood for a moment, listening to them enter her house, but she didn't call down to them. Instead she turned and went into the shower.

Elvira took her time in there; she heard Jack shouting up the stairs and made some vague reply. She wasn't going down until she was good and ready. She stood under the shower until it ran cold, smoothed cream on her skin, walked up and down her rows of clothes scrutinizing them until the right combination leaped out at her. She put on her favourite heavy silver earrings, a pair of beautiful turquoise-studded sandals from Naples, brushed her hair, and came downstairs.

They were standing in the hallway. Luke was wearing a lavender button-down shirt, a horrible clash, to Elvira's eyes, with his pink and white complexion and reddish-blond hair.

He was giving her what she thought of as a banker's smile, hearty, professional, watchful. She did not find Luke attractive. Annabel had her hand on his arm and was laughing; as Elvira came down the stairs she felt them look up at her and find fault. There had been a time when she wouldn't have noticed, when a critical look from such a person, from an Englishwoman who wore frosted pink lipstick and men's shirts would have made her laugh. But today Annabel's look seemed to Elvira as though it was part of something bigger, as though they were closing in on her, and she felt like crying. Or screaming. Instead she smiled.

'Good journey?' she said as lightly as she could, leaning forward to kiss first Annabel then Luke, barely brushing his cheek with hers.

Annabel sighed irritably. 'Luggage took its time,' she said. 'God, these budget airlines. The service is unspeakable.' Elvira attempted to look sympathetic. *Cheapskates*, she thought. *What do you expect for forty euros? Canapés and a foot massage? God, the English are mean.* She thought of Luke, who at lunch in Chelsea would stopper up a bottle of wine with a glass left in it when they had a thousand-bottle, temperature-controlled electronic wine cellar as the centre-piece of their gleaming steel kitchen.

'I know,' was all Elvira said. 'Let's have a glass of champagne, shall we?' And she saw them exchange glances.

Chapter Seventeen

Tiziana had attended the now derelict school that stood below the village, and so had her daughter, but by the time her grandson was of an age to start school it was long gone. Twenty years now it had stood empty, the tables with their spattered, obsolete inkwells, window-frames, roof tiles, all looted or broken and simply decayed over time. There were no children in the village any more so, unarguably, there was no need for a school. The place was dying.

Tiziana had a piece of land down below the village where the ruin stood, an overgrown piece of terraced ground just above the schoolhouse, but now she was getting on she didn't go down so often. She had once kept a couple of hutches with rabbits there, and a few chickens, but they were too much trouble. They needed feeding, cleaning out, and she didn't have to put so much food on the table these days. The terraces were poorly maintained now that Tiziana's husband had turned lazy in his old age, their dry-stone retaining walls crumbling, and she only went down there when it was time to gather the ripening fruit on the plum and peach trees. And after such a hot summer, broiling skies since April and not a drop of rain, it was time.

Tiziana waited until the temperature came down a bit, late afternoon when the sun had all but left the valley, and painfully she walked down the road, bowlegged and slow, herding her grandson ahead of her. They came to the lower edge of the village where the path began, Marco rattling a stick along the hubcaps of the parked cars, a battered Fiat, the foreigners' shiny Mercedes, right at the bottom a little grey van with a peeling decal from the bait shop on the windscreen. They came to the path and turned off the road and down into the green undergrowth, the path invaded by blackberries and wild vines. Tiziana was keeping up a running commentary on the dangers of Marco's behaviour, his skipping and hiding and cheeking her, his tendency to pull berries from bushes and stuff them into his mouth, when, just as they had drawn level with the broken-backed roofline of the old school, he stopped short in front of her. Tiziana almost tripped over him, and exclaimed loudly at his idiocy.

'For heaven's sake, child,' she said. 'What are you up to now?' The boy turned and looked up at her, his dark eyes wide in a face suddenly sallow.

'Nonna,' he whispered. 'It's haunted. Isn't it?' He jabbed a finger in the direction of the ruined school, although he didn't seem to want to turn and look at it.

Tiziana rolled her eyes. 'No, it's not haunted,' she said, exasperated, taking his small, bony shoulder in a vice-like grip. 'Who would haunt a school? Naughty little boys?'

Still the child didn't move, just squirmed a little under her

158

hand. 'But I heard something,' he said in a hushed, urgent voice. 'I did. I heard it yesterday when I was down here, then I heard it again, just now.'

'What something?' said Tiziana, losing patience. 'You heard a chicken scratching about, or a stray dog. Or some old fart tending his grapes. Why does it have to be a ghost? Now get on, those peaches aren't going to pick themselves, are they? And it'll be dark soon.'

At this her grandson seemed to quail even further; under her hand she felt him stiffen, stubborn as his mother, and for a moment Tiziana hesitated. Sometimes she didn't have the strength for this, not any more; perhaps she should come back tomorrow. In her day children did as they were told, or they were given a good crack. But in the brief silence, as she glared down at the child and he back at her in the gathering dusk, Tiziana heard something too.

It was coming from below them, behind the ruined walls or inside them, a kind of whimpering. It was impossible to say whether it was animal or human; there were no discernible words, or at least none Tiziana could understand. She hesitated, feeling the child take her hand now, gripping it hard.

'It'll just be a goat,' she said gruffly. 'Caught in something.' She extracted her hand. 'You just run back up to the house, if you're so scared. Tell Nonno to stir himself, he can come and help me this time.'

The boy seemed frozen. 'Go on!' she said, giving him a little push. 'Go.' And then her grandson seemed to register what she was saying and he turned and ran, head down, legs and arms pumping as if he had the devil after him. Tiziana sighed and turned back to survey the downward route to her peach trees, which led her past the tumbled stone wall of the school yard.

The way was congested with creeper, desiccated after months of heat and no rain. It rustled drily and showered Tiziana with seed as she began to make her way down, listening for the sound of whatever trapped creature it was they'd heard. A goat, she decided, certainly a goat. At first all she felt was annoyance that she was going to have to free the blasted thing. Goats were tricky beasts, almost as perverse and idiotic as sheep but with added malevolence. Tiziana hobbled on towards the grim old building in which it seemed she'd spent most of her childhood. And then the sound came again.

No more than five yards from Tiziana, Ania couldn't help herself. She had spent the hours since the sultry dawn, at least those hours when she hadn't been scraping and twisting at the ropes that bound her, wondering what she would do if anyone came within earshot. Should she call for help, or should she try to hide? If it turned out to be him, would he punish her for attempting to escape? In the event, though, she had been so far gone she couldn't stop the sounds that came from her mouth. Ania heard voices; one frightened, high-pitched, another angry. Then the sound of footsteps, hesitant but coming nearer. She wanted to form words in Italian, to sound human, reasonable, but she couldn't rationalize the shameful dread that gripped her. She didn't know where she was, she didn't know who was out there; suddenly the world had turned hostile and she was afraid of who might come. All she could do was blubber.

The steps that approached now were slow, deliberate. Ania shuffled upright against the wall. In the corner of the room something moved, a grey shadow low down ran along the skirting and she flinched. A feral cat, it was hunched against

160

the floor, and hissed, staring at her with its yellow eyes. Then it ran across the room in an odd, cowering, flattened motion, leapt up on to a window-sill and vanished. Outside the footsteps seemed to have stopped.

Tiziana saw the cat. So that was it, she thought. Funny, though; it didn't sound like a cat. She stopped, listened; there was no sound any more, she couldn't have said what it was but – there was something in the air, a vibration, as though the whole valley was resonating with it. She felt an odd reluctance, odd considering she certainly did not believe in ghosts, to go any closer to the school on her own. It was getting dark. Above her she heard the grumbling approach of her husband, and she called up to him.

'Rico? Enrico?'

'Yes, yes,' said her husband as he hove into view, plainly furious. The old bastard. Sometimes Tiziana wondered seriously about divorce. He stopped in front of her, his grey unshaven chin quivering with rage. 'What the hell are you up to? I was watching *Sarabanda*. Special holiday edition. And I still would be if that little devil would have let me, gibbering away about ghosts, I couldn't hear myself think.'

'Just have a look in there for me, will you?' said Tiziana, wheedling. 'In the schoolhouse. The boy said he heard sounds in there, what he said was ghosts.'

Enrico sucked his teeth, looking murderous. 'I'll give him bloody ghosts.' He pushed past her and stamped and slithered down the hill, wheezing with rage. Getting fat, too, thought Tiziana spitefully. She watched as he stuck his head through an empty window-frame, ripping angrily at the vegetation that clung to him. He stood there for a moment and when he looked back his face was sullen.

161

'Nothing there. No one there. None of our business, anyway; best keep our noses out. Those Albanesi can be vicious, you know? If they're sleeping rough out here, so what? We don't want them after us. The peaches can wait.' And he grabbed his wife by the elbow and pushed her ahead of him up the hill.

Ania had seen the face at the window, peering in, malevolent and suspicious. And he'd seen her, too. He'd seen her all right.

The phone rang, strident in the dusk, startling Rose who was sitting in the kitchen reading beside the open window. It was very quiet in the village this evening, and the air drifting in through the window was warm and humid after the long, hot day. Rose supposed, it being Saturday night, everyone was down in Levanto getting the breeze off the sea. Even the rackety house at the foot of the village had fallen silent, the amateur drummer wasn't pounding away, the Italian rock music wasn't howling up through the streets. When the phone rang, Rose had been gazing at the words – an entry in a film encyclopaedia on Elvira Vitale – but without focusing on them; instead she had been wondering about Richard Bourn. He hadn't spoken much about his wife, hadn't told her that she was dead, for example, but perhaps that wasn't surprising. Dead in a car crash, just a year after their separation, her blood alcohol level twice the legal limit. Perhaps that wasn't the kind of thing you mentioned over a light-hearted, flirtatious lunch.

Rose wondered what Richard was doing tonight. She found it hard to believe that he could live a celibate life out here, although perhaps she had old-fashioned ideas about men and their sex drive. Still, it would be strange if he had no social life, wouldn't it? Perhaps not; perhaps his social life resembled hers, something cobbled together out of acquaintances and shopkeepers. She imagined him in a bar like the Mare Blu, drinking a solitary Martini, or perhaps he was working at home, like her. His broad, strong hands. She thought of his pale blue eyes, looking at her across the restaurant table. She wasn't used to blue eyes; Tom had been dark, stubbly, thick-browed. Still was, save a few grey hairs at his temples. She really should stop comparing people with Tom.

Reluctantly Rose stood up and went to the phone; she heard a woman's voice and for a second her heart leaped, thinking it might be Jess. But the voice was deeper, husky and accented; it wasn't Cookie, either, not her clear upper-class English vowels. Rose was taken aback, trying to disentangle the name the woman gave from the accent in which she pronounced it.

'Sorry?' she said. 'I can't – who did you say you were?' In the background she could hear the murmur of voices, and some music.

The voice became clearer, although the words were still spoken softly. 'You are Rose Fell?' Rose admitted that she was. 'My name is Elvira Vitale,' the woman said; there was a trace of something in her voice, not quite slurred, but rough-ened around the edges with emotion of some kind – anger? Whatever it was, she seemed to make an effort to moderate it. Rose thought of the woman she'd seen in the Mare Blu, put the face with the voice.

'I had a letter today, from Giorgio Venturelli,' said Elvira Vitale. 'An old friend of mine. He gave me your number. About an interview.'

Rose's mouth fell open. *She's phoning me*, she thought. *Why?* It had not occurred to her that Elvira Vitale would make the first move. She wondered whether she might perhaps be drunk; there had been insinuations in some of the newspaper coverage about a habit. Veiled comments about living life to the full. *I'd better be careful*, thought Rose.

'Yes,' she said cautiously. 'I – I'm an admirer of your work. I've talked to Mr Venturelli about you – a little, and I think – you have quite a following.' She heard what she thought was a snort of derision from Vitale on the other end of the line and paused.

'I thought – I know you don't like giving interviews. But –' Rose tried to think why she should be favoured with an audience when so many others had been turned down.

'Mr Venturelli thinks it's time for you to make a comeback. I do feel – many people would be interested to know if that is a possibility. *Giulia* is a quite – extraordinary piece of film.' It sounded lame, forced, to Rose's ears, and her heart sank into the silence from the receiver. Again she heard the background voices, a burst of laughter in which Elvira Vitale didn't seem to share. There was a sigh.

'A comeback.' The voice was whispery, hoarse with some kind of suppressed emotion. 'Well,' Elvira Vitale said softly, sadly, 'what's tomorrow, Sunday? Perhaps not tomorrow. Monday, then? Not too early ... late morning. Shall we say eleven-thirty, something like that? Do you know where I live?'

Dumbly Rose stared at the receiver. She pulled herself together. 'Yes,' she said. 'I know. This is very kind of you.' 'No,' said Elvira Vitale, and Rose wondered what she meant. Not kind? Self-interest, then? 'I'll see you on Monday,' said Vitale in her whispered voice, and the phone went down with a clunk.

*

164

Elvira turned from the phone and looked back into the sitting room where Jack, Luke and Annabel sat on the long, L-shaped sofa, laughing. She was standing in the hall, in the dark, looking in. She thought of the plates piled in the kitchen, the grisly remains of her *maiale al latte* downstairs congealing in the sink. A disaster.

After too much champagne, her head aching with the heat and the alcohol and the effort of smiling at yet another of Annabel's anecdotes about the twins' accomplishments, Elvira had excused herself and gone to the kitchen. She could hear the murmurs of amused surprise starting up as she declared her intentions and pursuing her down the stairs to the kitchen; she couldn't hear Jack's words, but the note of conspiratorial laughter was unmistakable. And of course Annabel, who had done a Cordon Bleu cookery course as part of her expensive education and prided herself on her lavish dinner parties, could hardly wait to see what kind of dog's dinner Elvira, never known previously to prepare anything so elaborate as a canape unaided, might come up with.

What Elvira had forgotten, or perhaps never known, about *maiale al latte*, was that although it tastes good it looks disastrous at every stage of cooking. The meat was pale, the fat never crisped, the curdled milk in which it cooked looked like something regurgitated. Down in the kitchen Elvira grew hot and dishevelled as she waited for it to cook, and agitated as she realized how many separate things had to be remembered in the preparation of even the simplest meal. *I am too old for this*, she thought. *Old dog, new tricks.* The table had to be laid and therefore napkins and cutlery had to be tracked down in her still unfamiliar kitchen; a salad made, the delicatessen goods laid out carefully and not just plonked on a platter anyhow.

Bread; a fruit plate, cheese. Could it be so difficult? Elvira floundered, out of her depth.

All the same she persuaded herself it didn't look so bad, carrying the last dish upstairs to the dining room, the glass sparkling around the table, clean linen and even a couple of candles. But just one look at Annabel's face as the raggedly sliced meat with its curdled sauce was set down between them was enough. Her baby-pink upper lip curled fastidiously at the sight of the pale meat and she laughed in disbelief.

'What on earth is that?' she said.

'Now, darling,' said Luke, trying to look as though he disapproved but laughing too. 'It looks – um – looks very interesting, Elvira. Didn't know you could cook.'

Elvira said nothing, just sat, her face frozen in a smile to disguise the sudden furious loathing she felt rising in her. Doggedly she piled her plate high with the meat and, a piece of bread, took a side dish of salad, filled her glass with wine. Luke took one small piece of meat and passed the plate to Annabel, who gazed at it thoughtfully before passing it on to Jack.

'Let's say Elvira's talents lie elsewhere,' Jack said, smiling, as he accepted the dish and lowered it to the table without touching the food. And at that moment Elvira had hated him too. That was when she had thought of Venturelli's letter, and an idea had begun to form in her mind.

Now Elvira stood in the dark hallway and watched them as though from far away. Luke and Jack were leaning in towards each other, Luke shaking his head slowly. They were talking about the gallery; Luke's investment, perhaps. Annabel was leaning back on the sofa while the men talked, one long white arm stretched along the back, making circling motions with her long neck, Pilates or Alexander technique, some such thing. Luke sat up then, and stroked her arm proprietorially.

'It's all very well,' she heard him say to Jack, 'beautiful and all that, but – don't you find it a bit limiting? Rather provincial, isn't it?' Then he lowered his voice conspiratorially, but she still heard, standing there leaning against the frame of the door.

'I'd miss the action, if you know what I mean.' Elvira saw Annabel nudge him and giggle. 'It certainly misses you. A man of your – talents.' Then his voice became indistinct, and they all laughed again.

Elvira took a step forward, stood on the threshold and felt herself sway, as though the world was shifting around her. They turned to look at her, although she had not yet made a sound.

'I'm –' She stopped, unsure for a moment as they all looked at her. 'I think I'll go to bed,' she said. Annabel looked across at her husband, and her mouth turned down a little as though she was suppressing a laugh.

'Fine, darling,' said Jack, looking up at her lazily with his heavy-lidded eyes. His hair, Elvira saw from above, although dark was thinning enough to reveal a gleam of tanned scalp, and his tense jawline would sag, sooner or later. These, things appeared to her with sudden clarity; not that they mattered to her any more. Jack was getting old, and for a second she imagined his future.

He was still speaking. 'Of course. You do seem – tired. You don't mind if we –' He tailed off, looking around at his guests. They sat, complacent, on Elvira's linen sofa, among her things; she saw Annabel run her hand over the silk of a cushion. 'We thought we might head out sometime, to the bright lights. The night is young. Maybe Genova, even?' They all looked at her.

'Whatever you want,' Elvira replied vaguely. She leaned down between them to lift a glass – they'd moved on to grappa now – from the table and turned away to leave the room. As she walked upstairs in the dark with her drink she could hear them beginning to talk in whispers behind her, but she no longer cared.

Elvira stood on her balcony and watched them go; even with a warm wind off the sea the heat was stifling. The thought came into her head that this summer was extraordinary, the hottest she'd ever experienced; it wasn't just her age, that she could no longer tolerate it. The temperature, even here by the sea, hadn't dropped by more than a degree or two as it approached midnight. She stood very still, feeling the sweat bead her forehead, and watched the monstrous silver backside of Jack's car dip over the ridge and down into Levanto, blocking the narrow lane with its thuggish bulk. One of these days, she thought, he'll meet someone coming the other way.

Elvira wondered where they'd end up, their little *ménage à trois*; no doubt some nightclub on the harbour in Genova where they'd order a bottle of overpriced champagne and bray at one another. She thought of the lethal motorway in the dark, the tight bends, the ceaseless glaring headlights flashing up and around the ageing *chicanes* and battered barriers before swooping down into the old city. It was a dangerous drive, but she felt not a twinge of anxiety on her husband's behalf. Elvira imagined Jack sidling into the Luna di Miele, car keys jingling in his pocket, the doorman nodding to him, the girls' heads turning in the dark. Something in the picture tugged at the edges of Elvira's consciousness. She gazed down at the empty road without focusing, trying to remember. The bougainvillea that hung from the wall, still swaying in Jack's wake, shone luminous magenta beneath the single lamp at the gate. Taking one last breath of the scented air, Elvira drained her glass, turned and went inside.

Chapter Eighteen

He hadn't come back. Ania clung to that thought when she woke, long before dawn, crammed into a corner of the long room beside the shattered remains of a lavatory bowl. The man who brought her here had not been back and nor had the fat man who had peered at her through the ruined window. Perhaps they were one and the same; it was possible, but she thought not, somehow, and the fact that he looked at her with animosity was no proof either way. She was used to that look. Besides, Ania had felt not a flicker of recognition when his scowling face appeared thrust through the ivy, and she wondered if she might after all have stored some knowledge of her abductor in her subconscious. Perhaps, if she tried hard enough, if she went at it methodically enough, the memory would return. But at the moment Ania didn't feel able to be methodical.

Her right side was numb from the position in which she'd been sleeping, her neck cricked so violently she thought she might never straighten it again. Ania couldn't see her hands in the pitch dark but they felt strange, swollen into frozen sausages by the pressure of the ropes that tied them. She wondered whether the blood supply had been cut off for too long now. She had worked at the nylon rope, twisting her hands and feet, picking at the knots and rubbing them, on and off for hours the previous day. But despite her perseverance and determination she had managed nothing; the rope had not given a centimetre. She had hobbled across the room with her bound feet and tried to pitch herself out through the window aperture but it had been too high, her centre of gravity too low. When she had made her way to the door, a distance of some thirty feet through rubble and broken furniture that took her close to an hour, she found that it had been blocked by something leaning against it outside; whether it had been placed there deliberately was impossible to determine. Her shoulder still felt bruised and tender from her useless attempts to use it as a battering ram.

So Ania had ended up here, wedged into the tightest corner she could find, jammed up against a child's lavatory. She lay in the foul-smelling darkness and thought of her mother. Ania pictured her sitting at the table in the kitchen's gloom, a wooden box propped in her lap as she peeled potatoes for dinner. The box held the vegetables, on one side of her would be the pig-bucket for the peelings, on the other a saucepan of water where the clean white potatoes jostled.

Ania closed her eyes and willed herself into the picture, a small girl making earrings from the curled peelings, cross-legged on the clean, cool tiles of the floor and close enough to feel the warmth of her mother's body. But she couldn't get the rank odour of ancient urine out of her nostrils, the floor beneath her cheek was not swept smooth and clean but gritty

171

with plaster dust that had embedded itself painfully in her skin. What would her mother think? Her only daughter, whose hair she had combed and plaited until it shone every day of her life until the day she left home, lying on the filthy floor of a foreign latrine, bruised and soiled. Ania felt the tears well behind her eyes. Help me, Mama, she thought. Rescue me. But she knew she would have to help herself.

Ania squeezed her eyes shut to stop herself crying; she knew once she felt the wet on her cheek she would be lost. She pushed the thought of her mother away and slowly, in the dark, she tried to sit up. But her numb right arm failed her, giving way under her weight; she slipped back down again and banged her cheekbone hard and painfully on the porcelain. Seized in the grip of violent fury and frustration, Ania raged silently in the dark, and without thinking she brought her bound and frozen hands up, smashing them sideways against the broken lavatory pan, pounding pointlessly, uselessly until she felt the blood running down her arm. She lifted her hands to her face, wanting to hide herself, to stifle her noise, and then she felt it; something was different. She hardly dared trust her senses. The rope seemed looser.

Lying on her side in the rubble, Ania forced herself to breathe slowly and concentrate. Cautiously she tried to bring her palms apart and there it was again; a half-centimetre, perhaps even a centimetre's gap between the balls of her thumbs. She tried vertical movement now, shifting the hands clumsily up and down, and then she felt something give again. With her lips, then a thumb, she felt around the twist of rope and there it was; a thinner place, where the nylon twine was beginning to shred. It must have been the sharp edge of the broken lavatory pan, thought Ania, why didn't I think of that yesterday? Pain tingled and burned down her frozen right side as the sensation returned and she tried to sit up again, more cautiously this time. She levered herself up on one elbow, leaning her shoulder on the lavatory pan, edging her buttocks along the wall, and miraculously she was upright. But the effort left her clammy and panting and for a moment she realized how weak she had grown. Again she concentrated on breathing, slowly in and out.

As she gazed blankly into the room, slowly Ania became aware that the quality of the light that filtered in from outside was changing. The velvety blackness was fading just a little; barely perceptibly the dark was leaching out of the night and turning it grey. Turning it to dawn. It occurred to Ania as she sat there, trying to regain her strength, that this might be her last chance. He wouldn't come back before dawn, would he? Not in the dark. But perhaps . . .

She stopped, afraid. Perhaps in the first hours of light, before life begins again, before the old women come down to water their tomatoes, the tiny vans begin their descent to market, that would be when he would come for her. He hadn't come yesterday; Ania didn't know why. But suddenly she was sure that he would be back, and soon. How long would it take for them to find her body? To identify her? How long to get the news to her mother and father? Somewhere far off she heard a cock crow, a raucous, triumphant sound that pierced the darkness.

Inside the ruined building the shapes of things began to form out of what had been uninterrupted black, the lineaments of a door, a broken desk, a ripped and shredded piece of stud wall. Beside her Ania could see her saviour, a broken lavatory pan; one lethal shard of porcelain offered itself up as sharp as a

173

knife, at her service. She could still feel a stinging in the ball of her thumb where it must have cut her as well as the rope and she realized that she might have ended it all there and then, severed an artery and bled out on the floor. The thought made her cautious; should she wait for more light? Outside she could hear the liquid sound of birds greeting the brightening sky and somewhere far away, the whine of a moped. Ania hesitated.

Rose was woken by the bells. No cheery English village peal, this; no garrulous fraternity of bell-ringers who would be heading off to the pub for a pint after the service while their wives put on the roast. The bells that rang on a Sunday morning in Grosso sounded an insistent, doleful clang that somehow always spoke to Rose of centuries of poverty and oppression. Religion here, it seemed to her, wasn't a matter of fun, of guitars, Sunday best and leisure but of mortification and duty. Grim-faced, the arthritic old ladies of the village creaked up the hill in black with their unmistakable rolling gait, creaking back down later with no appearance of having lightened their souls or unburdened their hearts in the intervening hour. That wasn't the idea.

The bells rang for the first service at seven-thirty, which was later than Rose usually slept. She rolled out of bed and, rubbing her eyes sleepily, went to the window to see what the day offered. The colours of the hillside opposite, the parched grass and dark green trees, were dull; the glaring skies of the previous day had not lifted, and the high layer of white cloud had held the heat against the land like a blanket. Rose had passed a restless night as a result, which was perhaps why she had woken so late; she remembered stirring earlier, just before dawn. She had been disturbed by some noise from the village, an engine turning over, she thought, although she'd barely surfaced to register the sound before falling asleep again. Rose stretched.

She was hungry this morning and toasted herself a slice of yesterday's bread which she ate standing up by the kitchen door. It had taken her some time to get used to the bread of Liguria; it was saltless, crumbly, hard as a brick after an hour or so, but now she rather liked it. No more soft, cushiony sandwiches of white sliced or bloomer, no temptation to eat slice after slice of buttered toast, just the austere, almost religious satisfaction of something much closer to the biblical staff of life. One piece only, and even that would sit in her stomach like a rock for a couple of hours.

Rose's garden looked like a bombsite after the builders' visit on Friday. Two heaps of rocky, gravelly soil were piled at each end of her plot; the cement mixer squatted in between with a rusty mini-digger next to it. She sighed, wondering if this had been a mistake. Out of habit, she looked along the slope below the village houses to see whether Gennaro was about, although generally he didn't work his land on a Sunday, whether out of piety or self-preservation she didn't know. She could see the gas cylinder, the ramshackle rabbit-hutches, the heap of old wood and the little lock-up shed, but there was no sign of their owner. Then she remembered; she was supposed to be having dinner at his house this evening, and her heart sank. *I'll go and find him,* she thought. *I'll make an excuse. After all* – and at this Rose felt a surge of excitement – *I've got to prepare for tomorrow.*

The village was silent as Rose made her way up to Gennaro's house in the pale light; the early risers were obviously also the pious, and all in church. The house, which occupied a prominent position high up on a well-kept corner with ravishing views across the sea, was one of the smartest in the village. Its dark green shutters were all newly painted, the bright yellow stucco was fresh and the rows of geraniums on the two wrought-iron balconies were kept watered and trimmed. It was a good-sized house for a single man, particularly as she knew Gennaro also had a *cantina* further down the village which he used as a store. She'd passed him locking it up now and again, the whiff of anchovies and sour wine and mould pungent on the corner. And the house was expensively maintained; Rose wondered briefly where he got the money from. Perhaps he did all the work himself.

The green shutters, though, were all closed against the sun and the massive oak door, with its brass knocker and elaborate ironwork locks, stood shut. When Rose knocked, there was no answer. *Surely he couldn't be asleep? Not Gennaro.* It was unimaginable. But she found even the possibility that he might come stumbling to the door unshaven and in pyjamas faintly disturbing and took an involuntary step back, away from the house. It stood, blank and silent, in front of her.

Rose walked around to the side where there was a rear entrance through a small gated courtyard. The iron grille was locked, though, and only a small wooden table with a pair of chairs propped slantwise against it in case of rain was to be seen. The tiled floor was clean and swept, evidence that its owner was as fastidious and house-proud here as on his balconies. It occurred to Rose that Gennaro was quite mysterious to her; she could form no picture of his interior life. She had sat here on the little patio with him once at his invitation, making stilted conversation about his life at sea and the preparation of his anchovies, and sipping his wine. It was heavy, yellow stuff, very strong and resinous; she imagined him making it in his pungent, fishy-smelling *cantina*. Rose had only ever glimpsed inside the lock-up cellar over his shoulder in passing, seen rows of canisters and demijohns and steel barrels in the dark, a coil of rope, a jumble of cardboard boxes. Perhaps that's where he keeps all the mess, thought Rose, looking up at the immaculate façade and imagining the interior to be as tidy and ordered. Standing there, her head thrown back, she heard a sound behind her and jumped.

Gennaro was standing behind her, an expression of polite inquiry on his face. Rose felt flustered suddenly, couldn't gather her thoughts and remember what she was doing there after all.

'Good morning, Gennaro,' she said in Italian, trying to make her smile innocent and friendly. 'I – I came to ask you –'

'Yes,' he said, breaking into a smile. He looked almost handsome, strong and lean. 'This evening? Seven o'clock. That is what you wanted to know?'

'I – er – yes, I mean, it's a bit difficult this evening, Gennaro. I have some work I need to do, for tomorrow.' Gennaro frowned a little. He seemed bemused, and Rose shrank at the thought of summoning her excuses.

'Sorry,' she said. 'I'm sorry.' But he shook his head firmly.

'No,' he said, smiling again. 'You work too much, I think. And you must eat, sometime? Isn't that true?'

Rose noticed that he was breathing a little laboriously, as though he had had a long walk uphill, or had been hurrying. She felt guilty, and helplessly she nodded. 'Yes, but –'

'So,' said Gennaro. 'Come at eight o'clock, a little later. You must eat.' He caught his breath then, and wiped his forehead, pulled at his collar. Rose saw that he wasn't wearing his habitual overalls, but a white shirt and trousers which though

177

obviously old were clean and ironed; she wondered where he'd been. Church, perhaps, although no one else from the congregation seemed to be out just yet. She sighed, and gave in.

'You are very kind, Gennaro,' she said with resignation. 'At eight o'clock, then.' But as she said this it occurred to her that in fact she would rather have come at seven, when it was light, at least. Rose hesitated for a moment, wondering if she could backtrack, but then she realized that Gennaro must have things to do; he was standing with a polite smile on his face, waiting for her to go. She went.

Never mind, she thought, her pace quickening as she approached her home. It won't take more than an hour. Home by nine-thirty, maybe ten.

The spike of porcelain had been treacherously sharp down one side, blunt on the other, and fragile. Ania had needed to take some care so as not to snap it off and as a result it had taken her almost an hour to get through the rope around her wrists. At one point her hands, clumsy with fear and constriction, had slipped and she'd cut a deep gash in the fleshy part of her palm. But although it had bled profusely she'd missed the artery and eventually had been able to go on. Her hand was stinging now, and felt hot and swollen; with one part of her brain Ania registered that it was quite likely infected, given that the wound had been inflicted by part of a lavatory bowl. But it was as though she registered the information from a long way off, as though it applied to someone else. There were other, more immediate dangers.

Once her hands were freed, Ania had applied herself to the rope that held her ankles together. It proved more of an obstacle than she had expected. For one thing, the knot had tightened as a result of her laborious passage across the hall; for another, her hands felt almost nerveless now, her fingers about as dextrous as a bunch of bananas. Her back ached as she bent over her feet and occasionally she had to stop because she felt dizzy. She had not eaten or drunk for at least two days, probably more; she still couldn't tell how long she'd been there. Outside the light was strengthening every moment. Then she heard the bells.

Ania felt her throat constrict in panic. It was Sunday, then, and probably around seven thirty. He'd be here soon; she tried to slow her breathing, listened. Beneath the high, sonorous clang of the bells she felt sure she could hear something else; the snap of a twig, the rustle of creeper pushed aside. In blind fear she bent over her ankles again, fumbling desperately with the twined strands in the half-light. For what seemed like an age the stiff, hard nylon didn't budge, then something loosened. Ania tugged at it again, wriggled her foot and she was free. Without wasting a moment she stumbled upright, staggered across to the window aperture through which the fat man had stared at her the previous evening, and threw herself across the crumbling sill. She landed painfully, forearms first, on a heap of ivy-covered stones and lay there among the rubble and leaves, streaked with blood and half-stunned, her limbs like jelly. But she was out. Then she heard it; a definite footfall on the other side of the ruined school-house. He wasn't coming down from above, but up from below. The house lay between them still, and Ania had a chance.

The path led uphill and away from her in the grey dawn, up between wild vines, thickets of hazel, rowan and juniper. To reach it there was a short stretch of dense undergrowth, dry leaves and fallen branches; impossible to cross it in silence.

Even lying as still as she could and trying to control her breathing, Ania could hear her heart beating so loudly she felt sure it would betray her. She heard the footfall again, and another, the light, sinister rustle of fallen leaves. Someone was walking steadily up the hill towards the ruined building. Ania squeezed her eyes shut like a child, hoping against hope that if she couldn't see her pursuer this would mean he could not see her.

He was inside now; from the other side of the wall she heard the gritty surface of the schoolhouse floor crunch beneath a foot, then he must have stopped. There was silence.

Ania pressed her back against the stone, praying he wouldn't cross the floor to look out of the window. She heard a muttered exclamation from inside, and her skin crawled at the sound of his voice, the thick sound of clotted rage separated from her by only a few feet. She knew what would happen if he found her. Then swift footsteps, not towards her, not at first; he was looking behind the ripped stud wall, along the row of shattered lavatory bowls. There was a thud and a tearing noise, shockingly loud, and Ania imagined him kicking in the rotting doors. Every sound was harsh and brutal in her ears. Then suddenly she knew this was her chance; under cover of his noise she could run, she could make it to the path. She stumbled to her feet and went.

As she reached the path Ania heard a silence fall behind her and didn't dare look round. She knew that if she did he would catch her and besides, she didn't want to see him, see half a face looking after her through the ruined window, a blank, dead-eyed stare that would follow her wherever she went. Lungs burning, the whistle of her own laboured breath in her ears, Ania ran.

*

180

Awoken by the bells from the striped church on the sea front and then those more distant, from the far hills, for once Elvira was up before anyone else, or so she thought. The house was quite silent as she padded through it to the kitchen, but the atmosphere was thick with the presence of visitors she didn't want, and hot after a stifling, humid night. As she passed the heavy, gilded mirror on the landing she caught sight of a pale, haggard face and barely recognized herself. I'm going downhill, she thought. She made a cup of coffee and walked out into the garden with it.

Elvira didn't spend much time in her garden; a jumble of overgrown, sky-blue plumbago and some dense, rampant shrubs with scarlet flowers whose names she didn't know, it took second place to Jack's immaculate gravel drive. The garden was tended once a week by a man with a van who did all the villas. He did a bit of watering, some trimming, he had the patter that worked on the rich summer visitors, but he wasn't much interested. An old countryman would have been better, Elvira found herself thinking as she looked with some surprise at the pair of orange trees she hadn't realized she owned. They flanked the kitchen door in huge terracotta pots and their fruit lay on the flagstones, some of it rotten. A waste that a *contadino* would not have tolerated. Elvira bent to pick up one of the waxy fruits, and breathed in the bittersweet, oily scent. Mine, she thought.

It was some time since the bells had begun. She thought of the old people filing into church in the clean, pale light of dawn, taking advantage of the cool. Only the very devout and the old, those who could no longer sleep past five, would be at the six o'clock service. Elvira's mother, guilt-ridden, insomniac, desperate for redemption, had been one of those, at mass before her children woke, three times a week. Elvira felt an

181

unaccustomed stab of pity as she stood in her bright, fragrant garden and looked back down the years as through a telescope, her mother's small, shabby life at the other end. A life of degradation and hard labour, work and dirt and children, and still she needed to get up at five to pray for forgiveness.

Elvira weighed the fallen orange in her hand, gazing unseeing out across the glittering sea towards the horizon. Then she sighed, blinked, wondered why she was thinking of her mother now. *Getting old.* Dazzled by the dawn on the water, she turned away from the view and it was then that she noticed that the drive was empty. Jack's big silver car was nowhere to be seen, and for a fleeting moment she wondered whether they'd come back at all the previous night. But no; she'd heard breathing from the guest room, she couldn't have mistaken that alien scent on the stairs; the invisible, malicious chattering of unwelcome guests hung in the air, buzzed in her head.

She frowned at the empty gravel, but she didn't have to wonder for long; even as she turned to look down the steep narrow road into Levanto the car appeared at the bottom. Initially it seemed to her that Jack's face was dark, that he was angry when he saw her, but as the car approached she could see that he was smiling. He swung in in front of her on the gravel, so close that she had to jump back.

Jack was holding an armful of brown paper bags as he climbed out of the car, and smelled of the bakery as he leaned down to kiss her on the cheek. And aftershave, and a little light sweat; Elvira's senses, she thought, had been sharpened since she had stopped taking the pills, because she had never known Jack to sweat before. It gave her a different sense of him, something salty, almost feral, under his urbane exterior. She wasn't sure whether she liked it or not.

Elvira had never known Jack get up early to buy breakfast either, come to that. Perhaps it was the heat; certainly it seemed even hotter today. As she looked over his shoulder and out to sea the swell looked oily now, sweating under the glaring sky, and the horizon was obscured by haze.

'Breakfast!' said Jack, brightly, leaning away from her and holding the bag up triumphantly.

'Ah,' said Elvira. 'Yes. A bit early for you, isn't it?' She looked at Jack, impassive, trying to work him out. His expression was a little truculent, like a spoilt boy deprived of anticipated praise.

'And for you, for that matter,' he said lightly. 'You're looking a bit – tired, darling.' Elvira couldn't escape the malice in his voice, but she refused to rise to it. Soon, she thought idly, the future unfolding in her head, Jack won't want to be seen with me on his arm. He'll start suggesting plastic surgery. She smiled at him, had the impression they were at a stand-off.

'I'll make some coffee,' she said.

To her surprise Jack followed her into the kitchen.

'Who were you talking to last night?' he said. 'On the phone, before we went out?'

'Oh, no one, not really,' said Elvira vaguely; she had not yet made up her mind about this, about whether to tell Jack or not. She had a queasy feeling that she was playing with fire; she knew he wouldn't leave it until he knew. After all, who could she have been talking to? She had no friends of her own, not any more. Had she ever? She thought of Venturelli.

Jack snorted. 'Come on, darling. Your dealer? A secret lover?' For some reason the latter incensed Elvira even more than the suggestion she was out looking for drugs and had a dealer, the ridiculous notion that she might be loved. Why so ridiculous? She turned to him.

'You know Venturelli? The director, from Turin?'

Jack nodded, guardedly, his eyes narrowed. 'Won the Palme d'Or?' he said. 'That one? Isn't he an old flame of yours?'

Elvira ignored the needling. 'Not exactly,' she said haughtily. 'A – friend.' Jack didn't really believe in friends, she was aware.

'He called?'

'No,' said Elvira reluctantly. 'He wrote to me, to tell me about a journalist who'd been in touch with him, wanted an interview. So I called her. I was talking to her last night.' She waited, watching Jack's expression change.

'You what?' He looked startled, then furious. 'You – how could you be so stupid? You know nothing about this woman.' Elvira experienced a surge of unexpected satisfaction when she saw her clever husband wrong-footed, grasping to regain control, to understand what might have been going on.

Elvira shrugged. 'Too late,' she said. 'I said yes.'

In the dim half-light of the kitchen the flat, cold stare Jack gave her raised the hairs suddenly on the back of Elvira's neck. His eyes rested on her, incurious as a lizard's, for a moment, then he took the coffee pot from her hands, turned his back and began to fill it in silence. Upstairs Elvira could hear the sound of muffled footsteps.

'Someone's up,' she said. 'I should go and play hostess.' Jack didn't respond. Elvira looked at his motionless back and suddenly the cool, dark kitchen seemed oppressive, sinister; a buried place. She felt breathless and afraid; on the verge of panic, she wondered what she had done. *Got to get out.* She made for the stairs.

Chapter Nineteen

Cirri and his wife were among the last to leave the church; Chiara had fallen asleep in her pushchair during the service and they sat at the back, enjoying peace and the deep, incense-fragrant cool of the old building.

As, finally, they came out through the great studded doors Cirri felt the heat scald his face as though he'd opened an oven. He nodded blindly in the brilliant sunshine to the white-robed priest who stood by the door bidding his congregation farewell; in her pushchair Chiara squirmed as she felt the temperature change even through the heavy blanket of sleep.

'Shall we eat out?' said his wife as she turned to him, fanning herself and gasping a little. 'It's too hot to cook. And you've had a hard week, haven't you? With this – girl. The murdered girl.' Chiara stirred again, and Gloria bent over her, clucking a little under her breath, jiggling the pushchair to send her off again. She straightened. 'And it would be nice, while Chiara's asleep, just us two?'

'Yes,' said Cirri, 'that's a good idea.' He smiled at his wife in the sunshine, feeling suddenly flooded with a sense of his own good fortune. It was Sunday, his wife was kind as well as beautiful, his dark-eyed daughter was adorable, a treasure. He surveyed the piazza contentedly and for once it seemed an idyll, several generations of family life mingling, happy, poised for a day of leisure and good food. He even found himself wondering, as he watched a handsome blonde woman holding her baby up to her husband for approval, when might be the right time to have another child of their own.

'Shall we go to Piero's then?' he said, looking uxoriously at his wife.

Gloria raised her eyebrows, but he could see she was pleased with the suggestion. Piero's was one of the nicest restaurants in Levanto, on the picturesque edge of the town just up the hill towards Monterosso. The restaurant's terrace overlooked the sea, it was sedate but not too formal; the perfect place for a family Sunday lunch. It wasn't cheap, but it would be worth it, Cirri decided; and when Gloria slid her arm through his and squeezed him against her, his feeling was confirmed.

Although busy, Piero found a small but well-positioned table for the little family without difficulty, and the warmth of the *padrone*'s greeting improved Cirri's mood even further. Perhaps it wasn't so bad being a provincial policeman, he thought; perhaps there was, after all, some respect for his standing. More likely, he thought, Piero's fondness for Gloria had got them the table, but so what? His good humour remained intact.

The restaurant was still largely empty, the shade of its pergola cool and peaceful. As they arranged themselves at the table, careful not to disturb Chiara in her pushchair, Cirri's mobile went. Hastily he pushed back his chair and moved

186

away to the edge of the terrace so as not to wake the sleeping child.

It was Toto.

'Sorry to call you on a Sunday, boss,' he said straight away. 'Just a quick one, just something I thought you should know.' He paused.

'There's been another fire started, not close enough to be a danger, but it seems like they're getting nearer. This one's behind Santa Margherita. They think they've got it under control, but I thought you should know.'

Cirri nodded absently, looking out to sea. Over to the west there was just a smudge of grey drifting out to sea where Santa Margherita Ligure was hidden by the promontory that sheltered its pretty harbour. Smoke.

Forest fires were largely the responsibility of the fire department, but the police came into it if foul play was suspected. As it often was. 'Yes, thanks,' said Cirri slowly. 'You were right to let me know. Is there anything else?'

'Well, there's the toxicology report. On the Villemartin girl; that's expected tomorrow. And –' Toto hesitated. 'That maid of the Contessa's, the Romanian she reported missing? The girl was seen on the station platform, the evening before Ferragosto, seen by the stationmaster.' He paused again.

'She's a regular, the maid, arrives on the eight twenty-three, goes back to Genova at thirteen twenty-nine. They knew who I meant straight away. Everyone pays attention to who goes up to the Contessa's house.'

Cirri felt a twinge of pity for Elvira Vitale; every gossip in Levanto had something to say about her. What had happened last year – turning up at the station like that, all wild-eyed, making allegations – had set them all going like nasty little

187

clockwork toys, chattering and gossiping at the Mare Blu, heads bobbing every time someone came through the door in case it might be her. Cirri wondered why the husband hadn't had the presence of mind to stop her, calm her down.

Toto went on. 'Anyway, that particular afternoon she was later than usual, but then trains had been screwed up by forensics in the morning. She was seen being dropped off around three in that big fancy Merc the husband drives. He couldn't say – the stationmaster, that is – if she got on the train or not; there was a wildcat strike that afternoon, all the trains up from the south were delayed. He had some idea she might have got fed up waiting, been offered a lift; plenty of people had given up. The platform must have been pretty busy.'

Cirri nodded to himself thoughtfully, thinking of that big car muscling its way down from the hill and through the town. He could see Elvira Vitale's husband at the wheel in his mind's eye, a dark shape, languid, waiting, behind the tinted windows. He turned away from the sea and caught Gloria looking at him a little crossly. 'Right. Okay. Well, I'm going to the station in the morning, anyway,' he said. 'To talk to a guy who works in the bar. Maybe I'll have a word with the stationmaster while I'm there. See you tomorrow.' Thoughtfully he clicked the mobile shut and put it back in his pocket. The waiter was standing by their table, waiting to take their order.

'Sorry, *cara*,' he said to his wife, sitting down beside her and squeezing her hand. 'Sorry. It's turned off now.' He patted his pocket apologetically. 'So, what shall we have?' In the buggy beside them Chiara stirred, and impulsively Cirri leaned down and pulled her on to his knee, her compact little body still limp and heavy with sleep. He breathed in his daughter's sweetness, the clean smell of her fine, soft hair. Looking up, Cirri saw that his wife was smiling.

The restaurant was filling up and Cirri relaxed in the soft breeze off the sea, Chiara's head against his shoulder. Most of the voices around them were Italian; some local, although those only the more prosperous among them; Cirri recognized a Levanto businessman, manager of a chain of shoe shops, at the head of a long table with several generations of his family. *They must be doing well*, he thought automatically.

From where Cirri and his small family sat waiting for their lunch on the edge of the restaurant's wide terrace facing to the west, the silver undulation of the train track could be seen below them following the contours of the cliffs above the sea. Cirri could even see the dark mouth of the tunnel, the tumble of rocks where Anna-Maria Villemartin's body had lain. As he gazed down Cirri thought about the other girl, the one last year. He had resisted Toto's attempts to connect the murders; to his stolid, bourgeois sensibilities there was something cheap and disgusting about jumping to such a conclusion, about even using the sensationalist term. Serial killer. And his heart sank at the thought that these girls might be the beginning of something, that he would have to visit other grieving mothers in other shabby flats from which the light had suddenly disappeared.

But there were similarities; however much he wanted to ignore them, there were similarities. He wondered if Toto had found any connection. Both murders had occurred at the height of the holiday season, both victims were young, attractive women returning from a night out in Genova. But a year between them? That was the question that lodged in Cirri's mind. A seasonal visitor, this murderer? Not that that narrowed the field very much, he realized as he surveyed his fellow diners. Levanto's population more than doubled during August, and probably quadrupled for Ferragosto. He sighed.

'What's up?' said Gloria. 'You're thinking about work, aren't you? Come on, Leo, put it away for once. Look, our food's coming.'

She nodded towards their waiter, approaching them with a platter of fried fish held high, and on Cirri's lap Chiara began to bounce in anticipation. He set his daughter on her own chair and carefully tied a napkin around her neck. As he straightened up the policeman detected a change in the tone of the conversation on the terrace, a distinct hush falling over the thronged tables, and he saw heads turning towards the entrance. Elvira Vitale's husband was standing there, framed by orange blossom from the potted trees that flanked the entrance, his wife a little way behind him, with her face in shadow. Behind her stood another couple Cirri didn't recognize. He did, however, detect a kind of tension between the four figures; not at all the happy intimacy of a foursome out for Sunday lunch in holiday season. Beside them the manager was wringing his hands as he tried to see where he might seat them.

Gloria looked up from Chiara, registering the changed mood on the terrace.

'Who's that?' she said in a whisper, frowning across the tables at the couple in the entrance. 'Isn't that the – that Vitale woman? The film star? God, what's happened to her?'

Leo Cirri followed her gaze. 'That's her,' he said uncertainly. Elvira Vitale had moved forward into the light and he saw that Gloria was right: she looked terrible.

*

Rose emailed Cookie in triumph: *interview sorted with elvira vitale, tomorrow a.m.* No doubt Cookie would call with all sorts of prurient questions for her to pose, mostly concerning Jack Robbins, Rose suspected. Not many of Cookie's readers would have heard of Elvira Vitale, would have no more than the vaguest idea from the gossip columns of who she was; ageing foreign film star with an aura of faded seventies glamour and a whiff of notoriety. They might have read reports of the death of Vitale's drug-addicted first husband; he died in London, after all. They might even be aware of the intense second marriage that led to her abrupt fade-out at the end of the seventies; a Garbo vanishing act. But most of all they would know her from her reappearance on the arm of Jack Robbins. Had that been why she married him, to stage some kind of comeback? Rose doubted it. There was something about him that Rose could see sold magazines, a faintly sleazy, arrogant sex appeal. The readers loved him, but to Rose he was a kind of shell, quite hollow, just made to be photographed with a gleaming smile. Rose was more interested in her.

Elvira Vitale. When Rose had first seen her, in the Mare Blu, she had glittered like diamonds, something authentic, the real thing. A star. The trouble was finding out if there was anything of a human being left underneath. Rose had once or twice interviewed minor Hollywood royalty, interviews all conducted under the watchful eye of a public relations minder in the chilly, anonymous luxury of one Park Lane hotel suite or another. She had never managed to find anything resembling humanity under the mechanics of celebrity, the image consultants, the hair-cuts, the carefully rehearsed anecdotes chosen to illustrate compassion or a sense of humour. But this wasn't Hollywood. Italy was different; that, after all, was why she was here, where business was conducted on a human scale. She thought gratefully of Venturelli's intervention on her behalf, and with some residual astonishment of Elvira Vitale's phone call. She still couldn't quite believe it.

Rose clicked to send the message to Cookie with no small sense of achievement, stood, stretched and yawned, heard her stomach rumble. She realized she'd hardly eaten since Friday, when she'd had lunch with Richard Bourn. That wasn't like her; had he had that effect on her? She left her computer to make her way downstairs to the kitchen.

Staring into her near-empty fridge and registering with relief the absence of the bloodied rabbit carcass, Rose recalled Gennaro; he was having an effect on her too. His expression of polite interest, his strong, tanned arms, dark, opaque eyes, his neat movements. She thought of his invitation to dinner with a sense of impending dread and cursed herself for being too well brought-up, or too feeble, to have simply refused him. Rose closed the fridge with a shudder and turned away from the dark interior of her kitchen towards the light that flooded in through the open door from the garden. The smooth old tiles of the floor were warm under her feet, the hillside sloping away from her, bright and aromatic. It was beginning to feel like home.

As Rose stood in the doorway and gazed across the valley she concentrated on putting Gennaro out of her mind and trying to focus on Elvira Vitale. What must it have been like, to grow up in Genova in the fifties, and to end up a film star? By all accounts the city had been a decrepit, dirty, violent place, squalid and poverty-stricken, the northern Naples. Rags to riches, then. But Vitale was no Sophia Loren, all flashing eyes and heaving bosom, the soubrette of romantic comedy. From what Rose had seen she was subtler than that, more modern, more opaque.

On the hillside below, perhaps three hundred yards down, as her eyes adjusted to the light Rose became aware of a splash of white among the olive trees, moving slowly. She wasn't focusing on it at first, but then she realized there was something deliberate in its cautious advance, as though who-ever – whatever – it was was trying not to be seen. She took a step forward, her hand against the door which swung back with a creak and banged against the wall. The loud crack of wood against stone echoed in the Sunday-morning quiet of the valley. The smudge of white against the green of the hill-side – was it a shirt? Was it Gennaro, in his Sunday best, on his way to feed his rabbits? – stopped moving, seemed to duck and then abruptly disappeared. Behind Rose the telephone rang; she hesitated for a moment, frowned in an effort to find the white-shirted figure again, but it had gone.

Reluctantly she stepped back in and picked up the phone, which was just inside the door. '*Pronto?*' she said, still scruti-nizing the scrubby hillside. 'Hello?' she repeated in English.

Somehow she had been assuming vaguely that her Sunday-morning caller was Cookie, although if she had thought about it she would have had to be checking her mail even as Rose had sent the message to be responding already. It wasn't Cookie, though.

'Hello,' said Richard Bourn abruptly. It wasn't a good line; his voice sounded tinny and distant, and it was hard to believe he was just across the valley. Rose felt herself flush ridiculously at the sound of his voice; she stepped out on to the terrace and looked across at where his house must be.

'Hello,' she said. 'What are you doing?' Even as the question escaped her, Rose regretted the intimacy of it, but the truth was she wanted to know, suddenly, where he was sitting, if he was drinking a glass of wine, looking out to sea, what his house was like. It sounded empty, but perhaps that was just an echo on the line.

'I mean,' she qualified, 'where are you? You sound miles away.'

'Bad line, sorry,' he said. 'I'm at home. I'd –' He hesitated. 'I'd like to see you again.' He stopped short.

Rose felt breathless suddenly. 'Would you?' she said, unable to think of anything else to say, anxious not to misunderstand.

Richard laughed abruptly. 'Yes,' he said. 'I would. What about this evening? Will you come up here? I can drive you.'

Hell, thought Rose. 'I – no, I can't, not tonight,' she said, trying desperately to think of how to explain Gennaro. Reluctantly she went on, 'I've been asked to dinner by – oh, somebody in the village, I think he's trying to be friendly. I can't really get out of it.'

'I see,' said Richard flatly. It was obvious to Rose that he didn't see at all.

'No, really,' she said, exasperated. 'I'm not sure about him – he's called Gennaro – not sure at all. To be honest – I don't want to go at all. But what can I do? I don't want to look like a snooty foreigner.' She paused, but Richard said nothing, and she went on, desperately. 'But maybe some other time? I'm interviewing your neighbour, Elvira Vitale, in the morning, I could do with celebrating after that. I'm quite pleased with myself.'

Rose heard herself cajoling, trying to win him. *Don't try so hard.* But when Richard spoke again he seemed to be genuinely interested; intent, even.

'An interview?' he said. 'I thought she was hard to get. Just her? Or the husband too? Was it his idea?'

Rose was taken aback. She hadn't expected him to be interested at all and she felt warmed by his attention. 'Oh, just her, I think,' she said. 'She called me. I suppose I was a bit surprised.' She paused, remembered something.

'I didn't know you even knew who they were,' she said, curious. 'Your neighbours.'

'Oh,' said Richard. 'No, well, I didn't, not really, not until you told me. But after our trawl through the video shops, I suppose I got interested.' Rose could almost hear him shrug off the question. Something nagged at her, and she hesitated. *No,* she thought. *Let's get it out in the open.*

'Richard?' she said.

'Yes?' He sounded wary. Rose took a deep breath.

'Your wife – she's dead, isn't she?' She only realized then, once she'd said it, that if he asked how she knew she would have to admit that she'd been checking up on him. She felt a flush rise up her throat, but he said nothing. She heard him sigh, and wondered if she'd blown it.

'Yes.' There was resignation in his voice now, but Rose ploughed on.

'I'm sorry,' she said, and he cleared his throat, a startlingly harsh sound in her ear. When he spoke his voice was hoarse but defiant, as though when he thought of his wife his predominant emotion was not grief, but something fiercer.

'Well, yes,' he said. 'Me too.' There was a silence prolonged beyond a heartbeat, then two, and Rose wondered whether he'd hung up on her. But then Richard spoke again, and his voice was back to normal.

'Anyway, yes, maybe tomorrow, then. I'll let you know. You're sure?'

'Oh yes,' said Rose, catching her breath with a relief that took her by surprise, it came so close to euphoria. 'I'm sure.'

*

Ania heard the crack as the door banged back on itself, loud as a gunshot above her in the village. For an instant she froze, crouched helpless against the coarse, stubbly grass. Then in a panic she scrambled across to the dry-stone walling that supported the olive terrace above her and pressed herself against it in an effort to become invisible. Why? She tried to think clearly; this was just someone opening a door. But her head was swimming, she could hear things seething in the bushes. She swallowed, her mouth dry, and wondered if she was sick. Even in her hiding place she felt horribly exposed under the glaring sky; in this flat, merciless light even her grubby white shirt gleamed as though it was under a strobe. She could smell the scents of thyme, baked earth, sweet dry grass rising around her in the heat; a few inches from her face a small lizard flickered across the hot stone, stopping to rest its tiny, incurious amber eyes on hers. In the silence that fell as the echo died away Ania could hear her own ragged breath. She felt the sweat bead on her forehead and shivered.

It was partly the memory of her escape, so narrowly won and so fresh still in her mind, that made Ania tremble in the heat. The thought of her desperate panting scramble up the path away from whoever had been there, standing in the shell of the old building behind her. The road had turned out to be no more than five minutes away and when she reached it Ania had stopped on the verge in the pale morning light and gasped into her dirty hands, feeble with relief and almost hysterical. But then she had heard the sound of an approaching vehicle.

Ania had the impression that if she saw her abductor again, she would know him, her memory would return, but what if she didn't? She might not have seen him at all; it might have been dark, she might have been taken by surprise. It was like a fog; shapes hovered ominously just out of sight but they refused to form themselves into anything recognizable. In fact Ania still had no way of knowing who had taken her to that place, or why, and that frightened her more than anything. She might pass him on the road, and not know to run. When she heard the car she made for the far side of the road as fast as she could, the muscles of her thighs and calves aching from the unfamiliar exercise, and threw herself painfully into a tangle of the undergrowth on the verge. She stayed there, her shirt sticking to her back with cooling sweat, her greasy hair half-covering her face, while the car passed. It was a small, battered Ape van in the usual battleship-grey; from her hiding place she glimpsed the impassive, hook-nosed profile of the driver, an old man in a hat, a stout woman squeezed in beside him in the tiny cab. So familiar a sight, these little vans, stuttering up and down the country roads, owned by builders, peasant farmers, country people, battleship-grey, khaki, perfect camouflage against the hills. They disappeared around the uphill bend and the road was silent again.

Ania thought of going back down into Levanto; from where she stood she could see the green and white striped church nestling in the shadow of the cliff. If she went back to the station – but at the thought, the thought of the echoing waiting room, the tracks gleaming in the sun, the crowded concourse where her abductor might still be standing in wait, she was overcome with panic and began to tremble. She took a few deep breaths and forced herself to be methodical.

The only safe thing Ania could come up with was to stay out of sight completely and somehow make her way across country back to the Contessa's house. For some reason Ania put faith in the Contessa, for all her idle wealth; she had the feeling her employer would not turn her away. But she was weak with hunger and lack of sleep, and looking across the valley towards the sea and the house's distant silhouette it seemed impossibly far. She felt her legs tremble with the effort of even staying upright, let alone walking all that way, and she felt hollow with lack of food. From somewhere up the hillside, where the faded red plaster of a village house was just visible through the trees, a meaty waft of cooking smell brought the saliva into her mouth. She had to find something to eat.

In half an hour Ania managed to move perhaps a hundred metres. Her legs felt stubbornly heavy for lack of food and underuse, and every step brought her out in a sweat. Where she had cut herself on the lavatory bowl her wrist felt oddly numb, the skin of her hand stretched so tight and shiny she thought it might split like sausage skin, and now and again she shook her swollen fingers to try to bring them back to life. In some part of her mind she had recognized that her hand was becoming infected, but the need for food was a greater imperative. She passed a sickly-looking peach tree and pulled off a fruit but it was pale green, hard and underripe and instantly dried her mouth. She spat it on to the ground.

Ania came close to the red house, standing at its tumbledown garden wall to catch her breath. In Romania, she would be offered a glass of water at least, she thought, as the oven smell reached her. But then a heavy-set woman in a flowered overall materialized in the house's doorway; she made no offer, of water or anything else. Her square face darkened with hostility, she shook a tea towel at Ania and shouted over her shoulder, back into the house. A man appeared behind her in a dirty vest, his chin dark with stubble. Ania shrank back immediately and walked on as if she had never meant to stop for more than a moment. After that she moved as quickly as she could, working her way around the village on the slope below it, trying to keep out of sight.

She got lucky in the end, glimpsed a woman putting a tray of baked peppers out on her window-sill to cool and, made foolhardy by hunger, ran and snatched a warm, oily handful before she could stop herself, slithering back down the steep hillside to devour her booty in hiding. The peppers, red and yellow, were stuffed with crumbs and anchovies and parsley, pungent, salty and the most delicious thing Ania thought she had ever tasted. She could have slept, after that, in the warm shade of the hillside, but roused herself; she had to keep moving. She had gone perhaps another hundred metres when she had heard the sound above her, the crack of a gun going off, it sounded like, and there was someone up there, looking at her.

Feebly now Ania lay against the stone of the terrace as the lizard, having taken in her sorry state, flickered away from her down the wall. *I am sick*, she thought, hopelessly, and as she gave in to it she felt her skin turn clammy, her arms goose-pimpled despite the heat. A terrible, overwhelming thirst came over her. Ania remembered the blotting-paper texture of the underripe peach, tasted salt and fish, and she retched into the dry grass like an animal.

Chapter Twenty

It was ironic, Elvira thought with a kind of unnatural objectivity as she stood there in the doorway and tried to fix her gaze on the blue horizon beyond the lunch parties and the terrace. Ironic that just when she'd decided that clean living was the way forward, that's when her body should give up on her. Punishment for years of neglect, perhaps. She could see Luke and Annabel smiling at the manager just in front of her, ingratiating, Jack easing them through the door and past him. And then another wave broke over her, a cold slap of nausea, and she struggled for composure, all detachment gone. She thought she might lose control there and then, in full view of all Piero's Sunday diners, and leaned against the wall. Jack turned to look at her, assessing her through narrowed eyes. He knows, she thought.

In front of her it seemed to Elvira as though Luke and Annabel were about to turn to look at her too. 'Excuse me,' she said urgently, pushing past them. She broke away and made for the door marked *servizi* next to the kitchen as though it was the last lifeboat on a sinking ship, and as she went she could feel their eyes on her back. The brilliantly lit, pale pink powder-room was mercifully empty, and clean. Elvira knelt in a cubicle; she was sweating and she could feel the sour saliva come into her mouth. She shoved the door shut behind her, pulled her hair away from her face in an automatic gesture and threw up.

When it was over, Elvira found she could not move, or at least not yet. She sat back against the door and watched her hand tremble as she held it in front of her. She felt terrible, but she felt better. The nausea hadn't been the worst of it, not by a long way. When she felt it first she'd been in her own bathroom, making an effort for the lunch she didn't want to attend, trying to act like the wife she was supposed to be. Suddenly, as she leaned forward, squinting to see herself in the mirror, she could feel a dizzy, ballooning sensation in her head and the world shrank around her. Her heart pounded painfully against her ribs and she could taste the strong coffee Jack had made her, acid at the back of her throat. She had taken hold of the heavy basin, convinced that she was about to lose her balance and pitch forward on to her face.

'What on earth is she doing up there?'

At the sound of Annabel's high-pitched, complaining voice at the foot of the stairs where they were all waiting for her, and Jack's low, indecipherable reply, she had been seized by terror. *I'm going mad*, the thought came to her. The urge to hide, to fling herself down, to scramble into a corner and stay there was almost insuperable, but she'd gripped the basin and forced herself to remain upright. She thought with longing of the short walk across the landing that would get her to the sanctuary of her dressing room, where she could hide among the furs, the mothballs and chiffon. There'd been a short staccato burst of laughter from below and she'd broken into a sweat but held on tight. *One foot behind the other*, she thought. *One step at a time.*

And that was how she'd got here, vomiting her life up in Piero's *gabinetto*. Good job he did them up last year, she found herself thinking weakly, and rested her head against the ply-wood partition. Inhaling the harsh chemical bouquet of the cubicle, the tiled floor, air-freshener, disinfectant, the tang of urine, she felt as though this was it. She'd hit bottom.

For several minutes Elvira stayed there, crumpled against the thin dividing wall, her dress creasing under her, wanting to be sure it was over and whatever toxin it was had cleared her system. As she sat, concentrating only on her own shallow breathing, slowly, miraculously, the panic, the vertigo and nausea began to ebb and her head to clear. Elvira sat forward, thinking hard. She felt shaky but clean, hollowed out and clean, and then it came to her; that was what it was, poison.

For once Elvira felt quite clear-headed, even though she was entertaining such extraordinary ideas, and she understood quite suddenly: she knew the answer. It was quite obvious, really: Jack had done it.

Elvira thought of his back turned to her in the dim kitchen, the coffee pot in his hand, the angry silence. But poison? She walked around the thought, looked at it. With a growing sense of unease at the control she had surrendered she looked back down the years Jack had spent bringing her tea in bed, coffee, champagne, pills. He could be feeding her anything, couldn't he? It seemed to fit together, not just as an explanation for today, but before, too; why not? Elvira thought of the day she'd spent in bed, the blackouts and memory loss, the feeling that her life was slipping out of control. That she was going mad. Jack taking her down to Harley Street, she dutifully following. But why? Why would Jack want her to think she was going crazy? Why would he want her – sedated? With half her mind Elvira thought, *this is ridiculous. This is a joke.* But she knew with a crawling sense of dread that there might be reasons – all sorts of reasons – for Jack to want her like this. Before she had a chance to formulate them, however, she heard a sound; a door swishing open and then shut, the clack of heels on the tiles and an excited intake of breath.

There were two of them; she didn't recognize the voices.

'Well!' There was a pause. 'Did you see it? Where did she run off to, white as a sheet?'

'She actually looked green, to me. It's a disgrace. To allow yourself to get into such a state, in public. I mean, we all knew she had a – problem.' Elvira could imagine the pantomime gesture to indicate a glass raised to the lips that accompanied this portentous announcement, and involuntarily closed her eyes. *Did I? Do I?* She thought of the bottle of brandy she kept in her dressing room, for emergencies, and the way she felt if there wasn't champagne in the fridge.

The woman went on, her voice a little distorted as though she was applying lipstick as she spoke, and Elvira imagined her grimacing into the mirror. There was a click, a compact shutting.

The conversation was grotesque, and it seemed almost surreal to Elvira. She knitted her brows, wondering how she was going to extract herself from this situation. Her leg had gone dead beneath her and she shifted, the sound she made clearly audible. Outside the women fell abruptly silent and Elvira realized her cover was blown. She got to her feet.

As she approached the table Elvira registered Annabel's avid expression and on Luke's face a slight flush and that awful, evasive look with which Englishmen express embarrassment. She knew what she looked like, she'd looked in the powder-room mirror in full view of the two gossips who, she saw, were now seated back with their extended family on the long centre table and pretending not to look over at her, stage-whispering to each other. There were smudged dark circles under her eyes, her skin was white and papery with age and sickness, but she was beyond caring what Luke and Annabel thought. It was Jack's reaction Elvira was interested in; suddenly, hopelessly, she experienced a stab of longing; she wanted to be wrong; she wanted him to love her. A bit late for that, she thought savagely, and steeled herself. She sat down.

'My God,' she said, darting a glance at Jack. 'I feel like I've been poisoned.' And shakily she laughed. Jack put a hand up to her cold cheek and stroked it gently.

'Not feeling any better, then?' he asked softly. Elvira looked into his eyes and felt the tug of sentiment, but held her resolve.

'Oh, well,' she said. 'A bit rough, you know.' She squeezed his hand weakly, and caught a glance exchanged between Luke and Annabel. Elvira faltered. They think I'm mad, she thought, and wondered whether they were right. Cautiously a waiter approached the table.

At random Elvira ordered a steak she had no intention of eating, grateful for the flicker of concern she saw in the waiter's eyes. She heard the man's Genovese accent as he repeated her order, an echo of another life when she'd been a real person, not this stuffed dummy she'd turned into with sawdust for brains, and she felt obscurely encouraged. Across the table Annabel greedily scanned the menu, finally settling on a seafood salad with a virtuous air; Elvira gazed at her. *What on earth am I doing here, with these people?* she wondered. She'd rather be in the restaurant kitchens, washing up shoulder to shoulder with the Genovese waiter.

Luke and Jack were making a big deal of looking at the wine list, then she saw Luke glance over at her. He cleared his throat.

'Or perhaps we should just stick to water? Long flight this evening, after all.' He avoided Elvira's eye, and instead looked pointedly at Jack.

'Oh, well, the flight –' Annabel began to protest and Elvira suspected she was unwilling to manage without what she called a 'spritzer'. Elvira saw Luke catch his wife's eye and stop her in her tracks. 'Well, perhaps you're right.' Annabel's voice tailed off with a hint of petulance. The waiter stood patiently at Jack's elbow, his order pad at the ready.

Jack seemed not to have picked up on Luke's intentions. 'Oh, no, come on,' he said earnestly, 'It's your last day, after all. A nice red for your steak, sweetie?' Elvira wondered what he was up to. She shrugged.

'That's decided then,' said Jack. Luke and Annabel looked faintly bemused as he ordered a bottle of Barolo for Elvira – 'I'll share,' he said with a warm smile – and a local white wine for the fish. When the wine arrived the waiter set it down beside Jack. I wonder, thought Elvira, with a kind of dread. Jack's hand was slipped casually into his trouser pocket as he leaned back in his chair, saying something to Luke about airplane food: quite a natural place for his hand to be. Elvira thought of the powder she'd found when she'd gone through his pockets that morning – it seemed an aeon ago now. Coke, she'd thought, leftovers from an evening's clubbing. Where had she put it? The evidence. She felt as though she was on the edge of a precipice, sheer madness waiting below her.

Elvira's mouth dried and she swallowed painfully, pouring herself a tumbler of water and trying to keep her hand steady as she did it. They were all looking at her again. Only one way to find out, she thought, and pushed her wineglass over to Jack.

'Fill me up, darling,' she said, smiling. 'I'm dying of thirst.' And she looked away.

Across the packed restaurant Leo Cirri had seen Elvira Vitale turn pale and paler, a look on her face as though she was drowning, her eyes wide and dark, lips bloodless. She seemed to struggle against it, as a poor swimmer does when he finds the sea too much, his strength less than he thought; Cirri sat up and saw her make a dash for the powder-room, and fifteen, perhaps twenty minutes later he had seen her return. He wondered what was going on. Had she been taken ill? Could it be drugs? It had been known, even in so upmarket a place as Piero's. But Cirri had seen, too, the meaningful glances exchanged between Vitale's lunch companions as she pushed past them, and he felt sorry for her. She obviously wasn't well, and to his eyes, husband or no husband, she didn't seem to be among friends.

As he looked at Elvira Vitale's profile now, reflecting that although haggard she looked younger, somehow, Cirri thought of last year, when she'd come into his office with the bizarre allegation that someone was watching her, through binoculars or telescopes or some such thing. She'd been quite insistent, and almost reasonable; if it hadn't been for the alcohol on her breath and her reputation they might have believed her. In any case, to calm her he'd even agreed to pay a few calls, although for the most part the villas and mansions scattered across the cliff had been inhabited only by servants, waiting for their owners to turn up for the weekend.

They were a funny lot, in Cirri's book, but then that was the rich for you. That Englishman with his great big empty house; he'd been at home. He'd laughed when Cirri had asked him if by any chance he owned a telescope. Over Gloria's shoulder Cirri looked across the valley for the house and saw the distant tented shape of a sunshade on a terrace. Dimly he recalled the man, English, retired at, what, forty-odd? What did he do all day? On her father's knee Chiara wriggled and bounced, trying to get his attention back to its rightful place, the waiter approached with their order and for some moments Cirri was distracted.

When he looked back towards Elvira Vitale's table all seemed calm, a tableau of friendship and harmony. The two guests – English, Cirri thought, from their pink skin and faintly incongruous dress sense – were pointing, talking about something they had spotted out at sea. Vitale's husband was making a meal out of pouring the wine. Cirri looked at the man as discreetly as he could and wondered why it was that every time he saw Jack Robbins he found him more dislikeable. Something unsavoury about him. That big car for a start, the way he'd been looking at the girls on the beach, letting his wife get in such a state. With a start Cirri realized that Elvira Vitale was looking across the restaurant at him.

He found himself quite unable to look away, even though he could feel Gloria's eyes on him across the table, and it was Elvira Vitale who turned away first. She turned to reach for the glass her husband held out to her. Then something odd happened; there was a muffled exclamation, and Cirri saw a splash of dark red spread across the starched white of the tablecloth at Vitale's elbow. She had spilled the wine, but he could not see how. It seemed almost as though it had been done deliberately, and from the fleeting expression of thwarted anger Cirri caught on his face, her husband thought so too.

'Come *on*,' said Gloria, impatiently, and reluctantly Cirri turned back towards her. 'Look,' she said, 'you're letting your *frittura* get cold.' He smiled to placate her, but his mind was elsewhere, and she frowned back at him.

Chiara was babbling at him from his knee, grabbing at a piece of fried squid from his plate, golden in batter. As absently he restrained his daughter, held her tight with one hand while cooling a piece of fish for her in the other, Cirri was thinking of the spilled wine and the stain spreading like blood across the cloth. *What's going on there?* And perhaps it was out of prejudice, out of his instinctive antipathy for Elvira Vitale's husband, but he found himself casting his mind back to this time last year, Ferragosto, the day he'd heard about the other body beside the tracks around the coast; to the west. Had they been in residence then? Had that big car with its tinted windows been cruising the front last August, too? And the answer had to be yes.

Chapter Twenty-One

Away from the coast and the silver gleam of the sea, by six the light was leaving the land and the wooded slopes were turning velvety in the dusk; even in August night seemed to come quickly here. Sometimes Rose found herself thinking with nostalgia of a long, light summer evening in England, a cool blue twilight that seemed to draw out for hours, the scent of nicotiana and damp roses. Here in Grosso what she could smell was Tiziana's cooking, tomatoes and oil, parched grass, baked earth and an acrid, smoky bottom note. A mist had crept up the valley and as the lights of the villages further inland began to come on they shone through it with a blurred, ghostly luminescence. Upstairs in her bedroom, the window open to the soft evening air, Rose was wondering what to wear.

With an hour to go before she was due at Gennaro's she had decided a drink would be the thing to get in a little more of a celebratory mood. She could not turn up at his house, after all, with all the reluctance she felt showing in her face, like a sulky child. So she had a glass of wine.

Outside it was warmer than Rose expected; the thick stone walls of her house kept it cool inside, but when she turned into the alley that led up towards Gennaro's house through the centre of the village she felt stifled. It was as though the narrow passage had held and trapped the heat of the sinking sun, and mingled it with the pervasive odours of cooking, cats and a trace of something burning, somewhere far off. A deepening grey twilight muffled the shapes of things as she walked up between the houses; cracked flagstones, peeling doors, the grille over the window of a basement *cantina* that let out a gust of dank air as she passed. Gennaro's house, at the top of the village, stood in the last of the light, its sunny yellow stucco only just beginning to fade to pale lemon as Rose approached.

The wrought-iron railing around Gennaro's little patio was locked, the patio itself in darkness, and the chairs still leaning, unwelcoming, against the table. Rose walked around the side of the neat little house and found the kitchen door open a crack and light behind it. Gingerly she pushed it open.

The room that greeted her was very clean and orderly; two pans bubbling on the stove but otherwise no sign of cooking or preparation; a long wooden counter looked as though it had been scrubbed. Gennaro was standing motionless in the centre of his kitchen and turned towards the door as though he'd been expecting her just at that very moment. He wore heavy trousers with a clean cloth tied around his hips as an apron and a blue shirt that looked freshly ironed. *Does he do his own ironing?* His face above the bright cotton seemed very tanned, tough and smooth like good leather, his eyes a dark monkey-brown. Once again Rose found herself wondering how old Gennaro was. Fifty-five? Sixty-five? Something like that. Not so old that the thought that he was attracted to her was ludicrous, or disgusting. He came towards her with a hand out and awkwardly she took it, hoping her confusion didn't show on her face.

As though he could sense Rose's unease Gennaro released her hand somewhat formally, then tugged the makeshift apron from around his waist with a mixture of irritation and embarrassment.

'I'm sorry we couldn't sit outside, as before,' he said when he had disposed of the offending piece of cloth in a plastic laundry basket that stood behind the door. 'I think there will be a storm later, some rain, anyway. And sitting there – you know, when they see us the old women will gossip. They have nothing else to occupy them.'

He frowned a little, then seemed to recollect himself, brightening. 'But I have a beautiful dining room.' He gestured towards the door. This way.' As she walked ahead of him through the door into a dark hallway Rose felt a prickle of apprehension.

Silly, she thought as gingerly in the semi-darkness she negotiated a heavy piece of furniture that stood in the hall, trying hard to subdue a sudden and unaccustomed claustrophobia. She could sense Gennaro behind her in the dark. *You're a grown woman*. But she had no template for this kind of occasion, for what to expect or how to behave.

'Here,' said Gennaro, reaching past her to push open a door.

The room they entered smelled faintly musty and was illuminated by the uneasy, low-wattage light of a chandelier. It was rough-plastered and painted a deep terracotta and the floor, unusually for a village house, was a kind of shiny parquet. Set around the walls were more heavy pieces of furniture of walnut veneer dating from the era, Rose thought, of Mussolini: a glass-fronted cabinet filled with pieces of floral china and an ugly, highly polished sideboard. The centre of the room was occupied by a solid circular mahogany dining table, laid for two.

'Beautiful,' said Rose faintly. She felt her face ache with smiling as she stood and surveyed Gennaro's room with polite interest.

'An *aperitivo*?' Gennaro asked, indicating a low sofa covered in imitation leather. Rose sat down.

'Thank you,' she said, knowing that a refusal would offend.

At the sideboard Gennaro busied himself pouring a viscous colourless liquid from a stoneware bottle into a heavy tumbler. He brought it over to her with a small dish containing pretzels; Rose took the glass and raised it to him.

'Aren't you having one?' she asked with an attempt at gaiety.

'Later,' said Gennaro seriously. There is the cooking to finish first.' He indicated the door back into the kitchen, but didn't move, only stood there for a moment, looking at her.

Rose smiled uncertainly. 'Can I help?' she asked.

Gennaro laughed abruptly, and despite herself Rose felt a little offended. 'No, no,' he said, flapping his hand at her dismissively. He turned for the door.

When he had gone Rose took a sip from the heavy glass. It was warm, neat gin, and she choked as it hit the back of her throat and burned. To take the taste away she bit into a pretzel and found it stale and soft. It seemed clear that Gennaro did not entertain often, and with a qualm she wondered why he had chosen her for the privilege. If, for whatever reason, he didn't get on with the locals – and it seemed clear that he didn't,

212

that he discounted the 'old women' of the village even if they were considerably closer to him in age than she – Levanto was full of outsiders, and not just at this time of year. Foreigners. She thought of the policeman in the Mare Blu, blaming his murder case on them, the body of the young girl on the beach. Uneasily Rose shifted on the leatherette, and could feel it sticking to the back of her knees. She stood up, the glass in her hand. Absently she took another sip and it didn't taste so bad this time, bitter and aromatic. She felt the burn of the alcohol as it hit her stomach, and it wasn't unpleasant.

Turning in the dining room, Rose realized that it did contain a window but it was closed and shuttered, admitting no light, and with the realization the space seemed to draw in around her. Under the influence, perhaps, of the strong alcohol, she felt sorry for Gennaro, shutting himself away like this; she wondered if he missed being at sea.

Intending to examine the unusual bottle from which her drink had been poured, Rose wandered over to the sideboard. She looked at the expensive porcelain dinner service behind the glass – a wedding present? – she ran her fingertips along the walnut counter and found no dust. What kind of a marriage had Gennaro had? She couldn't imagine it; the room was so silent and untouched, spoke so clearly of decades left empty, that she assumed the marriage must have ended a long time since. As she looked idly at the pattern on the china she saw that inside the cabinet there also stood a perspex photo cube and without thinking, emboldened by the warm gin, she opened the glass door and picked the thing up.

There were yellowing views on one side of somewhere along the coast, Portofino perhaps, and a fuzzy snapshot of racing boats; on top was a more recent, formal photograph of a handsome elderly woman with a marked resemblance to Gennaro in the high cheekbones and strong jaw. Dressed in plain black with a rigid, iron-grey bouffant coiffure, the woman gazed out of the picture, a broad, sensual and incongruously lipsticked mouth the only colour in it. She wasn't smiling.

Rose pulled a face and turned the cube in her hands; on the bottom, where it had been turned to rest face down on the shelf, was a picture of a dark-haired young woman kneeling on a stony beach, facing the camera with her shoulders thrown back in a confident, happy pose. Although the photograph was a little blurred it was clear that the woman was bare-breasted, her golden skin gleaming as though it had been oiled. Rose felt queasy suddenly, not just from the gin and the sour aftertaste of the stale pretzel; she heard Gennaro in the corridor and suddenly what she was doing didn't seem acceptable. Hastily she thrust the cube back on to the shelf and pulled the glass door to. She turned away just as Gennaro entered the room, a platter in his hands.

The first course – somehow Rose knew there would be more to follow – consisted of at least a pound of anchovies swimming in oil and garlic. She had once liked the fish, in moderation anyway, but after a year in Liguria where they seemed to appear in almost every dish, her enthusiasm had waned. She tried not to think of Gennaro's *cantina*, the overpowering fish smell, and the anchovies in the murky depths of their huge rusty can, and smiled brightly at him. *Sisterly*, she thought, the inspiration coming at her from through the fog of gin. *That's what I'll be.* She laid a hand on Gennaro's arm as he served. 'That's plenty,' she said, laughing. 'I'll get fat!'

Gennaro took in the hand on his arm with an air of

puzzlement, and Rose withdrew it. He frowned. 'No, no,' he said. 'Anchovies are very good. They don't make you fat. Look at me; I don't need a diet, do I?' And he pulled up his sleeve, showed her a lean, sinewy forearm, then patted his abdomen. Rose hoped he wasn't going to pull up his shirt too, and quickly she nodded in agreement.

'All right, then,' she said. 'You win.' And she managed to get them all down.

The anchovies were followed by a dish of *trofie*, the local pasta, with pesto; this time when Gennaro left the room to get the dish Rose sat like a dutiful daughter in her place and didn't move.

'Is this your own pesto?' she asked as she lifted a pungent green forkful to her lips, asking out of politeness although she knew the answer. Gennaro gave her a look of mingled disbelief and injured pride, and snorted.

'What do you think?' he said. 'I wouldn't buy the stuff they sell down there.' He jerked his head in the direction of Levanto. Rose nodded and smiled, concentrating on forking the stuff into her mouth with every appearance of pleasure. And it was indeed good, but like the anchovies it was strong and salty, burning her tongue and reminding her that she was an outsider used to paler, blander tastes. She reached for her glass and took a gulp of Gennaro's strong, resinous yellow wine, regretting it even before she'd replaced the glass on the table. Almost immediately she experienced a tightening at her temples and the beginnings of a queasy sort of headache; imagining the oily mixture of gin and wine swilling together in her stomach, she looked for water on the table, but there was none. Somehow she didn't feel able to request it.

They were eating the fish Gennaro had caught now, a kind

of sea bass, Rose thought, full of bones. Gennaro was dissecting his food slowly, looking across at Rose. He volunteered no conversation and she wondered despairingly what he wanted of her; was she here just to eat, in silence? *I must say something*, she thought.

'Your house is lovely, Gennaro,' she began hesitantly. He nodded his head from side to side in grave acknowledgement of the compliment. It seemed to Rose that he was waiting for her to go on, and so she continued brightly, 'Did you live here with your wife, ever?' Gennaro frowned a little.

'No,' he said shortly. 'I came here – after.' So this house had been laboured over by Gennaro on his own. He shrugged a little and applied himself to his fish once again as though there was no more to be said. Emboldened by her relative success, Rose allowed her curiosity to take over.

'But she must have seen the house? And your daughter – it's a beautiful place ...' Rose tailed off, looking around the room, thinking of the bright neat kitchen upstairs, the sunny patio, the clean yellow stucco. 'They visit?' she asked helplessly.

Gennaro looked at her with a curious expression, as though examining her. Something flickered behind his dark eyes, and then was gone. 'No,' he said stolidly, taking another mouthful of fish, not looking at her now. 'I don't see them. They don't want to live like this.' He spread his arm in a gesture that took in the wider landscape around the house, the hills inland, and once again Rose was aware of the shuttered space in which they sat confined. 'They have different ideas – about everything.'

Out of some unreliable instinct, some reflexive curiosity, Rose persevered; this, at least, was conversation. 'What's your daughter's name? Does she have a family?'

Gennaro put his fork down and considered Rose patiently.

'We named her Maria Grazia. The last time I saw her she was calling herself Mia.' He looked down; meticulously he pushed the bones to the side of his plate. 'No family.'

Rose had been ready to say something teasing about the prospect of grandfatherhood but there was something in his voice that dissuaded her, something politely final. Suddenly she was afraid of Gennaro's patient, careful replies because behind them, she realized, lay the possibility that he might also lose patience. She had the impression that there were other things he might say, that there was something inside him that needed to find expression, but she didn't want to hear. She remembered the girl in the photograph cube and all at once she felt sure it was Gennaro's daughter. Rose found the thought that a man might possess a picture of his daughter half-clothed disturbing, and wondered whether that unease was just Anglo-Saxon prudishness.

Gennaro was looking at her. 'But you,' he said. 'You like this life.' He gestured around, fork in hand. 'The *paese?* You can share this with me.' It was said in a matter-of-fact tone, and he returned to eating. But Rose gaped, trying to work out what he meant. She fervently hoped that it had been an expression of – what? Community? Friendship? But with a sinking heart she suspected that it had been a proposal, and she had not the faintest idea of how to respond.

'Yes, of course,' she said, improvising wildly. 'I love the countryside. But I'm sure it's not just me, is it? There must be plenty of people to – share it with.' She flashed a quick smile at Gennaro, who was looking at her with an air, she thought, of quiet amusement, as though he was biding his time. Rose changed tack.

'And what about your mother?' she ventured.

217

'My mother?' said Gennaro, frowning.

Realizing that there was a possibility Gennaro might mistake her interest in his mother, Rose hurried to clarify her question, and heard herself gabbling.

'She must love your house, being from the country herself?'

'Oh, well,' said Gennaro, then paused, laying down his fork and standing to clear the plates. Rose made as if to help him but he held up a palm to stop her. He sighed. 'She doesn't come here.' He stopped again. 'My mother is too old,' he said with reluctance, the plates in his hands. 'She has – a neurological complaint. She can't walk far, and anyway she likes to stay put. She lives on this side of Genova; she didn't want to move there but it's easier – the hospital, doctors. And she's in an apartment block, so if anything happens there are people nearby ...' Rose had the impression he was rehearsing an argument for his own benefit, rather than hers. 'I visit now and then. Birthdays, and so on.' He fell silent.

Rose could see Gennaro in a suit and tie on the Genova platform on the way to visit his mother. She looked up at him; he was frowning a little, his mouth set with resignation, and she imagined a difficult relationship, guilt, perhaps, at leaving his mother alone. It occurred to her that all that familial closeness for which Italy was praised might be a mixed blessing, and, glad to be putting some distance between herself and Gennaro's proposal, smiled sympathetically.

'Well,' she said, 'it's hard, isn't it? My mother always complains she never sees me, but when I visit –' she spread her hands in a helpless gesture – 'she does nothing but grumble about all the trouble she's had to go to.'

Gennaro smiled a little, but his eyes were distant, and she didn't get the impression he was listening to what she said.

'Are you sure I can't help you?' she said, to change the subject. 'With the washing up?' Gennaro gazed at her blankly for a moment, then seemed to recollect himself and shook his head.

They had coffee after that, in a silence Rose tried to think of as companionable. Perhaps, after all, this was all he wanted; someone to sit with over coffee in this shuttered room, among the china and the lace. But when it got to ten o'clock she almost leaped to her feet.

'What a lovely evening,' she said.

'Ah,' said Gennaro. 'Thank you.' He nodded a little formally and she hurried on in an attempt to disguise the sudden eagerness to be gone that she felt almost overcome her.

'Your food – your pesto, it was wonderful. I'm so glad –' Rose hesitated, wondering how she might finish the sentence. What was she glad about, exactly? That Gennaro had confided in her? He'd hardly done that.

'I'm so glad you invited me,' she ended lamely. *I should invite him back*, she thought, but she said nothing.

Gennaro led her to his front door and unbolted it, letting her out. Rose felt a heavy, warm drop of rain on her cheek and remembered Gennaro had predicted it. She hoped he wouldn't notice; suddenly she knew she didn't want him to insist she shelter in the house until it was over, nor did she think she could even tolerate the delay necessary for him to fetch her an umbrella. 'Thank you,' she said breathlessly, pecked him hastily on the cheek, and ran.

It wasn't until she was halfway down the village that Rose realized she was still holding her breath and stopped, put out a hand to steady herself against a wall hung with jasmine. She leaned gratefully against the warm stone in the dense, scented darkness and exhaled at last, lungs burning, but even when she had recovered her breath she couldn't escape the feeling that she owed Gennaro something now.

They were gone, at last, they were gone. Elvira's cheeks burned as though she had a fever, her hair was lank, but she felt fiercely, exuberantly alive for once, and determined. Even the fact that if they could see her they would feel quite confirmed in their belief that she was losing her mind didn't lessen her euphoria as she sat, her back against the door of her dressing room and a bottle of cognac between her knees.

It had only taken lunch for her to realize that once she started to really listen to what was going on around her, straight away things began to fall into place.

Elvira had barely sipped at her wine once a new glass had been brought, saying in excuse that she still felt a little queasy. It didn't taste as though it had been tampered with, but she didn't want to take any risks and besides, she did still feel delicate. As her suspicions unfolded and became real to her, she was only now beginning to understand how momentous their implications might be. Her marriage, it seemed to her, was over, but she was not yet free of it, and she had to be very, very careful. She could see now how people perceived her, and how little credibility remained to her; at the table she had sat very still, and listened.

'So,' Annabel had said to Jack as they sat on Piero's terrace, 'Nick's serious, is he then? What a marvellous opportunity for you.' She sounded as though she was suppressing a laugh. They had finished eating, and the table was a tangle of crumpled napkins and smeared glasses. Annabel had had her spritzer, and another, they had just ordered limoncello and Annabel was letting go.

Elvira had been concentrating on the horizon, but she was listening. As she gazed at the water foaming white at the foot of the distant cliff she felt as though her hearing had been sharpened and in Annabel's languid voice she detected discontent, malice and clear insinuation. *Nick*, she thought, *Nick* . . . what about Nick? He was Jack's business partner; they'd set up the gallery together. Most of the money had come from Nick; Jack was supposed to bring the expertise, the front-man charm.

He wanted it back, was what Annabel meant; he wanted his money back, and Jack to buy him out. Elvira thought back to the last time she'd seen Nick, what, a year ago? And she hadn't wondered why he didn't come around any more, had she? It nagged at her that she hadn't noticed. What had she been doing for the last year, two years? Taking her pills, a bit of shopping, drinking coffee, waiting for summer to come. Sleeping her life away. Now she came to think of it, Jack might even have mentioned something about Nick here and there, without urgency of course. Dropped the odd hint, preparing her. A lamb to the slaughter.

She could also hear Annabel's unspoken question. *How do you think you're going to lay your hands on a million and a half sterling?* This could bankrupt him. She could see, now, that Jack had asked the two of them out here in the hope that Luke, with all his City money, would leap into the breach and come up with the cash, or some of it. Judging from Annabel's faintly derisive tone he would be turning Jack down, perhaps at this very moment as Jack was driving them to the airport, if he hadn't already. With friends like these . . . Still it nagged at her that she hadn't remembered Jack telling her they were coming. Had he really told her?

Elvira almost felt sorry for Jack. At any rate, she might have if she hadn't reached the conclusion that at least one of his reasons for wanting her doped to the eyeballs was to get his hands on her money, what was left of it. *Perhaps he wants me so gaga he can get power of attorney – or does he already have that?* Elvira realized with a flush of shame that she'd signed plenty of papers down the years and half the time with no very clear idea of what she was signing.

And then there was this place. Her beautiful house. She'd wondered why Luke had spent half the weekend going over the place like an estate agent, praising the views, commenting on the layout, how much the laws on building near the coast must have added to its value; at the time she'd put it down to vulgarity. But it occurred to her that it was just as likely Jack had implied, having made sure she was in no state to contradict him, that she was planning to sell, to offer Luke security on his investment. What else did Jack have to offer, after all? The stuccoed flat in South Kensington only had thirty years left to run on the lease and was mortgaged to the hilt anyway.

Elvira cradled the brandy bottle thoughtfully. Her mind was running ahead, like a ghost train in and out of tunnels, leaving skeletons rattling behind it. Perhaps Jack had been behind all that fuss last year, the flashing lights in the undergrowth over towards La Martinière, her panic about peeping toms and spying neighbours. To convince everyone she was losing it, or to turn Elvira against the place? *Never*, she thought. *Over my dead body.* But how could he have engineered that? She couldn't see Jack paying some local to spy on her.

Elvira set the bottle aside and got gingerly to her feet. Her ribs still ached from vomiting, her mouth was dry and she felt about a hundred years old. When had Jack left for the airport with Luke and Annabel? Their flight had been at eight, check-in an hour earlier, so they must have left around six. Elvira looked at her watch; it was now a quarter to seven. She had perhaps an hour, perhaps a little more, before Jack returned. Her first impulse was to go to the police. But after last year – and her heart sank at the memory, at the possibility that Jack had been setting her up for this even then – if she went without proper proof they'd dismiss her allegations out of hand. And if she went to the police and Jack found out – what might he do?

Elvira realized that she was afraid. The truth was, she didn't know what Jack was capable of, and it was her own fault. She'd spent most of their marriage alternately using him as her nurse-maid and indulging him, like a child, and don't spoilt children grow up to be monsters, eventually? The fear grew; Elvira felt it climbing in her throat, suffocating her, and she ran to the door and threw it open. She stood there on the threshold, at the centre of her own house, dizzy with panic. She badly wanted a drink now. *No*, she thought. *I've got an hour, I mustn't waste it.* She stepped out on to the landing.

At the top of the stairs Elvira hesitated, scanning the house in her mind, deciding where to start. The kitchen. She felt as light as air as she skimmed the stairs, down and down to the bottom of the house where the thick, warm darkness smelled of coffee. *Coffee.* She felt her way to the switch, and when the row of down-lighters sprang to life as though by magic, illuminating every surface brilliantly, they revealed a stack of cups in the sink. Elvira felt a bubble of triumph rise in her chest; of course, if Ania had been here they would have been washed and put away already. Which had been hers? Carefully she unstacked them, little heavy white cups; not that one, loaded with sugar, nor that one, with a tidemark of milky foam. There it was, the mark of her lipstick on the rim, and a coffeespoonful of gritty black dregs at the bottom. Elvira looked around, opened a cupboard at random and pushed the cup to the back, behind cans of tuna and coffee. She restacked the cups in the sink to cover her traces.

Seven-fifteen. Elvira barely glanced into the darkened drawing room before running back upstairs. Jack's dressing room, where a heavy brass standard lamp had been left on since this morning, illuminating the leather and wood with a warm glow. She registered the room's expensive fittings with a kind of disgust now, a disgust she realized was mostly for her own folly. On Jack's dressing table sat a leather cuff-box, the lid off and its contents half-spilled out on the polished wood. She sorted through them; studs and cufflinks, mother-of-pearl, gold, even a pair of novelty links shaped like racing cars a lovestruck girl from the gallery had given him. Nothing. Beside the cuff-box stood the camera still, and Elvira picked it up, hardly knowing why, and weighed it in her hand. She looked around the room.

Yesterday's jeans lay across the armchair but a quick trawl through Jack's pockets yielded nothing. Dimly she remembered that morning – or had it been afternoon? It seemed impossibly long ago now – when she'd last checked them, only for evidence then of infidelity. Elvira almost laughed; why had she cared? She thought of the Elvira who'd fretted about girls and nightclubs and gossips, and she experienced a strange kind of elation; she was free of all that now, even if it had been replaced by a larger fear. What had she found in his pockets, and what had she done with it? She had a muddled memory of a scrap of paper and something powdery on her fingertips, and looked around the room in an effort to remind herself.

Beneath the chair Elvira could see something white, a crumpled mass of fabric that seemed to have been kicked there, and she pulled it out. Her linen dressing gown. Had she left it there when they made love? The thought made her feel queasy, the thought of Jack's body in the bed with her, and the knowledge that her memory of that evening, like so many others, was in shreds. She set down the camera carefully, picked up the dressing gown and shook it out gently. Gingerly she felt the pocket: she could feel something like wadded paper and a gritty line of powder that had collected along the bottom. She tucked it under her arm and started on his cupboards.

At random Elvira pushed hangers aside and pulled out drawers; black silk socks, in pairs, expensive belts, monogrammed polo shirts. Delicately she pushed at the neat piles, trying not to disturb them, but only the scent of musk and cedar escaped from between the folds, expensively neutral. Then, in the bottom drawer, beneath a row of identical blue button-down shirts, she found a long leather box that rattled; it had a tiny brass keyhole, but no key.

Elvira took the box and carefully closed the drawer. Getting to her feet, she set about straightening the sweaters, the hanging suits, the ties and belts in the wardrobe that ran the length of one wall so that nothing looked out of place. Surveying the room one last time, she backed out, her haul clutched to her chest. Outside she heard the spray of gravel, the crunch of fat tyres in her drive. Silently she ran on bare feet across the landing and into her dressing room, pulling the door closed behind her and locking it just as she heard Jack's key turn in the front door below.

'Darling?' She heard his voice. 'Darling?'

The key, thought Elvira, her heart beating so hard she

thought it might come through her chest. If Jack saw that the dressing room was locked from the inside he would know straight away that she was in there. Would he bend down to look? In some part of her mind her behaviour seemed ridiculous, paranoid, but in another she felt saner than she had for years. Cautiously she knelt, turned and eased the little brass key towards her, every tiny scrape and rattle it made as it emerged sounding loud in her ears. *Done.* Jack climbed the stairs towards her.

Although it was a hot night Ania shivered; she couldn't get warm. She had crawled no more than fifty metres since she'd heard the sound that had made her think of gunfire. She'd gone uphill towards the houses out of some no doubt misguided instinct, at least partially hidden as she climbed, with painful slowness, by the shaggy, unpruned olive trees that scattered the terraces. Her dress was by now so dirty her camouflage was almost complete, but she felt like a vagrant; filthy and savage, and the sour smell of her unwashed body disgusted her.

By the time the light had begun to fail it had become clear to Ania that she was sick. She knew, in some distant, rational part of her brain, that she needed to find help, but the knowledge remained theoretical; her body would not cooperate. As she dragged herself onwards the landscape around her became something out of a dream, flat and gravelly underfoot, and then a digger stood in her way like a huge grazing animal, its scoop lowered to the ground. Ominously the hand itself no longer hurt at all, but it was swollen and shiny and she had seen livid red streaks beginning to track up her forearm, sending the poison crawling around her body. Ania's legs felt like lead, her muscles ached, and when out of the dusk the low shape of some half-ruined farm building appeared in front of her it was all she could do to shuffle inside and collapse.

When she woke out of a feverish half-sleep she had no idea of the time, nor even of where she was; she only knew that she was cold. The stars glittered overhead, cold and hard they seemed to her. Her cheeks burned, and she touched a hand to her face in a daze, surprised that she could be giving out so much heat when she felt cold to her bones. Her teeth rattled in her head, and in the distance she heard an answering rattle; a train, clattering through the night on its tracks beside the sea. She lay there in the dark, thought of the rails silver in the moonlight, a ghostly crowd on the platform. She saw a face coming out at her from the darkness, a face that appeared, smiling, beneath the archway at the entrance to the station and offered her a lift. Far off she heard a hoarse whistle as the train entered a tunnel, and as the fever rose Ania's body began to shake.

Chapter Twenty-Two

It was too hot to sleep; even at five in the morning the temperature had begun its inexorable upward creep. Cirri wished they'd put in air-conditioning, as Gloria's father had suggested. He gazed at the ceiling and imagined a fan there, something to create a breeze, even a warm breeze; anything would be better than this stifling blanket of stale air. But there were no fans left in the whole of Italy, it seemed, or even Europe, after such a summer. The temperature just kept on rising, and all the old wives' tales about rain on the feast of San Giovanni or some such seemed to have lost all currency. Cirri wondered what was happening to the world.

Beside him Gloria slept peacefully, a light sheen of sweat on her upper lip but otherwise quiet as a baby. If babies *were* quiet, which in Cirri's experience they hardly ever were. Certainly not the one lying next door in her cot, that great expensive pink monstrosity festooned with bumpers and friezes and mobiles and furry animals. Chiara had finally settled, he estimated, at about three-thirty, and now her father could hear her hoarse, snuffling little snore, regular as a heartbeat, occasionally punctuated by a small, shuddering gasp. Perhaps this is what fatherhood is, Cirri thought as he watched the thin grey light of dawn begin to show through the slats in the shutters. Lying awake and restless and listening to them sleep, watching for harm, fretting about the future, global warming, murderers on trains.

Cirri turned his head to the bedside table and squinted at the alarm clock. Five forty-two glowed green back at him. Decisively he sat up and swung his legs off the bed. The barman – what was his name, Nannini? – started his shift at six-thirty.

Cirri stood in the doorway and inhaled deeply in the gloom; even in a dingy railway café he loved that smell, the smell of early morning. The hopper full of coffee beans, the big Gaggia hissing steam, flakes of sweet pastry on the counter. Cigarette smoke. The place was empty except for a man in a clean white shirt through which a string vest was clearly visible, restocking the sweets on a stand in front of the till, his back to Cirri. Nannini. He was on the short side, muscular, and with tight-curled black hair. Cirri remembered he'd been in Campania for the weekend, and even from this angle he looked like a southerner. Cirri cleared his throat, and the man turned.

'Commissario,' he said, taking in Cirri's appearance through narrowed eyes. Cirri wondered how the man knew who he was; he was faintly disappointed that he was so obviously a policeman, even out of uniform. It occurred to him that the barmaid – Giovanna? – had called the man in Campania to say to expect him. Cirri nodded.

229

'Alberto Nannini,' he said, although he needed no confirmation.

'Yes.' The man seemed tense; the sound of one's full name recited by a policeman, Cirri found, often had that effect. 'It's about Tuesday night?'

'The last train through from Genova.' A piercing hoot sounded outside, and the gloom in the room intensified as the 6.43 hissed to a halt on the platform, blocking out the light.

'Yes,' Nannini said again, fiddling with the shrink-wrap on a big carton of chewing gum. He didn't meet Cirri's eye. 'I, ah, yes, I think I left before that train came in. The last train.'

'Mmm,' said Cirri thoughtfully. Yes. That's what the barmaid – what's her name, Giovanna? – said. I wanted to check.'

Nannini looked up at him now, perhaps thinking he'd been convincing enough to risk it, and Cirri held his gaze.

'Well,' said Nannini, with a hint of defiance. 'She was right. So that's it?'

Cirri smiled, changed tack. 'Giovanna – she seems like a nervous type.'

Nannini shrugged. 'You could say that,' he said. 'Yes, a bit. She's all right, though. Knows her job.'

Cirri persisted. 'But you left her on her own to lock up? With a load of Albanesi playing cards in the bar she couldn't shift?' He watched the barman; Nannini looked uncomfortable now.

'Well, I – I might have hung around normally, but I was – I had to get home. My mother's been suffering in this heat.'

Cirri sighed. 'Look,' he said, 'you know what this is about, don't you? You know it's about finding the murderer of a young girl, shoved off the train no more than half a kilometre from here? We're not talking about a bit of pickpocketing, this

230

isn't a tourist complaining about having her bottom pinched. It's important. And –'

Cirri paused. He had Nannini's full attention now. 'And if this is something to do with Giovanna's husband, or whatever – if you and she – if he doesn't like you working together –' Nannini opened his mouth to protest and Cirri held up his hands. 'For whatever reason, I mean I'm sure it's unfounded, whatever he might think. But in any case we could take steps to make sure he isn't involved. That he doesn't find out.'

Nannini looked at him a moment, then shrugged. 'She gets worked up about it, that bloody husband of hers is a pig. I mean –' and he rolled his eyes – 'it's not like there's anything going on. Just because he caught me pinching her arse while she was locking up one night. I mean, it was a joke.' He snorted incredulously, and Cirri nodded, trying to look sympathetic but beginning to feeling sorry for poor, plain, jittery Giovanna.

'Anyway.' Nannini sighed. 'I did see a few passengers get off that train, if it's any good to you.'

'Yes?' said Cirri neutrally. He didn't want to put the man off.

Nannini cleared his throat, looking over Cirri's shoulder at the door. 'We were locking up; I was at the platform side when the train came in. It was dark, but – I recognized a couple of lads – Ernesto and Fausto, from the Love Shack. I saw them heading off together.'

Cirri nodded; the Love Shack was one of the beach bars and he knew the boys. Not them, not the quintessential *paninari*, only interested in looking good in their beach shorts. And gay. Hardly the psychological profile they were after. 'Anyone else?'

'Yeah, yeah. I've been thinking – trying to remember, you

know, thinking about that girl.' The barman paused again. 'And there might have been a couple more got off. But I was in a hurry; there was some kind of argy-bargy going on in the bar, I could see Giovanna needed a bit of help. All I can be sure of is, I saw the English guy married to the Contessa, he walked past me – I was kneeling down to do the bottom lock and I saw these English shoes – you know how they make them? Stitched brogues, you know, English style, so I looked up.'

Cirri nodded, refrained from mentioning how this differed from the barman's earlier version of events; he was too interested in hearing what he had to say.

'You looked at him? Saw his face? Jack Robbins?'

'Yes,' said Nannini and he seemed quite confident now, had started restacking the shelves as he spoke. 'Looked pretty pleased with himself, as a matter of fact.'

'Thanks,' said Cirri, his mind racing ahead. Robbins, in his big car. What was he doing taking the train? And then – there was Robbins' maid, gone missing after he'd dropped her at the station. Robbins, here every summer, here last summer when the prostitute was killed. 'That's great.'

'That's all?' said Nannini, wary. When Cirri said nothing he ran on, his voice picking up with relief, 'I mean, is that okay? Will you need me to – what d'you call it, testify?'

But Cirri was hardly listening to the man, thinking furiously. *Robbins*, he thought, triumphant, *with your big hairdresser's car. What else would you be doing, slumming it on a train? Jack Robbins.*

By the time he reached the police station Cirri needed a shower; he changed into his uniform in the cramped bathroom at the back of the building. Toto was already at his desk, and on Cirri's lay a toxicology report on Anna-Maria Villemartin.

232

A small amount of alcohol had been in the girl's system, but there was no evidence of drug use of any kind. Interesting, thought Cirri. He'd somehow assumed that she might have been an occasional cannabis user, say; he'd had a vague idea that if the argument with her mother that had led her to storm off without her dinner hadn't been to do with sex, it might have been to do with drug-taking. There were drugs these days, of course, that left no trace, like Rohypnol, the date-rape drug; the screen didn't rule out that she'd been drugged by her killer. But recreational drugs would have shown up. So she was a good girl, after all. Straight. So what had the row been about? He put the report to one side. Underneath it was another piece of paper, a computer printout on thin paper, holes on either side; a list of names, hundreds of them, and dates. Some medical-looking abbreviations. He frowned. 'Toto? What's this?'

Toto appeared in the doorway, looking pleased with himself.

'You found it, then?' he said.

Cirri shook the pages at him in exasperation. 'I can't make head nor tail of it, though. What is it?'

'You know you said, go ahead, try to make a link between the Villemartin girl and the other one, Bosnic, the prostitute? Last Ferragosto?' Slowly Cirri nodded, scanning the page.

'They were both patients at the San Giovanni clinic.'

'The what?'

'Contraception. Women's stuff, gynaecology. Attached to the hospital of San Giovanni e Paolo,' Toto leaned over his shoulder, ran his finger down the scrolled pages until he reached first one highlighted name, then another.

'So what? It's not a VD clinic, is it? So they both used

233

contraception. It's hardly surprising.' The place was above board; a clinic attached to a state hospital, a place Gloria might attend. Or Chiara. Cirri wasn't quite comfortable with this conversation; women's stuff.

'They both had terminations. Abortions. See – Bosnic last year, Villemartin this year.'

Toto jabbed at the paper, triumphant, but Cirri felt brought down by the information, depressed once again. This case. Whatever the uses of abortion, he did not want to think of Anna-Maria Villemartin in that situation. He supposed he should feel the same about the Bosnic woman, but that hadn't been his investigation. He hadn't met her mother. He thought again of the woman sitting, tormented with grief and regret, in the darkened *salotto* among the portraits of her daughter. It came to him with a kind of glum certainty that this must have been the cause of their argument.

Sensing Toto standing expectantly by his side, Cirri struggled to regain some kind of professional distance, to look at the facts.

'Well,' he said. 'I suppose … I suppose it's a link. Some crazed anti-abortionist? They usually go for the doctors, don't they? Or could the same man have got them both pregnant?' It seemed hard to believe. Where would two such different girls find themselves seduced by the same man? At the MonteCarla? Cirri tried to link this information to Jack Robbins, and failed. The San Giovanni clinic seemed to him to be a red herring.

'Sorry, Toto,' he said. 'Look at all these women. Plenty of girls have – terminations. It might figure, but I can't see it, somehow.'

Toto looked crestfallen. 'Let me hang on to these, though,' said Cirri, relenting. 'You never know.' To placate Toto he

234

wrestled the printout into some sort of order and set it down with the toxicology report. Get back to first principles, he thought.

'What about the wire?' he said, musing. 'The stuff he used? Was it fishing line?'

Toto nodded. 'They've sent it off for DNA analysis. Expensive stuff, apparently,' he said. 'Could haul a half-ton shark in with that stuff.'

'Right,' said Cirri absently. *Shark-fishing*, he thought, as Toto turned to leave. *Off the back of one of those big motor-yachts out of Portofino.* That sounded like Robbins, all right.

The builders were back at eight; Rose could hear them long before they turned up on her terrace; large, loud and cheerful, they seemed to fill the village. She heard them come around the side of the house and when they waved to her from the terrace she offered them a coffee. Nervously she filled her pot, knowing how particular even builders were about their espresso.

As he knocked his cup back the foreman told her that today they would begin work dismantling the pigsty and cleaning up the old bricks for re-use. He spoke deliberately slowly, with pantomime hand gestures, and Rose wondered despairingly if she would ever come to be treated as anything other than a simple-minded foreigner. But she listened patiently with half an ear, while wondering what she should wear to interview Elvira Vitale, how she could get up to the house on the cliff without arriving in a sweat on a day like this. She tried not to wonder whether Richard Bourn was going to call.

Giunti had stopped talking and was looking at her as though waiting for an answer. 'Okay,' she said. 'Fine. Whatever.'

It took her half an hour to get down to a shortlist of linen

235

suit, two years old and looking a little past it, a sleeveless silk dress she'd spent too much money on last summer and had never worn, and a black number. How much could it matter, after all, what she wore? She put on the silk; it was comfortable and cool, even if when she looked in the mirror she hardly recognized herself, she looked so – feminine. She heard a shout from outside and went to the window.

The builder was standing on the terrace, and next to him was Richard Bourn, looking up at her. Feeling her heart jump, Rose ran down the stairs, three at a time, and had to make an effort to slow herself before she reached the kitchen door. He was standing at a polite distance from the threshold and looked tense, his shoulders square, hands jammed into his pockets.

'Sorry,' he said. 'I know it's early.'

'Oh – doesn't matter,' said Rose calmly but she felt her breath fluttering in her throat. 'How did you find the house?'

Richard shrugged. 'Followed the sound of the builders,' he said, and the tension in his shoulders seemed to relax a fraction. 'You said you were having work done.'

Had she? Rose couldn't remember. At any rate since Richard's arrival the builders seemed to have stopped work to look at what was going on. They hadn't even pretended to start dismantling the pigsty but were leaning casually against the concrete mixer, waiting to see what would happen next. Rose caught the foreman looking her up and down in her pretty dress and felt her cheeks begin to burn with a blush.

'But why – do you want to – oh, come in,' she said, flustered, and backed into the kitchen, just to stop them all staring. Richard followed, ducking his head to get through the door. The room seemed dark and small suddenly with the two of them in there, and she pushed open the shutters.

'Pretty house,' said Richard, looking around vaguely at the soft limewashed walls, the terracotta floor.

'Thanks,' said Rose, wondering what he was doing here. 'Would you like some coffee?'

Richard shook his head. 'No,' he said, 'thanks. I know you're busy. You're seeing Elvira Vitale this morning?'

Rose frowned, bemused that he'd registered her timetable so precisely. Yes,' she said, slowly. 'Eleven-thirty.'

'I can give you a lift,' said Richard, with the air of a man grasping at straws.

'Thanks,' said Rose, still unsure. 'Is that why you came?' Outside she heard the stutter of an engine as the mini-digger started up, the grind of gears.

Richard sighed. 'No,' he said. 'No. I came because I wanted to tell you something. I haven't been quite straight with you.'

Here it comes, thought Rose with resignation. *Still in love with his wife. In love with someone else.* She tried not to follow this line of thought, to look at him with nothing more than sisterly surprise. Why should she be upset, after all? It wasn't as if she'd had expectations. 'Really?' she said, raising her eyebrows. Richard sat down at the table and sank his face into his hands. His shoulders sagged and he rubbed his eyes wearily.

'I told you I didn't know them – Jack Robbins and his wife. But I do.' He stopped, looked down at his hands on the table.

Rose didn't understand. 'You do?' Why would he lie about knowing Jack Robbins? Even though the lie seemed to make no sense the thought that she had been deceived deflated her, made her feel obscurely let down. There was some story going on here she knew nothing about.

Richard Bourn looked up at her, and when he spoke this time his voice was so low she could hardly hear what he said.

'In a way. We haven't been introduced. But Jack Robbins killed my wife.'

Rose's first thought was that this must be a delusion. She stared at Richard Bourn; he was looking up at her intently, something desperate and fanatical in his blue-eyed gaze, and it occurred to Rose that she barely knew him. She wondered if he was mad. He had seemed so sane, so practical. She thought of those men who murder their children out of jealousy, bludgeon imagined rivals to death in their curtained houses – businessmen, family men, pillars of the community. Was it grief?

'Don't be stupid,' she said sharply. 'What do you mean?'

'She – Gemma, my wife, ex-wife – was having an affair with him,' said Richard. 'Not while we were married. At least,' he paused, frowning as though the thought had only just occurred to him, 'at least, I don't think so.' He stopped, white-faced. 'No,' he said hoarsely. 'She began it after she'd left me.'

There was something in Richard's voice that persuaded Rose that this, at least, was true. 'Go on,' she said, cautiously.

He sighed. 'He didn't understand her. Gemma was very – vulnerable. She was a romantic, you see, never did things by halves.' He sounded very sad. 'That's why she left me, I suppose – why she wouldn't put up with me spending most of our life at work.' Richard paused, musing almost to himself, and Rose knew that he was wondering why none of this had occurred to him at the time, when it might have saved their marriage. Knew that feeling.

Richard sighed again, a great, heavy sigh. 'I suppose he – Jack Robbins,' he pronounced the name with distaste, 'I suppose he might have been what she wanted, after me. He likes the big romantic gesture, by all accounts. Lives a – colourful sort of life.'

Rose thought about Jack Robbins with his slick black fringe and white smile, and Elvira Vitale beside him at the bar of the Mare Blu, weary and beautiful. *Creep*, she thought. 'So she wasn't married,' she said, slowly. 'But he was.'

Richard leaned forward, looking at her properly across the kitchen table. Outside the uneven roar of the digger's engine came through the window, coming and going as it bumped across the hill. 'Yes,' he said. 'You see, that's it.'

Rose nodded. 'Go on,' she said, beginning to see. Beginning to believe him.

'I had a drink with her, oh, six months after she'd gone. I wanted to make sure she was all right, you see. On her own. I met her in a bar in Piccadilly, some private place she suggested. Maybe he'd taken her there; it wasn't the kind of place I thought she'd have liked. Full of rich Europeans. French bankers drinking after work.' He frowned as if the memory was troubling.

Rose imagined him in such a place, ill at ease. Out of his element. 'And was she? All right?'

'No,' he said. 'Not really. Not that – I didn't have any illusions she was unhappy, wanted to come back to me. I knew it was over. She was actually very – full of life, plans, you know. Vivacious. But she was drinking a lot, and when she told me about him, I knew it was all wrong.'

'But you would have thought that anyway, wouldn't you? Whoever she was with?'

Richard shrugged a little, frowning. 'I – probably I wouldn't have been happy about her finding someone else. But she – it was as though she was losing control. No one was looking after her. She told me all these stories about the places he'd taken her, a weekend in Paris, restaurants, little hotel by the sea. But you could tell, in between she was on her own, flailing about, nothing to do. And as you say, he was married. Is married. I don't think that would have been enough for her, in the long run, having half, less than half of someone. Even half a decent bloke wouldn't have been enough, let alone someone like him. I mean, we wanted – I thought she wanted kids. And she said to me that night, it's not a real marriage; she's an old woman, losing her grip. He's going to leave her.'

Rose felt her stomach turn over at the knowledge that in not much more than an hour she'd be walking up Jack Robbins' drive, with all this information ticking away in her head like a time bomb. She stood up and took a step away from the table. She had to get it straight.

'So how – what do you think happened?'

Richard reached up and took her hand, stopping her as she paced. 'I'm sorry,' he said. 'I'm sorry you have to listen to all this.'

Rose looked at him, but she could only see the picture of his dead wife that had appeared on her computer screen, dark-eyed and melancholy. She shook her head impatiently. 'I just want to know,' she said. 'Did you want – did you want me to get to him? Is that why you came up here, took me to lunch, all that?'

'No,' said Richard. 'I mean, once I knew you were after them, I didn't want you to think – I didn't know. I didn't know what I wanted, so I pretended I knew nothing about them, Robbins and his wife. I suppose I did think I might find something out through you, but I hadn't, you know, got a plan.' He paused, uncomfortable. 'This – it isn't like me, all this. All this – emotion. Acting on impulse. When I first saw you, on the train – well – I had no idea then, I just –'

'All right,' said Rose, and she felt a spark of relief as she realized it was true, remembering the train. 'So what happened to her? To Gemma? That night?'

Richard looked at her searchingly, then sighed. 'She'd been drinking with him. It didn't come out at the inquest, I don't know how he managed that, although I suppose discretion's part of the deal at those private clubs. But when I went back there and paid a few people, one or two of them admitted it. There was a barman, he didn't seem to like Robbins much. He said Gemma wasn't Robbins' usual type; he said she seemed too old for him.' Richard's mouth turned down in anger. 'But he remembered that night, the barman; he said she had been very agitated. Upset. And he was pretty sure she had drunk most of a bottle of champagne, with Robbins sitting there pretending to drink with her. He knew *that* type, he said.'

'She was upset?' Rose felt her interest flare, her sympathy catch and turn to the pretty, dark-eyed woman she'd seen in the newspaper report on her death, drinking champagne in a seedy club with Jack Robbins. Poor cow.

'Angry. I suppose they could have had an argument about anything, but he wasn't going to leave his wife, after all, was he? You and I could have told her that, couldn't we?'

'So he fed her champagne and let her drive home?'

'At least. But another thing the barman told me was that Jack Robbins had a bit of a reputation. For slipping things into girls' drinks, some kind of sedative, I suppose, I don't know. There's a thing called Rohypnol? A girl once passed right out at a table with him, so the barman said, caused a bit of a stir, and he'd been spoken to about it by the membership committee.' Richard's voice was rich with contempt.

Jack Robbins, thought Rose. Spiking girls' drinks. Because he was a – a pervert, who liked women out cold? Vicious? Or perhaps he was just lazy, and couldn't be bothered to go through a routine any more. Cut to the chase. Suddenly she felt depressed, sickened; to her it was all of a piece with the girl murdered on the train from Genova by some psychopath, thrown off like a piece of rubbish, disposable to the likes of Jack Robbins. And of course, she knew with sudden clarity, he'd never get caught, not for this. She felt an access of sympathy for Richard.

'But the police found out none of this? There were no tests for drugs?'

'They tested her. Rohypnol doesn't show up,' said Richard flatly. And the police didn't like me much, always going in there shouting the odds. They gave me the brush-off; it wasn't as though we were still married.' Rose imagined Richard storming into the police station, raging at them. He went on. 'I think,' he frowned, 'I think they thought it was my fault, you know? As if *I'd* left *her*.' *No*, thought Rose. *But you think it was your fault, don't you?* His hands were still on the table between them, clenching convulsively, and she took them gently between hers.

'Did you follow them here, then? Jack Robbins and his wife? Do you – keep an eye on them?'

Richard nodded. 'I wanted to be sure. For myself, you know? Gemma's dead, it's too late to get her back. But I wanted to know I was right about him and maybe, who knows, catch him at it. I even bought a telescope.' He laughed miserably, looked down at the table, and suddenly he seemed very tired. Gently Rose let his hands go.

At that moment the rumble of machinery from beyond the open window fell abruptly silent, as if to allow the pathetic facts of Richard's story to resonate in the dim room, but before either of them had a chance to speak there came a volley of shouts from outside. Rose jumped up and went to the door.

The men were gathered around the pigsty, looking down at something. As Rose approached, she was aware of Richard following behind, but she didn't turn to look at him and she was glad of the diversion, her mind humming with what he had said. Then she saw what they were all looking at, and she stopped in her tracks.

Two of the men, the young plasterer and the beer-bellied older one who'd been operating the digger, stood on either side of a young woman, covered in brick dust and contorted in a frantic struggle to free herself from their restraining arms. She was making a high-pitched yelping noise, like an animal, and for a moment she did seem to Rose to be barely human.

'Wait,' Rose said impulsively. 'Don't hurt her.' At the sound of her voice the woman stopped her noise with a kind of choked sob, her knees sagged and she would have fallen to the ground if the men hadn't still been holding her by the elbows. They lowered her to the grass, but kept hold of her. Rose turned to Richard.

'Could you get some water?' she asked gently. 'A bucket, under the sink, to wash this off.' She indicated the powdery dust that streaked the girl's face and clothes. 'I think she might be hurt.' The men instinctively stepped back a little to give her some space, and Rose knelt beside the girl, crumpled on the ground, and took her hand. It felt very hot. When Richard came back with the water she dabbed at the girl's face and was shocked by what she saw. There was bruising around her neck and her face was puffy and discoloured, her eyes slitted by the swelling around them. The bruises were yellowish and well advanced, and Rose wondered how long they'd been there. And who was responsible for them.

'What happened?' she asked in Italian, peering into the girl's face. 'Do you understand? Can you hear me?' The girl looked at her through dull eyes, the cracked lips moved and she mumbled something Rose couldn't decipher, a jumble of slurred foreign consonants. Then Rose sensed rather than saw one of the workmen, the young, sweet-faced one, move nearer until he was standing at her shoulder, and she looked up. Out of the corner of her eye she saw faces further off, Tiziana on her terrace, her hands in her apron, Gennaro coming up from his vines below, doggedly climbing the hillside towards them. He raised his head and looked up, his gaze slid over them and Rose saw him pause for a moment before resuming his climb. She looked back at the plasterer.

'Romanian,' the boy said hesitantly. 'She's speaking Romanian.' There was tenderness in his voice. He knelt beside them and said something to the girl in a language Rose didn't understand and suddenly the girl began to sob weakly, like an exhausted child. Rose took her hand again to soothe her and the girl pulled feebly away and wailed, a thin sound.

Frowning, Rose took her cloth and dabbed at the skin. The hand was shiny and swollen and the swelling extended up to the elbow. As the dirt came off she could see that it was nastily mottled with red and at the wrist a piece of blue nylon rope cut into the puffed flesh. Rose turned and looked up at Richard; she saw that he had seen the rope too.

'What's this?' she said slowly, putting out a hand to the rope, looking once again at the girl's torn clothes, the bruising on her face, seeing other, terrible marks on her bare, dirty legs. 'Someone's done this to her.' She looked distractedly around at the soft green hills, the bright sky, and she saw Tiziana still standing there with her hands in the apron as though frozen to the spot. Richard knelt beside Rose, the plasterer on her other side, and the girl looked from one face to another, scrabbling upright, trying to see beyond them.

'Ask her what happened,' said Richard to the plasterer. 'You're Romanian too, aren't you?' The boy nodded, looking alarmed. Richard held up a hand to reassure him. 'It's okay,' he said. 'No one's going to turn you in if you haven't got a *permesso di soggiorno*.' The boy turned back to the girl and hesitantly asked his question again and this time she reached blindly towards him, taking hold of his arm with her good hand. She spoke to him insistently through dry lips, whispering the same sentence over and over again.

The plasterer looked back at them and shrugged helplessly. 'She doesn't make sense. She says her father is coming to take her home, that's all. I think it must be the fever.' Rose looked from his face to the girl's and saw that she was trembling a little now, as though a pulse was passing through her again and again. Rose made a decision.

'I think it's infected,' she said to Richard more briskly than she felt, nodding at the swollen hand. 'Shouldn't we get her to the hospital? And then I think – we've got to tell the police about this.' At the sound of the word, even in English, the workmen began to shift uneasily, and the little circle around Rose, Richard and the supine girl began to melt away. The plasterer disappeared into the truck, the builder following, the fat one busying himself suddenly with his bag of tools. Exasperated, Rose looked up at Richard who was still standing there beside her.

'Hell,' she said. 'And I've got to be at Elvira Vitale's in less than an hour.' She looked at him helplessly, not knowing what to do. Gennaro? she wondered, thinking of his strength and practicality, his little van. Could she ask him to help? But looking across the hillside to where she'd seen him walking up towards them she could see no trace of the wiry figure; he must have walked straight past them without pausing, on up to his house.

'Come on,' said Richard. And with one quick movement, apparently oblivious to the filth and blood, he bent and picked the girl up as though she weighed no more than a bag of washing.

In the stale, humid atmosphere of her dressing room, Elvira was waiting for Rose Fell to arrive. On the thick, pale carpet she assembled her hoard for the last time and for a split second as she looked at the random pile it seemed like evidence only of her own folly, junk collected by a deranged bag lady. She closed her eyes, wiped the image, and went on transferring it all to a carrier bag.

The polished leather box, scratched now and its tiny brass lock forced open crudely with Elvira's nail file, the pale suede interior containing two small hypodermic syringes in sealed cellophane and a blister pack of small blue, triangular pills. A napkin stained and stiff with spilled wine, a folded receipt containing some grains of white powder. Her empty pill bottles. Unease stirred as she placed each bottle in the bag; *it's not like this is cyanide, is it?* But she knew there was something in it, all the same, she wasn't this afraid for nothing. With trembling fingers she resumed her task.

A scrap of paper; Elvira unrolled the crumpled train ticket

she'd found in his pocket, how many days ago? The date, time and destination were still visible where it had been stamped: 0.28, 14 August. The date leaped out at her: the night the girl was killed. Elvira thought of the night train out of Genova; grubby, smoke-filled, low-life in the corridors eyeing up anyone who passed. Poor families on their way south to see relatives for the holiday. It was a long time since Elvira had been on any train, but that one she remembered.

Jack had been on the train that night. *Of course, that didn't mean* – Elvira knew he sometimes took the train in and out of Genova, for reasons, she realized, she had allowed to remain obscure to her. But that particular train? As the possibility sank in that this might not just be about her, Elvira leaned back against the panelled wall. *Of course for all I know, Jack could be capable of that*, she thought dully. *I've been out of it, after all, haven't I? All I could think of was that he might be sleeping with them, but of course it could be worse. Much worse.*

Elvira gazed sightlessly at her ranked clothes as they hung there, motionless, inhuman. The colours and textures no longer comforted her, the scent of old perfume and furs was cloying, choking her. She could taste bitterness on her tongue as though decades of toxins were rising to the surface, manifesting themselves in every membrane of her body, and she wished she'd thought to bring a bottle of water in with her. On the dressing table her faithful little clock ticked the time away stolidly, and Elvira thought of the hours she'd spent in here preparing, over the years, the little clock reminding her of what she had to do next. Time to get dressed for dinner, time for a drink, time for a little sleeping pill. She got to her feet. *Time to get ready.*

At the beginning, when Jack had got back from the airport

to what he thought was an empty house, she had heard him moving from room to room, his soft, measured step heading into her bedroom, and calling her name in that cautious way people have when they expect no answer, just checking the coast is clear. Then his dressing room; he spent some time in there, moving softly, picking something up, opening a drawer, considering. Her empty stomach turning over, she wondered then if he knew, and as she listened to his careful, meticulous movements a new Jack appeared to her out of the soft, padded darkness of her dressing room; one who took precautions, covered his tracks.

Elvira had heard him go downstairs after that, the heavy chunk of a tumbler filled with something in the drawing room, up again and out on to the terrace. She imagined the last of the light disappearing as he enjoyed the view, the dark blue sea. *This is my house*, she thought, and she had felt her anger rise at the thought that she was shut in here while Jack wandered at liberty from room to room, occupying her space. Elvira didn't banish the anger, she'd let it fill her with a kind of exhilaration that brought her to her feet, pacing the room. And then, of course, he'd heard her.

'Darling? Have you been in there all this time?' She'd heard his voice close up against the door, coaxing her. She heard wariness beneath his habitual breezy veneer. 'What on earth are you up to now?' She hadn't answered, and the door handle had rattled. An impatient exhalation.

'Come along, darling,' he said, and she heard the chink of ice in his glass. 'You can't stay in there for ever.'

Fear gripped Elvira. She thought of those wives, those mothers you read about, in denial when their husband, their son, is the one dragged out to the police car with a blanket over his head. *He'd never do a thing like that.*

When is she going to come? Eleven-thirty? Elvira gazed at the little clock as though it might save her. Eleven o'clock. She thought with longing of the warm sun outside, the sea.

I can't stay in here for ever.

Chapter Twenty-Three

'Look,' Richard said as they pulled up in front of the hospital, 'let me take you to the bottom of the road, at least. I can manage here.' Rose shook her head.

All the way down she'd been afraid the girl might try to leap out while they were moving, she had seemed in such a state. She had turned her matted head convulsively this way and that, looking over her shoulder as they left the village and peering down each slope as they wound down into Levanto. On one particularly tight bend she'd scrabbled to stay upright and had inadvertently taken hold of Rose's arm. Rose caught a whiff of her then; she smelled almost animal, pungent and wild, the smell of old sweat and earth and fear, something that had come in from the outside. She hadn't let go when the road had straightened, either, and even now held on with febrile tenacity.

'No,' said Rose, nudging open the door behind her, putting one arm around the girl's huddled shape to coax her out after her. 'Let's just get her sorted first.' She passed a hand over her forehead, smelled the girl on her. With weary resignation she went on, 'It's just an interview. I can be ten minutes late.'

Levanto's hospital was not Third World but not exactly impressive, either; a small complex of shabby modern buildings, their stucco cracked and greying, window-frames peeling. Rose's heart sank; she turned back and leaned down to the girl still inside the car. 'Come on,' she said gently. The girl sat motionless, framed by the car door, looking up at her with eyes that barely focused. Her mouth moved as though she was trying to say something.

Richard stepped past Rose, knelt and lifted the girl gently from the back seat and carried her in.

Inside, the hospital seemed down at heel, but clean. There was a long reception desk opposite them as they entered and behind it a middle-aged nurse stood, looking at them with fierce suspicion. She was a stocky woman dressed in a hospital green tunic, but above the uniform her make-up was impeccable, her hair gleaming and immaculate, gold earrings. Rose was taken aback; she had an idea such ornament was not allowed in hospital surroundings. It was allowed in Italy, obviously.

'She has a high fever,' she said, pointing to the girl in Richard's arms. She reached over and gingerly touched the girl's puffy forearm. 'An infection?'

The woman tutted exasperatedly and with impatience she called something over her shoulder. An unshaven orderly appeared around the corner with a trolley and an expression of ill-disguised truculence, and Richard gently lowered the girl on to it.

'We'll take her,' said the nurse briskly, making no effort

251

to moderate her Italian for foreigners. 'You have to go to *accettazione*. You have papers? *Codice fiscale?* If not, you must pay.' Rose's heart sank. She knew what that meant. An hour in a queue, then another explaining what had happened, filling in forms, applying for receipts, prescriptions, trying to remember tax codes and the number on her *permesso di soggiorno*. Bureaucracy. She looked up; above the nurse's head the hands on a large clock ticked loudly from eleven thirty-nine to eleven-forty. She closed her eyes in silent resignation, the interview with Elvira slipping through her fingers. She heard Richard's voice in her ear, his hand on her shoulder.

'Go on,' he said. 'I can manage all that. I'll go to the police after.'

Rose looked at him, thought of the girl's tight, hot grip. Could she leave this to him? She opened her mouth to protest but found she didn't want to; the girl was being wheeled away from them already, motionless beneath a clean white blanket.

'Go on,' Richard said again. 'If you hurry, there's a taxi rank outside, you'll only be half an hour late. Forty minutes at most. I'm sure she'll wait that long.'

The little clock's mother-of-pearl face told Elvira that it was eleven-forty. *She's not coming, is she?* As though she was ill, Elvira felt a light sweat bloom in the heat, on her back, her forehead, under her arms, and her stomach felt sour with fear. *What the hell do I do now?* Then, from outside the door, she heard a new sound. Not Jack's habitual soft, feline movements, padding about the house, never urgent, never hurried. She heard him run, up the stairs towards her, two, three steps at a time.

There was a thud, then a ripping, splitting sound of

splintering wood at the door. Horrified, Elvira scrabbled away from it; at the lock she could see the steel snout of a tool, a chisel working away at the lock, and Jack's voice, panting.

'I've had enough of this,' he said through the door and for a second Elvira heard anger turn his smooth voice ragged. She seized the plastic bag in one hand and with the other she reached for something, anything, to use against him. She took hold of the brandy bottle.

The lock didn't give; with a brief flare of pride Elvira remembered the carpenters and locksmiths from Genova who had done the work, their gravity and care. But Jack didn't give up; as he worked at it he pleaded with her, gasping with the effort, the rage put away. For the moment.

'You've been poisoning me,' she said. 'All that stuff you've been feeding me.' She heard a disbelieving laugh and steeled herself against him. 'And you were on that train,' she said suddenly, loudly, the words escaping her before she had time to think. She was shocked at her own boldness.

'What?' he said from behind the door, his voice shockingly close in the sudden silence. 'What are you talking about? You're mad.' Then with one last violent shove the chisel was through.

Now, she thought, and threw back the door in his face. Swinging wildly, she struck out at him with the bottle and felt it connect with a crack. When he just stood there swaying she didn't stop to find out if she'd killed him but dropped the bottle and made for the stairs. She took them two at a time and ran out of the front door with the bag in her hand.

Toto rang through at something like eleven, when Cirri was frowning down at the computer printout, his mind running

253

around in circles. Jack Robbins. He didn't want to believe that a decent girl would fall for a shit like him, would head home with him on a train; he'd formed quite a different impression of Anna-Maria Villemartin.

'*Un inglese*,' said Toto, and Cirri's heart sank. Not another one. Bloody foreigners.

'Apropos of what?' he said.

'He found some girl, had been beaten up; he's left her at the hospital. But he wants to tell you himself. He says it's important.'

Wearily Cirri passed a hand over his head. 'Give me a minute,' he said.

It was turning out to be a busy morning. Cirri rubbed his eyes and yawned, remembering he'd woken up at five, thinking longingly of his bed and Gloria's warm, soft body. Stiffly he rose from the desk with the computer printout from the abortion clinic in his hand, trying to make sense of the rows of numbers, the abbreviations. He couldn't get the image of the place out of his head, the San Giovanni clinic. He knew where it was, a beautiful old baroque building out on the eastern outskirts of Genova; what was the world coming to, the uses such places were turned to? A nice girl like Anna-Maria Villemartin sitting there on a hard bench with God knows who, waiting for her consultation, her 'termination'. She shouldn't have had to do it; she should have been protected. He walked slowly across the room, stopped beside the window where the morning light slanted through the shutters. *Un inglese*.

There was too much to think about; it was all happening too fast. Cirri had the uncomfortable feeling that his dislike of Robbins was interfering, somehow, with his ability to judge the facts. He should go and talk to him straight away, but he'd be happier if he had something more concrete. Cirri frowned at the printout from the clinic, a sour taste in his mouth from too much coffee, then something caught his eye amongst the jumble of letters and numbers. Another name. He didn't recognize the address, but he'd seen the name somewhere before. As he stared at the page there was a perfunctory knock and the door opened.

It was the Englishman who lived up on the hill, with the telescopes. Or not. Richard Bourn, Toto hovering behind him in the doorway. Cirri's head ached; he felt like sinking it into his hands, but he made an effort and gestured towards the chair across the desk. He shook his head at Toto's questioning glance.

Richard Bourn sat down without ceremony; he seemed tense but not nervous, had none of the anxious deference that usually afflicted those who occupied that chair. With a hint of impatience the Englishman waited for Toto to close the door behind him and leave them alone.

'Can I help you?' said Cirri, curious now, his headache ebbing. He didn't want to betray his intense interest in why Richard Bourn was here; as it happened, what the man said took him quite by surprise.

'Look,' said Bourn earnestly 'I've filled out all the forms, all right? Given all the details to your – the officer.' He paused. 'There's a girl in the hospital – have they telephoned you already?' He pressed on, taking Cirri's slight frown as an answer. 'I just left her there. We found her – a friend of mine, an Englishwoman who lives in Grosso, I was visiting her and we found this girl. Romanian.'

'Found her?' Cirri's interest quickened. Romanian. Like Robbins' maid.

'She was hiding in an outbuilding, out towards Grosso, on

the land of a friend of mine. She'd been bound –' He held up his wrists to indicate what he meant, and Cirri nodded. 'It looked like she'd been abducted, held captive up there somewhere. Perhaps tortured, certainly abused.' His voice was calm, laying out evidence much as a policeman might. 'It seemed she'd managed to escape.'

Cirri studied him, considering the situation, trying to remain objective. There might be no connection, after all. Was this girl able to tell you what had happened to her?'

Richard Bourn shook his head. 'She was in a bad way. We took her straight to the hospital. But she wasn't making sense; I don't even know if she speaks the language.'

Cirri stood up suddenly, walked the few paces to his window. He turned back to look at Richard Bourn. 'You're sure she's Romanian?' Bourn nodded, although he didn't elaborate on his reasons. He seemed to hesitate for a moment, then he said precisely what Cirri was thinking.

'I believe she's a maid,' he said carefully. 'Do you know Elvira Vitale? I believe she works for Elvira Vitale and her husband, Jack Robbins.'

Cirri nodded non-committally. 'Well,' he said carefully, 'that might be. May I ask how you can be so sure?'

Bourn stood up, and Cirri caught a hint of steely purpose in his blue, northern eyes. 'I know Jack Robbins,' he said slowly, choosing his words with care. 'I know all about his set-up up there.'

Even for a foreigner this phrasing struck Cirri as odd. 'He's a friend of yours?'

'No,' said Richard Bourn. 'Not a friend. I –' He hesitated. Cirri leaned forward, complicit, and the man spoke. 'I know a lot about him, though.'

'Tell me,' the policeman said. And when Richard Bourn had finished telling him what he knew about Jack Robbins, without even pausing to lift his jacket from the back of his chair, Cirri left for the hospital.

The bed was hard and high; the room held others but only Ania's was occupied. She could see three ranged against the wall opposite her, clean white sheets, a plump pillow at the head and a folded white blanket at the foot of each one. The wall to her left seemed to be all window and although there were shutters the room was filled with a clean morning light that hurt her eyes. As she turned her head towards the brightness Ania felt the small movement as a great and painful effort; it was as though her every muscle was inflamed. Gingerly she craned her neck, lifting her head from the pillow, and looked down at her body.

A single sheet covered the arrangement of knees —and hips, and underneath it she had been put into a starched white hospital gown. At the thought of having been undressed like a child Ania felt a prickle of unease and as she let her head fall back on the pillow in despair she heard an answering clatter. She turned towards the sound. It came from a tall metal stand by her left side to which she was attached, somehow; it held a plastic bag from which a colourless liquid drained down through a tube into a cannula that penetrated her body at the wrist, and this, she realized, was hurting. Her other arm was bandaged and supported in some kind of padded sling.

Ania struggled to raise her upper body and could not; her arms were restrained. She fought against rising panic. As she struggled images, dreams, terrible memories, seemed to jostle for space in her head, ugly fish rising to the surface of a dark

257

pond. She knew she must tell someone what had happened but all the right words in Italian evaded her and the sound she made was in her own language. She tried and failed to suppress a sob and as though in answer a woman appeared in the doorway.

Ania gazed at the apparition. Dressed in green scrubs and clogs, scolding and shaking her head, still the nurse appeared to her like an angel. The cool, dry hand she placed on Ania's wrist, the faint smell of perfume on her skin, the warmth of her body as she leaned across to check the drip, replaced her panic with something close to rapture, and Ania let her head sink back on to the pillow. The beds were clean, there was sunlight, and someone was taking care of her. Ania knew there was something she had to tell them, but it could wait, couldn't it? She was safe now; she closed her eyes.

A little while later the policeman appeared in the doorway in his shirtsleeves and pacing with impatience, but by then Ania was fast asleep. Her guardian, the nurse with the glitter of gold in her ears and scented skin, spoke seriously to Leo Cirri for some moments, shaking her head regretfully. Soon afterwards he left.

The back of the taxi stank of cigarettes and Rose was sweating on its fake-leather seats; she leaned forward, the backs of her thighs sticking to the plastic, and said in desperation, 'Okay, okay. *Va bene.* Here'll do fine. Put me down here.'

They'd sat behind a bus all the way through Levanto and now the driver was telling her he'd have to leave her at the bottom of the hill because of some one-way system or other. Rose didn't believe a word but suddenly she couldn't stand to be in the car a moment longer. Scrambling out, she fumbled for coins in her purse, dropped it, thrust a five-euro note at the man and didn't wait for her change.

Okay. Rose looked up the hill, took a deep breath and dusted herself off, trying to get rid of the smell of the taxi. *Okay.* She realized that she was going to be very late. Then she felt peace descend; it didn't matter, after all. She would have to apologize, sure, if there was no interview after all, then at least she'd done her best. She thought of the girl, wheeled away down the corridor under the white blanket, the clean, capable hands of the nurse. Done the right thing. The walk might give her time to think, anyway.

The road was steep and winding; she made her way up in the shade of a wall overhung with a great climbing plant, dark green leaves and brilliant orange, trumpet-shaped blooms. Rose would have liked to stop there for a moment, to rest against the wall and look at the flowers, inhale their scent. But up ahead the house was waiting for her, the last house on the road before it narrowed to a track along the cliff. Below it the sea glittered in the sun.

Rose went on, forcing herself to a slow, measured plod, smoothing her hair, her clothes as she went on up the hill, straightening her back. A little grey van puttered down past her with a load of wood, the driver a leathery old man in a cap who turned to look after her curiously. *They're everywhere*, the thought flitted into her head and out again, their little two-stroke engines the sound of the countryside, an old man invariably at the wheel. She passed a set of massive iron gates and saw a dark-skinned girl in a headscarf shaking sheets from a balcony and the troubling image of the Romanian girl's pale, sweaty face, her feverish, animal smell, returned to Rose. What had she been doing here in the first place? Prostitute, cleaner, kitchen hand? She supposed that they represented the flipside of the villas she passed, the girl they'd happened on and others like her, an immigrant community of near-slaves servicing the rich, willing to work for peanuts. Rose stopped in front of the gates of Elvira Vitale's house and looked up.

The villa was handsome, a soft yellow ochre stucco fading here and there, a deep terrace on the first floor overhung with starry white jasmine. The long shutters were all closed, though, a blank stare facing east along the coast, and from here, her eye following the coastal path, Rose could see Richard Bourn's house, La Martiniere, high up on the facing hill where he sat and watched Jack Robbins. She pushed the grey gate and it swung open in front of her.

The crunch of the gravel beneath her feet sounded loud to Rose; every step a rude intrusion on the garden's quiet luxury. *How quiet it is*, she thought, looking up at the shuttered house. *Where are they?* She edged past a huge car that occupied most of the drive, made her way up to the door and on the porch she hesitated. There was a flowerpot askew on its saucer and a dark spill of compost on the tile. The smear of an orange gone soft and rotten and trodden into the terracotta; no cleaner? No gardener to repot the plant? Rose frowned down at it but knew she couldn't prevaricate, and taking a deep breath, she rang the bell. She could hear it inside, an insistent sound followed by a brief silence. There was no answer. She pressed the bell again, and again there was no response.

Had Elvira gone out? The car was here. How late was she? Rose looked at her watch, and her heart sank. Twelve-thirty. It must have taken her longer to walk up the hill than she'd thought, and she cursed the idle taxi driver. She turned away from the door and to her left saw a small lychgate that stood

260

open, leading around to the back of the house. Could Elvira Vitale be in her garden, might she not have heard the bell? If the gate had been shut Rose might not have dared, but standing open like that – on impulse she went through it and round the corner of the house. She saw a stretch of short, coarse grass – no matter how many gardeners you employed out here, you never could manage a velvet English lawn – a low hedge at the end of it and some mounds of flowering shrubs, beyond them a great pale silvered expanse of sea and sky. There was no one there. She turned back towards the house, a porch along the length of it here supporting a wide, balustraded terrace. This was the grand, intriguing silhouette she could see from Grosso on a fair day. Rose looked up, aware now that she was trespassing, but the terrace, too, was empty. However – and she stepped back to get a better look – a window was open. Rose frowned, turned to go back to the gate, and as she went she saw something behind the glass of the lower windows, no more than a flicker of movement. Decisively she rounded the corner back to the front door and pressed the bell, a long, hard ring this time. She'd hardly had time to register footsteps before the door was pulled abruptly open from inside.

What had she expected? A servant, most probably, the place seemed to demand it; a decorous greeting, an intermediary placed between herself and the lady of the house. Not Jack Robbins himself, that was for sure, not Jack Robbins standing planted on the threshold, unshaven and glaring. Rose thought she saw a flicker of recognition pass across his face and for a moment she wondered whether he remembered her from the Mare Blu. But then he frowned.

'Yes?' he said roughly. 'What do you want?'

Taken aback, Rose stammered, 'I – I.' She held out a hand.

'I'm Rose Fell. I've got an appointment to speak to Mrs – to Signora Vitale. I'm afraid I'm a – a bit late.' She almost launched on an explanation, but she thought, no, why should I apologize to him? 'I'm a freelance journalist,' she ended, and smiled at him with as much confidence as she could muster.

Jack Robbins' frown deepened; he ignored her extended hand and she let it fall. 'No,' he said. 'I don't think so.'

He began to close the door against her. Rose's heart sank and instinctively she took a step back from the threshold. But as she felt herself giving up, rehearsing her excuses to Cookie Pearson, to Richard, the image of this man in a Mayfair night-club with Richard's wife came into her head, the thought of him pushing the glass of champagne over to her. *Have another drink.* She thought of Elvira Vitale's beautiful, worn-out face at the bar of the Mare Blu. *Come on*, she thought. *Not without a fight.* And instinctively she put out a hand to stop the door before it closed.

'I spoke to her,' said Rose with determination, addressing herself to the dark shape she could see through the door crack. 'Signora Vitale said to come this morning. She asked if I knew where she lived.' And then, before she could reflect too long, she stepped back up to the door, as close as she could get. 'Has she gone out? Where is she?'

She heard the accusation in her voice and thought, *I've blown it.* But the door didn't slam in her face as she had expected; instead it opened again. Jack Robbins was still there, and in the pale morning light admitted by the open door he suddenly looked – old. Rose looked closer, peering up at him, and she realized that he was in a state of some agitation.

'She's not here,' he said. 'She must have forgotten.' He spoke vaguely, as though his mind was elsewhere, and Rose didn't believe him. She took another step forward and automatically Robbins stepped aside to admit her. She was inside the house.

'Not here?' Rose could believe Elvira had stormed out in anger at the failure of punctuality, but forgotten? No. She looked hard at Jack Robbins, trying to get him to look back at her, but his eyes wandered, looked past her to the rectangle of sunlight through the doorway, his car parked on the gravel. Without looking away from him, Rose reached back and gently nudged the door to behind her.

'Perhaps I could wait?' she prompted. Robbins frowned at her.

'I don't know. You see, I'm not sure – I don't know how long she'll be.' He attempted a smile, and Rose felt him trying to restore social ritual. But she could tell that there was something wrong.

'Oh, I don't mind,' she said brightly. 'Really. I've been so looking forward to meeting your wife. She's an extraordinary actress.'

'Oh, yes, well, it was a long time ago,' said Robbins vaguely. 'She's an icon, of course ...' Rose had the impression this was a line he'd come out with many times; working his assets, she thought grimly. But the words petered out, and Rose wondered what it was that was so distracting Jack Robbins. Surreptitiously she looked around.

The front door opened into a spacious, light-filled hall that seemed the full height of the house; Rose could see polished wood, Persian rugs, pale walls, a broad staircase leading to a galleried landing. Nothing startling; precisely the kind of interior Cookie Pearson's magazine liked to feature. Only in Cookie's photoshoots every surface was gleaming, there were always fresh flowers, never any dust under the perfectly made beds. In Elvira Vitale's hall there was a ruck in the rug,

Rose noticed, and the roses on a console table to her left had dried up and dropped their petals. It was – surprising. Not full-blown squalor, far from it, but just neglect; it occurred to Rose that perhaps the rich and lazy didn't realize how quickly nature and dust reassert themselves, they need constant vigilance. They'd obviously let things slide in the past few days, which was odd if Elvira Vitale was expecting a journalist in her house.

Jack Robbins was looking at her now, with an air of growing perturbation as though she was a problem he wasn't sure how to solve, and Rose put on her bright, helpful smile again. He wasn't what she had expected; his smooth confidence was dissipated, and he seemed distinctly uneasy. Surely it couldn't just be that the place was untidy? Even if Jack Robbins was someone who set great store by how things appeared.

'So she's – gone shopping?' He said nothing. 'I could wait – outside on your terrace, perhaps?' Rose said, trying not to sound desperate. 'Wouldn't it be nice to say something about the view in the piece? Or perhaps we could talk – about your gallery? We could put something in about that, I don't think there would be a problem?' Rose heard herself gabbling and stopped abruptly. Why was Robbins saying nothing, just standing there, looking at her? He looked away now, the thick floppy fringe fell to one side and she saw a mark on his temple the size of an egg, red and raised. Rose thought of the overturned pot on the doorstep, and wondered. Looked over his shoulder, up towards the light flooding down from the landing through what appeared to be French windows. They must lead to the terrace; suddenly Rose felt she would very much rather be outside.

'Up here?' She took a step past Robbins on to the broad

staircase and a doorway came into view at the top of the stairs, an open door framed in some dark, expensive wood, cherry, walnut, she thought distractedly, looking for detail. She took another step and then she saw that at the lock the frame was splintered and the door hung askew from a broken hinge. Confused by the sight, she turned impulsively back to Jack Robbins to ask – what? – and there he was, his face up close to hers, sour breath hot on her cheek and one hand tight on her wrist.

'She's gone,' he said.

Rose backed up the stairs, one step away from him, then another, but he followed. This close she could see that the veneer of golden youth about Jack Robbins was just that; superficial. The skin at his jawline was beginning to slacken, his eyes were bloodshot, with a yellowish tinge to the whites. Rose tried to pull out of his grasp but he held on.

'Gone where?' she said, gasping, struggling to remain upright, to find her feet on the slippery, carpeted stairs behind her, with a horrible certainty beginning to dawn that he didn't mean just gone; he meant dead. But then Robbins let her hand drop and when she moved back another step he didn't follow. He put his face in his hands.

'Out there,' he said, jerking his head towards the French windows, towards the sea, and Rose heard a hoarse sound from between his hands. Without seeing his face Rose couldn't judge whether this was for real. 'She went over,' he said, his voice ragged. 'I couldn't stop her.' Rose's knees suddenly went, and abruptly she sat down on the stair. She felt very shaky, cold in the heat. *No*, she thought. *Not dead.*

Then from outside she heard the creak and clang of the gate, a crunch on the gravel, and for a brief, euphoric moment of relief she thought he was deluded, Elvira Vitale was there, back from a shopping trip, a morning walk. But when the door swung open the doorway was occupied by the uniformed figure of a police officer, with two more standing behind him and the light blue and white of a marked police car blocking the gate.

'*Permesso?*' The officer frowned as he took in the arrangement of figures in the hallway, Rose sitting on the stairs and Robbins standing over her, his face flushed. Rose noted that the policeman didn't seem aggressive or hostile, just sure of himself. He took a step forward.

'Signore Robbins?' The man's expression was one of polite inquiry now, and quite calm. 'I am Commissario Cirri, of the *Polizia dello Stato?*'

Rose looked from the policeman to Jack Robbins and saw his expression change from confusion to panic as he registered the uniforms, the police car, the ugly shape of a gun lying heavy in its holster on each man's hip. With a start he stepped backward and stumbled, and in a rush the leading policeman moved forward and grasped him by the elbow. The other two men took a step inside, blocking the doorway.

'I wonder –' Cirri began politely, then, perhaps seeing Robbins' distracted look, went on more assertively, 'You must come with us,' and as an afterthought, 'Please. We need you to make a statement, that's all. Something we need to –' he hesitated, looking for the right word – 'to clear up'.

No one spoke and Cirri looked from one to the other of them and back again. 'Excuse me,' he said slowly, 'but what has happened here?'

Rose felt quite dazed, wondering how on earth she had found herself in this situation, surrounded by police. Then she remembered. How could she have forgotten? She looked at Jack Robbins, waiting for him to speak, but his expression was slack and dazed.

'His wife,' she said, stammering. 'His wife – Signora Vitale – he says she's gone over the cliff. Into the sea. You've got to do something.'

The policeman looked at her, an expression of weary incredulity on his face.

'I'm sorry?' he said, frowning. 'Who are you? What are you talking about?' He looked down at Jack Robbins, whom he was still holding by the upper arm, and hoisted him up a little to address him.

'What does she mean?' he said. Robbins made an effort to stand up and extract himself from the policeman's grip.

'There's no need for this,' he said. The policeman reluctantly released his arm and Robbins attempted to assert his dignity by pulling vaguely at his clothing. Rose noticed that although he was wearing an expensive polo shirt and pale twill trousers, his feet were bare and scratched and the shirt was grubby.

'Your wife?' said Commissario Cirri patiently. Rose liked him. She saw him study Robbins' feet.

'Yes, yes,' said Robbins, his expression distraught. 'She's – she was hysterical, she ran past me. She'd locked herself in her dressing room all night ...' He looked around, then exclaimed, as though it had only just occurred to him. 'You've got to find her! A helicopter ... There must be boats?' Rose couldn't work out whether he was in shock or if his weird, distracted air was a product of some more sinister state.

Cirri said something to the policeman still in the doorway; the man withdrew a crackling radio from his breast pocket and spoke into it, without urgency. 'Show me,' said Cirri.

*

Tiziana watched the workmen on the Englishwoman's land. Although she had hardly exchanged a word with the woman she knew what her building plans were down to the last detail, having button-holed the builder the day he'd appeared to give Rose Fell a quote.

The builder now stood a couple of metres away from Tiziana on Rose's terrace, smoking and talking on his mobile phone, watching while his underlings worked, heads down, hard at it taking down the bricks and wire-brushing them. By the sound of it he was talking to his wife, wheedling her into cooking something nice for his dinner. Working women; Tiziana didn't know what the world was coming to, when a man had to sweet-talk his wife into cooking. *Mind you ...* She reflected, not for the first time, on what she might have got done instead if she hadn't spent the best years of her life feeding her useless lump of a husband.

Now he was talking about the girl they'd unearthed from that old pigsty, the runaway or whatever she was, a beggar from Levanto most likely, a prostitute. Tiziana cocked her head to listen. Romanian, he said. That's what happened if you went poking about in old buildings, digging up terraces, wasn't it? Find something nasty under every stone. She could have told the Englishwoman that, woman, girl, whatever she was, she hardly seemed grown to Tiziana, with no make-up and her clothes all over the place. *I could have told her not to bother poking about.*

Tiziana could have told her to steer well clear of that Gennaro, too; incomer, come to no good with a man like that, family all turned against him. But the English girl obviously had no sense, otherwise why would she be out here alone in the first place? Off to his house for dinner. Tiziana snorted at the thought, but she felt uneasy. Should she have told her about Gennaro? What was there to tell? His precious daughter got pregnant and got rid of it, he went down there to Genova and threatened to kill her if he ever saw her again and meant it, too, that's what Rico heard. She remembered the relish with which Rico had told the story, almost as if he approved of the old bastard. *That's how to treat women*, that was what he thought. Tiziana snorted. Still, to go so far as to tell all this to the Englishwoman; should she have done that? Gennaro Nutri might be an outsider, but there was a hierarchy; she was a foreigner. Tiziana hunched her shoulders and turned her back on the builder on his phone, looking away from Rose Fell's house.

Far below in the valley Tiziana could see the grubby orange of her grandson's T-shirt among the olives; from behind her in the darkened *salotto* she could hear the intermittent blare of the television as Enrico changed channels, endlessly. He liked the shopping channels; there was one local one, his particular favourite, a man standing in front of a bench covered with power tools shouting himself hoarse as if he was on a market stall. And when Tiziana wasn't around she knew he watched the ads for the slimming machine that were on around the clock, a woman face down on a massage bench with electrodes on her backside, buttocks twitching, bit of string up her bum. Disgusting.

Idly Tiziana watched her grandson making his way up the far side of the valley; *where's he off to now?* Her mind ticked over, returned to the haunted schoolhouse, put it together with the girl they'd found in the pigsty and her expression darkened; that had been no cat among the ruins, had it? What had Rico been up to?

'Rico?' Tiziana shouted over the blare of the television,

without turning, her eyes still on the boy. No answer. Across on Rose Fell's terrace the builder, mobile phone still clamped to his ear, turned to look at her and Tiziana stared him down. After a moment she turned and peered into her *salotto*. Rico sat there on the sofa in the gloom, skinny knees apart, big belly upturned like a turtle and the images from the screen flickering pale on his face. One hand held the TV controller immobile, raised towards the television.

'Enrico?' Her husband grunted. Tiziana crossed the room and turned the set off. Infuriated, Rico jabbed at the controller, but naturally nothing happened.

'I've turned it off,' she said. 'So you can listen to me for once.'

'In the name of God,' he groaned. 'What is it now?'

'That old place, the school. You did see something there whenever it was, day before yesterday, didn't you? What've you been up to?'

'Eh?' Rico's expression was of baffled rage. 'Shut up, woman,' he growled. 'You don't know what you're on about.' But Tiziana persisted.

'It was that girl, wasn't it? Someone had her down there, didn't they? Is it you and your cronies? Wouldn't put it past you.' Tiziana had never gone this far before; she was aware of coming close to a line and crossing over. *What the hell.*

'Don't be stupid,' snapped Rico sharply, pushing himself up from the cushions with a grunt. 'She's nothing to do with me, never seen her before in my life.'

'So you did see her then?'

'All right then, yes, I saw her. But like I said then, it's nothing to do with us, what they get up to, those Romany. No better than animals, anyway.' Tiziana stared at her husband, saw his vindictive little eyes and the saliva at the corner of his mouth as he spat his answer. The grey hairs sprouting through his vest, loose flaps of skin like breasts under the cotton. *Disgusting.*

'Who had her there?' Obstinately Rico said nothing, just humped his shoulders. 'You know, don't you?' But he said nothing; leaned across and turned the set back on. The noise and glare filled the room again and for fear that in her rage she might give in to the temptation to plant a knife between his bony old shoulderblades as he presented them to her, with a furious exclamation Tiziana turned and flung open the door.

In his orange T-shirt her grandson was climbing now towards the jumble of rabbit-hutches and gas canisters and junk that marked Gennaro Nutri's patch. *Hope the miserable old sod's not there*, thought Tiziana, distracted momentarily from her rage. That'd give the boy a shock if he was. But he wasn't there, was he? She'd seen him coming up the hill as they'd brought the girl out, and come to think of it, when he'd seen her he'd had that weird expression on his face, hadn't he? And then she remembered his van, parked down at the bottom of the village, she'd passed it on the way to her fruit trees, the boy had poked the sticks in his spokes and she'd clobbered him. Then they'd got to the old schoolhouse, and she hadn't connected the two. But now it all ticked down into place, click, click, click, dominoes in a box. *I've got you now, you old pervert.* Somewhere in the back of her mind she lumped them all together – Rico, Nutri, her own father, their sour, unforgiving old mugs, hands hard and leathery from work, always ready with a slap. *Got you now.* She turned and went back inside.

271

Chapter Twenty-Four

Elvira saw her brother, caramel-skinned in ragged shorts, running along the beach towards her with his face split into a smile, and the light around them fell warm and soft on the sand. The beaches of their childhood had been all stones, though; you could never have run on them. This one was empty, too, which on a lovely day like this was strange; her brother's were the only footprints and they were dissolving behind him. Of course the strangest thing of all was that her brother was dead, long ago, but that didn't seem to matter; what mattered was that he was here, come to help her again after all this time. She was holding something tight in her hand; perhaps he'd come to carry it for her, because her fingers were cramped and sore with holding it so tight. Then Elvira heard a sharp cry and she opened her eyes.

A gull napped away at the movement of her head; Elvira heard the beat of its wings. She looked up; high above her they circled on thermals, looking for a trawler, fish-heads and guts in its foaming wake. That feeling – what had it been? Joy? – ebbed away along with her brother's image, dissolving into the bleached sky above her. She was alone. And not only that; as she lifted her head Elvira understood that she was lying on a steep slope almost upside down, her head towards the sea. Her shoulder was jammed against the knotted trunk of some scrubby tree; it was the only thing that had prevented her headlong fall on to the rocks at the foot of the cliff a hundred metres below. And then in a rush that hammered at her temples and brought the hot blood to her cheeks she remembered. She remembered the panic in Jack's voice behind the door even now; she could see the astonishment in his face as he stood in the doorway and she'd come running out.

The bag. She looked down and there it was, her knuckles white around it. But the gates had been locked; she hadn't had the time or the coordination to attempt to open them. She'd run into the orange tree in its pot, something squashed and slippery under her feet, and she'd nearly gone over. She'd righted herself and there he'd been at the door, waiting, that awful blank look on his face. It had seemed to Elvira at that moment that she couldn't escape; it was too late, it was too difficult, there were too many explanations required of her. There was nowhere else to go, so she ran towards the sea. It seemed so simple, suddenly, the sea so calm and blue, there could be nothing more inviting than its blank blue silence to swallow up her wasted life and close over her as though she had never been. So Elvira had stumbled headlong over the layered stone of the low wall that marked the boundary of her garden from the scrub and rocks and scree of the downward slope, and all that kept her from the hundred-metre drop to the water. Or so she'd thought.

Gingerly, reaching behind her to take hold of the tree-trunk, Elvira raised herself to a sitting position and as she did so she felt a curious, languorous dizziness, as though she might faint, a narrowing of things; her hand felt wet and she lifted it to look. Blood. Quickly she looked away, anywhere but at the blood, at where it might have come from. So she looked down and then, light-headed with fear, she felt her stomach lurch as she saw how far there was to fall. The indelible image of a smashed body on the rocks appeared before her eyes, and she knew she didn't want to die after all. This was not what she had wanted. Hot tears started to her eyes, too late, too late; weakly she brushed at them. *Am I going to die?* Elvira closed her eyes and tried to see Nino again, but he was gone. She was on her own. She opened her eyes again and looked up.

A massive slab of stratified rock sloped up away from her, not quite vertical but near enough, barely softened by the odd bushy growth of gorse or juniper that had managed to find a foothold between its slanting layers. Did she have those scrawny shrubs to thank for the fact that she wasn't already dead? Elvira was glad she couldn't remember. Her neck ached with looking up; she couldn't see the house from here, nor was there any sign of Jack. But then it probably suited him quite well, she thought with detachment, his troublesome wife over the edge now, no more need to dope her and she'd even done it herself. Again she remembered that blank look as she had run past him, as though he was disassociating himself, stepping out of her way. Out here in the air she realized with sudden certainty that he hadn't been poisoning her properly, nothing so crude. A careful regime of drink and pills to keep her quiet. *Let's try this one, it's American, they've had good results in trials. One glass won't do any harm.* It was only that,

274

in the end, on Piero's terrace when she thought she'd been poisoned, what her body had been telling her was that it had had enough.

Suicide whilst of unsound mind. She wondered how long Jack would leave it before he went to the police, distraught, to say she'd been acting strangely, drinking, paranoid; there'd be enough witnesses to that, after all. The lunchtime trade at Piero's, Luke and Annabel. The police themselves; this was what he'd been after all along. Jack would leave it just long enough to make sure she was dead. Would he be able to keep it together? Had there been just a flicker of panic in those eyes as she'd run past? Perhaps it had got a bit too messy for Jack.

It was very quiet. Elvira wondered how long she had been here; she guessed it was around midday, the sun was high in the sky and very hot. She could feel it beginning to burn her face at the cheekbones, on the bridge of her nose; an unfamiliar sensation after years of wide-brimmed hats and sunblock, but oddly delicious as though she had turned back into a small girl after a long day on the beach. On the stones at Camogli with Nino, fishing for sprats with a net. Elvira shifted a little and felt the surface move beneath her, slippery pine needles sliding away as she tried to get a purchase, some loose gravel that skittered over the edge. She held still, knuckles stiff and white with tension, felt the sweat break under her arms and wondered how much longer she had.

The day was so bright, and she so exposed here on the cliff-face; it seemed impossible that no one could see her. But she'd chosen her house, chosen this cliff precisely because it wasn't overlooked, and the fishing boats at sea were too far off, bobbing specks. The morning was almost over; they'd be home soon with their catch. The journalist? Why hadn't she come?

Elvira felt disproportionately let down; only a journalist, after all. Why had she placed so much faith in her?

What if she was just late? Misremembered the time? Fervently she hoped that Rose Fell would after all turn out to be the most tenacious, dirt-digging type of journalist, one who wouldn't take no for an answer. At the very least, surely, Jack would not be able to pretend she'd just popped out for coffee; he'd have to come clean straight away, perhaps much earlier than he would have liked. But she knew she was fooling herself; the hope flickered and died. Again she listened, but still she heard nothing but the scream of the gulls and the wind flattening the scrub around her, no police sirens, no voices calling. *It's no good*, she thought. *No one's coming; there's no one.*

Cirri stood at the foot of the Contessa's garden and called out, but again his voice was carried off by the wind; he'd need the loud-hailer from the car boot. He peered over the edge. It looked like it was an awfully long way down but he couldn't see right over from where he stood, and he couldn't go any closer; on the cliff edges erosion from the rains and salt wind often softened up the rock. Just last week a couple from Milan on honeymoon had gone over the edge up towards Monterosso when they went too close to get a photo, the young marrieds with the silver sea as backdrop. A walker had found the camera sitting on a rock on a time delay; the footpath had to be closed.

Could Robbins' story be true? In a daze the man had shown him the room, the broken lock; Cirri had smelled the stale air and seen cushions on the floor with the imprint of a body. He could feel the adrenaline beginning to pump; something had gone on here.

'I didn't know what she was doing in there,' Robbins had

said, sounding helpless, puzzled, even guilty. A little. 'I lost my patience – you don't know what it's like, living with her. She had – pills. She was irrational – I don't know; I thought she might be planning to do something stupid. Perhaps I shouldn't have tried to get in, perhaps she panicked – I don't know.'

Was he just a good actor? It hadn't rung all that false, if Cirri was honest. At the memory of that room Cirri breathed in the fresh air on the cliff edge, the wind whipping his trousers at the ankles. *Bit of a wind,* he thought, *hope they've got that brush fire under control over to Bonassola.* Cirri couldn't help thinking with a kind of awe at the scale of the thing: *Robbins is in the shit, that's for sure.* His wife missing presumed dead, his maid found abused and wandering in the hills, and he himself seen by witnesses on a train from which a murdered girl was thrown. Cirri would have liked to have got to speak to the maid before coming here, but even he had seen she was in no fit state to be interviewed. As for Elvira Vitale – well, it was true, there'd been enough medication in the bathroom to kill an elephant, and if she'd gone over the cliff under the influence the likelihood was that she was dead.

He scratched his head. None of this seemed to fit together; it was altogether too much for one day and not yet lunchtime at that. Toto was talking into his radio still; he was trying to persuade them at Genova to scramble the helicopter of the *Polizia dello Stato*; it would be humiliating to beg one from the *carabinieri*, not to mention the fight over whose case it was going to be. Should he be waiting for the Romanian girl to wake up, or bring Jack Robbins in in the meantime?

Cirri ground his teeth in frustration; he couldn't hang about here, that was for sure, waiting for them to haul whatever was left of Elvira Vitale off the rocks. He felt a pang of pity for the woman, even though he despised suicides. He always thought, if they knew how they looked, a mess scraped from the wheels of a train or bloated beyond recognition after two months in the water, they'd stick it out. Not a pretty way to go. If it was suicide. He looked over at Jack Robbins, standing next to Toto outside the house. He had his hands jammed into his pockets, and for a moment Cirri thought he saw a curious smile on the man's face as he stared at the cliff, a kind of horrified excitement in his eyes. That did it. He beckoned Toto over.

'I'm taking Robbins,' he mouthed. 'I'll leave you the megaphone.' He jabbed a finger towards the car. Toto frowned, one hand raised telling him to hang on, ear pressed to his mobile.

Robbins, whatever it was Cirri had seen in his face wiped now, was watching as he approached. He was tense, shoulders hunched in resistance to their occupation of his territory, or so it seemed to Cirri. Was it his territory? Was it her house or his? Corporal Bruscolo's restraining hand rested on the Englishman's shoulder, just in case.

'I think it would be best if we had our discussion now,' said Cirri, making his voice gentle. 'Don't you?'

'But my wife –' The smile Cirri had seen was gone; now Robbins seemed scared, although whether for Elvira Vitale's sake or his own it was impossible to tell. His face was very pale, the stubble on his chin almost blue against it. Cirri saw a bruise on his forehead. He hesitated; was it humane to take the man in when they had no idea whether his wife was alive or dead? Robbins' eyes flickered, looking for an escape; it was fear Cirri could see.

'How did it happen, really?' he said softly, his face close up to Robbins'. This wasn't an accident, was it? It was you, wasn't it?'

Robbins gaped, panic in his eyes. 'I – I,' he stammered, and that was enough for Cirri.

'I understand you must be very anxious,' he said easily, as though no accusation had even be made. 'But you must see, there's nothing you can do? Even if she's still alive and down there, none of us can go down after her. We have to leave it to the helicopter.' *And perhaps the police boat,* he thought but did not say, grimly imagining the body fished from the water. 'This won't take long.' Although, of course, it might take a very long time indeed.

As he opened the car door he saw the woman who'd been there when they arrived, the journalist, standing staring at them, white-faced, arms folded across her body. He'd forgotten about her. Toto could deal with her.

Where was the helicopter? It seemed to Rose that only she cared about what had happened to Elvira Vitale, the face that had appeared in her dreams, beautiful and knowing and full of despair. *She can't be dead,* she wanted to scream, but all she could do was wait. In an agony of helplessness she stood and watched Cirri take Jack Robbins, unresisting, to the car. He bent his long body awkwardly to climb in, flinching as his forehead came into contact with the frame of the door. She watched as the car drove away, Robbins' motionless silhouette docile in the back seat beside the burly profile of the policeman next to him.

Rose supposed the third man – had Cirri called him Toto? – would deal with her; she didn't know. He was still talking urgently into his mobile. Perhaps they'd forgotten she was there, forgotten to ask what she was doing there at all, but no, he looked up at that moment and Rose saw he had his eye

279

on her. Briefly Rose thought of Richard Bourn; they'd made no arrangement to meet again. She wondered where he was now, whether she'd outlived her usefulness to him, with Jack Robbins in custody. This must have been what he'd been after all along, she thought with resignation. Did it matter?

The policeman's back was to her now, and cautiously Rose moved closer to the edge, to where Cirri had stood and dared go no further. There was a low stone wall, some kind of flowering plant – dianthus, she registered, little frilled pink flowers – and the grass beyond was coarse and bleached. She peered at it, saw a depression where a foot might have landed, and turned to the policeman, wondering if he'd seen it too. But he wasn't looking and before Rose could consider what she was doing she stepped over the wall. Ahead were a couple of low bushes, some scratchy, aromatic plant like myrtle or juniper; she took another step and then, with a gasp, she stopped.

The rock sloped away sharply in front of her, and yawning at her feet, the sheer drop down to the sea below opened up, the breakers, tiny with distance, foaming white against jumbled rocks. Dizzy at the sight, Rose swayed, saw the blue coming up to meet her and scrabbled backwards and sat down with a bump. Behind her she heard the policeman shout and as she turned towards the sound a gust of wind plastered her hair across her face. Blindly she groped about, but nothing she laid her hands on seemed to have substance, only loose stones, dry, slippery leaves. Struggling against panic, she pulled her hair out of her eyes in time to see the policeman reaching for her across the wall. This is madness, she thought, and put her hand out to take his. But then she heard it; a high, thin call from behind her, from somewhere down there, a living sound in all the inhuman din of the wind.

Rose's heart leaped and on her knees she tried to tell him, she pointed, gesturing towards the sound. He flapped his hands at her, pointing up at the sky. Rose squinted upwards, but she saw no helicopter. She turned her back on the policeman and lay flat, face down against the scree, and looked over the edge.

It was not, after all, a clean drop; a scree scattered with loose stones, lethally steep, but perhaps twenty feet below Rose there was a tiny outcrop, not even a ledge, no more than a scab on the cliff-face. Rose could hear her own hoarse breath in her ears as she pressed herself flat and looked; she saw a couple of weedy bushes and immediately below her, a stunted tree, its trunk no thicker than her wrist. Wedged between the tree and the steep, rocky hillside was – something. A body. But as Rose squinted down to see it, to find out what she had to know, that Elvira Vitale was alive, that it was not too late, something flapped before her face, screaming in her ear, and she beat at it with her hands. A seagull, shockingly close to her; she saw its greedy eye, its needle-sharp beak, then it wheeled away, and she looked down again. Turned up towards her, the beauty stripped from it and white as bone, was Elvira Vitale's face, framed by the sea.

It took less than half an hour for Jack Robbins' lawyer to arrive; Robbins had seemed paralysed by the sight of the police station's interior, the row of holding cells, interview rooms marked two and three. He stopped still and stared at the doors with horrified fascination, passing his tongue nervously over dry lips.

He hadn't been charged with anything; all Cirri had said was that it was to do with the train journey he'd made, he'd been seen to make, on the night before Ferragosto, but

Robbins had wanted the lawyer present anyway. The speed with which the guy arrived from Genova, the shine on his big silver-grey Maserati, were indicators to Cirri not only that Jack Robbins had some connections, but that he knew, one way or another, exactly how serious the situation was.

He'd turned to Cirri in the car. 'Am I being arrested?' he asked, trying to make light of it, Cirri thought, as though it might all turn out to be a joke.

'Just a chat,' Cirri said. 'Helping us with our inquiries.'

He didn't try to sound too reassuring, and he could tell Jack Robbins knew there was more to it than that. So far there hadn't been much help given. Cirri was finding the man much trickier to make out than he'd expected. He wasn't stupid, but he wasn't cocky, either, which disappointed Cirri somehow. Cockiness was a good start; bravado always disappeared, in the end, to disintegrate into panic, and the truth. No, if he was honest, the impression Cirri had of Jack Robbins was that he was bewildered and very, very frightened.

Cirri didn't want to kick off with the maid, Ania. He needed to talk to her first, after all; she was alive, eventually she would be able to talk to him, perhaps tonight. One thing at a time, and Cirri knew where he wanted to begin.

'You come over every summer, is that right?' he said easily, and Jack Robbins gave a guarded nod. 'Last year, you were here around this time? Ferragosto?'

'Yes,' said Robbins, wary still, and uncertain, 'I think so. We arrived in July last year.'

Cirri nodded. 'Right,' he said, without enlightening Robbins as to the significance of his question. He leaned forward. 'Okay. Now, last week. Do you remember where you were on the evening of fourteenth August? Tuesday night?'

Robbins looked properly confused now. His face was very pale, and Cirri could see that his hands, resting on the chipped formica of the interview table, were trembling very slightly.

'Why?' He seemed genuinely taken aback. 'I can't – it seems like a long time ago. I don't see what it's got to do with my wife.'

'This isn't about your wife,' Cirri said gently. 'We'll talk about your wife later. Try to think. Tuesday night, early Wednesday morning.'

Robbins stared at him, expressionless. 'I –' he began hesitantly, 'I went –' His voice slipped a little and he cleared his throat. 'I went to Genova for the evening.'

Cirri pursed his lips. 'Alone?'

Robbins nodded, his eyes fixed on the policeman. 'I went on the train,' he said slowly, and Cirri looked at him impassively, letting it pass. Robbins went on. 'I arrived at about nine o'clock, I think. I spent most of the night in the Luna di Miele, if you know where that is.' He spoke quietly; beside him the lawyer from Genova sat, primed and watchful as a bird of prey.

Cirri nodded neutrally but he felt his pulse quicken; the Luna di Miele was the sleek nightclub up the street from the MonteCarla. He tried to suppress the feeling he had that whoever killed Anna-Maria Villemartin might have tried to place himself at a greater remove from the club where she was known to have spent her last evening. But maybe Robbins was too clever for that. There must have been witnesses, after all.

'The barman could probably tell you I was there,' Robbins went on, his voice a little firmer now.

'And when did you leave, exactly?'

Robbins shrugged. 'It's important,' said Cirri, trying not to lose his temper.

Robbins shrugged again. 'Midnight? Something like that?'

'And were you alone then, too?' Cirri kept his face neutral. Not many people did leave the Luna di Miele alone, even if they arrived that way.

Robbins was expressionless. 'As it happens, I was.' Perhaps Jack Robbins wasn't quite such a ladies' man as Cirri had imagined. He thought of George, the bouncer, who'd seen Anna-Maria walk to the end of the road, and wondered how sure he could have been. He tried to read Robbins' expression; maybe he was getting too old to pull, and maybe he didn't like it. All he saw now was hostility, a kind of resistance.

Cirri placed Anna-Maria Villemartin's scuffed identity card on the table. Her pretty, oval face, thick brows, dark eyes gazed defiantly up at him; he leaned forward and turned the card round to face Robbins.

'This girl ...' Cirri paused, studying Robbins' face for a sign of recognition, but saw none. 'Was this girl outside the club as you were leaving, by any chance?'

Robbins pursed his lips. 'Not that I remember,' he said, shrugging a little, forgetting himself; Cirri couldn't suppress a frown of disapproval at the insouciant gesture and Robbins seemed to sit up straighter in response. 'It was late, I was ... preoccupied. Wanted to get home. There's always plenty of people around at that time of night, I seem to remember there was a queue to get into the place down the road ... People going in. Not coming out.'

'Preoccupied?'

The lawyer drummed his fingers on the table, but Robbins looked down. 'My wife ...' He tailed off. 'She's been – Elvira's been – I was worried about her. She forgets things. Drinks too much.' He looked up earnestly; Cirri returned his gaze levelly.

This – no, he thought. *Is this an act? The concerned husband?* The look he'd seen on Elvira Vitale's face at the restaurant came back to him. Had she been asking for his help? The thought made him uneasy; he had felt sorry for her, but he'd done nothing.

'But you went out for the night, despite that? On your own?' He gave Robbins a frank smile. Robbins looked away. 'I need a life,' he said shortly, distantly examining a spot on the wall behind Cirri's head.

'All right,' said Cirri. 'Fair enough. But what I really want to know,' and he leaned forward to catch the man's eye, 'is, why you were on the train. I mean, you have a beautiful car.' He spoke with sober respect. 'Do you often use the train?' He allowed a note of incredulity to creep in.

Robbins' face turned blank and obstinate, his eyes hard. 'Why shouldn't I use the train? What business is it of yours?' His voice was soft, polite even, but there was a steely resistance behind it.

'Well,' said Cirri patiently, but something about the man's response bothered him. Surely Robbins knew by now what this was about? 'Shall we come to that in a moment?'

The lawyer began to protest, started to open his briefcase on the table in a gesture Cirri recognized as a drawing up of battle lines. But Robbins paid no attention, his head hanging so low that his face was almost completely hidden. Cirri too disregarded the lawyer, leaning towards Robbins.

'Let's just say a matter of life and death,' he said softly. 'Now, will you tell me what you were doing on that train?' Slowly Robbins raised his head and Cirri saw a flush rising from his throat.

'I sometimes take the train,' Robbins said, a little too

casually. 'See how the other half lives. Do you have that expression?' Cirri said nothing, and Robbins shrugged. 'It can be fun.'

Cirri leaned forward. 'Fun?' He didn't understand. Robbins said nothing, his mouth set obstinately.

'Do you know what this is about?' said Cirri deliberately. Again Robbins shrugged, turned and spoke to his lawyer in an undertone, in English. He shook his head, once, twice, firmly, then sat back in his chair.

'My client doesn't see where this is leading,' the lawyer said. 'His private life, surely ... ' He opened his palms in a gesture to indicate that they were all men of the world. Cirri leaned forward.

'If you don't know already,' he said slowly, 'let me make this quite clear. We need to know exactly what you were doing on that train because,' he looked at Robbins now, not the lawyer, 'there is a witness to your presence on the twelve thirty-two from Genova – the train which Anna-Maria Villemartin – this girl here,' and he tapped the photograph that still lay in front of Robbins, 'took, perhaps with her killer. It is certainly the train on which she was murdered, and from which her body was thrown, just on this side of the tunnel.'

Jack Robbins' face was more than pale now; it was so white Cirri thought he might be going to pass out. He opened his mouth as though to speak, but nothing came out. He stared at the photograph.

'So it interests me, as you can see,' said Cirri, 'to know why you like to travel by train, really. Do you understand?' Robbins nodded as though in a daze, and when he spoke his voice was frightened.

'It offers opportunities,' he said, his voice trembling. 'For – encounters.' He looked at Cirri with a kind of despair.

'Encounters?' Cirri was having trouble with this one.

'Of a – particular kind. A sexual kind.' The head went down again.

Cirri sat back in his chair. 'On a train? A crowded train?'

Robbins shrugged, looked at his hands. Cirri looked too; long, tapered fingers, pale, soft palms. He tried to imagine them around a girl's throat. He hadn't used his hands, though, had he, the murderer? A garrotte; fishing line or some such. Cirri frowned at the hands before him.

Robbins spoke again, still looking down. 'There are places on a train where no one can see you. If that's what you want.' He shifted uneasily in his seat, saw Cirri looking at him, and seemed to realize the implications of what he had said. 'But not, I mean not –' He stammered to a halt, running out of breath as he stared at Cirri with dawning fear.

Impervious, Cirri continued. 'Are these encounters – commercial transactions? You pay?'

Robbins gave a small, hopeless shrug. 'Not always. It depends.'

'And that night?'

Robbins looked away. 'Yes,' he said, and the words were barely audible.

'With Anna-Maria Villemartin?' Cirri spoke deliberately, his enunciation clear and loud in the room, and Robbins started as though burned.

'No! No! I don't even remember seeing her on the train, I don't remember. She might have been on it but I didn't – we didn't –' He was stammering again now, desperate to get the words out. 'It wasn't her. The girl I – she was –' He put both hands to his forehead in desperation, pounding with the palms. 'She was blonde, even, I think she was blonde, the one I –'

Ignoring Robbins' protestations, Cirri tenderly picked up the identity card, tilted it towards him. 'Did you try it on with her?' he asked. 'Did she say no, and you got angry?' He tilted his head to one side, thinking of the other girl, the prostitute the year before. Too young, both of them, too young for their bodies already to have been turned inside out by abortion clinics. Too young to die. 'Or is it part of the deal? Do you like to hurt them?'

Robbins shook his head slowly. 'No,' he whispered, staring at the picture.

'Your wife,' said Cirri softly. 'Did she know that you liked – to travel on the train? Is that why –' Robbins looked trapped and he made as if to push his chair back from the table.

Just then Cirri heard a soft knock and the door opened behind him.

'Just thought you'd like to know,' said Bruscolo, his head around the door. 'They've got her. They've got Elvira Vitale. She's alive.' *Now*, thought Cirri, triumphant, and turned back to Jack Robbins. He looked terrified.

'No,' he said desperately, 'no, no, I didn't touch my wife. She's – she's got a problem, she'd really lost it – look, she's alive, she'll tell you.' Robbins was almost gibbering now, as if at last he understood the situation he was in, and Cirri raised a palm to calm him.

'Okay,' he said softly, 'okay'. Robbins put his face in his hands, and Cirri could see the lawyer's expression as he placed a hand on his client's shoulder, aghast at his disintegration. Cirri paused a moment, meditating. *Have I got him now?* The man seemed about to cave in completely, just one last little push might do it.

'Your maid,' Cirri said slowly. 'She's turned up.'

Robbins looked up, his eyes bloodshot, dazed. He seemed utterly confused now, shaking his head a little as if to clear it. 'What?'

'We found her. She's in a pretty bad state.' Cirri waited, but saw no understanding in Robbins' eyes. *React*, he thought. 'But she's alive. She'll make it.'

'She's been hurt?' Robbins tilted his head, wondering. Cirri didn't answer immediately. He studied Robbins through narrowed eyes, gave him room to falter, but he could see nothing but surprise in his ashen face. Was Robbins that good an actor? What the hell, he thought, and he decided to push it.

'Were you sleeping with your maid, Mr Robbins? Were you having a sexual relationship with her? Because Richard Bourn says you were.'

And Jack Robbins began to laugh.

Chapter Twenty-Five

Gennaro Nutri's house was all closed up once more in the warmth of late afternoon, the chairs on his little patio had been taken inside and the kitchen door locked and shuttered. But then Tiziana had known it would be; she had waited until he went out, until she saw his little grey van winding down the hillside below her terrace. She didn't wonder where he might be going, not on this occasion, although in the past she had applied considerable scrutiny to Gennaro's comings and goings, his trips into Genova to see his old mother, to look for that daughter of his. Always back late, and who knew what he got up to, walking the streets, looking for something, that was for sure. This time, though, she simply needed to know that he wasn't at home.

Tiziana turned. 'Tsst,' she hissed. 'Marco!' The boy was driving her mad. 'Go back to Nonno,' she said, flapping her hands at him.

Marco thrust out his lower lip. What are you doing, Nonna?' he asked slyly. 'He's not in, you know.'

'It's none of your business,' she snapped, giving him a little shove. 'Scram. *Via, via.*'

'D'you want one of his rabbits?' the boy persisted. 'I know where he keeps them. He's got hundreds, he wouldn't miss one.'

Hands on hips, Tiziana scrutinized the boy. 'What else has he got over there?' she asked. 'Anything – funny?'

Marco frowned. 'Like what?' Tiziana moved around the house to the side, peering in at the shutters. Nothing. She squinted back at Marco over her shoulder. 'Has he got a shed? Somewhere to keep tools and stuff? Any – you know, secret places?' Marco shook his head slowly.

'Oh, never mind,' she said impatiently. 'Just go on home, all right? I won't be long.'

Marco looked as though he was about to sulk, but then suddenly he brightened. 'What about his *cantina*, Nonna?' He looked around, to make sure there was no one to overhear. 'I even know where he keeps his key.'

As she watched the boy run ahead of her, light and fast as a little goat on his bare feet, Tiziana felt a momentary and unfamiliar impulse to wrap her arms around the child and plant a kiss on his grubby cheek. He's not so bad, she thought grudgingly as she lumbered painfully after him. Not as much of a pain in the neck as his father was, that's for sure.

Gennaro Nutri's *cantina* was down at the bottom of the village, on a gloomy corner Tiziana rarely passed. The key was buried in the loose soil of a potted plumbago that stood opposite the door; like the door to Gennaro's house, and unlike any other *cantina* door in the village, all of them half-rotted away and peeling, it was brand-new and robustly built, painted green. She'd always thought of this as incomer's ostentation, a sign that he hadn't wasted his life working the land, or slaving on a trawler dragging for sardines; for him it was a hobby for his old age. What was it he'd done? Steward on a liner. What kind of a job was that for a grown man, pandering to spoiled foreigners, turning down their beds, running their errands? Enough to turn you sour and nasty, or worse, she supposed. The door opened without a creak, hinges oiled to perfection, and a gust of dank, fishy air billowed out from the darkness.

Marco was behind her now, holding on to her skirt, and Tiziana felt a pang of conscience. She turned and knelt beside him, her fat old knees painful on the cold stone. 'Off you go now, darling,' she muttered, the endearment taking her by surprise. 'There's some ice-cream in the freezer compartment, your favourite, *bacio bianco*.' Rico'd be furious; it was his favourite, too. But she didn't want the boy here, not now.

'Tell Nonno I said you could have it.' The boy grinned suddenly, as much at the thought of annoying his grandfather, she could see, as at the prospect of ice-cream, and he shot back off up the village, taking the stone steps at speed on his skinny little legs. Tiziana turned back to the *cantina*, and groped inside the door for the light pull. The first thing she saw as the yellow light came on was a coil of faded blue nylon rope, hanging from a nail beside a stack of fishing reels.

Back at Tiziana's house Marco sat in a hideout of his own making behind two chairs on the terrace, a tub of *bacio bianco* between his knees, his chin dripping with ice-cream. He heard the sound, of course, but like the cicadas and the sea it was a sound so familiar as to be background, the whine of a two-stroke engine as it strained to pull a small grey van up the hill. But he was too preoccupied with staying hidden from his grandfather for as long as it took to finish the tub of ice-cream to recognize this particular vehicle. Marco didn't watch it park below the church, nor did he see Gennaro Nutri climb out and head off, not uphill to his neat little yellow house at the top of the village, but down towards the *cantina*.

That had been it, the laughing; that had been the end of Cirri's run of luck. He couldn't even persuade himself it was hysteria.

'Richard Bourn? Come *on*.' Robbins seemed almost elated; the transformation was extraordinary. 'It's hardly as though he's objective, is it? I mean, you do know the history there?' He leaned and muttered something to his lawyer, then turned back to Cirri. 'And the maid – I could do better than a dumpy little Romanian peasant, couldn't I?'

'Like a prostitute on a train?' But it bounced off this time.

'So what?' said Robbins. 'So I use prostitutes now and again. It's not a hanging offence, is it?' He sat back in the chair. His face had the washed-clean, born-again look of the newly reprieved. 'You've got nothing on me, have you? Just gossip, just circumstances.' It was as if Cirri had given him his life back by that one reckless question. Cirri cursed himself for asking it, cursed himself for taking Richard Bourn at face value.

It was downhill from then on. After half an hour more of fruitless interrogation, the lawyer back on form and batting half the questions out of court, Cirri had had enough. He suspended the interview, left them to stew a while with Bruscolo in there to keep an eye, and went to his office to think.

There was a new cardboard folder on his desk. A couple of forensics-trained officers had been through the Contessa's house and found nothing much, although they'd got excited when they found out Robbins had a darkroom. But on balance that had turned out a disappointment; sure, there'd been plenty of surreptitious pictures of girls on the beach buried away among the arty shots. But you couldn't accuse a man of murder for photographing women's breasts; they hadn't been kids or anything.

This was all going too far and too fast for Leo Cirri; he wanted everyone to stay right where they were. He needed to talk to Elvira Vitale when she came round and with the bloody *maledetto* Richard Bourn. And what about the journalist? He almost groaned. He should have known not to take the word of one witness at face value. What was left of that house of cards he had built? The wife. Elvira Vitale. If he looked back at the interrogation she'd been Robbins' real weak point throughout the whole interview; he'd swear that even if he hadn't pushed her Robbins had something to do with her going over that cliff. But the rest? Could pampered, weak, self-indulgent Jack Robbins have put his arms around a girl's lifeless body and heaved it from a moving train? Cirri thought of those soft, manicured hands, and with dull certainty he knew they'd never pulled fishing wire tight around Anna–Maria's neck. No.

Cirri passed a hand across his eyes. *Move on*, he thought. *If not Robbins, then who?* He stood for a moment, thinking. *Go back.* Had there been something, before he embarked on this headlong pursuit of Robbins, something he'd shoved aside? He stood very still, waiting for it to come to him. The room was dim, long windows shuttered as usual, although by now the sun had moved around to fall on the other side of the old building, to the west. Suddenly, furiously impatient with the atmosphere of profound gloom in which he conducted his professional life, Cirri strode over and shoved the shutters behind his desk open, and the light flooded in from outside.

Below his window was a dusty little garden, begonias wilting in the dry shade; beyond it the small piazza in which the old people would gather at this time of day to exchange gossip, talk about who'd died, whose children and grandchildren had left home and abandoned their roots. Two old men, brown trousers pulled up over their elderly paunches, white shirts, vests, skinny, liver-spotted forearms resting on walking sticks, turned at the rusty scrape of the shutters opening and stared at him in mild astonishment, their conversation suspended.

Old men. They were everywhere. Cirri nodded a sheepish greeting and turned back inside. His office seemed dusty and unfamiliar in the afternoon sunlight. Anna-Maria Villemartin's identity card lay there on his desk, together with the computer printout, and for the hundredth time he stared at it. This time, though, the name jumped out at him again and this time he remembered where he'd seen it before. Nutri. The nameplate beside Anna-Maria's mother's apartment. The neighbour, the old woman who'd eyeballed him through the crack in her door as he waited to go in.

Cirri looked at the numbers beside the name on the flimsy paper. Nutri, Maria Grazia. Was that a date of birth? Born July 1979; couldn't be a daughter, then, could it? Granddaughter more like. Cirri frowned; he couldn't remember what Anna-Maria's mother had said about the woman. And why, with Jack Robbins right here and looking as guilty as they come, was he hedging like this anyway?

Cirri turned to look outside again, the paper in his hand, at the bleached scene framed by the window, at the old men gossiping on their bench. That train wasn't empty, he mused; it was the week of Ferragosto. Why hadn't he thought, if someone as visible as Jack Robbins had been with Anna-Maria

Villemartin, someone as foreign, there would have been witnesses on the train, surely? It bothered him. Something stirred in his memory. Who else had been on that train? Whom had the barmaid seen through that murky window?

Cirri sat down at his desk, picked up the phone and dialled; in that muffled, gloomy sitting room on the thirteenth floor of a suburban tower block, among the Tiffany glass and the photos of Anna-Maria Villemartin, he heard it ring.

The din inside the helicopter was deafening, the atmosphere heavy with gasoline and testosterone. The pilot wore huge headphones and dark glasses, and his mouth below them was unsmiling as the helicopter lurched and swung in the wind. He gestured to the policeman, waving at something beyond the curved glass. The policeman looked, if anything, even grimmer than the pilot, and strapped to the stretcher between them Elvira Vitale lay as white and motionless as though all the blood had already drained from her body, a surgical collar bracing her neck. The male paramedic had fixed a line into her arm, and was attempting to make notes on a chart that fluttered and tugged in the wind. Trembling, Rose sat on the other side of Elvira, wondering what on earth she was doing here.

It had seemed to take for ever, even once the helicopter had arrived, to lower the stretcher; swinging in the wind, it had slammed into the cliff-face on the first attempt, sending it spinning out of the helmeted and harnessed paramedic's control. For what seemed half a lifetime Rose had lain there, ignoring the policeman's shouts, buffeted by the downdraught from the helicopter's rotors, and stared. She hadn't even known if Elvira Vitale was alive or dead – her open eyes, after all, meant nothing, did they, the dead had to have their eyes closed for them – and every muscle in her body was tensed to will her alive. She felt as though nothing save Jess's birth had ever been more momentous in her life, and out of idiot desperation she had even found herself praying, *let everything be all right,* although to whom her prayer was directed she couldn't have said.

I only came to do an interview, Rose had thought as she lay on the cliff edge with her face pressed into the prickly grass, her eyes streaming in the wind and the smell of the sea in her nostrils. She was awed by the speed with which things could change, when a morning walk under the bougainvillea could end in a matter of life or death. *It's just there, under everything,* she thought with a kind of terror, *a speeding car, a moment's madness, and everything could be finished.* Below her the paramedic in his luminous jumpsuit succeeded in getting a grip on the body beneath the shoulders, he hauled, Rose held her breath, and Elvira Vitale was on the stretcher. Rose saw an arm flail and reach for the man, a voluntary movement. *She's alive.*

The stretcher inside, the helicopter had touched down briefly on the expanse of grass behind Elvira Vitale's house and the policeman, ducking to avoid the whipping rotors, had motioned to Rose to get in. Without questioning, she had obeyed; when she reached the man she felt his arm heavy on her back, grasping her firmly and shoving her inside. *I'm in trouble,* she thought, realizing that the holster on his hip, the handcuffs at his belt, weren't just for decoration. *Oh well.*

In the roaring din of the helicopter's interior Rose was surprised by how little she cared that there would be explanations required of her, and questions asked, all the oppressive bureaucracy of Italian officialdom. She just wanted them to get to wherever they were going, to the hospital, where the terrible responsibility of keeping Elvira Vitale alive could be assumed by machines and doctors in a place of warmth and light and reason. Here, it seemed to Rose, in all this noise and among only men, that burden was partly hers, and in the deafening, turbulent space of the helicopter cabin, the narrow space between life and death, she tentatively reached down and took Elvira Vitale's hand.

She had a son. The neighbour had a son, that's what Cirri remembered.

'Yes,' said Anna-Maria Villemartin's mother, bewildered. 'As it happens, he was there that day. Visiting his mother, in the afternoon. It was her birthday.'

Thank you,' said Leo Cirri, trying to keep his voice even, to keep the brief flare of triumph at bay. It wasn't so hard; even the sound of the woman's voice subdued him, the flat, dead sound of it when she picked up the phone, as though she knew that whoever was there, they wouldn't be bringing good news, not any more.

Besides, he wasn't sure what it meant, if it meant anything at all. The neighbour's son had visited his mother on the day Anna-Maria was killed. To find out more, he knew, he would have to proceed very softly.

'Signora,' Cirri said carefully. 'The argument you had with your daughter on the day she – the last time you saw her –' There was no gentle way of putting it, he realized. He began again. 'Did you argue with her about – a boyfriend, for example?'

There came a heavy sigh. 'It doesn't matter any more, does it?' she said. 'It wasn't about him,' she said in a listless mono-tone. 'He was just a boy, you know, someone from college she

298

fell in love with one night and out the next. She wasn't seeing him any more. It was about – what he'd left behind.'

Cirri nodded, invisible, holding his breath. 'What he left behind?' he prompted.

'The baby,' she said hopelessly, as though nothing mattered any more. 'She – got rid of the baby. Six weeks ago now.' Cirri thought of the names and dates on that paper, that particular date burning in someone's memory. 'It doesn't matter now. No one can think any worse of me now. I wish I'd never said any of it, it's just – she was my only one. My only baby. A grandchild – it would have been –' She let out a kind of gasp and stopped.

After a moment she went on in a tone of dull shame, 'I should never have said any of it. Screaming like a fishwife for the neighbours to hear.' *One neighbour in particular*, thought Cirri. She stopped. 'She was right, it was her life, her decision. There would have been other grandchildren, wouldn't there? But she was my only child.' Her voice grew muffled as though by hands over her face.

I should leave her alone, thought Cirri. He hated this part of his job, wheedling, softening his voice, inflicting pain.

'You mustn't – blame yourself,' he said lamely. 'What you said didn't kill her.' But the woman said nothing. He hesitated, then went on, as gently as he could, 'One last thing, to do with your neighbour again. I'm sorry –'

'Yes?' she said wearily.

'Her son –'

'Gennaro.'

'Does he have a daughter, too?'

'Yes,' she said, and her voice was hollow with bitterness and despair. 'He has a daughter.'

*

Back on the drugs, thought Elvira through a fog of pethidine, and she smiled hazily up at the faces, or thought she did. They didn't smile back. *Don't look so frightened*, she wanted to say to the one holding her hand, *we'll be all right*, but she couldn't grasp at the right words. She squeezed the woman's hand instead and felt an answering pressure; it was enough. She closed her eyes.

Chapter Twenty-Six

The helicopter had circled the hospital, from this angle an untidy arrangement of pitted grey concrete boxes, a scrubby patch of grass to the back and emergency admissions marked by a large, painted red cross on the flat roof to the front. Where they'd left the Romanian girl only a few hours earlier, Rose realized with a start; it seemed much longer ago than that. The closer they got to the ground the more wildly the helicopter seemed to swing and lurch; *I hope I never have to ride in one of these again*, thought Rose. With a jolt, they set down.

The tarmac was scalding, with no shade from the afternoon sun; the hospital was perhaps a mile inland and any breeze off the sea had, by the time the air reached it, long since been absorbed by the hot stone of the town and the dense, dark canopy of trees around it. Rose walked slowly beside the stretcher, unwilling just yet to release the hand now holding tight to hers, taking shallow breaths; the boiling air felt as though it might burn her lungs if she inhaled too recklessly.

They pushed through the doors to the emergency room and immediately they were surrounded by equipment, nurses, three doctors; even a confused elderly patient ambled up, unhindered in the melee. There was noise too, people asking questions and shouting instructions, but to Rose, temporarily deafened by the roar of the helicopter, it was like noise coming at her from underwater. She stood in the marvellous cool of the air-conditioning and closed her eyes for a moment, still holding on to Elvira Vitale's hand. When she opened them again she saw Richard Bourn.

He was at some distance from her, through a set of swing doors and across another reception area, a desert of plastic seating beyond the doors, standing at this end of a corridor. She saw him across it all, looking at her. Under his gaze Rose felt the burn of the wind and sun on her face, and was aware of her hair tangled into rat's tails after the ride. Then the doors swung shut, someone tugged on her sleeve, and she turned away to see the policeman at her side.

'They're taking her up to the operating theatre,' he said in Italian. 'There may be a spinal injury. You can let go now.'

Rose looked down at Elvira Vitale; she was still very pale but seemed quite calm. She gazed up at Rose.

'You'll be all right now,' Rose said, painfully aware of her clumsy accent, and gently she withdrew her hand from Elvira's. Elvira tried to nod, but the collar prevented her; instead she smiled, a crooked smile. But then something seemed to occur to her, an anxious, distracted look passed across her face and she tried to raise herself up. Rose leaned down towards her, half-kneeling beside the stretcher.

'*Il sacchetto*,' Elvira whispered. 'My husband's things.' She paused, then, in a more emphatic whisper, she said, 'Not mine.

His.' *Plastic bag?* thought Rose, puzzled, then remembered there had been something in Elvira's other hand, clutched to her body as they hauled her off the cliff. Rose looked across her strapped body on the stretcher and there was the bag. The policeman was talking to the doctor; she wondered if he'd seen it. Questioningly she looked from the policeman to Elvira and saw her make a tiny movement of the head, shaking no. *She wants me to have it,* thought Rose, and felt a tiny flare of gratification. She leaned over and in one quick, deft movement took the crumpled plastic bag; Elvira smiled again, and closed her eyes.

The policeman turned. 'That's enough,' he said gruffly. 'Come on.' He turned back to the doctor, said something and watched as the trolley was wheeled away, the strapped shape of Elvira's body on it suddenly insubstantial. Rose bit her lip, wondering if she would see Elvira Vitale again. The policeman turned back to her.

'Okay,' he said, prising a notebook from his back pocket. 'I need some details from you, Signora. Your name?'

Rose lowered herself into one of the grey chairs, a row of them welded to a metal stand. There wasn't much to say. She had arrived too late, seen almost nothing; how could she explain a feeling, a premonition? Elvira Vitale's weary face at the bar, Richard Bourn's suspicions? She could only describe Jack Robbins' demeanour when she arrived, the small things that had made her anxious, the stain on the doorstep, the wrenched door-frame. The officer nodded, writing everything down; they, too, had seen these things. He stood up.

'Thank you, Signora.' He hesitated. 'You are a resident? Not on holiday?' Rose shook her head. 'Not on holiday.' 'Good,' said the policeman with satisfaction. 'Because we may need to talk to you again.' He raised a finger in warning, then pushed

303

his cap back on his head, revealing a forehead gleaming with perspiration and giving him a rumpled, surprised look.

Rose got to her feet, went over to the doors and pushed them open. She saw a reception desk with a computer console but no receptionist to tell her whether she could come in or not. A half-empty waiting area, a few bowed, greying heads, an old woman being comforted by a younger one, a middle-aged daughter with grey hair greasy and limp in the heat, the kind of dishevelled look about the pair of them that comes from grief and anxiety. A bored-looking young mother with a child at her feet, wriggling under the seat. Beyond them a wide corridor with several doors led off the waiting area; this was where she had seen Richard. He had gone.

Oh, well. Rose sat down on the nearest chair. At the far end of her row sat an elderly lady, bundled in layers of faded black despite the heat, even thick brown tights on her legs; she, too, clutched a crumpled plastic bag on her lap, a husband's personal effects perhaps. Rose looked down at the bag Elvira Vitale had given her, and cautiously she pulled it open, to see this husband's things.

The bag at first seemed to hold rubbish, scraps of paper, bottles of pills, and for a moment she wondered if Elvira Vitale had had some – episode. Manic, delusional, whatever. She turned one of the bottles around; the name on it was Elvira Vitale's, although they called her Robbins. Mrs Elvira Robbins; it sounded lumpen and ugly. Prescribed in England, then, where she was known by her husband's name; in Italy not only film stars, Rose knew, but all women were called by their maiden name, and briefly she felt a swell of pride in her adopted home. So much more – dignified. To keep one's name.

One bottle was something called Xanax, another Seroxat,

a third Temazepam. Most of the prescriptions had been filled in London, one bore the label of a Los Angeles pharmacy. She weighed them in her hand; they were big, family-sized containers. So many pills. Wasn't that dangerous, in case – in case someone had suicidal tendencies? Rose delved further into the bag, sorting the pieces of paper, unfurling an old train ticket, pulling out a stained napkin. Bewildered, she stopped, gazed ahead, trying to make sense of it. Her husband's things. What had she meant by that? She gazed at the bottles spread on her lap, thought of all these drugs in Elvira Vitale's name. Rose didn't know much about drugs but she had a vague idea that these all had a sedative effect. She understood, then; he supplied them. Jack Robbins. To keep his wife happy, and quiet. What a good husband.

At the end of the corridor she focused on the policeman, talking to a doctor in a white coat and clogs. The policeman was asking something of him, gesticulating, and the doctor was shaking his head slowly. Rose looked back at the bag, poked around inside it.

In the bottom was the only thing that didn't seem to be rubbish; a longish leather box with a gold band and Jack Robbins' initials embossed on the lid. Someone sat down beside Rose but she hardly registered it; she went on looking at the box. Smooth, polished brown leather, shiny and grained as walnut, but the tiny brass lock had been crudely forced.

'Rose?' She looked up and saw that the man beside her was Richard Bourn. He looked at her gravely, and she thought she saw concern in his eyes. She realized he knew nothing of what had happened.

'What are you doing here?' he asked. 'Are you all right?'

'I'm fine,' she said slowly, 'But – the interview never

happened. Things all went a bit haywire. Elvira Vitale —well, it looks like she'd tried to kill herself. And they – the police – came while I was there. I think they were arresting Jack Robbins.' She saw Richard Bourn look away at this. 'Did you know about that?' He looked down at his hands, and slowly she went on, 'And anyway, what are *you* doing here? Have you been here since this morning?'

'No,' said Richard, looking at his hands. 'I – I went to the police straight after you left. Then I came back.' He seemed uncomfortable. Just then the policeman walked back down the corridor and past them, hardly glancing their way. They paused, watched the man walk towards the glare of the late-afternoon sun that flooded through the hospital's wide glass doors, a patch of sweat darkening his pale blue uniform shirt between the shoulder-blades. The doors swished and the policeman vanished, swallowed up by the light. Richard stared back down at his hands, then looked up at Rose; she thought he looked unhappy.

'I wanted to know if she was okay; Ania. She's called Ania. She's down there.' He pointed down the corridor to a pale blue door at the end; as they watched a nurse emerged, closing the door firmly behind her.

'They won't let me see her. Only relatives, they said.'

Rose sat up. 'She's not –'

'No, no,' said Richard Bourn with a weary smile. 'I think there's no danger. She's just very weak, they said. It's just –' He seemed to notice the bag in her hands then, frowning at it. 'What's that?'

'Oh,' said Rose, 'I'm not sure myself, actually. Elvira Vitale gave it to me.' She stopped, too weary suddenly to go into it all. She handed him the bag. 'She said it was her husband's stuff.'

306

Richard pulled out a couple of pill bottles and held them in his big brown hand. 'Huh,' he said, examining the labels. 'Sleeping pills. Tranquillizers. Prozac.' He looked at her and shrugged. 'He hasn't been taking this stuff, has he? Prescription stuff. They'd pack a bit of a punch if you took the whole lot together, though.' He frowned. 'Not his style, falling asleep on Valium, I'd say.'

'No,' said Rose slowly. 'I think – I think he was doping her with it.' Richard nodded wearily. 'Yes,' he said. 'That would figure.' Rose looked at him curiously; surely this confirmed everything he had suspected about Jack Robbins? But there was no elation in his tone; in fact he seemed almost downcast at the discovery. She watched as he pulled the stained napkin from the bag and regarded it with bemusement. The folded receipt fell out of it into his hand, leaking a little powder into his palm, and he lifted it to his face, picked up a grain or two with his tongue, grimacing. 'Coke,' he said meditatively. 'No surprises there.'

Then Richard saw the leather, box, extracted it carefully from the crumpled plastic and hesitated, weighing it in his hands like a prize. He looked at Rose as if asking permission, and she shrugged. He sighed, and opened the box; Rose couldn't see what was in there, but she heard Richard give a kind of joyless laugh.

'What?' said Rose. What is it?'

Richard looked up, his eyes dark. 'Well, it's not Rohypnol,' he said quietly.

'So? Do you know what it is?' He turned the box towards her and she saw two silver blister packs of pills, small, blue, triangular. Four pills had been popped from one of the packs.

'Viagra,' he said flatly. She didn't ask him how he knew.

'Jack Robbins couldn't get it up,' he said, and she couldn't tell if the disgust in his voice was for himself or Jack Robbins. He laughed again, a harsh, dry sound, dropped the box back inside the bag and held it out to Rose. When she took it he buried his face in his hands, and when he looked up again he looked very tired.

Rose frowned. 'What's up?' she said. 'You look worn out.'

Richard sighed, rubbing a temple over and over. 'I – I did come to make sure the girl was okay. But there was something else too.' He stopped, and Rose said nothing. 'I've done something wrong,' he said.

'What have you done?' she said quietly.

'You've got to understand,' he said. 'It's all been going on so long. Since I retired, that's all I've been doing, trying to nail Jack Robbins. And in the end I had to –' He stopped, shaking his head in a dazed sort of way.

'Yes?'

'I lied,' he said flatly.

Rose's heart sank. 'To me?'

'No,' he said, shaking his head. 'No, no. To the police. I lied to the police; I was just so desperate for them to get him, once and for all. And I was so sure, I even convinced myself.'

'Of what? That he killed your wife?'

Richard sighed and looked up at her. 'Not that – I'm still sure of that. As sure as anyone can ever be. He might not even have positively wanted her dead, but I think – he didn't care if she died or not. That's the same, in my book.' His voice was hollow with loss.

'Then what?' said Rose gently.

'When I went to report finding Ania, I told them about – my wife. But not just that. You see, Ania – she's Jack Robbins' maid. She was reported missing last week; last seen on Wednesday. And, well –' He paused. 'I knew he'd taken her to the station that day, I saw them pulling up when –' he ducked his head again – 'when I was leaving the station with you, just after we met.' His voice was low and ashamed. 'And I told them –' Richard hesitated, stared up at the ceiling at the harsh strip lighting, anywhere, it seemed to Rose, but at her.

'Go on,' she said quietly.

Richard sighed, his face set with resignation. 'I said I was certain he was having an affair with her and I thought he wanted to get rid of her because she was going to tell his wife.' He sat, elbows on his knees, face between his hands, and stared at the floor.

Rose was staggered. 'You knew all this?'

He looked up at her. 'That's the problem,' he said slowly. 'I didn't know. Don't know. I mean, I'd even more or less convinced myself it was true, but I – the truth is, I made it up. So they'd go after him. And now – I know it was wrong. The wrong thing to do, and quite likely just wrong. Inaccurate. Because –' he hesitated briefly – 'because he dropped her there, that's it. He let her out of the car and drove away. So unless he came back again, he wasn't the one who killed her, was he? Because that's where she was last seen, the police said, that day.'

'So even when you were saying it you knew it was a lie?'

'I suppose I did. Yes, I did. And I came here – yes, sure, I wanted to know she was all right. But I wanted to ask her – Ania – if it was him; tell the truth, I might even have tried to talk her into saying it.' He stopped.

'What changed your mind?'

He looked at her. 'It was something – when I wanted to see her, they asked me if I was family. I said no, and then thought,

I felt so – so –' He paused, lost for words. 'Sick of myself,' he said finally, his voice full of self-disgust. 'To end up here, that girl half-dead, and all I could think about was myself, and bloody Jack Robbins. This isn't me. I hate this. If it has to be done like this, by lying, then I'm not going to do it.'

Rose looked at him, at his tired, crumpled face, and felt a wave of pity for the way his life had eluded his control; she could see all at once the kind of man he was. One who needed order and clarity, who believed in taking care to get things right, who'd been led into deceit as though down a blind alley and now he didn't know how to get out.

'Right,' she said. 'Look, it's not too late, is it? If it's not him, they'll find out, as soon as they talk to Ania, won't they?'

Richard stared at her, and slowly his brow cleared; gratefully he broke into a smile. 'You're right,' he said, and she heard his relief. You're right. It's not too late.'

'We'll wait together,' said Rose, looking into his exhausted face with concern, and to her surprise Richard put his arms around her. He rested his head on her shoulder, and she found herself pressed tight against his chest; they both stood there for a long moment, and Rose was in no hurry, she found, to let go. When eventually she stood back and looked at him, he smiled, and she thought he looked different. His face was pale with tiredness, but the haunted, distracted look had gone.

'Look,' he said. 'I want to wait until I'm sure she's all right.' He hesitated, looking at her earnestly. You don't have to – I mean, if you'd like – let me take you home, then I can come back.'

He wanted her to stay; Rose knew it with a kind of under-standing newly acquired, some instinct she felt she'd always lacked before. She felt the knowledge that she was wanted warm her.

'No,' she said. 'I'll wait.'

Cirri put his hands to his head, thinking. 'Toto?' he called absently through the half-open door. 'Toto? Before I forget, get someone down there to the hospital, will you? Keep an eye on that girl, talk to her when she wakes up properly.'

He didn't wait for an answer, stared down at his leather desk top, thinking. Villemartin's neighbour had a granddaughter who'd had an abortion at the same clinic, the year before. Discharged last year on the same day as Myriam Bosnic, and Bosnic's body had been found the day after. Like the snow in one of those glass toys, the pieces whirled and floated in Cirri's head, and slowly they began to settle.

Almost as an afterthought he'd said to Anna-Maria's mother, 'The son. The neighbour's son. Where does he live?'

She couldn't think at first, couldn't remember, she knew of course, it was just that everything was getting so muddled, she couldn't seem to get a grip. Somewhere out east, yes. Somewhere on the coast . . . did he go fishing? Yes, she thought he did. Cirri said nothing, thought of fishing line in an old fisherman's hard hands. He waited. Anna-Maria's mother fell silent and he wondered if she'd wandered off. Then she spoke.

'Levanto, that's it. One of those villages up behind Levanto.' Slowly Cirri exhaled, a careful, controlled sound.

She went on now, rambling a little in a pitiful, melancholy way. The son came out on the train to visit his mother, now and again, not a frequent visitor but he was always there the day before Ferragosto, because that was when his mother's birthday fell. Did Signora Villemartin know Nutri's daughter had had an abortion too, Leo Cirri asked as gently as he could. *On her grandmother's birthday*, he realized with a start. There can't be much love lost between those two, either.

No, Anna-Maria Villemartin's mother had whispered down the line, her voice barely audible, the voice of a ghost. No, she hadn't known that. They kept things to themselves, and it wasn't the kind of thing you told people, was it? She spoke as though to herself, wonderingly. Except old Signora Nutri had found out about Anna-Maria somehow, didn't need to be told. She'd overheard something probably, then wheedled around with her insinuations to find out for sure and Anna-Maria's mother had given in, sobbed her heart out, the betrayal of it pouring from her, the grief. They'd sat in the dining room, polished wood table with lace on it, the mother said, as though recalling events under hypnosis, transfixed. The old woman might have just said, I know what it's like, that would have been such a comfort, but she'd said nothing. Old Signora Nutri had sat in stony silence, let her go on thinking this was a singular shame, a great sinful millstone to bear on her own. No doubt she'd felt it her Christian duty to tell others. She might even have told her son, that good man who thought of Anna-Maria almost as another daughter, and what would he think of them now? Her voice rose, thin with mourning. What indeed?

Suddenly Leo Cirri couldn't listen any more. He said goodbye to the woman as gently as he could, said he'd keep her up to date with developments, but in the pit of his stomach a sour mixture of dread and triumph stirred. He replaced the receiver; there was a bitter taste in his mouth and then he knew what that elusive memory was that had tracked him as he spoke to Anna-Maria's mother. Giovanna, the daft, chattering barmaid, had seen the boys from the Love Shack, hadn't she? A man in a white shirt, that would have been Jack Robbins. And someone else, the invisible man, someone they all overlooked. A *contadino*, with a bag. Gennaro Nutri.

The maid had been found up there too, hadn't she? Last seen at the station, not far from where Nutri, if Cirri was right, had killed Anna-Maria, then found beaten and bound, wandering in the hills above Levanto – what village had Bourn said, Grosso? He'd bet his life that was where Gennaro Nutri lived. Leo Cirri stood up from his chair, reached for his coat, then hesitated. He thought of Jack Robbins, still in that interview room, and of where rushing in had got him so far. *Get your facts straight*, he told himself. *Talk to the daughter. But make it quick.*

He needed to get hold of Maria Grazia Nutri. But as he called for Toto to track down the number, he remembered Jack Robbins' maid, still in the hospital, and sat up. 'Toto?' There was no answer. Of course, Toto had gone in the helicopter. He was already at the hospital, wasn't he? Just as well; strictly speaking he should get a guard posted at her door. Deep down Cirri knew he had to get over there, but then his eye fell on the printout from the San Giovanni clinic; of course, they'd have contact details for Maria Grazia Nutri. He dialled the number.

But Toto wasn't at the hospital any more, because Elvira Vitale had committed no crime, made no allegation, brought no charges, and there was no justification for a police presence at her bedside. And although of course he was itching to find out what had happened he couldn't even talk to her, because although she was out of danger, the doctors had told him very firmly that she couldn't be questioned until the following morning at the earliest.

So Toto should have been on his way back to the station

but there'd been a traffic incident on the road to Bonassola: one of those big monster trucks – hairdresser's cars, the boss called them – had tried to overtake a camper van on a blind bend and met another coming the other way. A right mess, and when it had come through on the radio Toto happened to be just around the corner, on his way back to the station on foot. So when Leo Cirri thought he was at the hospital Toto was in fact standing beside the Bonassola road laboriously taking down details from a ponce from Milan, who only cared about his crumpled bull-bar, and two sets of irate Germans. And as he stood there, doggedly going through the motions as the motorists gesticulated and threatened across him, Toto looked down the valley and saw smoke.

He gaped; this was no garden bonfire, no backyard inciner-ator. At the lower end of one of the villages, Grosso, perhaps, or Doppo, hung a pall of grey smoke that covered half the hill-side, and as he watched it puffed and billowed down towards the town.

'Jesus,' Toto whispered, and his pencil fell to the ground. At the sound the Milanese turned and followed his gaze. They all stopped then, Germans and Italians alike, their altercation evaporating as they became aware of the new and sinister scent to the air, the distant gun-metal glitter of smoke particles on the heat haze. At that moment Toto felt the wind stir and rise off the sea behind him, and in the sudden silence they all heard the distant crackle of flame.

Chapter Twenty-Seven

Tiziana heard him coming. A lifetime of sitting on her doorstep in this village with an ear cocked for comings and goings had given her a sixth sense; she knew the sound of every car door as it slammed, every footfall, and particularly this one. He moved softly, Gennaro Nutri, like a cat, placing his feet carefully on the uneven surface of the village's paths and alleys; he could sneak up on you, that one, if you weren't careful. But Tiziana was careful.

She'd been right inside the *cantina* when she heard the sound; she'd been feeling around for a light-switch in the dank darkness, a smell of rancid oil and fish in her nostrils. She'd been able to see the rope, though, in the light that fell through the door. There were fishing lines beside it in reels, a couple of cans for gasoline and diesel below, and a neat row of tools on a shelf at eye level, mole grips, a wrench and knives: pruning knives, filleting knives, boning knives. She'd stared at them, suddenly beginning to wonder how good an idea this had been. And a frayed loop or two of blue nylon rope carefully coiled, just like the rope she'd seen on that girl's swollen wrist.

Tiziana had just bumped against a big oil drum and stubbed a toe, an agony with her feet, all hammer-toes and ingrowing nails. She was rubbing her foot and cursing when she heard him coming, up by the church; she heard the sound of his footsteps change as he passed under the covered walkway two hundred metres up the village. Without a second's hesitation Tiziana straightened up, whisked the rope from its nail and inside her overall. On slippered feet she was out through the door, locking it behind her and dropping the key back in its hiding place at the base of the plumbago before there was any sign of the *cantina*'s owner.

Where now? She couldn't get out of sight in time, the downhill corner was too far for her to round it before he appeared at the top of the alley. Could she risk ambling off as though she'd just been passing? But on her way where, and with a piece of his rope making an odd bulge beneath her flowered apron? Opposite the *cantina* the broken paling gate to a foreigner's sunny courtyard – the Swedish family? Or were they Germans? – swung idly on a broken hinge and in a blink Tiziana was through it, a sweat breaking on her forehead as she reached back to stop the gate from banging behind her. She hadn't known she could move so fast.

The soft footsteps descended at a leisurely pace; he was in no hurry. Stopped. Painfully Tiziana doubled over to get a look. Beneath the gate she could see a pair of stringy brown ankles, the bottoms of his canvas trousers, and, as he bent to retrieve his key, Tiziana glimpsed the sharp line of Gennaro Nutri's jaw. She swallowed, suddenly aware of how ridiculous she would appear if the door were to decide to swing back open in the wind. And how suspicious. Nutri set something down on the ground, and she bent further over, straining to see; something wrapped, a tub in florist's paper. She frowned, momentarily distracted; he'd been to buy a pot plant of some kind, a trailing spiral of shiny ribbon brushed the path. Was he on his way to visit his mother? The *cantina* door yawned open with the faintest squeak from well-oiled hinges, a gust of cold, fishy black air, and Tiziana held her breath. But there came no exclamation, no sign that he'd noticed anything wrong, anything missing. Just the hollow clang of a jerry-can being moved, the slop of a liquid, and the oily, unmistakable odour of gasoline filled the air.

Restless in the heat, Ania turned on her bed. Whatever sedative they had given her was wearing off, and although the fever had abated she was sweating. The shutters to the little ward were closed but she could feel the relentless heat of the evening sun behind them through the wood. Even the wall behind her head felt hot to the touch, as though she had been incarcerated in an oven and was being left here to roast. Above the door hung a heavy dark crucifix. Ania felt fear sitting in her chest like a stone; she couldn't put it off much longer.

The beds around her were still empty, neatly made up in the gloom, but now Ania was beginning to wish someone else would be admitted. Just for a bit of company, to ward off this feeling, to distract her. She raised her hand, tubes trailing, and examined it without much interest; she noted that the swelling had gone down, and she could even move her fingers. The door into the long corridor was just ajar, and through the gap she could glimpse shadowy figures moving up and down and

317

talking in lowered voices, too soft to understand. Ania laid her head back on the pillow and closed her eyes.

Perhaps it was the drug they'd given her; perhaps it had opened something up in her head, but the pictures came without being requested. Ania moved uneasily on the bed, but it was as if whatever it was that had kept her going, had got her here, was all used up. She gave in, lay still and remembered. On the station platform she had turned away in frustration from the glare of the sun on the tracks and gone into the cavernous interior of the ticket hall. Another strike, and a platform full of waiting passengers, foreigners seated on their backpacks and chatting, with no particular place to go. All right for some, Ania had thought, playing at being gypsies with a comfortable house to go back to, somewhere clean and smart, hot water and a mother to cook for them. She thought of her own mother now, and tossed her head on the pillow, distracted with longing, close to tears with it.

All right for some, was what Ania had thought standing on the platform in the afternoon heat, *but I've got to get somewhere, got to get some rest.* It had seemed too much, suddenly, that she should have to wait like this, not to know when she would get to her own bed, a burden too far. So she had turned to leave the station; made reckless by the injustice of it, of a train strike that punished only the workers, she'd had some idea that she might catch up with her employer and ask him for a lift. As if. And then she'd seen the man standing there right in her way, his eyes narrowed as he saw her as though he was trying to place her. Then he smiled and she'd smiled back.

Ania wasn't prone to smiling at strangers, but in some strange way she had felt as though she knew him. He might have been her own father, with his strong lined face and eyes hooded from a lifetime working under the sun, and besides, she did know him. Had seen him before, at least. Only the night before she'd seen him on the platform in Genova with his arm around his daughter, seeing her safe home. Or so she'd imagined.

What had he said? A man of few words; that in itself had put Ania at her ease, hadn't it? Shared disgust at the striking workers, an exchange of grievances. He was waiting for his daughter, but if there was a strike he might as well go and fetch her himself, from Genova. And as an afterthought, was that perhaps where she was headed? Perhaps he could ... And the little grey van had been there in the station car park, the cab hot from sitting in the sun.

The memory of it made her shudder, the terrible misjudgement. His hand across her on a bend, the sudden violence. *You saw me*, he said regretfully, and she'd felt his strong hand fasten on her. Feeling bile rise in her throat, Ania sat bolt upright in the dark, and screamed.

Along the corridor Rose and Richard heard the sound, and turning in unison towards it saw a nurse, a stout, motherly woman, emerge further along the corridor and make for the door from which the cry had come with an unhurried, rolling gait. Rose heard the nurse say something soothing as she rounded the door, *now, now, what's all this then?* And the girl's panicked voice pleading in a confusion of languages, half Italian and half something else. There was the sound of retching, and another nurse hurried past them with a basin, fishing in her pocket for something as she half-ran. They heard Ania's voice rise again and the sounds of gentle remonstration from the nurses, a brief metallic clatter, a soft grumbling sigh, and then silence returned.

After some moments the first nurse, then the second, emerged from Ania's room, pausing to confer for a moment in lowered voices. They seemed to Rose not to be able to agree on something and one of them pointed down towards the reception area.

'Was that her?' said Rose to Richard. 'Ania?' He nodded slowly. 'I think so.' Overhead Rose heard the sound of a helicopter, then another, passing over, a heavy, ominous roar.

'Do you think we should ask if there's anything we can do?' Rose felt helpless; the voice had held such a note of panic and fear. She remembered the rope around the girl's wrists; she had been tied up somewhere like a dog.

Richard smiled wryly. 'I did try that when I got here,' he said. 'These nurses don't accept interference very readily. But I'll ask, yes. Find out what's going on.' He frowned. 'Where the police have got to.' He stood up, stretched and yawned. 'Want a coffee?'

Leaden-eyed and heavy-limbed after so many hours of tension and uncertainty, Rose thought of a little cup of treacly espresso and realized that it was exactly what she wanted. Because she had become more Italian than she realized. She nodded, and sat up.

'No, no, stay there,' he said. 'I'll bring you one back from the bar. Talk to the nurses on the way. Okay?'

Gratefully Rose settled back in her seat and watched him go. She liked being there with Richard, she realized, never mind where they were, or why. Liked being two, not one, for once; everything seemed so much easier. There was no sound, now, from Ania's room, and no one in the corridor; on impulse Rose stood and tiptoed to the door. It was open an inch or two, and she peered into the gloom. All the beds but one were empty, all but the one next to the window, and its occupant lay quite still. As she listened Rose heard a harsh snore, the mechanical response to heavy sedation. Ania was asleep.

On her way back from Ania's room Rose passed another door, open on to what appeared to be a staff room; some shabby armchairs, a row of lockers and a coffee machine. It was empty.

No one had asked Rose if they could help her, or what she thought she was doing. Levanto's forty-year-old hospital, the *policlinico*, was a sleepy little place as a rule, a basic emergency room, an obstetrics ward, orthopaedics for broken bones, and it had grown sleepier as the permanent population declined. At this time of the year, of course, midsummer, the population it served more than doubled with the arrival of holidaymakers, but still it had never been thought necessary to introduce anything more than the most basic of security measures. There were no access codes required, no proof of identity, no surveillance and barely a skeleton staff at reception most of the time; only the odd fierce ward sister stood between visitors and patients.

Even if there had been security cameras in the hospital car park, the arrival of a little grey Ape van would barely have registered, puttering in through the broken barrier and parking neatly beneath a tree for shade in the early-evening sun. The *contadino* who climbed out of it, a wiry individual whose age might have been anything between forty-five and seventy and was dressed carefully in his Sunday best, would have been close to invisible. It was nearly visiting time, and such figures were ten a penny; the nurses would often remark that the old country relatives were the only reliable visitors for sick loved ones, their children and grandchildren being too busy these

321

days, off snorkelling in the Maldives or holding down office jobs in the city. As a consequence the well-worn clothes and weathered faces of farmers' wives and fishermen were like camouflage in these dull grey hospital corridors, and they came and went unnoticed.

The car park was almost empty, anyway; perhaps this evening's visitors had been drawn away by all the commotion up the valley, where the helicopters were dropping their load of sea water on yet another forest fire. This one, it seemed, had all but blocked the main road into Levanto; strangely, though, it didn't seem to have started in the obvious way, a cigarette carelessly discarded out of the window of a car, nor, as was usual in cases of arson, somewhere off the beaten track in the middle of the forest where there were no witnesses. This time the fire had started in one of the hill villages, down on the edge of Grosso where there were *cantinas* and storerooms carved out of the rock and where the *contadini* kept their oil drums and gas bottles. Which was perhaps why it had got so far and spread so fast, fuelled by God knew what lethal substances, carelessly stored. At any rate, it had certainly been noticed now; the bright livery of fire engines was clearly visible even through the haze of smoke, standing guard at the lower edge of the fire.

The man paused for a moment in the car park and looked back at the layers of smoke that hung across the valley inland, unsmiling, eyes narrowed against the low sun slanting in from the west. His lined face betrayed no curiosity, and only the odd little nod, almost of approval, that he gave as he turned back towards the hospital's entrance gave a hint that he had even noticed the commotion. A lean, upright figure carrying a cellophane-wrapped gardenia, Gennaro Nutri approached

322

the wide glass doors of the hospital and disappeared through them like a ghost.

Maria Grazia Nutri – my name's Mia, now, she said – had been succinct on the subject of her family.

'My grandmother,' she said, enunciating carefully, 'is an interfering old woman. And my father is a cold-blooded bastard.' There was a silence. 'I hate him,' she burst out with sudden savagery, and as her voice broke Cirri could hear something else, something more than anger, something like grief.

'All those years,' she spat, when he said nothing, 'waiting for him to get back from some cruise or other, nine months on, six weeks off, and I'd be all dolled up in my party dress, lace tights, the lot, a kiss for Daddy, and he'd walk me round the town, showing me off, then he'd be back to sea. But when he came back one time and I wasn't a little girl any more ...' She tailed off briefly, sighed.

'He came home for my fourteenth birthday, a surprise visit. He came through the door, spotted a love bite on my neck, and he didn't say a thing, just hit me so hard I saw stars. I had dizzy spells for a year after that. Had to go to the hospital. That's when Mum left him.'

'How long is it since you last saw your father?' Cirri asked her quietly, trying not to think of his Chiara in her little white lace dress, round-eyed like a china doll.

'A year, maybe,' she said, but her voice was subdued.

'Ferragosto last year, then?' She said nothing.

Cirri took a deep breath. 'Did he know you'd had a – a termination?' There was no point in hedging.

Maria Grazia – he couldn't think of her as Mia; did that make him like her father? – was silent for a long moment.

When she spoke her voice was dull. 'I saw him when I came out of the clinic,' she said. 'I don't know how he found out, but I expect Nonna told him. I should never have said anything to her, but – I wanted – I don't know, to shock her.'

'On her birthday.' It was not a question.

'So? Just because she's old doesn't mean she's a sweetheart. She's a nasty old woman, wants everyone else to be as miserable as she is.'

She was defiant, daring him to act the father with her, but he said nothing, and when she spoke again the bravado was all gone.

'You have to stay in three, four hours after the – operation; I didn't know that. If it had been down to me I'd have been out of that place straight off and never mind blood clots or whatever, but they made us wait, all sitting around staring at each other in some waiting room. And when they let us out – there he was, on the pavement.' Her voice shook then, just a little, and he imagined the man, one of those country characters standing there in his old clothes, unsmiling, watchful, patient. Registering the girls' faces as they emerged from the clinic. What did he see? Messed-up, promiscuous teenagers, cheap little tarts, whores? Kids. His daughter among them. And Myriam Bosnic, dead that night.

'Did he speak to you?'

'He took hold of my arm and said, all quiet, I wasn't his daughter any more, and if he ever saw me again he'd kill me,' she said simply. 'He didn't even shout, just said it as if he was asking me not to get home too late. No one batted an eyelid.' She sounded incredulous. 'I just walked on. I didn't look back at him.'

Cirri nodded to himself. 'Did you tell your mother?' he

found himself asking, thinking of the girl walking away, alone. In the distance he could hear the sound of rotor blades in the air, more a vibration than a noise but getting louder. The helicopters were on their way back to the sea to pick up more water. The glass in his windows shivered, a tinny, ghostly sound.

The girl's voice was hard and suspicious now. 'Why do you want to know all this, mister? All right, yes, I told her, eventually. I shouldn't have done, though, she went up there to that miserable little village, Grosso, to have a go at him but he wouldn't listen; told her he'd kill her, too. I bet that gave his neighbours something to gossip about.'

There was a sudden, deafening roar as the helicopters passed overhead; Cirri shouted into the receiver, but the line was dead. Maria Grazia Nutri had gone.

The phone went again almost immediately but Cirri was already half out of the door, trying to think what to say to Robbins and his lawyer and what was the quickest route up into the hills to Grosso. It took him a minute to work out what the hell Toto was on about.

'Up the valley,' he was saying, 'smoke coming down like a bloody great cloudbank, you can hardly see a thing. We'll have to close the road.'

'What – Toto – wait a minute. Where are you? Aren't you at the hospital?'

There was a crackle and a roar of static that swallowed Toto's voice up, and when it returned he was saying something about the coast road and a collision. In the background Cirri could hear angry foreign voices. *Shit*.

'Look, Toto,' he said urgently. 'I think we've got him. Forget Robbins, it's not him; it's a local, after all. It was all in the clinic printout – that was good work.' He was itching to go now. 'I'll tell you later. Get back to the hospital.' Hopeless, he thought, Toto'll be half an hour getting out of that mess. But then Toto spoke and this time the line was clear as a bell.

'Boss,' he said. 'No way you're going to Grosso. That's where the fire is.'

Robbins and his lawyer were right where he'd left them, sitting calmly side by side at the interview table. Bruscolo, the officer he'd left keeping an eye on them, was standing in the corner with his arms folded and looking fed up. The lawyer stood up immediately but before he could speak Cirri said brusquely, 'All right, you can go now. Thank you for your help.' Outraged, the lawyer began to bluster about unlawful arrest, shaking a sheaf of papers in Cirri's face. Ignoring him Cirri looked down at Robbins, whose gaze was fixed on a distant point – he was half-smiling still as though in anticipation of victory. Cirri had to wipe that smile from Jack Robbins' face.

'No one was arrested,' he said to the lawyer, but still looking at his client. 'Mr Robbins came of his own free will. A girl was murdered, that mustn't be forgotten.' He paused. 'And besides, there is still the matter of Signora Vitale's accident.'

He studied Robbins' face and watched as the realization that he was not quite off the hook yet dawned and the dangerous edge Cirri had perceived in him before evaporated. His unshaven jaw sagged, and at the corner of his mouth a fleck of dried saliva gave him a vagrant, unsavoury look.

'I'd like to see her,' he said in a whisper. 'My wife.'

Cirri barked a laugh. 'Not now,' he said. 'Perhaps not ever. She's critical. How long had she been down there, and you didn't even call emergency? Why didn't you want to see your wife then?'

Robbins' eyes darted away, and Cirri turned to the lawyer.

He paused. 'Take him home,' he said. 'And make sure he stays there. If there's an officer available after all this I might send someone over to accompany him to the hospital in the morning.' Cirri watched as that prospect registered in Robbins' face, that like a criminal he could not even visit his wife without a police escort. He was no longer a free man. Two red spots appeared on his cheeks and Cirri saw that he was shamed. *About time*, thought Cirri as at last he made for the door. *About time*.

Elvira took some time to come round from the anaesthetic. She felt dehydrated, the membranes of her mouth, nose, even her eyes felt gritty, and her head throbbed. She couldn't feel her legs at all.

The surgeon, a gentle man with curly greying hair and wire glasses who rested his long, cool fingers on her forearm absently as he spoke, had explained to her in the room where they administered the anaesthetic that this would happen. They could not be sure what the outcome would be, but he was optimistic. All the same, she should be prepared for an initial period of paralysis. And after the operation he had returned to the recovery room to tell her that her spinal cord had not been damaged, but she had cracked a vertebra at the base of her spine and the bruising was severe, the swelling considerable. The operation had gone very well, on the other hand; they had succeeded in removing a shard of bone that had threatened to cause further, irreparable damage. Quite calmly Elvira had looked up at the man as he spoke gravely to her; he reminded her of her old friend Venturelli, and she trusted him. What a thing it was, she realized, trust.

'Do you understand?' he had asked her. Elvira understood.

She could move her arms. She could still feel the cool touch of the surgeon's fingers on her forearm; it was as though, paradoxically, her senses had been sharpened by her accident. Like the first day at school, Elvira thought out of nowhere, nearly half a century ago, when her mother had kissed her goodbye and she had stood in the long, unfamiliar hall full of echoing voices and strange smells and watched her go. All that day she had thought she could still feel the warm imprint of her mother's lips, had every now and then put her hand up to her cheek in class, certain that there would be something there. *That was my mother, too*, Elvira thought with a kind of amazement; she had forgotten all this. She turned her head on the pillow towards the window and felt a hot tear trickle down one cheek.

Elvira lay there for a long time, it seemed, listening to the sounds of the hospital around her and watching the sky change through the window above her. She could see a dark ridge of mountain and above it the last of the light fading from a violet sky. Night was coming, and something else; there was a blue haze at the ridge as though of low cloud, or smoke. The door opened and a nurse came in.

'We'll move you downstairs soon,' she said kindly after she'd checked the drips, made notes on a chart and taken Elvira's temperature. Elvira accepted the information, smiling a little at the woman's reassuring face, her expression of concentration. 'You're doing very well. But someone will have to come in with some things for you.' She looked at Elvira's ring finger. 'Your husband?'

My husband. The words sounded very odd to Elvira, all

wrong. She realized that she had quite dispensed with her husband, in her mind. She understood at the same time that this absence was the key to the preternatural calm that had descended on her. Whatever her future held, it would not hold Jack. And everything would be all right.

'I don't think so,' she said, her voice a little hoarse, but firm. She felt it was the first time she had spoken in hours, days. 'I wonder –' She hesitated. Had it been her imagination?

'Yes?'

'Did – there was a woman, came in with me. Wasn't there?'

The nurse frowned a little, half-turned towards the door as though trying to recall. 'Yes?' she said. 'Is she still here?'

Gennaro was methodical in his search, as in all things; it was a small hospital, after all, and he would start at the top and work down.

The recovery nurse reflected in the lift on her way down to reception, only two floors below but it had been a long day and her feet were killing her, that the old man with the pot plant was on the wrong floor. There were no wards up on the top, only theatre and recovery suites and administration; he must have got lost, pressed the wrong button, got out too late. She should have stopped and asked him where he was going, who he was looking for, but it was always happening. The old folks would be anxious and confused so they easily lost their bearings and they could be talkers; she didn't want to get stuck there for hours promising this and that, listening to an old man's tales of woe. And she'd promised to track down this woman, whoever she was, and if she hurried, she might catch her.

Elvira saw the outline of a man, not tall, standing in the

doorway. He wore a hat, carried flowers, and for an instant she thought, on her cloud of sedative drugs, *it's my father, come to claim me.* It had been one of the things she'd wondered during her brief five years or less of fame, when her face appeared on the cover of *Gente* and *Oggi* every other week. She'd wondered if he would come, would remember whatever short-lived liaison he'd had with her mother and come for money or something, but he never had. Of course, he was long dead, and had probably never known he was her father. There was a tiny creak, a breath of air and he was gone; there was only yellow light falling through the door. Elvira felt nothing but relief.

Rose saw Richard coming back, picking his way from the bar through the reception area. He held a tiny plastic cup and had a nurse in tow.

'Someone's been asking for you,' he said, as Rose downed the syrupy spoonful of coffee. He stepped aside and the nurse inspected her.

The long corridor yawned emptily in front of them as the lift doors opened. It was very quiet on the top floor, and warm. The nurse looked up and down the corridor for a moment with a faintly perturbed expression as though she was looking for something, but whatever it was didn't delay her for more than a moment before she apparently decided it wasn't worth her time. She set off briskly down the hall and showed Rose into a small, dimly lit room with the ominous shapes of resuscitation equipment ranged against the walls, pumps and masks and dangling tubes, and one bed beneath a large window. Elvira Vitale turned her head very slightly on the pillow and looked at Rose.

'Hello,' she said. The nurse beside Rose stood there for a

moment, as though trying to gauge the situation, but then she seemed to give up.

'Five minutes,' she said with an admonitory look to Rose, and left the room.

Elvira was still looking at her as Rose approached the bed. There was a small hard stool beside it, and she sat down.

'I wanted to say thank you,' said Elvira. And then, almost as an afterthought, 'Who are you?'

Rose laughed, and at once the atmosphere in the room lifted. Elvira's hands lay on top of the bed's worn cotton cover and she lifted the one nearest to Rose. It seemed almost to float up of its own volition and without thinking Rose took it.

'I was coming to interview you,' she said. The thin, cool hand relaxed in hers.

'Ah, yes. The journalist.' Elvira Vitale's voice sounded quite unlike the one Rose had heard on the phone only three days earlier, quite contented now, and peaceful. It was as though they were having an ordinary conversation. 'Venturelli sent you. He's a nice man, Venturelli, don't you think?' She said it wonderingly, as though the thought was quite novel, and Rose supposed that if you had married the men Elvira Vitale had married, the dry kindness of the Torinese might well appear like a revelation.

'Yes,' said Rose, then, hesitating, 'They've arrested your husband. They've arrested Jack.'

'Ah,' said Elvira, and Rose saw the ghost of a smile on her pale lips. 'He won't like that.'

'What happened?' Rose asked. 'Do you remember?'

Elvira turned her head away a little and gazed at the ceiling. 'Oh yes,' she said. 'It seems like a long time ago. Don't you think?' Rose nodded slightly.

Elvira turned back to look at her. 'I jumped,' she said.

331

'He didn't push you?'

Elvira laughed; the sound was dry and painful enough to be a cough. 'Jack couldn't push anyone. I think it would make him sick. He's a coward.'

Rose remembered Jack Robbins' sour breath on her cheek as they stood on that wide, baronial stairway. 'He didn't hurt you?'

'I thought he was poisoning me,' Elvira said conversationally. 'I didn't know if I was just going crazy, or if – I did feel it. I felt like I was being poisoned. That's why I kept all that – that junk. Napkins, coffee cups. It does seem crazy now.'

Rose nodded. 'Well,' she said, and meant it, 'it's not too far from the truth. You shouldn't have been on all this stuff.'

Elvira closed her eyes briefly. 'I just wanted to clear my head,' she said. 'All those pills ... ' Her voice tailed off and Rose wondered if she'd fallen asleep. Then she opened her eyes and her gaze wandered to the bag in Rose's lap. '*That* was Jack,' said Elvira, her voice quite clear and sure now. The pills. I didn't have to take them, of course; not to begin with. But there was always a good reason, I mean, why be anxious or unhappy if you don't have to be? And then I was afraid of what would happen if I stopped.'

Rose felt distaste for Jack Robbins coil inside her, and on impulse she reached into the plastic bag. She brought out the blister pack of triangular blue pills, leaned towards Elvira and held them up so she could see. 'Do you know what these are?'

Elvira frowned. 'No,' she said slowly. 'They're Jack's. I found them in his room.'

'I know,' said Rose, nodding. She narrowed her eyes, watching, and chose her words carefully. 'It looks like he needed a bit of help himself. They're Viagra.'

Elvira looked at her, eyes wide, and put a hand to her mouth. Then, as Rose watched, a smile, a proper smile this time, curled the edges of her mouth and creased the corners of her eyes, and just for a moment Rose saw what Elvira must have been like as a girl. With no more than a twinge of regret she thought of the scoop she would never deliver to Cookie Pearson. She dropped the foil strip back into the bag, placed it gently at the end of the bed and stood up.

'There's someone waiting for me,' she said. 'But I hope I'll see you again.'

It had looked good to start with, the roads quiet in the dusk. Cirri rounded a bend, and immediately he had to stamp on the brake. There ahead of him sat a tailback of twenty cars and just visible beyond them the banners and flags of yet another summer parade twirling and swaying over the heads of a modest crowd. This was where everyone was. *Shit*. Overhead he felt the pressure go in his ears as a helicopter thundered in from the sea and up the valley.

Chapter Twenty-Eight

It was dark but the fire was still burning. It had covered three hectares of land by now; orchards, vines, olive groves and a derelict farmhouse stood blackened and smoking, reeking of destruction. Elsewhere the flames seemed to lick straight up the bare trunks in an instant, then billow and take hold in the canopy of foliage like a great head of hair catching light, the blaze suspended in mid-air. It was unusual to find a fire in such a place, not on the coast where land values were sky-high and arson was lucrative; there it would have been easier to control, too, as the helicopters had less ground to cover with their great water bombs. Little by little, though, despite the rising wind, the firemen seemed to be making headway at last.

The road out of Levanto, however, the road that connected the town to the inland villages and the rest of the world and had been so long coming, was impassable now, and once again the town's inhabitants found themselves cut off from the interior. Striped yellow barriers stood across the road half a kilometre from where the fire burned, and its glow was reflected in the faces of the curious as they pressed up against the cordon and watched. From behind them came the sing-song siren of an ambulance, and the spectators stood aside reluctantly and allowed it through.

Behind it Cirri arrived at the cordon in a sweat, spraying gravel from the verge as he pulled in. The fireman manning the barrier watched him come over.

'I've got to get to Grosso,' Cirri said with as much authority as he could muster, coming to a halt in front of the burly figure. 'Can you let me through? It can't wait.' *Damn*, he thought. *Looks like Toto got it right.*

'Sorry, sir,' said the fireman imperturbably, eyeing him. 'Not a possibility. Grosso's right in the middle of it. We've been evacuating the inhabitants for an hour and a half, and even we're having to pull back now. It's too dangerous.'

Cirri looked from the fireman to the billowing bank of smoke. He could taste it, hot and acrid, at the back of his throat, and his eyes stung.

'This isn't just a forest fire, is it?' he said, distracted momentarily. The fireman put his head on one side. 'Not this one, no, sir,' he said. 'I wouldn't say so. Started in some old country feller's *cantina*, they're saying, and a lot of accelerants involved. At least one casualty.'

Cirri's eyes were beginning to stream and he wiped them with his sleeve; he knew he had to think fast. There was only one place he could go now. 'Thanks,' he said to the fireman, already turning back to his car at a run. He tore at the door, feeling the fear rise up inside him. *As long as it wasn't too late.*

*

335

On the first floor Gennaro stood in a concrete lobby, looking in through reinforced glass at the ward. There were a couple of metal seats but he was standing. A long, bright, broad corridor stretched away from him, and as he watched a midwife wheeled a perspex cradle through from one room to another, then a woman in a thin hospital gown came to the door of one of the rooms. She was very pale; a swaddled bundle was held high across her body and supported by a stomach still visibly soft and distended beneath the gown. From where Gennaro stood you could only see a tiny blurred oval for a face, all wrapped and folded as the baby was in the cotton blanket, but the mother didn't look away from it all the time he stood there.

A midwife coming on shift brushed past him on her way through the door and when he didn't move she paused. A fisherman, this one, she thought, looking at the bag at his shoulder, pockets for fishing line and bait, funny things to bring into hospital with you. He was carrying a plant wrapped in paper and gold ribbon and she turned to face him with a professional smile.

'A bit late for visiting,' she said cheerfully. 'They need their rest, these ladies.' He said nothing, looking at her blankly, and she tried again. 'Come to see a grandchild?'

She couldn't have said what it was exactly that brought her up short then, but the fisherman stared at her with a look so dark and empty, so lacking in any of those feelings she expected to see, that she took a step back.

'Come back tomorrow, eh?' she said briskly. 'Only dads after eight, see?' And she fixed the polite smile on her face and stood her ground until, at last, he turned and headed for the lift, his footsteps slow and soft on the polished tiles. And even when the midwife was sure he was gone, after she had come on to the ward and clocked in and greeted her colleagues, she still couldn't shake off the feeling she'd had when he looked back at her. She made a note for the technicians to sort out that entryphone.

'You've had enough, haven't you?' said Richard, taking one look at Rose as she emerged from the lift. She felt somehow lighter for having seen Elvira and given her back her bag, but drained. 'I'll take you home. They're both okay, after all, in no danger. The police'll sort it all out now.'

Rose nodded tiredly, trying to summon the energy to make a decision. Thanks,' she said gratefully, stretching. She could smell herself, sweat and gasoline, but it didn't seem to matter to Richard. As they passed the lift it pinged and the doors opened; someone came out but Rose didn't turn to look; she just wanted to get home now, looking only ahead at the big glass doors ushering them out into the sweet night air.

But as she came outside Rose stopped, and sniffed. She turned to Richard.

'What's that smell? Smoke?'

Richard frowned and shrugged; beside them a young man in motorcycle leathers, a helmet hanging from one arm, was leaning against the wall taking a last deep drag on his cigarette and Richard turned to him, sniffing the air. It wasn't cigarette smoke on the wind.

'What's that?' he said in Italian. 'Is there a fire somewhere?'

The boy nodded, his heavy-lidded eyes taking the two of them in without curiosity. 'Yeah,' he said. 'Up there.' He nodded inland, but when they followed his eyes they saw no more than a fading glow against the hills. 'Road's blocked while they sort it. Looks like we're stuck here for a while.' He smiled, dropped the cigarette butt on to the concrete, ground it with his booted foot and turned to go back inside.

'What do we do now?' said Rose in despair as the prospect of home, shower, bed all receded.

Richard passed a hand over his forehead.

'Well . . .' he said slowly, but then, from the direction in which the boy had nodded, came the rising wail of a siren and within seconds two ambulances hurtled through the barrier to the hospital car park and round to the emergency bay, followed by two or three cars. They must have come from the fire, Rose thought, and it dawned on her first that this was serious, and then that if the blaze was blocking the main road up the valley it couldn't be far from Grosso. She put her hands to her face, trying to think.

'What?' said Richard. 'What's up?'

'Let's go inside,' said Rose. She didn't want him to see her jumping to ridiculous conclusions – after all, the fire could be anywhere inland, couldn't it? – but she wanted to know. The ambulance men would know, surely; someone would be able to tell her.

Inside the atmosphere had already changed; a small crowd had already gathered at the reception desk. The crying woman had gone, but her daughter was still there, staring straight ahead quite blankly. Down in the quiet corner where she and Richard had been sitting someone had replaced them; she could see only the back view of a small brown figure in a dusty trilby with a wrapped plant on his knee. Otherwise people were on their feet, and the noise levels were rising.

'I don't know,' Rose could hear the nurse say. 'Only one casualty so far. Just sit down and wait.' Rose put a hand to her head, longing for home.

'It's chaos in here,' Richard said. 'It can't be worse in casualty, can it? Let's ask in there.'

Gratefully Rose nodded; it was all she needed, someone to agree, someone to give her permission. 'Okay,' she said, then hesitated. 'Look,' she said, 'I'll do it on my own, all right? Five minutes.'

He'd been wrong, though; casualty *was* worse. The space was more confined and the noise – of twenty anxious voices pleading, shouting and threatening at once – even more clamorous.

Beside her a door opened and Rose saw a stretcher roll out, a body mounded white and still on it with a tented structure over the legs. There was a white-clad male orderly on either side of the trolley, the one nearest her blocking her view of the upper body and the face, but the reek of smoke and something worse, a sweetish smell like charred meat, emerged from the room with them. Rose shrank back, her stomach contracting in horror. The stretcher stopped, its path half-blocked by a woman's stout back, and as the woman shuffled slowly out of the way the orderlies tutted.

'They might send her somewhere else, anyway,' one said to the other. 'Once they've freed up a helicopter, take her to the burns unit in Genova. Not much we can do for her here.'

'If you would be so kind, Signora,' said the other heartily to the fat woman in their way, 'we haven't got all day, have we?' Then he spoke to the first orderly in an undertone. 'You're right, though. She might as well stay down here, for all the good they'll do her up in surgery.'

'I'm not deaf, you know.' The voice was hoarse and weak but defiant, and the words were followed by a prolonged bout of coughing, a tearing, painful sound. But something about it drew Rose and, curious, she leaned across to see more. The stretcher moved on an inch or two and she saw two hands wrapped in clingfilm, raw and bloody as Gennaro's skinned rabbit, and then the face, or what remained of it.

'Stop,' said Rose instinctively, and put out a hand to stay them. 'Tiziana?'

Tiziana looked up at the Englishwoman and her first thought was, *this is all your fault*. Why hadn't you seen what kind of man he was, the worst kind of hard-handed old bastard, why had you gone along with it, so foolish and trusting? Any one of us could have told you, don't touch him with a barge-pole. *But we didn't, did we?*

Although they'd dosed Tiziana with something for the pain it hurt when she closed her eyes, and when an angry tear trickled against her will from one of them and down beneath the dressing on her raw left cheek. She felt the bandages holding her face together and blinkering her view; she didn't dare move for fear of what she might feel. *Where's Rico when I need him?* she raged silently, glaring up at Rose Fell's pale, shocked face, never mind that for all she knew Rico was dead, and the boy too. They said it was under control, the village was safe, but they weren't here, were they? They might just be saying that to keep her calm.

She hadn't cottoned on at first, she'd smelled the petrol, heard the glug and splash, but she hadn't worked it out. She'd just sat there like a fool in the foreigners' yard, watched the puddle spread down into the *cantina* opposite and then a trickle meandering towards her beneath the broken gate, but she thought he was still out there, waiting for her, and she couldn't move. Then she'd heard the steps further away, his small, soft

340

steps and a tiny sound she'd registered in her head but whose significance she didn't understand until it was too late. The sound was the scrape of a match on a bit of strike, and then the great breathless whoomph that followed as it went up wiped out everything else.

Had he known Tiziana was there all along? She thought he had, and it filled her with a kind of triumph. *Attempted murder, you bastard.* He would have managed it, too, if the Swedes hadn't had a water butt in their yard, topped with green scum and slime but a metre or more of water underneath it. She'd tried to get out through the gate and burned her hands so they stuck to the iron latch; she'd turned back, seen the butt and jumped in before she had a chance to think about it. Had that saved her life? Or perhaps she was going to die after all. For some reason the thought of the boy came into her head; *I can't go and leave him,* she thought, outraged at the thought, *that mother of his is no bloody good.*

All Rose recognized in the crusted, blistered, bandaged face were Tiziana's black eyes, beady and inscrutable, glaring up at her. Tiziana's mouth was moving a little but the words seemed to have gone.

'Tiziana?' she said again, and the old woman's mouth opened, the lip trembled.

'I – I . . .' Tiziana's voice was rusty and feeble, she faltered, then her mouth clamped shut.

'It's all right,' said Rose in Italian, hoping she was making sense, trying to inject reassurance into her voice. She put a hand out gingerly, not knowing what she might touch. Tiziana's papery eyelids closed, and moisture leaked from beneath them; what Rose could see of her face seemed to sag with hopelessness. 'It'll be all right,' said Rose again, and leaned closer. *Was she asleep? Or* – The eyes flew open, and for a moment she seemed to struggle against something, wanting to get up.

'Hey,' said one of the orderlies sharply. They'd been watching, in no hurry, it seemed. 'Please. *Calma, signora.*'

'It was him,' said Tiziana, hoarse and urgent, and somehow Rose was instantly sure of what she meant. 'Who?' she said cautiously, staying close despite the hand of an orderly on her shoulder now. 'Who was it?'

Tiziana's head fell back on the pillow. 'Nutri,' she said. 'Why did you . . . Couldn't you see what he was like? Had that girl, didn't he? Tied up in his rope. And now look –look at all this.' Despairingly, Tiziana's eyes moved down her motionless body; they seemed to be the only part of her capable of independent movement now.

'Gennaro? What girl – not – you mean Ania? The girl we found?' Rose felt her face go slack, stunned into silence because she knew it was true; had known it all along. Had known it in the stale air of his shuttered dining room, the photograph of his daughter turned face down in disgrace. She thought of Gennaro plodding up the hill towards them when they found Ania, not even looking up. *Wait*, she thought, and something she'd only just seen, the image of a small, bowed figure in a brown trilby, waiting patiently with a gift on his knee to be allowed a visit, sprang into her mind. *Where* –

'Come along now,' said the orderly, and the hand pulled at her, prising her off. 'Plenty of time to talk later.' And Rose stood back helpless as the stretcher moved away.

Standing on the edge of the crowded lobby, watching Rose as she disappeared, Richard had seen the old man but at the same time didn't see him; he was so still, so anonymous, so humble, with his offering on his lap.

Over at the reception desk there was a small crowd now, and a man was banging furiously on the desk with his fist. The nurse who had administered a sedative to Ania an hour earlier looked over and, seeing what was happening, made the decision to leave her post to assist the receptionist. A minute or so later, when her colleague's arrival seemed to have only made things worse, the second nurse came in an attempt to restore some kind of order. The corridor now stood empty, and in one quick movement the small, patient man got to his feet, placing the plant carefully on his empty seat.

Ania was dreaming again, she was back on the station platform with her father and there was a train she had to get on. But the station wasn't in the forest like the one at home, it was the vaulted, echoing concourse of a great city terminus. There wasn't just one train, there were hundreds, they slid in and out silently and she waited for the right one. Her father put his hand on hers and it was warm. She opened her eyes and saw him.

She'd read in magazines of operations that went wrong, they gave you the anaesthetic but it didn't take and you lay there watching them cut you up and unable to move, unable to make a sound. She couldn't have said whether it was the sedative or simple terror, but Ania didn't believe she could even blink once she opened her eyes and saw him there beside her. He must have pulled a chair up close to the bed because he was sitting there, his hand over hers on top of the bedcover. He was leaning forward a little and smiling at her.

'How are you feeling now?' he asked softly in Italian. 'A

'bit better?' Ania stared; that was all she could do. Her mouth hung open. But he didn't seem to mind.

'You'll soon be able to come home,' he said. 'I can take better care of you than they can.' He didn't have the voice of a *contadino* or a fisherman; he spoke fluently and easily, as though trained to it, and Ania's heart dipped as it came back to her.

She moved her head on the pillow, just a fraction. His breathing was shallow, she could hear it whistle in her ear, and she gazed at him as though hypnotized. He was watching her closely and Ania could see him waiting, waiting for a signal. She'd seen that look before, the maniacal restraint of a wife-beater, the hair-trigger waiting for an excuse, the food too hot, the pepper on the wrong side of the plate. She'd seen that look on his face when they came out of Levanto on the road into the hills in his little dirty van and he'd reached across and casually hit her. Ania concentrated on breathing, in and out, holding his gaze, trying to remember where that button was, the red button on a panel behind her head to call the nurses. But she couldn't take her eyes from his to look behind her. *It's good I can't move*, she thought; *that way I can't get him started*.

He looked down at his hands for a moment; there was something in them but she couldn't see what it was. When he looked up he wasn't smiling so much; he looked more vacant, as though he was looking right through her to somewhere else, someone else.

'I should really have done it quick,' he said, 'because it's easier, just as it is with a rabbit. But you hadn't done anything wrong, had you? I couldn't get that thought out of my mind. Not like the others.' He scratched his head and the hat moved back so that she could see his face more clearly, even

344

the dusting of white bristle on his chin, in the light from the door. *Where is everyone!*

'The train made it easier,' he said then, out of nowhere. 'Those night trains particularly, you see. They're all drunk or on drugs or half asleep on those trains, no one sees. Make sure you find a window that comes down easily, and it's all over, nothing left behind. All clean.' He made a little whistling noise and brushed his hands one against the other as though dusting them off. Whatever it had been in his hand he'd left on his lap but she could see red lines across his palms as though something had cut into them. 'If we'd got on the train – but there was a strike, wasn't there? They're layabouts, those railway workers.'

Ania looked at him and tried not to listen, only beseeching him silently to have mercy. But his eyes were black and bottomless, not looking at her at all.

'You shouldn't have been there in the first place,' he said then, almost to himself. 'You shouldn't have been coming home so late. Then you wouldn't have seen me with that one, that little whore, and I wouldn't have had to come and find you.'

He nodded a little at that thought as though agreeing with himself. *He came after me*, thought Ania, *because he needed to shut me up. That girl*, she thought sadly, *she wasn't his daughter, was she?* And she felt hot tears well up behind her eyes, a sob in her throat of pity for the girl, whoever she was, and for herself, because she knew what was coming next. He looked down again at his hands, made a winding movement with one slowly, as though skeining wool, and Ania suddenly felt a tiny breath of cooler air. A draught was coming in from somewhere and the door moved barely a millimetre and creaked. He turned his head a fraction at the minuscule sound and she knew this was the time to do it if she ever did anything again.

As though struggling against drowning, as though under some momentous weight of water, she made one huge effort and threw her arm out and back behind her, flailing and struggling to find the button. Her hand flapped useless and desperate as a fish on a trawler's deck as he rose up over her, lifted his hands as though to play cat's cradle and she saw the silver line, fine as a spider's web, strung between them.

'Daddy,' Ania said sadly in her own language, and her eyes filled with tears. 'Daddy.'

Rose crashed through the doors and saw Richard turn towards her, astounded, his mouth open in a question. She could not speak, couldn't answer his look; her heart pounded in her chest as she ran towards him. Her breathing was raw with panic, that long-forgotten feeling of having lost sight of Jess in the supermarket and standing there, not knowing what to do next, paralysed with fear. *Of course it wasn't him*, she told herself, *some innocent old man*, just as she had always said to herself, *she'll be in the next aisle, behind that display.*

As she propelled herself across the room it felt as though she was dragging an anchor. How impossibly slow and obstructive all these people seemed suddenly; well-meaning, they tried to step out of the way but moved in the wrong direction. In the background some insistent mechanical noise echoed her panic, pulsing like an accelerated heartbeat; an alarm.

Rose reached the place where they'd stood and only then did she pause, skidding a little on the polished floor, but there was no one there, their corner was an oasis of emptiness. She took another step and saw it, a plant in florist's paper with a spiral of gold ribbon trailing, sitting where he had sat on the plastic chair facing down the corridor to Ania's room. The noise was still in her ears, that same urgent noise, and a light was flashing somewhere but she paid no attention, she just bolted down the corridor. She heard voices behind her and the clatter of nurses' clogs on the tiled floor, but she got there first.

The door was wide open and in the light that fell through it into the darkened room Rose saw a chair overturned by the bed and Ania, sitting up with her hands at her throat and gasping, a terrible, hoarse sound, while tears streamed down her face. There was no one else.

Chapter Twenty-Nine

The place was in uproar when Leo Cirri ran through the door, his shirt sticking to his back with sweat. *It's the fire*, he told himself. *She'll be fine.* He looked for Toto, praying that he'd already got there. And then the chaos in front of him took shape and Cirri didn't have time to think about Toto any more; this was something else, something terrible had happened here, and the instinct Cirri had developed over twenty years' service told him it wasn't over yet.

At the reception desk ahead of him there was a small crowd and Cirri could see the shock in their faces. They stared at him as he approached, and fell back to let him through. Even before he looked down the corridor where the girl had been sleeping earlier he knew that it was here that everyone's attention was focused, and he felt his stomach turn over. *No.* He turned his head to look and a woman appeared from the first door, a nurse beside her; he recognized the woman as the journalist who'd been at Elvira Vitale's house. He stopped at the desk.

'What's been going on here?' he asked, unable to keep the dread from his voice. The nurse behind reception began to stammer.

A voice came from his left; the nurse standing at the door to the girl's room. 'There's been – an incident,' she began, but then the Englishwoman cut in.

'He's tried to kill her,' she said, her voice calm, but Cirri could hear it was only by exercising some control. 'He came back for her. He's called Gennaro Nutri.'

Cirri didn't ask how she knew the name; he just nodded. His heart sank at the knowledge that he'd been right, and that he could have been too late. Could still be. 'Where is he now?' he said, and the women looked from one to the other.

'I don't know,' said the nurse. 'No one saw him. But he can't have got far – I don't understand how he got past us. He must have been in there only a matter of seconds before, but I just didn't see him.'

'Right,' said Cirri urgently, turning to the receptionist. 'Do you have anything in the way of security personnel?' With a stunned look the woman nodded. 'Get them to the exits, please,' said Cirri. Inwardly he cursed himself, over and over. *Too slow, too bloody slow.* Cirri pulled out his radio and got Toto; the line roared and spat.

'Where the hell are you?' he hissed.

'Getting out of the car,' said Toto. 'A call came through from the firemen, this woman, this story about a piece of rope –' Cirri, thinking furiously, interrupted him, almost shouting. 'Are you in the parking lot? Can you see some beaten-up old van, an Ape van?' There was a bemused silence, then slowly Toto responded.

'Yes,' he said. 'I can.'

So he was still here.

As it turned out they didn't need to monitor the exits; Gennaro Nutri found another way out.

Valeria Rondoni, the woman he'd seen carrying her baby out into the corridor of the maternity ward, was waiting for her husband to come and see his son for the first time. She couldn't understand why he was taking so long; they said a fire had blocked the road, but surely he should be here soon? The midwives were attending to a woman in the next room whose baby wouldn't feed, and Valeria wandered out into the corridor again. She felt loose-jointed and precarious and she walked gingerly, holding tight to the child whose tiny red face pouted up at her in sleep. He was three hours old and Valeria thought she might never stop looking at him. She came up to the door and looked through the wired glass at the world outside.

An old man was sitting there, slumped in sleep, a hat down over his eyes and a fishing bag on his knee. One of his hands rested upturned on the bag, the other had fallen to his side. Valeria frowned, and pressed her face closer to the glass, turning the warm bundle in her arms to one side. The upturned hand held something she'd seen in her own father's workshop, a cork with a razor blade embedded in it for cutting stubborn knots and trimming nets. Then as Valeria continued to look, puzzled, at the motionless figure she saw that something was slowly dripping from the old man's hanging arm and forming a dark puddle on the tiles. A thin, high, breathless scream issued from her open mouth, and the midwives came running.

Chapter Thirty

It had been something to talk about through the winter months, that was true, through the low season when the worst storms in living memory had kept everyone indoors. It had stopped them dwelling on the olive trees the wind was bringing down, the boats smashed up one particularly foul dawn, the broken slates and leaking roofs. *Of course*, they said, *he wasn't from around here, wasn't born here*, by which they meant the five-mile radius around Levanto, the neighbouring villages drawn tight in the town's net over winter, no longer beyond the pale. And of course it was a local woman who'd practically brought the man in single-handed, old Tiziana, the deep furrowed scarring on one cheek and the palms of both hands testimony to her bravery. Tiziana, who could no longer come to market without being offered a drink – *just a small one*, she'd say, *something sweet to build up my strength* – in every bar along the front. They'd been right, after all, that was the word in the *gastronomia* where Elvira Vitale bought her stuffed peppers, in

351

the Mare Blu, in Paolo's bar under the dusty limes; he'd been Italian, sure, but a foreigner all the same, the murderer.

It had kept them going, then, the story worked and reworked to reflect well on all concerned, the fire service, the police, the town's foreign community, even down to Valeria Rondoni and the scream with which she managed to raise the alarm despite having barely given birth. Over that hard winter everyone involved was awarded a place in local mythology; it was decided that they belonged. But as Easter approached and with it the real beginning of a new year, a new season on their beautiful riviera, the events of the previous Ferragosto were quietly consigned to history. The sun was shining again, at last.

Leo Cirri sat on the promenade and gazed at the sea. The sky was clear and blue but the morning air was cool still and the beach below them was pristine and deserted. The board-walk was busy with churchgoers holding their palm crosses from the morning's service and taking the air, but it was peaceful. As they passed they nodded at him, and some even touched their hats.

Chiara climbed on to his knee and laid her round cheek against his chest; he rested a hand on her soft hair, fine as silk, and turned to look at Gloria beside him. He found she was already looking back at him and when he took in the whole of her silhouetted against the sun, from her dark eyes crinkled at the corners in a smile and her wiry hair lit up by the light behind her, to the curve of her seven-month belly, he thought, *Yes. That's it, let none of this change.*

On Elvira Vitale's terrace Ania was sweeping in the sun and looking down at the stream of tiny figures still emerging from the green and white church. Behind her the house stood clean and empty, in the kitchen lunch was ready in the cool beneath white cloths. Ania had prepared a salad with the first of the tomatoes sprinkled with thyme, her mother's meatballs of chopped pork and lamb spiced with paprika, stuffed peppers. Elvira – that was what she had been asked to call her employer now – liked her food, these days; she had even gained a pound or two over the winter, and Ania had discovered a talent for cooking that both boosted her confidence and reminded her of home. Not that she needed to miss home any more; she had her own room here now, the room with a view of the sea that Elvira's husband had once occupied, and she had Anvar, who came to call for her every evening, his hands still dusty with plaster. They would go for a walk into town even when it was cold or blustery, mostly in peaceful silence, but if they wanted to they knew they could speak in their own language and be understood.

One Sunday in Advent they had been to Florence on the train to attend a service at the Orthodox church there. Anvar had put his arm around her proudly and introduced her as his fiancée to the one or two faces there who knew him, a cousin of his and an old workmate. But as she looked down at the flat, glittering sea and the promenade and the people walking, Ania thought that when the time came, she might prefer to be married here in the striped church by the sea.

She turned and looked the other way at the house high up along the coast that had been named, so she'd been told by Richard Bourn, for a birds' nest. La Martinière. She used to look up there what seemed like a hundred years ago but was only last summer, but she had never known what it was called. The heavy white umbrellas had been put up for the first time this year and as she watched she saw a tiny distant arm raised to wave. She lifted her arm in return.

In the cool shade of the white umbrellas Rose, her mind elsewhere, was distracted from her waiting by the movement and looked across at Elvira as she stood and raised her hand to wave. If you looked closely you could see that Elvira had to lean quite heavily against the balustrade for support, and that getting to her feet was not effortless. But it was hard to believe that she had spent five months in a wheelchair. She had been out of it since Christmas and she walked everywhere now, along the coast paths and into town for the *passeggiata*, sometimes very slowly at first but never allowing herself to be put off. As a result she had gained strength and muscle and a kind of energy she had not had since she was a girl. She had not been back to London and nor would she; Jack Robbins' gallery had gone into receivership, he was bankrupt, and everything she had left there, from the expensive, neutral clothes Jack had liked her to wear down to the last pair of tights, was gone. And good riddance.

Elvira's hair was red now, a rich, fiery pomegranate colour; it cheers me up, was what she said. It made her look more ordinary, was what Rose thought, more like every other well-preserved woman in this small town, but then, perhaps that was what Elvira wanted. As Rose watched she turned away from the view and smiled.

'I should go,' she said. 'I don't want Ania to have to wait around.' She leaned down and brushed her cheek against Rose's. 'Come when you're ready.'

Richard came out through the long French windows and stood at Rose's shoulder as together they watched Elvira go. Rose leaned her head a little until her cheek touched Richard's side and as she closed her eyes and felt the warmth of his body against hers, his hand came around and held her there. On

354

the table Rose's mobile sounded, a jaunty little tune, and she looked up at Richard.

'That'll be her,' she said. 'That'll be Jess.' And she reached for the phone.

Below them Elvira made her way down through the fragrant rooms of the garden in which her future had once been decided, a lifetime ago, washed in the scent of English roses and wild thyme. She walked slowly and painfully but ahead of her lay the wide, flat, glittering sea of her childhood, and every step she took on the sweet, warm earth said to her, *you are home.*